BLIND SPOT

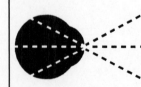

This Large Print Book carries the
Seal of Approval of N.A.V.H.

BLIND SPOT

BRENDA NOVAK

WHEELER PUBLISHING
A part of Gale, a Cengage Company

GALE
A Cengage Company

Farmington Hills, Mich • San Francisco • New York • Waterville, Maine
Meriden, Conn • Mason, Ohio • Chicago

Copyright © 2019 by Brenda Novak, Inc.
Dr. Evelyn Talbot Novels.
Wheeler Publishing, a part of Gale, a Cengage Company.

LIBRARY OF CONGRESS CIP DATA ON FILE.
CATALOGUING IN PUBLICATION FOR THIS BOOK
IS AVAILABLE FROM THE LIBRARY OF CONGRESS

ISBN-13: 978-1-4328-7134-5 (hardcover alk. paper)

Published in 2019 by arrangement with Macmillan Publishing Group, LLC/St. Martin's Publishing Group

Printed in Mexico
1 2 3 4 5 6 7 23 22 21 20 19

To Kate Kenyon. It was such a pleasure meeting you, your handsome husband, and your beautiful children at my book group event in Boston. Thanks for coming out and taking the tour with me — and for being such a great member of my online book group. I always smile when I hear from you.

For all of these things, I am not the least bit sorry.

— Carl Panzram, American serial killer, arsonist, rapist, and burglar

1

Dr. Evelyn Talbot sat trembling on a cold cement floor, blinking into pure darkness. No matter how hard she strained her eyes, she couldn't see so much as a glimmer of light, had no idea of the dimensions of the room where she'd been tossed or who'd thrown her in it before locking and bolting the door.

Considering all the psychopaths she'd studied over the years, she was afraid to find out who it was.

She had to calm down, she told herself. If she didn't, she wouldn't have the presence of mind, or the physical strength, to save her own life. Not only did she have to manage her fear, she had to remember everything she'd learned as a forensic psychiatrist who'd spent the past twenty years studying serial killers. In this moment, her education was the only weapon she had.

She removed the suit jacket she was wearing over a matching beige dress and rubbed the arm she'd landed on to see if it might be broken. Whoever had grabbed her as she was getting out of the car at her own house had attacked without warning. He'd come up from behind, thrown a bag over her head, hauled her off her feet and shoved her into the back of a van. Before she could even reach up to try to remove the bag, she'd felt a knee in her spine as her hands were jerked behind her and tied. Then the door had slammed shut and she'd heard an engine rev and tires squeal as she was launched to one side with the motion of the vehicle.

She didn't believe her arm was broken, just bruised or sprained. Fortunately, the rope that'd been used to tie her up had been cut off as she was dumped into this room, so she had feeling again in her hands. Until this moment, she hadn't realized that her ankle was tender, too. She must've rolled it in the brief scuffle. At least whoever kidnapped her hadn't been particularly rough when he forced her onto her stomach, so nothing had happened that would've injured the child she carried — *yet*.

But who'd abducted her? She hadn't

caught a glimpse of her attacker, but she assumed she knew him.

Her mind sifted through the dangerous men she'd studied since graduating from college, but she couldn't even venture a guess.

It was frightening not knowing what she was up against.

It was even more frightening to acknowledge that no one would have any clue where she was — or even that she'd been taken — least of all Sergeant Benjamin Murphy, or Amarok as the locals called him, Hilltop's only police presence and the man she loved. It was summer in Alaska, that brief period where the days lengthened to almost twenty hours and tourists came from all over the world to enjoy the natural beauty of the last frontier.

She and Amarok — his nickname came from the Inuktitut word for "wolf" and went all the way back to junior high — had finally relaxed and begun to believe that the danger Evelyn had faced for so long, until Jasper Moore had been caught and imprisoned seven months ago, was over. They'd been so sure of it they'd begun planning their wedding. She was supposed to meet Amarok at the Moosehead today — possibly right now; she'd lost track of time — to talk about the food they'd serve. On the eighth of July, they were going to be married in a small ceremony in Alaska, where he'd been born and raised. Then, after the birth of their baby, they were going to fly to Boston, where she'd grown up, for a second reception in the fall.

Struggling to even out her breathing and slow the pounding of her heart, she hugged her knees tighter to her chest — as much as her swollen stomach would allow. If the person who'd kidnapped her was one of the psychopaths she'd worked with, she had some inkling what to expect. He was probably someone who was easily threatened. Someone who lived to dominate others. Someone who had to win no matter what the cost. Someone who enjoyed torture and/or killing.

She could go on simply by ticking off the traits named on the PCL-R, which was what Dr. Robert Hare had created to help diagnose a psychopath. She knew what such people had in common. Glib charm. Impulsivity. Grandiose estimation of self. Cunning and manipulative. The list went on. The real question was: Could she tolerate what her captor had in store for her? Hold him off long enough to get away?

She had to. If she wanted to live, if she

wanted the unborn child she carried to survive, she had to be both strong and smart. But the most debilitating of memories exacerbated her panic and fear. This wasn't the first time she'd been victimized. She'd been only sixteen when her boyfriend, intelligent, popular and well-loved Jasper Moore, had killed her best friends and tried to kill her. It was a miracle she'd managed to drag her broken and bruised body from the shack where he'd left her after torturing her for three days. Had she been any less determined to survive, she wouldn't have made it.

That experience had changed her life in so many ways. First and foremost, it was the reason she'd decided to make the study of such individuals her life's work. Jasper had been an only child who'd come from a good family. His wealthy parents had *doted* on him. There'd been no abuse or deprivation, nothing one would think necessary to "create" such a monster. That was the most puzzling part of the equation, and what had prompted her to establish Hanover House, the first prison of its kind. Located in a town of only five hundred people an hour outside of Anchorage, it housed over three hundred inmates, including 110 of the worst serial killers in America. According to some estimates, psychopaths made up 4 percent of the general population and over 20 percent of America's prison populations, so *someone* had to figure out a way to treat them.

Too bad it was such a dangerous job.

Evelyn had a terrible feeling she was about to be reminded of just *how* dangerous.

Tilting her head back, she hauled in a deep, calming breath as she tried to estimate the length of time she'd been in the van so she could attempt to determine where she might be in relation to Hilltop. Had her kidnapper driven an hour? Longer?

Tough to say. Shock and fear — not to mention disorientation — made it almost impossible to come up with an accurate estimate. Ten minutes in such a situation felt like ten hours. Her captor could've taken her to a remote cabin in the middle of the wilderness on the far side of Hilltop. There was no snow on the ground right now, nothing to make those mountain roads impassable. Or he could've taken her to Anchorage or some other town or community where it would be easier to get groceries and necessities.

She held her breath, listening, but she couldn't hear anything. When would her captor make himself known? *Where was he?*

That the attack had been so well co-ordinated, so efficient and restrained, told her she wasn't dealing with a disorganized personality. This wasn't the kind of crime that came without much, if any, forethought or planning. But what did that tell her?

Her attacker was probably smart. And she knew him. Or he knew her.

After a few more minutes, she gathered the nerve to move from the spot where he'd dumped her. By pressing her ear to the door, she thought she might be able to make out a noise or two that would provide some clue as to what was going on.

She managed to find the door by crawling on her hands and knees and feeling her way across the rough, hard floor. If her captor had left the premises, maybe she could bang on the door or the walls of her prison and bring help. It might even be possible for her to kick the door open and escape —

That tantalizing hope was dashed the second she felt the door. It wasn't the usual somewhat flimsy wooden panel found on most houses these days. And there was no crack underneath. It felt like the heavy steel door of a walk-in cooler. She couldn't hear anything through it, and she couldn't break it. There wasn't even a handle on her side, just what felt like a six-by-twelve-inch slot

15

in the middle with a metal cover over it on the outside.

Once again, her unease began to spiral toward panic. Was she about to run out of air? Had whoever grabbed her tossed her in here to suffocate?

"Oh God, oh God, oh God," she whispered as she began to crawl around the room, searching for any opening or other possibility of escape.

On the opposite wall, in the corner, she ran into a small commode. She had no idea how dirty it might be, so she hesitated to touch it once she figured out what it was, but she could tell it was a toilet. There was no tank, but there was a handle and a round seat. There didn't seem to be an accompanying sink, however. There didn't seem to be *anything* else in the room except a cot, which was bolted to the floor, with a lumpy mattress, a pillow and a blanket.

By the time she made it all the way around her small prison, she'd determined that it was only about six feet by seven feet: the size of some walk-in coolers. She was fairly certain it *was* a cooler, or had been. The walls felt like a smooth, hard plastic. But the presence of the toilet and the bed made her think she hadn't been put here to suffocate. Those items wouldn't be necessary if she was going to run out of air.

Forcing herself to stand, despite her wobbly legs, she made a second circuit. The blackness was so complete she doubted she'd find the window she was praying for. It had been daytime when she'd been abducted. No way had enough hours passed for it to be night — not in June. There should be some glimmer, somewhere, and there wasn't.

Determined to learn as much as possible about her surroundings, to perhaps find a light switch, she kept investigating. There was nothing on the walls, not so much as a picture or a nail. But once she gathered the courage to walk straight through the middle of the room, waving her arms to see if she could determine whether there was a high ceiling or a low one, she encountered a thin chain. It hit her face, startling her before she gave it a hesitant tug.

A small snap sounded and a single lightbulb flickered on, buzzing with the flow of electricity and painting the stark white walls of the narrow room a dull yellow.

Evelyn felt infinitely better just being able to see. Darkness made *everything* more frightening. But her situation hadn't improved otherwise. There was nothing else in the small, enclosed space besides what she'd already discovered — nothing except a drain in the floor so the cooler could be easily washed out and what looked like an HVAC vent to one side of the light on the ceiling. As she stared up at it, she realized that she would have air, but her captor had taken great care in selecting and preparing this place.

No way would she be able to escape on her own.

Hilltop, AK — Tuesday, 3:30 p.m. AKDT
"She get caught up at work?"

Amarok swiveled on his stool to see Shorty, the short, wiry, bowlegged proprietor of the Moosehead, wiping down the bar. "Must've." He'd been having a beer, his Alaskan malamute, Makita, lying at his feet, while watching the Giants play baseball. He'd figured Evelyn would arrive any minute. She had more to do than most people, so he could understand why she might be a little late. Now that Shorty had interrupted the game, however, Amarok's eyes were drawn to the huge clock between the two moose heads, which hung on the wall staring sightlessly down on the most popular gathering place in town. That clock indicated she was more than "a little" late.

She would never make Shorty or Shorty's

18

sister, Molly, both of whom were supposed to be meeting with them to go over the menu for the wedding, wait for thirty minutes without some form of communication.

"Want to give her a call?" Shorty asked.

"Yeah." He could've walked to the pay phone back by the bathrooms, but Shorty did him the courtesy of putting the business phone within reach. Since there was no cell service in the area, he and everyone else in Hilltop couldn't communicate as easily as most of the rest of the world. But Evelyn had a landline at the prison. Why hadn't she taken a minute to let them know she was running so far behind?

Had something gone wrong at work?

Anxiety began to roil in the pit of Amarok's stomach. Something could always go wrong when dealing with the men she studied. But the biggest threat to her had been Jasper Moore and Amarok had arrested him seven months ago. Although Evelyn had worked with other killers — still did — none had become quite *that* fixated on her, not any who were now in a situation to harm her, at any rate.

He'd believed any danger to the woman he loved was finally under control.

But was it really? She'd had Jasper transferred to Hanover House. Not only had she deemed it poetic justice that he would become her captive instead of her becoming his, she'd also longed for the opportunity to study the one man who'd sent her on the odyssey to understand evil in the first place.

Sensing his sudden anxiety, Makita lifted his head and twitched his ears forward as Amarok dialed the prison. Amarok told himself he was getting worried over nothing. In a few moments, he'd hear her voice. Maybe she'd sound a bit harried — she was probably trying to get out of the office so she could make their appointment — but she would apologize for the delay and he'd finish his beer and the game while she drove over.

That didn't happen, however. When Penny Singh, her assistant, told him Evelyn had left three hours ago to grab some files from home and hadn't returned as expected, the fear he'd shoved away suddenly lunged at him again. "Why didn't you call me?" he asked.

"I-I don't know," she responded, obviously flustered by the question. "I figured she must've decided to work at home for a few hours this afternoon. She doesn't have any appointments on her schedule until four fifteen."

Because she'd kept the afternoon mostly clear so they could meet with Shorty and his sister.

"Is something wrong?" Now Penny sounded alarmed.

"No, nothing's wrong," he replied. But when he called home and couldn't get Evelyn there, either, his concern ticked up another notch.

"Any luck?" Shorty's sister sauntered close while drying glasses.

Amarok hung up, slapped some money on the bar and dug his keys from his pocket. Knowing that was his signal, Makita jumped to his feet. "No. She's not at the prison and she's not at home."

"Must be in the car on the way over," Molly suggested.

He hoped to God that was it. She could've fallen asleep when she went home or something. With the pregnancy, she was always tired. Even so, taking a nap in the middle of the day would be unlike her. She was too driven not to make the most of every minute. "Maybe."

"Don't freak out," she warned. "You put that Jasper fella away, remember?"

"I remember." But when Jasper wasn't standing trial for one of the many murders for which he had yet to be convicted, he

21

was at Hanover House. As a matter of fact, Amarok was fairly certain he was there now. Maybe he'd engineered a way to get to Evelyn. Or someone else had, someone just as dangerous. "I'll give you a call when I figure out what's going on," he said, and walked out, Makita at his heel, without waiting for a response.

The five-minute drive home seemed like it took forever. Makita paced on the seat, even though he was too big to be walking around the cab while they were moving. Amarok felt just as uneasy, so he didn't stop him. But he breathed a sigh of relief when he found Evelyn's SUV parked in their driveway.

As he pulled in behind it, he decided she must've gotten busy and forgotten their appointment. But why wouldn't she answer the damn phone? Why the hell would she give him such a scare?

He planned to ask. Jamming the transmission into Park, he hopped out, and Makita immediately followed. That was when he found something that made his blood run cold. One of the shoes she'd had on when she left for work this morning lay on the concrete only a few feet from the driver's side of her vehicle. And her purse, its contents sprayed in an arc, wasn't far away.

2

Time was *everything*. Each and every second was valuable, and yet second after second zipped away from him. Amarok had never in his life felt such urgency, such desperation. Nothing could be more shattering than realizing Evelyn was gone, because she wasn't just "gone." Her cat, Sigmund, was home, but she'd been *taken*, and, considering the kind of person who'd most likely taken her, he knew what that probably entailed. He had to get her back before she was harmed or, worse, killed. But how? This had come out of nowhere! There wasn't anything to indicate who'd abducted her or why, not with Jasper behind bars.

As a police officer, he understood how critical the first few hours were, but the fear flooding his body was quickly robbing him of strength and clarity when he needed them most. His feet felt like they were encased in concrete and his chest constricted, making it difficult to breathe.

Makita licked his hand in sympathy and followed as he somehow forced his legs to carry him back to the truck. The woman who'd been about to become his wife and the mother of his child was counting on him. He could be all she had as far as help. But he didn't have anything to go on. He'd checked the security video on his computer — thanks to the Internet, he'd been able to install a camera at his front door for a fairly modest price — but it showed only the stoop and Evelyn hadn't made it that far. She never even entered the frame. He'd also called everyone he could think of in town. No one could say where she was. No one had seen anything suspicious or spotted any strangers in the area.

So where did that leave him?

Flipping on his strobe lights and siren, he ordered Makita to sit still in the seat so he couldn't get hurt prancing around as he tore out of his own driveway and raced over to Hanover House. Fortunately, his strength began to return as a white-hot anger welled up, overcoming the hormones that had swamped him at first. Once that happened, he felt like he could tear apart the person who'd taken Evelyn with his bare hands —

if only he knew who to blame.

There *had* to have been something to precipitate this, he told himself. And he was going to find out what it was. He wouldn't lose the woman he loved, not after everything they'd survived so far, especially when she was carrying their child! That she'd been able to conceive despite the skepticism of her doctor had been a miracle, a source of joy and hope to them both. He wouldn't allow anyone to rob them of that.

His gut twisted as he remembered touching her belly after they made love last night. Their child had been moving, and she'd been eager for him to feel it. Usually when she tried to show him, he couldn't discern anything. At only six months along, the baby wasn't big enough to kick very hard.

But last night had been different. The faint sensation that had registered on his palm was his first contact with their child, and it had affected him deeply, made the fact that he was going to be a father real in a way he'd been afraid to hope for in the first trimester and even after. The doctor had gone over the risks of this particular pregnancy with them both. Evelyn would be turning forty this year. Her age, in conjunction with what her body had been through when she was tortured, made miscarriage more of a possibility than it would be otherwise. Amarok had been trying to maintain some emotional distance, so he wouldn't be devastated and could help *her* through the heartbreaking ordeal, should that happen.

The guards at the checkpoint, startled when his tires screeched and his back end swung around far enough to almost clip the fence, stepped out.

"What is it, Sergeant?" Officer Bailey asked, obviously concerned by the lights and the noise as well as Amarok's seemingly reckless driving. "What's wrong?"

"Have you seen Evelyn today?" he asked without preamble.

"Not for several hours." Bailey looked over at his younger counterpart, Officer Derby, who stood in the shade of the building. "You?"

Derby moved into the sunlight with Bailey. "She left after lunch. Must've been one or so. I'm not sure *exactly,* I can check the logbook —"

"No. I've spoken to Penny," Amarok told them. "I know when she left. The bigger question is . . . has she come back?"

Bailey exchanged another glance with Derby. "No, sir."

"Did she have anyone with her when she

26

left? Did she seem upset or say where she was going?"

Both correctional officers looked utterly bewildered as they shook their heads. "No. Has something happened?"

"I think so." What other answer was there? She wouldn't stand him up, especially when they were planning their wedding, wouldn't skip out on work when she was expected back, wouldn't drop her purse in the front yard and walk away with only one shoe.

"What is it?" Bailey asked, wide-eyed.

"That's what I'm here to find out. Can you tell me if Jasper Moore is still locked up?"

"Last I saw, he was," Derby said. "I searched his cell yesterday when I searched the whole block."

That was good news. Jasper getting his hands on Evelyn was the worst possible scenario. After being so terribly scarred and traumatized by what he did twenty-three years ago, she was finally beginning to conquer her fear of him. Amarok couldn't remember the last time she'd come awake thrashing around and crying in bed due to another nightmare. It'd been months.

But it could be that someone just as bad was the culprit this time around — maybe even someone she'd dealt with before she

27

moved to Alaska, which would mean he'd *really* be searching for a needle in a haystack. He'd have to go through all her old files and records before he could do anything else, and by then —

He cut off that thought. "Can you let me through?"

"Of course. One sec."

Amarok gripped the steering wheel, squeezing tightly to keep his hands in place as Bailey circled the truck with the pole-mounted mirror to check the undercarriage. Such tight security felt like a waste of time. As far as Amarok was concerned, the worst had already happened. It was all he could do not to pull his gun and demand he be allowed to pass. And Makita could tell he was on edge. He barked, then gave a low growl to signify he was ready to fight, too, if necessary.

Fortunately, Bailey gestured the all clear and he was able to roll through only seconds later, without having to do anything that could cost him his badge.

He didn't bother parking. He pulled under the covered sally port, rolled down his windows so it wouldn't get too hot for Makita, told his dog to stay put and left his truck at the curb before he jogged in.

"Hello, Sergeant." . . . "Amarok." . . .

"How's it going?" . . . "What's up, man?"

Most of the COs, even though the majority commuted from Anchorage, had grown familiar with him. Not only had he been to the prison a number of times on official business, but he also stopped by occasionally to bring Evelyn lunch, visit with her or pick her up if there was a storm.

As he put his firearm and belt on a tray so they could circumvent the X-ray machine and walked through the metal detector, he asked everyone the same questions he'd posed to the guards at the gate and received the same answers. Evelyn had left around one, she'd been alone and she hadn't seemed upset or distressed in any way. And, yes, Jasper was locked up.

He told them to bring Moore to an interview room. Then he got on the elevator and headed straight up to Evelyn's office on the third floor.

As soon as he pushed through the double glass doors that separated the mental health headquarters from the rest of the prison, he encountered Penny, who was agitated and moving around the office instead of sitting at her desk, working, like usual.

"Have you heard from her?" she asked right away. "I've tried calling her at home several times. She doesn't pick up."

"She's not there," he replied. "And I *haven't* heard from her. Have you checked with the rest of the mental health team?"

"I've spoken to the ones who aren't in the middle of a session with a patient or doing research that shouldn't be interrupted."

"And?"

"They don't know anything."

"Interrupt the rest," he said. "I don't care what they're doing. Tell them I need to talk to them *now.*"

The color drained from her face. "This is *that* serious?"

"It appears so."

She covered her mouth. "She's pregnant!" she whispered between her fingers.

He could barely speak for clenching his jaw. "I'm well aware of that."

Determined to keep a cool head, so that fear and despair wouldn't gain the upper hand again, he dodged Penny in order to reach Evelyn's office. "Do you know what she's been working on lately and who she's been working with?"

She hurried to keep up with him, but she was less than five feet and he was nearly six three. She had to take two steps for every one of his. "Do you mean inmates or — or doctors?"

"Both."

"She interacts with all the doctors, but probably Dr. Ricardo more often than the rest. Seems like he's always in her office for one reason or another."

He switched on the light and crossed to the desk. "Like . . ."

"She says they aren't ready to publish their findings, but he keeps pushing her. They're also doing a lot of testing together, some of them empathy tests and . . . and IQ tests to determine how mental acuity might interface with psychopathy. They've even been doing a lot of experiments to see if psychopaths can better fool a lie detector and why that might be the case. Lots of stuff."

He checked Evelyn's desk calendar, saw her appointment with him at the Moosehead and the four fifteen Penny had mentioned, which was with Dr. Ricardo, but nothing else, and began going through the papers on her desk, her phone messages, her drawers. "And inmates? Which ones has she been focusing on lately?"

She frowned as she watched him. He wasn't being particularly careful to leave things as he'd found them. He was in too big of a hurry. "She's been frustrated with Mary Harpe, our only female psychopath."

"The former nurse who murdered those babies."

"Yes."

She rounded the desk, pulled open the filing cabinet against the wall and handed him Mary's file. He'd heard Evelyn talk about Mary. Other than Jasper, she liked Mary less than any other psychopath she'd ever studied. "Is there anything in particular Evelyn has been saying about her?"

"Not really."

She watched as he leafed through Mary's file, skimming Evelyn's handwritten notes on their sessions — mentions of her lack of remorse, her total indifference to the parents of the babies she'd killed as well as the pediatric doctor whose practice she destroyed. He also came across several graphs showing the number of deaths that had occurred in the hospital where she worked before the hospital got rid of her — by laying her off while still giving her a recommendation — and she went to work for the pediatrician.

"Nothing stands out to you as unusual or worrisome?" he pressed. Evelyn often talked about her work when they were relaxing together in the evenings, but he hadn't heard anything of note lately, certainly nothing that would put him on high alert.

32

Penny seemed at a loss. "She just told me that some psychopaths are more charming than others and Mary is way down the list."

Essentially what Evelyn had said to him. "Does Mary dislike Evelyn?"

"She dislikes everyone, but maybe she dislikes Evelyn more than the other doctors. Evelyn sees through her crap from the get-go. The men give her more leeway, more understanding."

"Does Mary get many letters or visitors? Have any family to speak of?"

"I don't know. I'll have to check with Dr. Jones."

Amarok glanced up. "Why Dr. Jones? Has he been working with her, too?"

"Yes, and they seem to be on friendlier terms."

When Amarok closed Mary's file he noticed another file sitting on top of the cabinet, as though Evelyn had recently accessed it. He grabbed it so he could read the name on the tab. "What about this guy — Robert Knox?"

"He's not a violent offender. He'd be unlikely to harm anyone."

"But he *is* a psychopath. A con artist or con man, right?" He'd heard Evelyn mention Knox before, too. Knox had callously bilked several old ladies out of their retirement savings with his investment schemes.

"Yeah. But Evelyn seems to like him okay."

"Does he have any visitors, mail, that sort of thing?"

"I have no clue. You'll have to check with the mailroom. Or I can do that for you. . . ."

"Please do," Amarok said, but he was skeptical that Bobby Knox was behind what'd happened today — that he'd hired someone, or convinced someone, to kidnap Evelyn. Amarok was grasping at *anything.* "Have you heard of him or anyone else making threats or creating any particular problems for Evelyn?"

She wrung her hands as she thought the question over. "No. Since you caught Jasper last November, everything has been peaceful around here — or as peaceful as it's going to get in a maximum-security prison that houses so many psychopaths. There's always danger, but we have protocols to minimize that. To be honest, I've never seen Dr. Talbot so carefree and happy, not in the two and a half years that Hanover House has been open."

He felt the same about Evelyn's state of mind. After twenty-three years of feeling as though it was only a matter of time before Jasper followed her to Alaska and attempted to finish what he'd started when he attacked her the first time, that threat had been eliminated. They'd *both* felt more secure knowing he was finally behind bars.

So what the hell was going on? This shouldn't be happening!

"Sergeant Murphy?"

Dr. James Ricardo, a slender, rather nondescript man in his late forties with close-cropped dark hair, and the only neurologist on staff, appeared in the doorway of Evelyn's office. Although none of the doctors on Evelyn's team had any more authority than the others, James had made it clear that if Evelyn ever left Hanover House, he wanted her job. He'd stated as much when things went awry last winter. "Yes?"

"Where the heck is Evelyn? She was supposed to join me on the situational-versus-dispositional empathy tests I'm running right now, but I've been waiting for fifteen minutes."

Preoccupied with the desperation he felt to find some clue, something to tell him what he should do next, Amarok turned in a full circle. "We don't know where she is, Jim. That's why I'm here."

His eyebrows came together. "What do you mean?"

"She's in trouble, and I need to get her out of it."

"What kind of trouble?"

"I wish I knew. Is there one inmate, in particular, anyone on Evelyn's roster, who's had it in for her lately?" Amarok had heard various names since he'd entered Evelyn's life, men who'd given them both cause for concern. Jasper Moore, of course, but not only him. There'd been Anthony Garza, Hugo Evanski and Lyman Bishop, all psychopaths she'd studied here at Hanover House. Even her onetime colleague Tim Fitzpatrick, the very psychiatrist whose reputation and support had helped make Hanover House a reality, had become a problem in the end. He'd quit two years ago, before he could be fired, and returned to Boston.

But none of those men were likely culprits. Jasper was in prison and, as an only child who'd murdered his parents not long ago, he didn't have a lot of friends or family who might be willing to assist him in getting revenge on Evelyn. Anthony and Hugo were both dead. Lyman, nicknamed the Zombie Maker because of his penchant for performing ice-pick lobotomies on his victims to render them dependent and compliant, was in a mental institution, being fed through a tube, after suffering a severe brain hemorrhage. And Tim Fitzpatrick was grateful to

Evelyn for helping to get him out of prison after he served time for a crime he didn't commit. He'd had a thing for Evelyn when they worked together, an obsession that'd caused him to cross certain boundaries. Maybe there was still some of that left. But, surely, he hadn't had anything to do with *this*.

"No one that *I* know of," Ricardo said. "There's been *nothing* out of the ordinary, not since she insisted on having Jasper Moore transferred here."

The disapproval in his voice prompted Amarok to ask, "You were against that?"

"I thought it would be better for her to get him out of her life at last."

Amarok had felt the same. But he could also understand her reasoning. If the man she feared more than any other was at Hanover House, she would be able to keep an eye on him, and that was important to her peace of mind. Jasper was *so* cunning she didn't trust anyone else to use sufficient caution with him, couldn't believe he wouldn't eventually be able to manipulate those around him by convincing a female guard that she should help him escape or whatever. He was a fit, handsome forty-year-old, which made him even more dangerous than a run-of-the-mill sadist. People tended to trust men who looked so well put together and were as intelligent and articulate as Jasper Moore. "What could've happened to her?" he asked Ricardo.

The other man lifted his hands palms up. "I have no idea."

Neither did Amarok. This day had started out like any other and should've continued that way. But if he didn't come up with a lead soon, he might never see Evelyn again.

A CO by the name of McKim rushed into the mental health department. Seeing them gathered in Evelyn's office, he hurried over. "I've got Jasper Moore waiting in Interview Room Eight."

Word of the emergency was spreading. Amarok could sense the concern in the CO's manner. Everyone loved the doc, as they called Evelyn. No doubt they were all hoping for a quick resolution. But Amarok had a terrible feeling that wasn't going to happen. From where he was starting from, which was ground zero, how would he ever find Evelyn in time to save her?

Maybe she was already dead.

If she was in the hands of someone as sadistic as Jasper Moore, he hoped that was the case. He couldn't bear the thought of her being tortured again. In his mind's eye, he kept seeing their baby being ripped from

38

her womb, which caused bile to rise up and burn his throat.

"Sergeant?"

Silencing the sinister little voice in his head that insisted he was already too late, Amarok started for the door. He had to do *something,* had to keep fighting, no matter what — if only to bring the person who'd taken her to justice.

If it came to that, he'd hunt the son of a bitch to the ends of the earth, wouldn't rest until the bastard was caught and punished, so he figured he'd better get started on his revenge, if that was easier to believe in. "Show me the fastest way to get there," he said.

Anchorage, AK — Tuesday, 4:00 p.m. AKDT
A noise woke Evelyn. She'd worried herself into a fitful slumber, but she had no idea how long she'd been fading in and out of consciousness. It hadn't been long. An hour? Two? She came awake quickly and, afraid she'd miss the opportunity to escape, talk her captor into letting her go or better her situation in any other way, jumped off the thin mattress that covered the coils of the cot.

She'd left the light on. Since that was all she had as far as creature comforts, besides

39

the bed and blanket, she wasn't willing to turn it off. She didn't like the idea of being alone in the dark. She'd never experienced such total blackness. It felt like a tomb, and she was afraid that's what it would become.

Once on her feet, she steadied herself by putting a hand to the wall. She'd gotten up too fast, hadn't given her heart a chance to pump enough blood to her brain.

Bending over, she took a moment to ward off the dizziness but straightened as soon as she could, her eyes riveting on the small slot she'd noticed before.

Someone was out there.

"Hello?" she called.

No answer.

She crossed the small space to bang on the door. "Hello? Who's there? Let me out, *please!*"

Again, she got no response, but as the slot came open she realized that it was the slide of the bolt that had awakened her.

She crouched down, trying to peer out, but the door was so thick it was like looking through a pipe. She couldn't see anything except the midsection of a man. He seemed fit, was most likely in his twenties or thirties and wore camouflage pants with a black T-shirt. She didn't know if that meant he was in the armed forces, had once been in the armed forces or merely liked the military. She couldn't see his face — not that his face would necessarily answer that question.

"Who are you?" she asked. "Have we ever met?"

He stepped out of sight before reappearing with a metal tray of food, which he slid through the opening.

She didn't want to take it. She wanted some type of explanation or understanding of her situation. But she wasn't sure when she'd have the opportunity to eat again and didn't dare let the food fall to the floor, for fear that would be all she got. Even if she was too upset to eat right *now,* she had her baby to think of, couldn't go *too* long. For all she knew, she could be locked up here, subsisting on very little, indefinitely.

She grabbed the tray before he let go, and was glad she did. She got the impression he didn't care whether she accepted it or not, that he would've let it clatter to the floor if she hadn't caught it. That would teach her to be quicker the next time.

The slot closed and the bolt that held it shut slid home. As far as she could tell, that was the end of the encounter.

"Wait!" She pounded some more. "Don't leave! Just . . . tell me who you are. Why

I'm here. What do you want from me?"

She put her ear to the door and thought she heard movement, but the walls of her prison were so thick she could've been imagining it. "Hello?" she yelled, pounding some more.

Nothing.

Her knuckles were sore, her voice hoarse, by the time she gave up and slid down to the cement, still holding her food tray with her free hand. What was going on? Was this about revenge? Rape? Torture?

She stared at what looked like a hastily prepared peanut butter and jelly sandwich, a bag of plain potato chips, some carrot sticks and an apple. A carton of milk, like what a child might receive in a school lunch, took up one of the small sections of the tray.

Tears welled up, but knowing they'd do her no good, she battled them back. After carefully setting the tray beside her, she opened her milk. "Amarok, *please* come for me," she whispered. *"Please."*

She imagined him arriving home to find her shoe in the driveway, along with her purse, and knew he had to be frantic. He'd do anything to save her. She trusted that.

But this had come as such a surprise. How would he even know where to start?

3

"What do *you* want with me?" Jasper asked, obviously surprised when Amarok walked into the room. Protocol for a prisoner as dangerous as Jasper dictated that prison staff follow certain safety precautions to the letter, and one of those precautions was speaking to him from the other side of the room, behind plexiglass. That was where Evelyn normally sat whenever she met with inmates of his classification. But Amarok wasn't prison staff, and this was a unique case — a very personal one. He wasn't about to let Jasper believe he had any fear of him.

He *didn't* have any fear. He was hoping Jasper would attempt to harm him. Then he'd have an excuse to unleash the pent-up rage he'd long felt toward the monster who'd hurt Evelyn so terribly, not to mention the thirty or so other women he'd

43

tortured and murdered over the years (no one besides Jasper himself could give an exact number and he wouldn't admit to anything).

Instead of confronting him or threatening him in any way, however, Jasper took a step back. No doubt he could tell that Amarok wasn't messing around today, that he was more than willing to take his chances in a physical altercation. To prove it, Amarok asked the CO standing outside the door to come in and remove Jasper's shackles and belly chain.

"Are you sure?" Officer Hatch was already unhappy that Amarok had insisted on meeting Jasper on *this* side of the plexiglass. He wasn't eager to forgo yet another layer of security.

"Positive."

Reluctantly, Hatch did as he was told. "Anything else, Sergeant?"

"That's it."

The CO hesitated. "Maybe I should stay in the room, in case you need backup."

"That won't be necessary."

"But this one's wily, sir. Always trying to cause trouble in subtle ways."

Jasper snapped his teeth, causing the guard to jump, at which point Jasper laughed and Hatch gave him a baleful glare.

44

"It's not a good idea for you to be in here alone with him, and there's no need," Hatch said. "We have a place where you can talk to him safely."

Amarok's cheeks ached as he forced a smile. "No one knows this bastard better than I do, Officer Hatch. I'll be fine."

"*Evelyn* knows me better," Jasper crooned. "After all, I've felt her warm blood pump out all over my hands."

When he closed his eyes as though savoring the memory, it took every bit of willpower Amarok possessed to keep from grabbing Jasper by the collar of his prison-issue jumpsuit and shoving him up against the wall. His muscles bunched, but he didn't move. As much as he was tempted, he couldn't be the aggressor. "Which is why, if anything happens to her, I'm going to hold you *personally* responsible, even if you're not to blame."

Jasper lifted his eyebrows. "Now you're just giving me a hard-on. I admit I've never had sex with a man, but I'd be happy to make an exception for you."

"I'm out of your league," Amarok said.

The amusement fled Jasper's face.

"Sergeant, I really don't think this is a good idea." The CO glanced suspiciously at Jasper before returning his attention to

Amarok. No doubt he could feel the powerful animosity between them.

"You can go," Amarok said.

With a heavy *suit yourself* sigh, Hatch moved to the door. "I'll be right out here if you need me."

"*I* won't need you — but *he* might."

"In that case, if I hear someone yell, I'll take my damn sweet time," he muttered. "Because I won't lift a finger to save that animal."

When the door closed behind the CO, Jasper took another step back. He was no longer so cocky, so ready to taunt. He was on his own, and he knew it. "So . . . you've finally come for revenge?" he asked uncertainly.

Amarok didn't feel like sitting down. He had too much adrenaline flowing through him. But he forced himself to adopt a casual demeanor as he walked over to the only furniture in the room — a metal chair bolted to the floor. It faced the desk on the other side of the plexiglass, so he sat sideways, in order to see Jasper. "That depends . . ."

"On . . ."

"You." Amarok had never felt anything even remotely akin to the hatred he reserved for the man who'd tortured Evelyn for three

46

days before cutting her throat and leaving her for dead when she was only sixteen, so it wasn't easy to speak in a civil manner. Maybe that was why, after Jasper's initial arrest, he'd never paid the man a visit. The investigators in Peoria had approached him to see if he would be willing to try to get a bit more information out of him, but Amarok had left that up to Evelyn, who was better at it, anyway.

The reason? He didn't trust himself.

"How does it depend on me?"

"If you give me what I want, we might not have a problem. *Today.*"

Jasper was sizing him up. Amarok could tell. Amarok didn't get the impression Jasper was scared of him, exactly. Jasper didn't experience fear, at least not the way most people did. But there was little question he understood, even though he was no longer restricted by chains, that he didn't have the upper hand in this situation. Since Amarok knew who and what he was, Jasper couldn't ply the normal tools of his trade — surprise, lies, trickery, flattery, manipulation. Even brute strength wouldn't be the asset it was when stalking women; Amarok was bigger and probably stronger, too. "What is it you want?"

Amarok had heard Evelyn mention Jas-

47

per's eyes — how dead they were, how bereft of any kind of humanity. She said that was common among psychopaths. Since they didn't feel the same emotions as other people, that lack of feeling often revealed itself in their eyes, making them sort of dull in appearance, like a shark's.

But Amarok was surprised to see just the opposite. He could hardly believe that someone so twisted could look so normal, even in the eyes. As far as he was concerned, there was *nothing* about Jasper that would warn an unwary stranger that he or she was dealing with a deadly predator. No doubt that was part of the reason he'd been such an effective killer. He was handsome and muscular with blond hair and blue eyes. He looked anything *but* dangerous. "Information."

Jasper's expression grew suspicious. "Go to hell. I'm not confessing to anything, and I'm not talking about where certain women might or might not be buried."

"This is about something else entirely."

"What else could you want from me?"

"Someone's taken Evelyn."

His mouth dropped open. *"Taken* her? You mean she's been *abducted?"*

His surprise seemed genuine. That was one of the reasons Amarok had come to see

Jasper; he'd needed to be sure Jasper wasn't involved in any way. "That's what the evidence indicates."

"What evidence is there?"

Jasper didn't seem to feel any pleasure at the news of Evelyn's abduction. He probably still had plans to kill her himself and didn't want anyone else to remove the pleasure of that possibility. "I don't feel like going over that with you," Amarok said flatly. "I just want to know if you've heard anything in this place, anyone talking about having it in for her, threatening to get even with her, bragging that they will soon have their revenge or anything like that."

Jasper started to laugh. "That's all anyone talks about. Most of the men in here are sadists!"

"I'm asking if anything in particular stands out in your mind, if there's something I should be aware of."

"Oh my God! You don't know who took her! You don't have even the first clue, or you wouldn't be standing here, talking to me."

Amarok clenched his jaw. "Have you heard anything or not?"

"What will I get out of it if I tell you?"

"I can make your life in here a hell of a lot easier." He hated to bargain with the devil, but right now, as desperate as he was, he'd sell his soul, if only it would help. He didn't have the luxury of time, needed to find some direction.

Jasper began to pace across the small room. "Tell me what happened. You've got to give me *something* to go on, something that might jog a memory or inspire an idea."

Again, Amarok was tempted to refuse. But since he'd already stooped, in a sense, to taking Jasper into his confidence, he figured he might as well swallow *all* his pride. He'd do *anything* to save Evelyn and their child, and, while the culprit could be any of the antisocial assholes she'd studied over the years — or even consulted on peripherally, whether it was by doing a Violence Threat Assessment or something else — she'd been in Hilltop for the past three years. The odds were much better that her abduction had to do with someone associated with Hanover House. "She was supposed to meet me this afternoon at the Moosehead, and she didn't show up."

"So . . ."

"When I couldn't reach her by phone, I drove home to see what was going on."

"And . . ."

Somewhat reluctantly, Amarok continued, "And when I got there, I found her purse spilled all over the front yard and one shoe on the drive, just outside her vehicle. She pulled in and got out — but never made it into the house."

"Someone grabbed her right in the middle of the day."

Amarok sensed some admiration in his voice but tried to ignore it. "This time of year, it's light until late, but yes — at a time when I wouldn't be home."

"Whoever kidnapped her knows you," he said simply.

"He knows where we live, but that isn't hard to find out, not in a town the size of Hilltop. *You* did it easily enough."

"So did Lyman Bishop," he said. "He got your address from that waitress he killed and hanged in the center of town to distract you so that he could get to Evelyn, remember?"

How could he ever forget? He'd known Sandy and her family for most of his life. None of them had forgiven Evelyn for bringing such dangerous men to town. "You didn't hear?"

"What?"

"He suffered a brain hemorrhage from the beating you gave him. These days, he's almost a vegetable."

At first Jasper seemed pleased by the idea

51

of having hurt Bishop that badly, but then his eyes narrowed with obvious skepticism. "Who says?"

Amarok came to his feet. "It's documented. A brain hemorrhage shows up on an MRI. They have the scans."

"Maybe he *did* have a hemorrhage. That doesn't necessarily mean he's completely incapacitated. He could have exaggerated the effects. That's what I would've done. And even if he *didn't* fake more damage than he sustained, hemorrhages affect people to greater and lesser degrees. It could be that he's improved — to the point where he's capable of plotting revenge."

The odds of that were remote, which was why Amarok hadn't seriously considered Bishop when he thought of him earlier. But perhaps he'd discarded the possibility too soon. The Zombie Maker was no ordinary psychopath. He'd been a cancer researcher with a genius IQ. Was it possible he still had enough brain cells to escape and come after Evelyn? Or, as Jasper suggested, had he been exaggerating his impairment from the beginning to avoid being locked up for the rest of his life?

If so, it could be that he'd been lying low this whole time, waiting for the perfect moment to strike — which meant he'd had a whole year and a half to recover and prepare.

If Bishop was behind Evelyn's abduction, she was in even more trouble than Amarok had assumed. Lyman Bishop used an ice pick to give his victims a frontal lobotomy. That was why they called him the Zombie Maker. Sometimes scrambling the brains of his victims killed them; other times they survived, severely impaired. Death had never been his goal. What he craved was total acquiescence, total control, total *enslavement*. "You think it's him."

"It sure as hell isn't anyone in here — unless there's been an escape I don't know about."

"Not all psychopaths are locked up. There are still plenty of people like you on the outside," Amarok said dryly. "Evelyn was on the news several times while fighting to establish this institution. The challenge could've drawn someone else. It doesn't *have* to be Bishop."

"True. But you have to ask yourself, who'd want to get to Evelyn worse than Bishop?" Jasper pursed his lips, making a show of considering his own question — and then he answered it. "Only me."

Evelyn tried to remain calm. Whoever had kidnapped her wasn't Jasper. It *couldn't* be Jasper; he was locked up. And she wasn't quite as scared of anyone else. She took some solace in that.

When nothing happened, no one else came for quite some time, she slowly began to relax, despite the questions that swirled in her mind. Who'd taken her? What was his intent? And why hadn't he confronted her? What could he possibly be waiting for?

She had no answers and the unknown was driving her crazy. In an attempt to occupy her mind, she started doing math problems. "If Suzie plans to unload a refrigerator from the back of her truck, and the truck's thirty-eight inches from the ground, the ramp sixty-four inches long, what is the length of the distance from where the ramp touches the ground to the back of the truck?"

She solved that before making up a bunch of others, which required such focus that more frightening thoughts couldn't intrude. But she'd skipped breakfast, been kidnapped before she could have lunch and hadn't been given enough dinner, so she was hungry again.

She returned to the tray her captor had left before and nibbled at the core of the apple she'd discarded. While such a small amount of food didn't do anything to ease her hunger, it tasted good.

Her body ached from sitting on the ground. She'd stayed close to the door, wanted to get out so badly she hadn't dared move away for fear she'd miss her one and only chance. But she was beginning to believe she was wasting her time. It wasn't going to open anytime soon. Her captor or captors didn't seem to be on the premises. If they were, they were good at ignoring her presence in what used to be a walk-in cooler.

Why would someone kidnap her but not harm her? she asked herself. Was she being ransomed?

She hoped she *had* been taken for money. If that was the case, maybe Amarok could raise the funds to get her back. They weren't wealthy, but they both had decent jobs. And he could go to her family and friends. Her parents had a significant fortune. While she hated the thought of anyone having to sacrifice for her release, especially her parents after all they'd been through when she went missing for three days in high school, if the only thing her captor wanted was money maybe she wouldn't be put through the hell she'd experienced before.

She decided to believe that whoever had

taken her *was* negotiating with Amarok, that Amarok was trying to free her, and picked herself up off the floor in order to cross to the bed. She was so weary she could barely move. Fatigue had become an issue since she'd started her third trimester. Never before had she been tempted to put her head down on her desk for a catnap during the middle of the day, but she'd done so twice the past week.

"We're going to be fine," she whispered to her baby as she rubbed her stomach. "We just need to be smart. To eat whenever we get the chance. To get plenty of rest. To conserve our strength for the right moment."

She heard the heat kick on, felt the warmth blowing through the small vent overhead and was slightly reassured. She'd been given only one thin blanket. It was nice to know she wasn't going to be miserably cold on top of everything else. It wasn't as though she could tell anyone if she was getting uncomfortable. Even on the temperature, she had to tolerate whatever someone on the outside decided.

Scooting down in bed, she pulled the blanket over her and fell into a troubled sleep.

4

Hilltop, AK — Tuesday, 7:10 p.m. AKDT
From Amarok's best guess, Evelyn had been gone for five hours or so. Five hours wasn't long in most respects, but in this regard, it was an eternity. On the way back from the prison, he'd stopped at his house to scour the empty land around it, just in case Evelyn had been killed quickly, her body dumped nearby. He saw nothing out of the ordinary. No drag marks through the summer moss, no footprints. Not a trace of anything different at all.

He had Makita with him as usual, but Makita wasn't an official police dog. He hadn't been through the training in New Mexico that so many police dogs had. That training, together with the price of the dog, could cost upwards of fifteen thousand dollars — money the state wasn't willing to spend.

But Amarok had been around dogs all his

life, so he trained Makita himself, step by painstaking step, teaching him to help enforce the hunting laws, which was a large part of a trooper's job in Alaska, especially in a small outpost like Hilltop. Because he had to confront groups of hunters who were often drunk and jacklighting — shining spotlights on deer or bear, causing them to freeze so they could easily be shot — or doing other illegal things, he'd trained Makita to hide behind him and remain completely silent. If the hunters who were breaking the law wouldn't obey verbal commands and grew threatening, ganged up or started to shoot, he'd whistle for his dog just as other cops would call for backup, and Makita would come charging out of hiding, take them by surprise before they could shoot and put an end to the fight, most of the time before it could even get going. Makita knew how to knock a man down. If Amarok *really* got into trouble and gave a certain command, he could put his opponent out of commission permanently.

But now that Evelyn was missing, Amarok wished he'd trained Makita as a search dog so that he'd be more useful in finding Evelyn. As it was, the dog kept returning to him as though asking when they were finally going to confront what he would consider a "pack" of hunters, so the fight could begin — especially because this was hunting season, the time of year they worked the most, in tandem.

"Evelyn," he told Makita, having him smell her shoe. "Find Evelyn." But the dog didn't fully understand, and they didn't turn up anything. Neither did Phil Robbins, a middle-aged local who helped out by clearing the roads in the winter and acting as a Village Public Safety Officer throughout the warmer months. Amarok had sent Phil to check the closest rivers at various choke points where broken branches and floating debris typically got snagged, but Phil had called on the radio just as Amarok finished to say that he was back and the rivers were clear.

Amarok was hoping to get better news from Shorty, who also helped keep the peace during the summer months when they had such an influx of rowdy hunters and fishermen. He'd sent Shorty to various hunting cabins in the mountains, and because of how long it took to get from one to the other, he hadn't yet radioed in a report.

"Hey, I don't like the look on your face," Phil said as Amarok entered the small trooper post. "I can tell what you're thinking, and it isn't good."

Amarok didn't reply, just glanced up to see Phil with a paper cup at the water cooler as he closed the door behind Makita.

"We've been up against tougher things," Phil added in an effort to encourage him.

Amarok shook his head. "No, we haven't."

Phil's forced cheer crumbled beneath Amarok's leveling gaze. Instead of continuing to act chipper and overly optimistic, he downed the water, crushed his cup and tossed it in the wastebasket as he walked over. "We're going to get her back, Amarok. And she'll be fine. That doc of yours has already been to hell and back. She knows how to survive. She's tougher than all the rest of us put together."

"How tough can she be at six months pregnant, Phil?" Amarok wiped the sweat from his forehead as he dropped into his chair. "She's so tired at night, she falls asleep on the couch almost as soon as we have dinner. Sometimes, I have to carry her to bed. Her feet swell if she doesn't put them up enough. Her back aches if she doesn't change her position as often as she should. She feels nauseous if she doesn't eat at regular intervals. And, sometimes, if she overdoes it, she starts to cramp, which the doctor has warned us could mean trouble. The stress alone of what she's going through could bring on early labor and —" His voice cracked, so he shut up.

Phil squeezed his shoulder. "I understand what's at stake. But she knows you're out here doing everything you can to get her back. That's what she's clinging to. You have to believe you can do it, too. You have to keep fighting as though it's a given — and thinking what you were thinking a second ago won't help."

Those were strong words for Phil. He wasn't someone who typically took charge. But he was right.

With a nod, Amarok picked up the phone to give Beacon Point Mental Hospital in Minneapolis another try. He'd left three messages before he exited the prison, but the person on duty kept insisting that, what with HIPAA laws these days, she couldn't even confirm if they still had a Lyman Bishop at their facility.

He'd explained his situation and asked to speak to her superior, and she'd promised he'd be hearing from someone soon, but, probably because it was three hours later there, so after ten, it wasn't happening soon enough.

"Hello?"

He recognized the woman's voice. "Sarah? It's me again."

"I know," she said. "I'm sorry. I've been trying to get a hold of someone who can tell me what to do, but the on-call doctor hasn't responded yet."

Amarok struggled to keep his voice from rising. "I just need to know if Lyman Bishop is there. That's it."

"I understand. But I've already told you —"

"I'm a police officer."

"That's what you say, but how do I know it's true? Anyone can call up and pretend to be a police officer. You need a search warrant or a court order to get medical information —"

He could hear Makita lapping up the water in his dish after the time they'd spent outdoors. "I'm not asking for medical information."

"This is a mental hospital. I can't share *any* information, not unless you have the patient's written permission or private code."

"I don't have Bishop's permission or his private code because I'm no friend of his. And I can't get a search warrant, because I don't have probable cause for believing a man who's been ravaged by a severe brain hemorrhage and is being fed through a tube in Minneapolis might've just committed a crime in Alaska. I'm merely trying to get a lead on a woman who's been abducted. He's attacked her before, so I need to rule him out."

"I understand."

"No, I don't think you do. Her life could hang in the balance — her life and the life of her unborn child. You don't want to be responsible for their deaths, do you? Please, tell me if he's there."

She'd been adamant in her refusal, completely unresponsive to his entreaties, but when she didn't answer right away, he got the impression she was finally softening.

"Please?" he said again. "Rules are just rules. Sometimes doing what's right — what's most humane — requires breaking them."

"I agree, but —"

"This isn't just any woman who's gone missing. It's Dr. Evelyn Talbot." He'd been reluctant to mention that before, to start up the media circus that would result. Those who didn't believe in what Evelyn was doing tried to capitalize on any setback in order to shut her down. But now that she hadn't turned up as he'd hoped, he was beyond trying to protect her work at Hanover House. "You've heard of her, haven't you?"

63

"I have. Anyone who works in a psych-related field has heard of her. She researches serial killers."

Makita padded off to his bed, but even after he curled up, he kept lifting his head as though he was trying to figure out what had changed, what was going on.

"That's right," Amarok said. "At Hanover House in Alaska. And I'm calling from Alaska. You can tell by the area code, right?"

"She's missing?" she said uncertainly.

"Since one o'clock today. At least, that was when she left the prison. It was nearly four when I found the contents of her purse scattered over the ground and only one of her shoes."

There was a brief pause. Then she said, "Fine. He's here, okay? You can quit worrying about him and look elsewhere, because it's not Bishop. He's no longer on a feeding tube, but he isn't capable of much."

Amarok dropped his head in his hand and began to massage his forehead.

"Sergeant Murphy?" she said. "Did you hear me?"

"Yeah. I heard. Thank you," he said, and hung up.

Phil watched him expectantly. "So? What'd they say?"

"It's not Lyman Bishop. I can't believe I

64

let Jasper convince me it might be."

"Who then?"

"I'm going over to speak to the Led-stetters."

"Sandy's family? Why? They've never hurt anyone."

"They hate Evelyn, blame her for Sandy's death. You should see the way they look at her if they happen to see her at the Moose-head or elsewhere. She pretends she doesn't notice, but I can tell it bothers her."

"Sandy died eighteen months ago, Ama-rok. Don't you think Davie or Junior would've done something by now — if they were going to?"

He scrubbed a hand over his face. "Of course I do. I've always liked Davie *and* Junior. But right now, it's the only lead I've got."

Minneapolis, MN — Tuesday, 11:00 p.m. CST
Lyman Bishop frowned as he lifted the remote to turn off the television that hung on the wall.

"What the hell?" Terry Lovett, a janitor about thirty-five years old, paced beside Lyman's bed. "Why wasn't it on there?" he asked, referring to the late-night news.

"Because it's too soon." Lyman too had thought Evelyn's abduction would be re-

65

ported right away. He'd been counting on it, but he couldn't let on that this wasn't something he'd anticipated. He had to maintain Terry's confidence, pretend as though he had everything under control. Seeing Evelyn's abduction on the news tonight wasn't critical, anyway. They'd just have to wait an additional day for word to spread. He wanted to be in Minneapolis when the news broke.

"How long can it take?" Sweat beaded on Terry's forehead even though it wasn't the least bit hot. And Terry wasn't overweight. He was just worried, anxious.

Lyman watched him curiously. He found this manifestation of Terry's anxiety rather odd, since he'd never been nervous enough to have that kind of physiological reaction. "It'll probably be tomorrow."

He pivoted at the wall. "And if it's not?"

"It *will* be. Dr. Talbot's a prominent figure. The press will pick up on her disappearance soon. Then, as Sergeant Murphy — or anyone else who gets involved — starts searching for her, they'll check to make sure I'm still in this terrible place. And once they confirm it, they'll assume I couldn't possibly be responsible, that it was a stretch to even consider it, and you won't have to worry about anyone pointing a finger in your direction when I come up missing."

"After everyone knows she's been kid-napped, that's when you'll escape?"

Lyman shoved his glasses higher up on the bridge of his nose. "Yes. I'll put on the change of clothes you brought me and walk out the back door."

"Which I'll leave unlocked for you. You have the burner phone I picked up? You've hidden it well?"

"It's taped to the bottom of the bed. No one's looked under there since I got here."

"Why would they? *I'm* the janitor."

That was Lyman's point. Even *he* hadn't gone under the bed, and he was supposed to clean there. "Exactly." Bishop liked him, but there was no question he was lazy.

"Be sure the door latches behind you when you leave," he said. "I'll need to repair the emergency alarm before anyone discovers I deactivated it."

"I'm not likely to forget." Lyman adjusted the covers on his bed. "We couldn't have any of the lunatics in here getting out on the streets, now, can we?" He laughed at his own joke. Some of the patients in the psych ward were scary, and not only the schizo-phrenics. But Terry was too worked up to enjoy a little levity.

"What if things don't go the way you've

planned and the police jump all over this?"

Lyman waved him off. "They won't. They'll assume I got up, rambled around and somehow managed to get out of the building, at which point I wandered off."

"They'll need to account for you somehow. They might even call Hanover House to let them know you've gone missing."

"Why would they? They think I'm an incoherent fool these days, not capable of surviving on my own."

Terry picked up a piece of trash Bishop had thrown at the garbage can earlier. "And if you're wrong?"

That was always a possibility. He couldn't control everything. He could only put the odds in his favor and, statistically speaking, he felt his chances were good. "Let them search. They'll never find me. I'll be Mr. John Edmonson at that point. The ID you got me is flawless. No one will ever be able to tell it's a fake."

"Should be good. Cost enough," he grumbled.

Lyman smoothed what hair he had left over the top of his head. His male-pattern baldness was getting so much worse as he aged. "I'm going to pay you for that. Don't worry. I'll pay you for everything, just as soon as I get out of here and can access my money."

"I'm counting on it. You don't know my brother-in-law like I do, but he'll come after you if you don't."

Bishop wasn't worried. An ounce of brainpower could overcome a ton of brawn. "You've made that clear."

Terry retied the drawstring on his scrubs. He enjoyed looking like one of the medical staff, probably because it was more prestigious than being a janitor. "If they *do* find you, tell me you won't drag me into it no matter what. I got a family now. I can't go back to prison. And Emmett is not the type of enemy you want to have."

"Again, you've made your point. Anyway, I would have no reason to bring either of you down with me. Like I said before, relax. Everything's running according to plan." *His* plan, which, even he had to admit, was brilliant. Maybe his mind wasn't quite as sharp as it used to be. But now that the seizures he'd suffered right after the brain hemorrhage were gone, his situation could be a lot worse. He could be sitting on death row with little or no chance at freedom.

"I'm *trying*," Terry said. "But Emmett is unhappy. He doesn't like that she's pregnant."

Bishop found that aspect of Evelyn Talbot's situation especially appealing, but he couldn't say so. He'd spent too long crafting a far different image of himself for Terry. "He must be afraid she'll go into labor."

"Do you blame him? He doesn't want to be responsible for delivering a baby — or having the baby die while he's in charge. He told me he's about to bug out."

Lyman felt his first real jolt of alarm. He'd finally made his move, had it all set up. He couldn't have Emmett ruining everything. "He'd better not. We had an agreement!"

"I've told him that, but if he decides to go there's nothing I can say to make him stay."

"What about the money? Doesn't he care about getting paid?"

"I'm sure he does, but —"

"You assured me he was dependable. I told you what I needed, and you said you could make it happen."

"And I *did* make it happen. It's just that Emmett's a little . . . unpredictable."

"Your wife's his sister. Have *her* say something."

"Are you kidding? She doesn't know anything about this. Besides, he makes up his own mind, and he has this weird code of ethics. Some things he has no problem with, others are a big deal."

"Then you should've gotten someone else."

Terry threw up his hands. "I was lucky to get him! How many people do you think I know who'd be willing to kidnap a woman, especially someone like Dr. Talbot?"

Lyman toyed with the anxiety medication they gave him each night, along with a sleeping pill. He'd been saving his meds instead of swallowing them almost since the day he arrived at this facility. They made him feel tired and dull, and he couldn't have that. "Ten grand is a lot of money. And I'm paying *you* the same amount. So if you want to keep your demanding wife happy, you'd better make sure her brother doesn't let us down."

He heaved a sigh as he came back toward the bed. "I'm doing my best. I had no idea Emmett would get this jittery. He talked so tough when we were in the joint. How much longer do you think we'll need him to stay?"

"Could be as long as a week."

"A *week*," Terry repeated, as though Lyman had said a year.

"In order for this to be successful, we have to be patient. Tell him I'll give him an additional two thousand dollars if he'll stay."

"What about me?" he asked.

Lyman considered handing him the medication, so he could dispose of it — or sell it, which was far more likely. Lyman had already stockpiled so much. That sort of thing was likely to come in handy when dealing with a recalcitrant prisoner. Knowing that, he'd prepared from the beginning and hidden it all in a small shoe box he kept with his few personal things. But, at the last second, he decided to keep even these last pills. One could never have too many, he told himself. "You're getting paid well enough," he said, and slipped the pills into the pocket of his pajama top.

Terry arched his eyebrows when he saw him do it. "You know you can't keep them there. The nurse will come by in just a little bit to make sure you took all your medication, and if you do anything that's out of the ordinary, it'll draw attention we don't need."

"I plan to take them," he lied. "I just don't want to do it while you're here. They'll knock me out in no time, and what kind of company would I be then?"

"Go ahead," Terry said, his concern melting away that easily. "I have to get my work done, anyway. This place isn't going to clean itself." He started for the door, pausing at the last second. "I've promised Emmett you're not going to hurt Evelyn Talbot.

72

That's true, isn't it?"

"I've told you, many times, I've never hurt *anyone.*"

"So the Zombie Maker stuff — with the ice pick through the eye socket and all that other gruesome bullshit — that wasn't you?"

Bishop knew how benign he looked, lying in a bed with half his face paralyzed. As an educated man, a man who came off as a calm intellectual, he wasn't anything like the thugs Terry associated with criminal behavior, a fact he continued to use in his favor. "You know it wasn't. The detective who was investigating those murders planted the evidence in my house. Otherwise, they wouldn't have let me out of prison, remember? I've shown you the archived newspaper articles online."

"I remember. You just want her to sign some paper so you can get your life back; I got it."

Bishop hid a smile. It wasn't difficult to convince someone who *wanted* to believe him.

"So how long will you keep her locked up?" Terry asked.

"Not for long. Once I've had my say, really made her hear me, she can go, if she wants."

"*If she wants?* A woman like that would never *choose* to stay with a man like you," he scoffed, incredulous.

Bishop smiled as he imagined how easy it would be to change her mind — in the most literal sense. "You never know."

5

Anchorage, AK — Tuesday, 10:16 p.m. AKDT
Evelyn was far more exhausted than ever before in her life, but she fought sleep, didn't feel as though it would be safe. She had to remain as aware as possible and *do* something about her situation, couldn't sit back and suppose Amarok or someone else would be able to find her.

But what could she do?

She asked herself that over and over as she stared at the ceiling. Her situation seemed hopeless. She didn't have a door or window that could be breached. The walls were solid, too; there was no way to break through them. But once she quit trying to think of a way to break out and started looking for other options, she had an idea. She'd associated with prison inmates long enough to have learned that it was possible to make a weapon out of almost anything. And something Herculean — like digging a tunnel to freedom — could be accomplished with only a *little* progress each day, given enough time.

She had no idea how long she'd be held captive, but in case this wasn't as simple as being kidnapped for ransom, she wasn't about to waste the time she had lying on a filthy cot, worrying and waiting for the worst to happen.

So what were her options? She'd known inmates who'd heated up chocolate bars to throw on prison staff or rival gang members, causing severe burns; inmates who'd created shivs out of magazines or even toilet paper (strengthened with papier-mâché); and inmates who'd made spears from the metal framework of their beds. Most simply filed down the end of a toothbrush. With enough thrust, that could be lethal and seemed the easiest way to go. But she hadn't been provided with a toothbrush, had only one roll of toilet paper and no magazines.

For that matter, she had no chocolate, either, let alone something to heat it with. Her cot provided the only hope she had of creating a weapon, and she already knew it wouldn't be as fancy as a spear. She couldn't remove part of the frame, not without a screwdriver. It might even be too optimistic to believe she could remove one of the springs, but she intended to try.

She pulled the mattress off and studied the interlocking coils. It wouldn't be easy, not when she had only her bare hands to work with, but if she could untwist one of the thick steel wires, straighten it out and sharpen it by filing it on the floor, she could tear the lining out of her jacket and wrap the fabric tightly around one end to create a handle.

When she was finished, the weapon would look a lot like a screwdriver. And if she ripped out a short length of the seam in her mattress, she'd even have a place to hide it. Then, if her captor tried to torture or rape her, she could at least *attempt* to defend herself and her baby.

She squeezed her eyes closed as past memories assailed her and, once again, had to remind herself that this wasn't Jasper. Yes, she was pregnant and physically compromised because of it, but she was also older and wiser.

Humming a song, so she couldn't think too much while struggling with those coils, she fought to undo one. She'd been hungry for hours, it seemed, but focusing on something else, especially something so difficult, helped her ignore the pangs in her stomach.

Both thumbs were bleeding at the edge of

the nail by the time she gave up. She'd managed to untwist one of the wires halfway down but couldn't finish. She was too nauseous and weak.

Being careful to bend the part that was now sticking out so it wouldn't poke through, she replaced the mattress. She hoped if she slept for a few hours her morning sickness would be gone when she woke up. But she wasn't overly optimistic, doubted it would go away if she didn't eat.

She'd barely closed her eyes when she heard the telltale rustle on the other side of the door.

"Hello?" She rolled off the cot, nearly tripping in her haste to reach the slot as it opened.

"Give me the tray."

Her captor had spoken, but she didn't recognize his voice, which was odd. For someone willing to risk a lengthy prison sentence by abducting her, she felt they should have some shared history — a vendetta between them like the one she'd had with Jasper. It was the man she'd seen before, however. She could tell because he was wearing the same camouflage pants and black T-shirt.

Now, he barked. "Or you'll skip dinner."

She grabbed the tray that held the seeds

from her apple and slid it through the opening.

He responded by giving her a bottle of water and a plastic bowl of oatmeal.

"This looks more like breakfast. Is it morning?"

"It's nighttime, for your information. But this isn't fucking McDonald's."

"How am I supposed to know what time it is?"

"You don't need to know. You just eat what I give you."

"Fine. Okay. No problem." For the sake of keeping her hands free and preserving the meal, she put everything on her bed before rushing back to the opening. "Will you tell me what I'm doing here?" she asked. "What I can expect? Is this a ransom situation?"

He didn't answer.

"Who are you?"

He gave her a banana, which she eagerly accepted. She was hungry enough to eat almost anything, but she had no idea what the oatmeal would taste like and figured fruit could only make it better.

Although he started to close the slot, she put her fingers in the way — and prayed he wouldn't simply crush them. "Wait! I'm going to need more water. This isn't enough.

79

I'm carrying a baby. I have to have enough water."

When he walked away and returned with another bottle, she took heart. This was the first time she'd been able to improve her situation. "Would it be possible to get another banana?"

"Move your hands or you won't have any fingers left," he growled.

She pulled back, and he slammed the covering and rammed the bolt home.

"Bastard," she whispered as she slid to the floor and twisted the top off her water. Fortunately, she could feel somewhat confident that what she was about to drink was clean, since it had been previously unopened. It turned her stomach to remember the substances Jasper had forced down her throat when he held her captive in that shack. He'd taken such pleasure in her revulsion, in his power over her.

But, of course, that wasn't the worst of what happened. . . .

She drank one whole bottle before getting up to eat the banana and oatmeal. The food wasn't what she'd call *good.* She could tell the oatmeal was instant, probably cooked in a microwave. But at least she was able to stop her stomach from growling, and the banana did improve the taste.

After she finished, she drank only half of the second bottle of water before making herself save the rest. After all, she had no idea when the man in the camouflage pants would be coming back. If this was dinner, it would be a long time until breakfast.

Hilltop, AK — Tuesday, 10:30 p.m. AKDT
"*Excuse me?*"

Prepared for anything, Amarok spread his legs about eighteen inches apart, the right foot slightly behind the left, so he'd have better balance if one of the Ledstetters came at him, and stood with Makita at least five feet from the door. They were good folks, but Davie, who was in his mid-fifties, and Junior, who was Amarok's own age at thirty-two, were known hotheads — not the type to take an insult of this magnitude lightly. "Have you seen Evelyn?" Amarok asked, repeating his initial question.

"You have hundreds of criminals, a large majority of which are serial killers — *the worst of the worst* — just five miles down the road and you show up at *my* house after ten o'clock with this kidnapping bullshit?" Davie demanded.

"I didn't say anything about kidnapping. I just asked if you've seen her."

"Yeah, well, I've heard what's going on.

81

It's all over town. So I know what you're really asking."

"So? What's the answer?"

"Seriously? I've never even had a DUI!"

His son had been arrested for fighting on more than one occasion, but Amarok let that go. "I'm sorry," he said, and meant it. "With what you've been through . . . It's not that I *want* to be here."

"Then why'd you come?" he demanded. "You've known me your whole life. You *know* I'm no criminal."

"Heartbreak and hatred can twist a man's heart."

"So now *my* heart is twisted?"

"I've seen how you and Junior glare at Evelyn whenever she's around." His wife, Betty, did the same. To a lesser extent, so did the two younger girls. But Amarok didn't want to accuse the women in the family, too. "I'm just asking if you've seen her, Davie. Let's try not to make anything more out of it."

"You believe I might've done something to her. I can tell by your face."

"I'm hoping you haven't."

The television went off as more members of the family came to see what was going on. Amarok noticed how Betty's expression grew accusatory when she saw him. He used to be good friends with the whole family, but that relationship had been destroyed since Sandy's murder. They didn't like seeing him with Evelyn — took it as a betrayal of sorts, as if he'd chosen the other "side" — and these days he was always with Evelyn.

"Davie would never harm a woman, even Evelyn," she said.

"You know what she's suffered in the past, right?"

Betty squeezed in front of her husband. "Everyone knows what *she's* suffered. She's made a big deal of it on the news. Talking about the man who attacked her, garnering sympathy. Those were the antics she used to put that damn prison in our backyard. Doesn't seem to matter what she's doing to the rest of us." When she started to tear up, Davie pulled her back, out of the way.

"I've got this," he murmured. "Go finish your show."

"What's happening, Dad?" Junior emerged from somewhere, probably his bedroom.

"Amarok is asking about Dr. Talbot."

"He's here? Why?"

"Wants to know if we've seen her."

"Us? What the hell! One of those bastards finally got to her. That's what happened. We all knew it was only a matter of time."

Amarok didn't hear any regret in that statement. "The question is . . . which bastard?"

"I'm only going to say this once, Amarok," Davie broke in. "You're jumping to the wrong conclusion."

When Makita growled deep and low in his throat, taking exception to their tone and body language, Amarok barked a command for him to stay where he was and looked past Davie. "Junior? What do *you* have to say for yourself?"

Junior nudged his father aside. "I say the same thing as my dad. You're going after the wrong people."

"Now we've *both* told you," Davie said, reasserting his authority. "I'm going to try to forget that you came over here to accuse us of a felony, because you're probably out of your mind with grief. I know what that's like, so I'm willing to cut you some slack — *this time.* But unless you have some kind of evidence, besides the fact that we hate the woman who cost us the loss of our oldest daughter, you'd better not ever come back here."

Amarok rested one hand on the side of the door and leaned into it to make himself appear friendlier, more relaxed and less

84

defensive and accusing, but he was carefully watching everyone he could see — and he knew Makita was doing the same. "Evelyn didn't cause Sandy's murder, Davie. She was about the only one fighting to keep Lyman Bishop behind bars. You seem to forget that."

"And you seem to forget that Lyman Bishop would never have been in Alaska, if not for her."

"*Someone* has to do the research. And it can't always be someone else." Amarok was using Evelyn's line — one she'd used in various arguments with him — but after living with her for so long he'd become convinced that her work was important.

"Yeah, well, we'll see if that's any solace to *you* now that *she's* gone."

He started to close the door, but Amarok stopped its forward motion. "She's six months pregnant, Davie."

For the first time, he seemed to feel some empathy. "Then I'm sorry for the baby."

There was nothing more he could say. Amarok let the door close, after which he stood on their front porch, staring at the ground, feeling more bereft and helpless than ever before in his life. Evelyn had been missing all day, and he didn't have the slightest clue who'd taken her or why.

When Makita licked his hand, he started toward his truck, but before he could reach it, the door opened again and a teenage girl, their youngest daughter — a caboose born a decade after the last child — poked her head out. "Sergeant Murphy?"

He pivoted to face her. "Yes?"

"I don't know if this means anything, but I saw a man I've never seen before in town earlier. He was driving a blue carpet-cleaning van. It had yellow writing on the side."

"A carpet-cleaning van? Could you make out the company name?"

"No. That part had been painted over. It just said carpet cleaning. But he didn't look like any kind of carpet cleaner to me."

"What *did* he look like?"

"He was sort of scary. He had this terrible scar on one eye."

"Where did you see him?"

"At the Quick Stop. I was at work, talking on the phone to my boyfriend, when he pulled up. After he left I mentioned that some guy had come in with a nasty scar who made me sort of nervous, and my boyfriend joked that he'd probably just been released from Hanover House."

"What time was it?"

"Now that I'm a senior, I get out at noon, so I've been starting earlier. I hadn't been at work long, so . . . around one?"

The timing was certainly suspect. Evelyn had gone missing shortly after. "What was he wearing?"

"Camouflage pants and a Black Sabbath T-shirt."

"Do you remember anything else about him? The color of his eyes, maybe?"

"Just that scar that barely missed his eye and the fact that he was all roided out, like The Rock."

"Would you say he was as tall as The Rock?"

"I don't know how tall The Rock is, but he wasn't short."

"How old?"

"Maybe . . . thirty?"

"Did he speak to Garrett? Have an accent?"

"Didn't say much. Just asked for a pack of Camels. From what I could tell, he didn't have an accent."

"Did he mention me or Evelyn? Ask where I lived? Where Hanover House was?"

"No."

Which, if this stranger was the culprit, meant he probably already knew. The question was . . . *how*? And how did he know Evelyn would be home at such an unusual time of day? That was the part that puzzled

Amarok the most. He'd checked her schedule, spoken to the other doctors and staff at HH. Other than meeting him at the Moosehead, no one knew of any appointments she'd made. And she certainly wouldn't have hired someone to clean their carpets. They had only hardwood floors. "How'd you see what he was driving?"

"I was by the door when he got there."

"Did you happen to get his license plate number?"

"No. I was too preoccupied with the sight of him, and I didn't follow him out when he left. I was just glad to see him go."

"Thanks, Kaylene."

She gave him a shy but sympathetic smile. "I'm sorry for what you're going through. I know it wasn't *your* fault — what happened to Sandy. *You* were against the prison coming here. I did a report on it in eighth grade and interviewed you. I'm not sure if you remember."

"I *do* remember," he said, although he hadn't until she reminded him.

"Well, I hope you can find Dr. Talbot and that . . . and that your baby's okay."

"Appreciate your help," he said, and whistled for Makita as he hurried back to his truck so he could head to Quigley's Quick Stop.

Anchorage, AK — Tuesday, 10:40 p.m. AKDT
Evelyn's captor returned for her bowl. Because he'd left the tray before, she hadn't expected to hear from him so soon, but it couldn't have been more than twenty minutes before the slot opened and she could see the now familiar torso of her captor as he demanded her empty water bottles, banana peel and bowl.

When she shoved those items through the hole — all except for the water she was conserving — he caught her hand so she couldn't withdraw it.

"Why is there blood on your fingers?" he demanded.

A fresh deluge of adrenaline ripped through Evelyn. She was just trying to decide what to say when he added an impatient, "It's not the baby, is it?"

"No. I-I fidget when I get anxious, sometimes bite my cuticles." Although she'd wiped the blood on her jacket, it'd left a telltale smear. She'd been unwilling to waste her drinking water by pouring it over her hands, and there was no way she was going to wash them in the toilet.

"You make yourself *bleed*?"

"A lot of people do." She prayed he'd believe her. She didn't want him to come into the room. If he figured out what she

89

was up to, the punishment could be severe. There was also the possibility that, even if he *didn't* discover she'd been trying to pry her cot apart, he might take the opportunity to abuse her.

At the same time, she needed to engage him, try to befriend him. She'd spoken to enough violent criminals over the years to understand that the victims who survived were those who managed to make themselves more than mere objects, to be used at will. They connected with the person who was confining or abusing them, made themselves *human,* and they often did that by pretending to be supportive of their attacker and empathetic with his motives, needs and situation.

Her heart pounded loudly in her ears while she waited to see how he might respond — and what she might be able to make of it.

"You're a shrink and you're self-destructive? Isn't that ironic."

"I've been through a lot, and being locked in a cooler is reactivating some bad habits."

He seemed to accept that. No doubt he had a few bad habits himself. "How much longer until the baby's due?"

"I just started my last trimester."

"What the hell does that mean?" He

tightened his grip on her wrists. "Speak English, for God's sake!"

She drew a calming breath. "I still have twelve weeks left, but this is a high-risk pregnancy, so . . ."

"So the baby could come at any time. Is that what you're saying?"

"Yes."

He cursed as he let her go.

"If that happens," she added, "if I go into labor, I'll need a hospital if the baby's to have any chance of surviving. So I hope there's one close by."

"You'd better not deliver while I'm here. That's all I've got to say."

She'd been hoping he'd reveal something about their location. She'd gotten nothing along those lines, but *while I'm here* seemed to suggest he was leaving soon. Where was he going — and when? "You do realize I can't stop labor. Can't do anything to change when the baby will arrive."

"Just keep your legs crossed, because you'll be in a world of hurt if you don't."

His hands were massive, leading her to believe he was a large man. And she'd noticed calluses that suggested he wasn't someone who worked in an office. Did he do construction? Some other kind of physical labor?

91

Possibly . . .

She doubted he was married. He didn't know *anything* about childbirth — just that he didn't want any part of it. She didn't see a wedding ring, either. "How will I call you if I do go into labor? Surely you won't leave me in here to have this baby alone."

"I told you. It's not going to happen on my watch."

"Your 'watch'? Is someone else coming? Jasper Moore doesn't have anything to do with this, does he?" She couldn't imagine how. Not too long ago, Jasper had killed his wealthy parents, who'd helped him escape after he slit her throat and left her for dead way back when. She was fairly certain they'd helped him financially through the years, too. But now that they were gone, who else would come to his aid?

No one. Unless . . .

Was the man outside the cooler a brother or a friend to one of the women in Jasper's life? One of his ex-wives, or someone who'd started writing to him since he'd been caught? Jasper looked a lot better than most serial killers, and, like Ted Bundy and even Charles Manson, he received more than his share of love letters, money and gifts from women. Since all prison mail was monitored, she'd read a few of the letters. The

Bonnie and Clyde Syndrome, or hybristo-
philia, was a very real phenomenon where
some women were sexually attracted to
high-profile, dangerous criminals. Evelyn
had seen the same thing over and over again
through the years with other notorious killers.

He didn't answer. He disappeared and
then returned. "Stick your hands out here
again."

She hesitated. *"Why?"*

"Just do it!"

Someone like Jasper would take great
pleasure in cutting off her fingers. She was
afraid to take the risk. But this man could
come in and do whatever he wanted, so
refusing wouldn't save her for long. It would
probably only make him angry.

She swallowed hard as she put her hands
through the slot.

He poured a bottle of water over them and
then dried them, roughly, with a paper
towel. "Who knows what kinds of germs are
in this place? If I were you, I wouldn't risk
so much as a paper cut."

"It's stress," she lied.

"Then you'd better calm down."

Although it didn't help, she craned her
neck, trying to see his face, and that was
when she noticed the five dots tattooed on

his hand. He was an ex-con; that was a prison tattoo. "Where'd you serve time?" she asked, still trying to figure out who he was or who he might know.

"That's none of your business," he said, and jammed her hands back through the slot.

6

Hilltop, AK — Tuesday, 10:40 p.m. AKDT

There was video! That came as a shock to Amarok. "When did you put in a surveillance system?" he asked Garrett as Makita lay by the door so he wouldn't have to venture too far from the cool air outside.

The owner of Quigley's Quick Stop stood behind the counter wearing his usual flannel shirt with jeans and suspenders, slightly stooped, his gray beard hanging down to the middle of his chest. "Few months ago," he replied.

"Why didn't you say anything about it?" Since Amarok was in charge of keeping their small town secure, he would've expected Garrett to mention such a change.

He shrugged. "Wasn't a big deal. Only cost me four hundred dollars, cameras and all."

Maybe Amarok shouldn't have been surprised. Garrett was never unprepared. Like

95

many of his generation, he wasn't well educated in technology, but technology had become so easy almost anyone could use it. "You never used to have any security. . . ."

"Never needed anything except this." He lifted the sawed-off shotgun he kept behind the counter. "But with the trouble we've had since Hanover House came to town, I decided it was time. Nothing against you," he quickly added. "You do all you can to keep this community safe."

So *that* was why Garrett hadn't told him. He'd been trying not to offend Amarok. Not only was Amarok the only police officer in town, he also was marrying the woman most local people blamed for the trouble they'd had in recent years. "Better safe than sorry," he said. "I just wonder how I missed the cameras."

"I haven't had 'em long. And there are only two. That one right there." He pointed at one corner of the ceiling. "And another tucked up under the eaves outside."

"Does that mean you have a visual record of every customer you served today?"

"Since the weather has improved, I have a visual record of every customer I've served for the past *week*. As long as the Internet doesn't go out, like it does so often in the winter, the new system works great."

96

A clock was ticking in Amarok's mind — one that felt like a time bomb. "Finally some good news. How can I view it?"

"My laptop's almost out of battery. I just plugged it in, so you'll have to come around." With one gnarled hand, he motioned for Amarok to join him behind the counter. During hunting season, Garrett sometimes stayed open until midnight to make up for the slow winter months. And since it wasn't yet dark, he usually had customers.

Tonight, however, it was quiet. He'd been counting out the till when Amarok arrived.

He put the piles of money back in the drawer as he made room for Amarok and pulled up the security files on his computer. "I take this computer upstairs with me when I close for the night. That way, I can see what's happening in the parking lot and down here in the store. I get an alert whenever there's motion. That's the only time the cameras turn on. Course, it's usually just a skunk or possum or something, but having some sort of security in place has given me more peace of mind."

Amarok could relate. He'd felt better since putting a similar system in his own house. He couldn't look at a smartphone to check his front door like those who had cell service, but he could use his computer at the trooper station. Providing Evelyn had her laptop, she could do the same.

Too bad she hadn't made it far enough to trigger the motion detector when she was abducted. Whoever nabbed her must've taken into account the prevalence of such devices these days, which was why he struck in the driveway, out of range.

Or maybe that was simply where the perpetrator felt he could grab her the quickest. Maybe the perpetrator knew about Makita and feared the dog would be home.

"You just click on the date," Garrett explained. "And see this? This link makes it possible to go to a specific time."

Amarok already understood how it worked. "Go to noon and show me everything you've got moving forward."

"Oh, you're looking for the guy with the scar on his face, right? I should've known."

Amarok looked up from the computer. "He stood out to you, too?"

"Looked a bit rough. But then . . . we get a lot of rough-looking characters come through here during hunting season. A few days in the wild and they all look like serial killers."

"To the animals they encounter, I imagine they are," Amarok muttered, but he didn't bother to laugh. He was too focused on looking through the clips.

It didn't take long to find the one he wanted.

Anchorage, AK — Tuesday, 10:45 p.m. AKDT
She'd done it! She'd removed one of the metal springs from her cot. Her thumbs were paying the price. They were so tender she could barely use them, and they were bleeding again, so she was taking a much-needed break. But she felt a small sense of victory at the accomplishment.

Evelyn put a hand to her abdomen as she lay on her cot. Her baby was active. She'd been worried that the terror of her situation alone would harm the child, but if her little girl was moving, she was obviously alive.

That was comforting, but Evelyn also found the reminder that she had a child to protect incredibly daunting. If she couldn't save herself, she wouldn't be able to save the baby growing inside her.

She closed her eyes and tried to picture Amarok. What was happening at home? He was the best man she'd ever known and a damn good cop, but she had no idea if her captor had left enough evidence behind for even the most experienced detective to be able to find her. It could be that she was completely on her own — that whether she survived depended on convincing the man who'd been bringing her food to have mercy on her, which didn't seem likely. Her captor seemed to be inoculating himself against any kind of entreaty by limiting his contact with her.

She imagined how upset Amarok must be and couldn't help wincing. He didn't deserve the problems she'd brought into his life. He'd asked her, many times, to change her profession and do something safer, like going into private practice or teaching. But he, of all people, had to understand that in order to keep society safe, dangerous jobs had to be done. Being a firefighter was dangerous. Flying a rescue helicopter was dangerous. Being a soldier was dangerous. Heck, being a cop was dangerous, too, but she'd never asked him to quit his job. Fighting psychopathy was her life's calling. How could she walk away from it? There were people who did despicable things, with absolutely no remorse, and it was vitally important someone figure out how to treat them. She couldn't give up, not unless she reached some sort of breakthrough. Until then, the innocent would never be safe.

However, if she *had* quit as Amarok asked, maybe she wouldn't be in this situation.

And her child would be safe, too.

Closing her eyes, she pretended that Amarok was lying beside her, imagined him pulling her into the cradle of his big, warm body and felt tears well up. She'd finally let herself love again, *trust* again — which was the harder of the two, given her past — only to be ripped away from the security he provided.

Gathering her fortitude, she got off the bed. She couldn't fall into despair. She had to think of some way to save herself. Besides what she was doing to create a shiv, knowledge was the only other weapon she possessed. So what information had she gleaned about her captor?

He was an ex-con, but she no longer believed he was or ever had been one of her patients. She didn't know him, doubted she'd ever met him before. She could also say he wasn't some middle-aged, frumpy or overweight opponent. He was strong and physically fit. She couldn't expect to overcome him physically, not without an equalizer. No matter how badly her fingers hurt, now that she'd removed that wire from her cot she needed to sharpen it.

Fortunately, the concrete floor made the sharpening part fairly easy. That would've been impossible if she were being held in a room with carpet or linoleum, especially because the walls weren't made of cinder block, like those in so many prisons. But a wire could puncture even without sharpening, so maybe that wasn't a *great* deal to be grateful for.

What else could she put in her favor? If she were consulting on a case and evaluating the man who'd grabbed her, only by what he'd revealed about himself so far, what would she make of it?

A couple of his comments led her to believe he wasn't in this alone. Even if he hadn't said what he'd said about his "watch" and while he was here, she would've guessed someone else was involved. If that *weren't* true, they wouldn't be in this holding pattern. He would've done something to her by now. Raped her. Beaten her. Demanded a ransom. Were he like so many of the men she'd studied, he wouldn't have been able to stop himself. She was completely defenseless; there would never be a better opportunity.

That made her feel somewhat safe — for now. But the possibility of someone else arriving, someone who might be *more* dangerous, made her blood run cold. It indicated that, although this terrible waiting would come to an end, things wouldn't get any better. Chances were they'd get exponentially worse. . . .

Drawing a deep breath, she pulled the mattress off her bed to provide a cushion as she sat on the floor and went back to work on her homemade weapon. She didn't know how long she'd have to create it or when she might have to use it, so she needed to get it done as soon as possible.

"You've got this," she coaxed, trying to keep going even after her arms and hands began to ache. She was *so* close to having it finished.

When she finally stopped, the end was razor sharp. She watched a large drop of blood ooze out when she pricked her thumb and found the sight gratifying. She'd equipped herself with some small defense. But she was still trying to work out other possibilities, ones that might not include violence, since her captor didn't seem to have a thirst for it himself. He didn't even want to look at her, hadn't so much as bent down to peek through the slot.

A psychopath, at least one who'd taken her for sadistic pleasure, would've been eager to see the terror in her eyes, to enjoy her pain and discomfort and fear. This man had given her an extra bottle of water when she'd told him she needed it for the sake of the baby, and he'd washed the blood off her hands so they wouldn't get infected. Those actions, small though they were, indicated he had *some* level of humanity.

Given all of that, why had he kidnapped her?

The most obvious answer was money.

Maybe she could buy him off by promising to pay more for her freedom than he'd get for holding her captive, talk him into letting her go before whoever he worked for arrived.

In order to have the chance, however, she'd need him to come to the door. And she wasn't sure he was listening — or that he could hear her when she banged and called out for him.

She'd try to negotiate with him the next time he brought her some food, she decided. And if that didn't work? She'd hide her shiv close to her body, pretend she was going into labor and, the second he opened the door to see if it was real, stab him and make a run for it.

Hilltop, AK — Tuesday, 11:00 p.m. AKDT
Amarok watched the video of the van guy with the scar very closely. The man was tall and muscle-bound — he had to spend a great deal of time pumping iron to maintain

that kind of bulk — and he looked hardened, mean in a junkyard dog sort of way. He walked into the store, his legs slightly bowed from the thickness of his thighs, glanced around and spotted Kaylene, whom he seemed to like. But when he noticed Garrett watching him, he pulled his gaze away from her and walked down the aisles. He lifted this or that as if he was considering purchasing it, but Amarok got the impression he was just wasting time.

After several minutes, during which he paused at the magazine rack, he put back the latest issue of *Sports Illustrated* and sauntered over to the register to request a pack of cigarettes. His voice sounded normal, as Kaylene had said, no accent. But he had a mark or bruise or something on the web of his hand between his fingers and thumb.

Amarok had Garret stop the playback. "What's that?"

"A tattoo. But there wasn't much to it, just some dots. Pretty stupid, if you ask me."

Now that he could see it close up, he knew what it was. "It's a prison tattoo."

Garrett stroked his beard thoughtfully. "How do you know?"

"They're common enough. It signifies that he's served time. The four dots on the outside represent the walls of the prison and the dot inside represents the prisoner." Impatient to get on with it, he gestured for Garrett to hit Play and watched as the van guy handed Garrett the money for the cigarettes, put the change in the small dish near the register and walked out. The date stamp on that video segment read 1:05 p.m. "Didn't you say you have an outdoor camera in the eaves?"

"I do."

"Can you switch to that?"

"Sure. Just a sec." After a few keystrokes and some time spent searching for the appropriate segment, Amarok was looking at the carpet-cleaning van Kaylene had described. The unknown man climbed inside, took out a cigarette and sat in the driver's seat to smoke it. When he was done, he tossed the butt onto the pavement and backed out.

Amarok grabbed Garrett's arm, which caused Makita, ever watchful that it might be time to work, to come to his feet. "Freeze it there."

"What do you see?" he asked.

"The license plate."

"But isn't it too small to read?"

It was. Amarok couldn't make out a single letter or digit. "Can't you zoom in?"

"I haven't used this program enough to know how to do much more than click on it if I get an alert. But there's got to be a way."

Amarok certainly hoped so. He could use a break. Problem was . . . blowing up the freeze-frame could make it too pixelated to read even after he spent the time to make it happen.

But what else could he do? Without this, he had nothing.

Anchorage, AK — Wednesday, 12:15 a.m. AKDT

The television droned in the background as Emmett Virtanen did fifty push-ups, then a hundred burpees, in sets of twenty-five since those were so grueling, and fifty squats. He was stronger than ever. He'd relapsed when it came to smoking, but he wasn't going to be too hard on himself over that. He'd only picked up cigarettes again since accepting this shitty job. Regardless of the damage the nicotine did to his lungs, it helped take the edge off his nerves and, without that, he didn't think he could get through the interminable wait.

It wasn't that he minded breaking the law. But harming a defenseless woman? Especially a *pregnant* woman? That was beneath him. That fell under the slimy bastard

107

category of pedophiles, wife-beaters and rapists — the kind of men he'd targeted in prison. He'd actually killed a dude who'd fondled and raped the young boys he coached, and he was proud of it. As far as he was concerned, he'd done the world a favor.

But this . . . He never should have let Terry tempt him into getting involved. He wouldn't have, except he needed the money. And he'd justified it by convincing himself that *he* wouldn't be responsible for whatever happened to Evelyn Talbot. If he didn't nab her, for that kind of money someone else would. It was the guy footing the bill who was to blame.

If he'd been told she was pregnant, however, if he'd seen it mentioned in *any* of the things he'd read about her online, he wouldn't have done it, especially if he'd known she was so far along.

Shit! What kind of man had his former cellmate and brother-in-law gotten him involved with? And what did he have in store for the woman who was now locked in the old cooler? Emmett hadn't heard of Dr. Talbot until Terry had given him her name, but he'd learned quite a bit about her since — everything except that she was about to have a baby.

He tried telling himself that she'd wind up dead at some point, regardless. She was surrounded by men as evil as Ted Bundy and John Wayne Gacy, for God's sake. Considering her choice of profession, she was asking for it.

That calmed him down a bit — until the feeling of her rounded stomach pressing into his arms as he grabbed her flashed through his mind again. What would his grandmother say if he was ever charged with the death of a pregnant woman? His "nana" was the one person in this world he loved. Lord knew she was the only one who'd ever stuck by him.

He wiped the sweat from his forehead and squinted at the clock, which still hung on the wall from when this building had been used to clean and process eggs. He needed to get some glasses, but, with effort, he could make out the time. He'd guarded Evelyn for only ten or eleven hours, but they were the longest ten or eleven hours of his life, and that included prison. He'd been worried the whole time that the stress of her situation — and the memories it *had* to evoke given what he'd read about her background — would put her into labor. He didn't want her baby to come while he was in the picture.

What would he do if the baby did? He couldn't call for help, not without giving himself away. Maybe there'd be no time to get help, anyway. And he didn't know the first thing about childbirth, except that his mother had lost her life giving birth to him, which told him how dangerous it could be.

Stupid ass Terry! He should never have introduced his old cellmate to his sister.

Emmett pushed the tattered couch he'd bought from the local Goodwill store, along with a rickety old table he used for his laptop, farther out of the way and grunted as he forced himself to do another fifty push-ups. When could he get out of this place? What had happened to the phone call he'd been expecting?

He grabbed his cell and held it up only to realize that he'd missed the call he'd been waiting for. *What the hell?* His phone hadn't even rung! The cell service in this old plant sucked. Cell service in Alaska sucked in general. He hadn't been able to use his phone at all when he was in Hilltop. Even now that he was in Anchorage, there were spots where thick stands of trees or mountains blocked the signal.

He stared at the cracked linoleum while waiting for Terry to answer, which happened on the second ring.

"There you are!"

"Don't know how I missed your call. I've been here the whole time."

"You scared the hell out of me. I thought you'd split, man."

"I'm about to. This place stinks."

"I thought it was empty, that it had been vacated. Isn't that what you told me when you rented it?"

"It *is* empty. The husband of the old woman who owns it died, the business failed and she's been trying to sell it for over six months, with no luck. She was excited to make the five hundred dollars for two weeks I offered her, even turned the electricity back on when I told her I was going to make one of the buildings that used to house hens into a temporary dog shelter."

"You don't think she'll check, do you?"

"I stuck some stray dogs in there to bolster my cover, just in case. I should be fine if she comes snooping around, as long as she doesn't get *too* nosey."

"That was smart."

"I am going to start a shelter one day."

"I'll help you with that."

Emmett wasn't sure Terry would be around to help. Bridget wanted out of the marriage, and that could prove the end of their friendship. "Sounds good. You haven't

111

said a word to my sister about this job we're doing, though, have you? Because I told you from the beginning that you'd better not. She'll be mad as hell if she learns we're involved in something that could land us both back in prison."

"Of course not. I'm not *that* stupid."

"Good thing, because I guarantee she would leave you and refuse to talk to me." Emmett wrinkled his nose. "Damn, it stinks in here."

"What from?"

"I think it's the candling machine in the next room."

"The *what*?"

"That's what the owner called it. Apparently, it's the machine that was used to wash the chicken shit off the eggs and separate them into sizes so they could be packed."

"Can't you just throw that junk outside?"

"No, it's huge! And it's fastened to the wall."

"Then base out of a different room while you're there."

"I am! I'm camping out in the staff area, but it's tiny, and this part of the building is no picnic, either. I guess after losing her husband and her business, the owner wasn't very excited to come in here and clean, the lazy bitch. Anyway, when's your boss going to relieve me?"

"*My* boss? You mean *our* boss? Last I heard, you were making as much as me."

"But I'm the one doing all the work. I came to Alaska and scouted out this place, put in a toilet and a bed and nabbed her. What have *you* done?"

"I'm the one who figured out how to get her to leave the prison alone so you could nab her. I've also fronted the money for everything until we can get paid, and now I'm tapped out and your sister is nagging the hell out of me because we can't make our house payment."

"Yeah, well, Bridget has never been easy to deal with. I warned you about that when I introduced you."

"I was in prison! When you're doing time, a great set of tits trumps a bad temper any day of the week. Anyway, we'll both be better off when this is all over."

"I hope so, because I'm telling you, if the doc in the box goes into labor, I won't have a clue what to do. And I'm not going to be responsible for the death of a baby. So your man just better get his ass up here and fast."

"You know he can't come right now!"

"Why not?"

"I told you in the beginning it would be a week or longer."

113

"But you *didn't* tell me I was kidnapping a pregnant woman! That changes things."

"Look, he's going to pay you extra. He's sorry for not mentioning the pregnancy, but he didn't know himself."

Somehow that mollified Emmett, made him feel less set up. "How much extra?"

"Two grand. That's a lot of money."

"It is, but he should've done his homework. Then he wouldn't have had to sweeten the pot."

"She's nearly forty, and she's never had kids. How was he supposed to know she'd start now?"

"Okay, fine." He toed off a piece of linoleum, making the hole that was already there that much bigger. "So when can he get here? How much longer do I have to sweat this out?"

"It'll be a few days."

"Why doesn't he jump on the first flight?"

"Because he's tied up! You'll be fine until he gets there."

He rubbed his forehead with his middle fingers, trying to decide if he should bail out. He wasn't an expert on pregnancy, but he did know that a woman didn't have to be due in order to go into labor. His mother had delivered him early, hadn't she?

And she hadn't survived the experience. . . .

Still, he'd come this far. If the lack of intel was truly an honest mistake, he figured he might as well see it through. "I'll give him until Friday. That's two days. If he's not here by midnight, I'm turning her loose and taking off."

"Whoa, whoa! Wait a minute. Don't do that. Just sit tight. You can't screw this up. If you do, neither one of us will get paid and Bridget will leave me."

"You heard me. Friday. What does your guy want with her, anyway?" He'd been reluctant to ask, but now that a baby was involved he had to know.

"He wants to convince her that she was wrong about him."

"That's bullshit! He had her kidnapped. You don't kidnap a woman just to talk."

"You do if you can't get her to listen any other way. He needs her help getting his sister back. It's legit, man. I promise. I know this dude."

"He's not going to hurt her. . . ." Emmett couldn't help being skeptical.

Terry busted out laughing. "I doubt he could even if he tried. A strong child could kick his ass. That's why he hired *us* — because he's useless himself. He just needs her to sign a few papers so he can regain custody of his sister. That's all."

"Why can't his parents raise the sister?"

"He doesn't have parents anymore. Never had a dad to begin with, and his mother abandoned him and his sister when he was sixteen. At least that's what he told me. Anyway, his sister is only six years younger than he is, but she's retarded or something. In a facility."

Someone who was willing to take care of his retarded adult sister couldn't be *all* bad. Who'd volunteer for a tough job like that?

"Okay," Emmett said. "I'll give him through Saturday. But stay in touch. I'm nervous as hell that this will turn into something we never expected."

"I'm only a phone call away, but I'd better get back to work. I swear my boss hates me. She stares daggers at me every time she sees me."

"Because you're a lazy ass." Emmett spoke as though he was joking, but he knew it was true. That was his sister's greatest complaint about Terry.

"Fuck you," he said, joking back. "I gotta go."

With a sigh, Emmett disconnected. At least he hadn't snatched a pregnant woman for the use of some sadistic monster. He could hold out through Saturday. It wasn't as if he had to worry about being found. He'd rented this place via a recommendation from someone else he'd called after seeing a listing on the Internet, when their place was already taken, and there weren't any neighbors close by.

So far, so good. Come Saturday he'd return to Minneapolis and never look back.

7

Evelyn had finally slept solidly. It felt as though many hours had passed. What time was it? She hated not knowing, not being able to do something she'd always taken for granted. She was hungry again — another sign that it had been a while since she'd last eaten — but her captor hadn't yet brought her breakfast, so . . . she couldn't have slept *that* long.

She listened to see if he might be coming now, but didn't hear anything. Just for something to do, she got out her shiv. She'd created a handle by tearing the lining of her jacket into strips, which she wound tightly around the coil.

She squeezed it to get it to form to her hand. She liked possessing a weapon, even an improvised one. It was better than nothing, but she'd have only one chance to use it. If she stabbed her captor and for some

118

reason *didn't* manage to get away . . .

She didn't even want to contemplate what he might do in retaliation. Probably kill her, which was why, when she made her move, she'd have to *completely* incapacitate him. Otherwise, she'd face the consequences.

The thought of killing someone made her woozy. Like most people, she could act in a violent manner if she was feeling directly threatened. She'd fought for her life — and won — before. But this guy hadn't done anything to *seriously* harm her. *Not yet,* she told herself, unable to shake the memory of what Jasper had done. So while she was frightened and uncertain and even angry, she wasn't feeling the same level of "kill or be killed" desperation that had fueled other actions. She just knew she had to get out of this place, guessed it was going to get a lot worse if she didn't, and he was standing in her way.

She heard the lock bolt on the slot begin to move, so she hurried to slip her shiv back inside her mattress. If only this guy would give her some idea of what was happening and why! Then she'd know whether she had to stab him in order to escape — or a ransom was forthcoming and she could simply wait.

"Hello?" She bent down to peer out.

He stepped out of view without answering, but she could hear him moving around, knew he was most likely preparing her food.

"Not knowing what I'm up against is scaring me," she said. "Are you *trying* to put me in labor?"

No comment.

"I should probably tell you that I've been feeling some contractions."

"I hope that isn't true," he said flatly.

That wasn't exactly *friendly,* but at least she'd gotten a response. "It's not as though I can control when the baby comes."

"That's what you've said."

"It's true! I'm not all that likely to carry this baby to term. When I was sixteen, I was tortured for days. A body doesn't go through what mine went through and come out of it without sustaining a few scars. My doctor has said it a dozen times."

He brought her a tray with another peanut butter and jelly sandwich, a bag of chips and some more carrot sticks, but she refused to accept it. "If you'd just talk to me for a minute, give me some reassurance, it could make all the difference. I'm going out of my mind in here."

He cursed under his breath. "Fine. This is your reassurance: relax."

"You expect that to be enough?"

"You'll only be here for a few more days. Try to make the most of it."

"But I don't understand! Where will I be going?"

"Home."

"You mean you're going to release me?"

"Someone else will."

"Who?"

"I don't know!" he snapped. "And I wouldn't tell you even if I did."

Evelyn was pushing her luck, but she had to find out as much as possible before she faked labor and plunged a sharp instrument into this man's neck. "Why is it a secret?"

"Look, this is just a job for me. Nothing more. Now take the food, or you'll go hungry until dinner."

She believed him, so she accepted the tray. "Please. Don't go."

"I told you. You have to sit tight."

He closed the slot with such force she nearly dropped the tray. "Give me a few more seconds!" she yelled. "If this is only a job for you, if this is all about money, maybe we can work something out between us!"

She waited, hoping the slot would open again, but it didn't.

"I'll *pay* you to let me go!"

More silence. "Hello? Can you hear me?" She held the tray with one hand while bang-

121

ing on the door with the other — until she was too exhausted to continue.

"Damn it!" She slid down the wall and stared glumly at her food. Who'd hired the gym rat on the other side of the door?

She took a bite of her sandwich before realizing that in all the excitement, he hadn't given her any water. She had to have something to drink. She was already thirsty.

She set down the tray and stood to beat on the door some more. "I have to have water! Hey! Can you hear me? I'm not getting enough to drink!"

A moment later the slot opened and he handed her a small bottle.

"So you *can* hear me!"

"Why don't you make it easy on both of us and go back to sleep or something?"

Did that mean he'd looked in at her earlier? Found her sleeping?

That he might've been watching her sleep and she hadn't heard him made her skin crawl. "Because I'm frantic! Who's coming and what will he do to me?"

"He won't do anything to you! He wants you to sign something so he can get his sister back, okay?"

Evelyn froze. "His *sister*?"

"Yeah. He's trying to regain custody of his retarded sister. I guess you had her put

122

in some sort of facility."

Her hands and feet began to tingle and the room started to spin. She leaned against the wall to hold herself up. "Where? In *what* facility?"

"I don't know," he said as if it didn't matter, but Evelyn knew it did. She'd only ever been in *one* situation where she'd had to make sure a dangerous psychopath could no longer victimize his mentally disabled sister, whom he'd used as a sex slave for years — after giving her a frontal lobotomy to make her completely docile, compliant and unable to think for herself.

This guy had to be associated with Lyman Bishop! But how could that be? Lyman had suffered a massive stroke and was in an institution himself. Sure, he'd once been a brilliant cancer researcher and a cool and calculated killer, but these days he couldn't think any better than his sister, Beth, and had no motor skills to speak of.

Or had he, against all odds, managed to recover?

She supposed it was possible. The brain was an amazing organ. There was even a chance he'd managed to fool the doctors from the beginning. If anyone could pull off a trick like that, it would be the harmless-looking Bishop.

"Oh my God . . ."

"What is it *now*?" he grumbled.

She knew what Lyman would do to her if he had the chance. In less than ten minutes, *she'd* be the vegetable. "You're working for a man by the name of Lyman Bishop. Do you know who he is? Have you heard that name in the news? He's a psychopath *and* a serial killer! You need to go to the police right away!"

She was breathing hard, hoping she'd shocked him into doing the right thing.

Bishop's hired thug stood there for a moment, as though uncertain.

Was he going to let her out?

She was hoping and praying for all she was worth — only to be disappointed when he closed the slot without another word.

"Wait! Please!" she cried. But it didn't make any difference. He wouldn't open it again no matter how much she pleaded with him.

Anchorage, AK — Wednesday, 7:00 p.m. AKDT

Amarok had taken only one quick nap in thirty-seven hours. He felt like the walking dead, and yet he was driving. But he couldn't crawl into bed and collapse knowing that Evelyn was being held against her

124

will. The thought of some sociopath harming her goaded him on like a red-hot poker.

Thanks to the security cameras at the Quick Stop, Amarok had been able to determine the license plate number on the carpet-cleaning van. He'd considered that a win, a huge step forward — until he ran it through the Division of Motor Vehicles database and found that the van had been reported stolen the Sunday before Evelyn went missing, early in the morning.

The registration showed a forty-year-old Anchorage man named Dax O'Leary as the owner. Amarok had spent most of last night and much of today trying to locate him. Not because he thought Dax was responsible for Evelyn's abduction. Whoever had stolen the van was probably the man he was looking for, but Amarok still wanted to talk to Dax. Maybe once he described the ex-con with the scar and the prison tattoo, Dax would remember having seen him somewhere or be able to provide some other information.

Amarok wished he had something more solid to go on than the owner of a stolen vehicle, especially because it was going on two days since Evelyn was abducted. He was growing more and more desperate, but all he could do was take what the investigation gave him, go from one bread crumb to the next, and pray the trail didn't end before he found her.

He was afraid it might've ended already. Locating Dax was proving to be difficult. The phone number on the DMV records was disconnected, and he no longer lived at the address listed — Amarok had just left that house — which forced him to spend valuable time tracking down information that should've been relatively easy to confirm.

He was bleary-eyed by the time he arrived at Dax's brother's place, which was also in Anchorage about twenty minutes from where Dax had lived when he registered the van. Shoving the transmission into Park, Amarok sat in the cab of his truck in a bit of a stupor, trying to summon the energy to climb out. The nerve-racking race against time combined with the lack of sleep was making him punchy. He couldn't think straight, would *have* to sleep more at some point.

But as long as he had the strength to overcome the need, that point wasn't now.

Pushing through his exhaustion, he ordered Makita to stay in the truck and went to the door. The neighborhood wasn't a *bad* one. It was blue collar, but there were no burned-out buildings or drug dealers standing on street corners.

Elroy O'Leary's house was the worst on the block. The paint was peeling from the trim, a broken chair was overturned on the porch and bristling weeds had swallowed the yard. Amarok couldn't help noticing every sorry detail. But at least he had the right place. A fairly new carpet-cleaning vehicle sat in the drive, leading Amarok to wonder if the O'Leary brothers were in business together — or if Dax owned that van and lived here, too.

Surely he couldn't get that lucky, not with the way things had been going so far.

It took real effort to rouse someone, but after he banged on the door several times a small man wearing pajama bottoms and a T-shirt peered out at him while putting on a pair of wire-rimmed glasses. "Can I help you?"

Amarok flashed his badge. He was also in uniform, although he didn't always bother with such formalities in Hilltop. There everyone knew who he was, so it didn't seem necessary. Out on the road, on a desperate quest for information, he had to look authoritative, do anything and everything he could to save time and get people to talk. "Elroy O'Leary?"

"Yes."

"Sorry if I woke you."

"It's early yet. I was just dozing on the couch while watching TV."

Amarok could hear a sports announcer in the background. "Watching the game?" He kept his tone casual and friendly.

Visibly relaxing, Elroy opened the door wider. "Yeah. Kinda. When I can keep my eyes open."

"I know what you mean," Amarok said with a smile. "Listen, I just want to talk to your brother, Dax. He around?"

Elroy yawned and scratched his stomach. "No."

"Can you tell me where he lives?"

"Not off the top of my head. But I hope this means you've found the van I gave him."

That answer was unexpected. "You *gave* him the van?"

"The mileage on it was getting up there, so I was planning to replace it, anyway. And he didn't have a vehicle." He rolled his eyes. "You know how that goes."

Amarok had a brother — an identical twin — but he *didn't* know how that went. He'd never had to sacrifice for or help his brother; he hadn't even known he had one until he received a call from Jason on his eighteenth birthday. He and his brother had been only two when their parents split. When his mother moved to Seattle, she took Jason with her and left him with his father. After that, no one bothered to mention that he had a sibling. He grew up believing he was an only child.

But he tried not to think about all that, even on good days. And this was definitely *not* a good day. "Do you know anything about what happened to the van the night it was stolen?"

"Only what Dax told me, but I can't say whether or not it's true." Elroy used his fingers to comb his hair over the bald spot on top of his head. "He's not the most trustworthy guy in the world, and since I'm the one who gave it to him in the first place, it's not likely he'd tell me if he lost it in a poker game, crashed it or handed the keys over to some stripper in exchange for a blow job. You hear what I'm saying?"

Amarok's eyes were so tired they kept going blurry. He blinked to clear his vision. "What was his version of events?"

"He said he went into a strip club and when he came out it was gone."

"Which strip club?"

"Didn't ask. I'm a good Christian." He lifted his chin to show his pride and commitment. "I don't go to those kinds of places."

Amarok was getting a headache. He hadn't eaten *or* slept. He squeezed the muscle between his own neck and shoulder, trying to ease the tension. "Did he say if there was anyone around that night who looked suspicious when he went in? Anyone he thought might spell trouble?"

"No."

"When I went to the address on his DMV records, I met a woman who told me he moved out three months ago. She said she has no idea where he is now and she doesn't care. But she gave me this address as a possibility."

Elroy made a clicking sound with his mouth. "Yeah. That must've been Serena. His relationship with her tanked in a hurry. My brother wasn't the best husband in the world. Hardly ever worked, came and went at all hours. She claims he has a porn addiction, and I believe it. If he doesn't settle down and get his life sorted out, I'm afraid he'll be homeless one day."

"Is he homeless *now*?"

"No. I helped him get a room with some other guys. At least, that's what he told me the money was for. Even if it's true, who knows how long it will last? I tried to give

130

him some work, thought he could help me with my business, but he's not reliable. I don't make enough to support both of us, anyway."

"Hard times," Amarok said, playing the sympathy card. "Can you give me his new address?"

Elroy glanced back over his shoulder as if he wasn't sure where to find it. "I wrote it down, but — Never mind. He has a new phone. Let me see if I can reach him."

While he waited, Amarok stared out at the other houses. Was Evelyn being held in a house like one of these on some normal, quiet street, a barn out in the middle of nowhere, some shabby outbuilding like what Jasper used for his crimes or something else? Did she even have a place to sleep? Food to eat? Or was she being tortured all over again —

The door opened, and he shoved the morbid images crowding into his brain back as fast as he could.

"Just spoke to him," Elroy announced, and handed Amarok a slip of paper with an address scrawled on it. "Said you can come by. He's waiting for you."

"Thanks for your help." Amarok took the note and returned to his truck to key Dax's address into his maps. It was only ten

131

minutes away. Amarok had to pay him a visit, but he doubted Elroy's brother would be able to tell him anything more than Elroy just had. And if Dax couldn't tell him anything new, he was wasting his time.

The second that realization hit, he felt his muscles bunch and the anger, fear and panic he'd been holding back since he found Evelyn gone erupted. Pain shot through his hand as he slugged the steering wheel, but he didn't care. Once he'd taken that first swing, he couldn't stop. Crying out with all the anguish he was feeling, he punched everything within reach, which freaked out Makita and got him barking and turning in the seat. The dog couldn't understand where the fight was.

A knock on the driver's side window finally drew Amarok's attention.

"You *okay*?" Elroy called through the glass, his eyes wide with shock. "Or should I call someone?"

Amarok could easily imagine what Elroy had to be thinking after witnessing such a spectacle. But he didn't understand what Amarok was going through; no one could understand.

Amarok was breathing hard, but he forced himself to regain control, ordered Makita to sit still and rolled down the window. "No,

I'm fine," he managed to say in a somewhat normal voice. But he wasn't fine. He'd never felt so helpless. And the rage that filled him as a consequence was consuming everything else — all objectivity and control.

"Are you *sure*?" Elroy looked skeptical, and for good reason.

"Yeah, I've got it. I'm okay," he lied, and threw the gear-shift into Drive, jamming down on the gas pedal so he could get out of there.

As he rocketed away, a glance in the rearview mirror revealed Dax's brother standing in the street, looking after him. He had to think Amarok had lost his mind, but Amarok didn't care. He didn't care about anything except bringing Evelyn home.

"God help you when I finally get my hands on you," he muttered to whoever had taken her.

Minneapolis, MN — Thursday, 1:00 a.m. CST
"They're letting me go." When Terry pushed his mop and bucket into Lyman's room, his face was red and sweaty and his hair was standing up as though he'd been combing his fingers through it over and over again.

Lyman blinked at him. "What do you mean — letting you go? You're getting off early tonight?"

133

"No. I got canned. The new night manager just gave me my two weeks' notice." He spat on the floor he was supposed to be cleaning. "That fat bitch has had it in for me ever since she started here."

The night manager *was* severely overweight, but Bishop didn't mind the extra pounds as much as the hair on her face. He'd never seen anything like it: her five o'clock shadow was worse than his. "She might be fat, but she's efficient."

Terry's scowl deepened. "So? What are you saying?"

Bishop could tell by Terry's tone that he'd said something wrong. But Patricia Skousen *was* efficient, so he didn't understand why it would be a problem to acknowledge it. "She *is* good at her job, isn't she?"

"She just fired me, you asshole! Do you think I want to hear that?"

Lyman couldn't help bridling at Terry's response. He'd been treated poorly, even cruelly at times, for most of his life, so that spiteful tone was a trigger for him. "I'm just saying that I'm surprised you were able to keep your job *this* long."

"That's exactly what I thought you were saying! God, it's impossible to like you! You know that?"

The open hostility he sometimes encountered never ceased to amaze Lyman. His inability to understand emotional nuances put him at a disadvantage. He tried to compensate with his intelligence, but he'd never had any friends to speak of, and only two girlfriends, both of whom dumped him after only a few months. *Nothing* he did seemed to change the way people treated him, except his career, of course. He'd enjoyed the respect he'd earned through his cancer research, but Evelyn Talbot had stepped in to rob him of even that. "You don't have to be so rude."

"You think *I'm* the one being rude? I wasn't getting by on what they paid me and now I got nothing! And you tell me I had it coming?"

Bishop used his good arm to pull himself up higher in the bed. "Do *you* think you did a good job?" he asked in confusion. "Were you even *trying* to do a good job?"

Terry shook his head. "You're crazy. Just like the rest of the assholes in here. The point is, this place doesn't pay shit, so no one else is going to do any better."

"I agree with you there." Cleaning a mental hospital wasn't exactly what anyone would consider an ideal job. Some of the patients spread feces on the walls! Lyman had even observed some coprophagia since he'd been committed.

He shuddered at the pathogens that could be spread by human waste and the illnesses that could result — cholera, typhoid fever, E. coli. He didn't belong in here, was glad to be getting out. "So how will you get by? Can you live on unemployment benefits?"

Terry shot him a dirty look as he grabbed the mop/ bucket combo he'd wheeled in and started haphazardly mopping the floor. He was doing an especially poor job tonight, but, as Lyman had already said, he never did a very good one.

"You're not going to answer me?" Lyman asked. "I didn't mean any harm in what I said."

"You never do. And yet you say the wrong thing. Over and over again."

"I apologize." It galled Bishop that he had to mollify such a lazy idiot, someone with an IQ that was probably half of his. But he'd been doing stuff like that his whole life. No wonder he'd done what he'd done! He'd never been liked, never been accepted. The people around him treated him so poorly he had no choice.

Finally, Terry seemed to calm down. He leaned on the mop handle as he said, "I'll have to find other work right away. We're already behind on our bills. If I can't make rent, Bridget will leave me."

"Oh. I'm sorry. That's not good."

"No, it isn't. Now the money you've promised me is more important than ever. I need that, man."

Lyman gripped the remote that raised and lowered his bed a little tighter. "You'll get it soon."

"Why not today?" he said, and Lyman saw the hope of immediate relief from his worries dawn in his eyes as he hurried over.

Lyman tried to wave him off. "I don't have access to any of my accounts, not while I'm in here. You know that."

Terry glared at him. "But we need to speed things up, make this happen before something goes wrong that I had nothing to do with. I've done my part."

"Not all of it. Besides, we had a deal, remember? I'll pay you when I'm free."

"Why don't you go tonight? You can head to Alaska, relieve Emmett, and we'll all be happy."

"I *can't* go tonight." Lyman had to modulate his voice so that his own irritation didn't leak through. "It has to be when you're not working, remember? We don't want anyone to think you had anything to do with my 'escape.' Otherwise, as soon as they realize I'm gone, they could come straight to you."

"So? I'll play dumb."

"It won't be that easy. Let's do things right to begin with. That will save us from having any problems later."

"But Emmett is freaking out, threatening to leave. He's giving us through Friday night. That's it. Even if you take off tonight, you'll have travel time and . . . and you should be prepared in case there are any delays. Let's do it while we can!"

Lyman stared at the television without really seeing the program that was playing.

Terry lowered his voice. "Don't you hear me? If we wait, Emmett might set Evelyn Talbot free. This could be your only chance."

Lyman had spent the majority of his time since the hemorrhage trying to rebuild his mind and strengthen his body. At first he could barely open and close the hand on his weak side and wiggle his toes, but he'd come a long way since then. The past year or so he'd been limping into the bathroom, where he wouldn't be observed, using the grab bars to steady himself while he did basic exercises, building enough muscle to do calisthenics and other, more intense therapy. He never missed a day. Sometimes he added a night workout, too. Now he was stronger than anyone would imagine. He hadn't regained *all* of his fine motor skills or all of his mental acuity, but it didn't matter. Evelyn would be there to give him the love and comfort he'd need to continue to improve.

The thought of touching her again gave him an erection, which was even more encouraging. These days it was extremely difficult to get his body to function properly, and he was far from old. He wasn't ready to give up that aspect of his life.

She was going to make a big difference, he promised himself. He'd never had a woman like her, and he'd never considered kidnapping one. Accomplished, intelligent females, especially ones who were also beautiful, drew too much attention when they went missing. But Evelyn had so many enemies the authorities wouldn't know which way to turn.

All of that gave him a distinct advantage when it came to her.

"Hey! I'm talking to you!" Terry cried.

Maybe Terry was right. Maybe he *should* leave tonight. Even if he disappeared only two days after Evelyn, Minneapolis was so far removed from Alaska it was entirely possible the police would never connect the two events. Especially because he'd been careful

139

not to let anyone see his progress. No one would ever *dream* he'd be capable of pulling off something like this.

"Yes, I can hear you," he replied, his mind made up. "Go do the rest of your cleaning. Make sure you stay on that side of the hospital so no one sees us together, and I'll be gone when you come back. But you don't want to be the one to report me missing."

Terry looked as befuddled and stupid as he was. "Why not?"

"Because tomorrow, when they contact you, you're going to tell them I was here when you left."

"And you'll get the cash you owe me and give it to Emmett when you get there as planned, right?"

Greed was so many people's downfall. "I'll make sure you get what's coming to you," he said. "I'll make sure you both do."

8

Emmett had tried to ignore what Evelyn Talbot had said. He'd told himself it was none of his business. If he did his job, he'd get paid and whatever happened from there wasn't on him. And he'd stuck by that for hours. He'd drowned out her cries by listening to music with headphones and working out. Then he'd gone out and checked on the dogs. He'd even filled the van up with gas and gotten a few more groceries. Now he was slumped in front of the television.

But the memory of her voice — _You're working for a man by the name of Lyman Bishop. Do you know who he is? Have you heard that name in the news? He's a psychopath_ and _a serial killer! You need to go to the police right away!_ — kept coming back to him.

Finally, unable to push those words out of

141

his brain any longer, he used a search engine to look up the name. Terry hadn't told him who they were working for. It wasn't that he'd kept it a secret; he just hadn't volunteered the information, and Emmett hadn't asked for it. He preferred less information to more. Keeping things impersonal prevented his conscience from getting too engaged.

But if Evelyn was right . . .

He scanned the links.

Cancer Researcher at University of Minnesota Arrested for Murder . . .

Fruit Fly Geneticist Indicted . . .

Panties of Eight Murder Victims Found in Attic of Geneticist Lyman Bishop . . .

Authorities Say the Zombie Maker Used Ice Pick to Perform Lobotomies. . . .

"Son of a bitch!" he muttered. Surely he wasn't working for someone called the Zombie Maker.

He tried to call Terry, but Terry didn't answer, so he went back to those links and read the articles. Most claimed Bishop had cut into his victims' brains to make them more docile. If a victim died during or after the procedure, he'd simply kidnap someone else and try again — until one survived whom he could keep as his captive. Hence the nickname.

This time when he tried to call Terry, Emmett left a voicemail message: *You'd better get back to me right away. Do you hear? I mean right away!*

While he waited, he did a Google search on transorbital lobotomies. He hoped they sounded a lot worse than they actually were, but that didn't turn out to be the case. From what he learned, an American neurologist named Dr. Walter Freeman, a Yale graduate no less, began scrambling his patients' frontal lobes in the late 1940s in an attempt to cure them of various psychological complaints. He believed an excess of emotion caused mental illness and severing certain nerve connections would relieve that emotion.

He started out by drilling six holes into the top of a patient's head. Later, he streamlined the process by shoving a regular, kitchen-variety ice pick through the patient's eye sockets, where the bone was much thinner.

Emmett shook his head in amazement as he read one survivor's account of how his stepmother took him to Dr. Freeman to have the procedure done because he was "a bad kid."

"What a bitch!" Emmett muttered. He hoped she got what was coming to her. His own stepmom had hit him in the face with a Jack Daniel's bottle when he was fourteen, which nearly cost him his eye. He'd always hated her. But this kid had it even worse. And, according to another article, he was only one of thousands who underwent the procedure. Most were older, but Dr. Freeman performed over thirty-five hundred ice-pick lobotomies during his career — some in front of spectators.

Lyman Bishop had used an ice pick in the same way, but he hadn't been putting on a show and he hadn't done it with the intention of helping anyone — except himself.

Emmett had hung out with some pretty tough dudes, especially while he was in prison. But what Bishop had done was barbaric.

Or . . . was he innocent?

As Emmett dug deeper, he found other links and articles that suggested Bishop might *not* be the Zombie Maker. The detective who'd investigated the case had planted the panty evidence that convicted him. Bishop had been sent to Hanover House but was released after only a short time. Extensive media coverage labeled his conviction a tragedy that never should've happened, especially to a highly educated scientist and distinguished advocate of medical progress like Bishop. Their take: an overly ambitious cop tried to make a name for himself by solving the high-profile case.

Emmett jumped when his phone rang, startled by the sound. Caller ID showed his brother-in-law's number.

He started to pace as he punched the Talk button. "*There* you are!"

"What's up, man?" Terry's voice was wary.

"I need to talk to you."

"You need to chill out! I just lost my fucking job, okay?"

Damn. That wasn't going to go over well with Bridget. "What happened, dude?"

"I don't want to talk about it. I work for a bitch who's been trying to get rid of me since she started. And now that she has, I'm especially glad we're about to get paid. Our guy should be there tomorrow or the next day. He's coming early, so this is almost over."

Terry was talking fast, in hushed tones, and he sounded stressed — for good reason — but Emmett was stressed, too. "Did you know that we're working for a serial killer? A *psychopath* who cuts into the brains of his victims to control them?"

"No, no, no. That Zombie Maker shit is all wrong. He didn't do any of that."

This was exactly what Emmett had hoped

145

to hear, but he was far from convinced. "How do you know?"

"Because I've talked to him about it. And I've told you why he wants Dr. Talbot. He needs her to sign something so he can get his retarded sister back. Would a psychopath even care about a sister like that? Who'd want to take on such a burden? That makes him a saint, not a psychopath."

Emmett rubbed the beard growth on his face with his knuckles as he considered Terry's response. "How do you know he doesn't want revenge on Dr. Talbot? From what I've read, she fought his release even when everyone else was rushing to apologize and kiss his ass."

"Maybe she believes he's a psychopath, but who's to say she's right?"

"Her degree says she should know a little something about that!"

"A degree doesn't always mean anything — just that she spent a hell of a lot of years taking classes that may or may not have taught her a thing or two."

"Still, you should've told me about all this bizarre shit in advance."

"Look, Emmett. Stop worrying. Bishop's not out for revenge — he's already got revenge. He won. He's a free man."

Emmett grabbed the remote and shut off

the television. The noise was getting on his nerves. "One article I read said he tried to *kill* Evelyn."

"That isn't true," Terry argued. "That was Jasper Moore, the dude who tried to kill her before. You know her background, right? Bishop was simply in the wrong place at the wrong time. That's all."

Could that be true? Emmett didn't generally believe in coincidences. But he had seen the photos of Bishop that went with those articles. The guy didn't *look* dangerous. The way he hunched in on himself as if he didn't want to be seen gave Emmett the impression he was like a dog who'd been kicked too many times and skittered away at the first sign of confrontation.

"I don't know. . . ." He crossed over to the small kitchenette and opened a bag of chips. "Something about this doesn't feel right to me."

"This isn't about what you feel, dude. You need the money and so do I, especially now. I've got bills to pay. What else am I supposed to do?"

Emmett didn't have a good answer. He was in a similar situation.

"Anyway, Bishop is hardly dangerous," Terry went on. "Jasper Moore beat him to within an inch of his life the night they both showed up at Dr. Talbot's. Bishop has been in the hospital where I work ever since. That's how I met him. I'm telling you, it was Moore who tried to kill Evelyn Talbot."

Swallowing a mouthful of barbecue-flavored potato chips, Emmett stepped back to glance at the cooler door separating him from his prisoner. He could so easily open it and let the psychiatrist go.

He was tempted, but Terry was right. They both needed the money. Besides, they were *so* close to the end of this thing!

He popped another chip into his mouth and spoke around it. "If he doesn't let her go after a day or two, I'll *make* him do it."

These words were met with silence. But, after a moment, Terry said, "You planning to double-cross him?"

"I won't be double-crossing him. I'll be holding him to his word."

"That's true, I guess. Okay. As long as we get paid, I don't care."

"He's bringing the cash with him, isn't he?"

"That's the plan. He won't have access to it until he gets out of here, and he can't come anywhere near me after that in case someone sees us together. So he's bringing it all to you."

"Good. I'll give you your share when I get

back. But before I leave here, I'll make sure he releases the pregnant shrink."

"You shouldn't have any trouble. He's a weird little man — think Danny DeVito but without the personality — and he's had a stroke because of that beating I mentioned, so the left side of his body doesn't work very well. You could easily overpower him."

"I was never worried about that," Emmett said, and hung up.

Anchorage, AK — Wednesday, 10:15 p.m. AKDT

Dax O'Leary was quite a bit younger than his brother. He still had his hair and he wasn't wearing glasses, but he looked emaciated. Amarok was fairly certain he was an addict, which explained the way his wife felt about him and what his brother had said, too.

"Elroy told me you wanted to talk to me." He stepped outside an old duplex wearing a T-shirt with a stretched neckband, a pair of holey jeans and no shoes. "It's about time the police did something to find my van."

Amarok heard a television blaring inside, got the impression others were there — Dax's roommates, no doubt — but they were minding their own business, didn't seem to care about what was going on at

149

the door. "Your van wasn't stolen in my jurisdiction."

"What does that mean?"

He glanced back at his truck to see his dog staring out the window at him as though he wasn't pleased to have been left behind. "It means I'm here because I believe it was used in the commission of another crime."

Dax seemed mildly surprised. "What kind of crime?"

"An abduction."

"*Really?* Don't tell me it was one of the dancers!"

"At the strip club you visited that night? No. Have you ever heard of Dr. Evelyn Talbot?"

"I haven't." Dax sounded completely confident in his answer but a second later looked a bit uncertain. "Wait, yes, I know the name. She runs that prison for psychopaths in Hilltop, right?" He shoved his hands in his pockets. "I've been thinking about applying there, as a correctional officer."

Amarok decided not to mention the drug testing that would be required. "Dr. Talbot's been kidnapped, and the person who took her was driving your van."

He blinked several times. "Wow, no kidding?"

"No kidding. Does anything stand out in your mind about the night it was stolen? Did you meet anyone suspicious? See anyone eyeing your van after you parked it?"

Dax glanced at Amarok's swollen and aching hand. "No one. There were some guys hanging out by the door, talking to the bouncer. But I didn't think anything of it. There're always a few smokers there."

"The man I'm looking for has a scar on his face right here." Amarok indicated his eye. "I'm guessing he was in some sort of accident, maybe a car accident where he went through the windshield."

Dax's face lit up. "Yeah, I saw that dude. I remember wondering if he was blind in that eye."

"Could be."

"Looked that way to me. He was one of the men who was out talking to the bouncer. I did a double take when I passed him and noticed that scar over his eye. Thought it was tough luck, since he would've been a fairly handsome dude otherwise."

"Did you talk to him? Have any interaction with him?"

"No, but he had to be as tall as you, and he was completely *yoked.* I assumed he was a new bouncer, going through training."

"What strip club was this?"

"Roxanne's, down on Spenard Road."

"Who was working the door that night?"

"Greg. He's always there on Saturdays."

"Did he seem to know our friend with the scar?"

"Hard to say. I got only a general impression of them."

Amarok peered closer at him — or as close as his blurry eyesight would allow. "You're not lying to me, right?"

Dax stiffened. "*Lying* to you?"

"You didn't loan this guy your van and then report it as stolen when he didn't bring it back so you could cash in on the insurance? Or *sell* it to him and then report it as stolen so you could get paid twice. Nothing like that?"

"God, you sound like my brother. *No!* I didn't loan out my van. Didn't sell it, either."

Amarok pinched the bridge of his nose. He was struggling to keep his head clear, to remember the answers he'd already been given and connect them into a cohesive whole. "Good, because Dr. Talbot is supposed to marry me this summer and I'm still counting on that happening. You hear what I'm saying?"

Dax flicked a mosquito off his arm. "I didn't know you had a personal tie to her, but, either way, I'm not lying. I wouldn't do that to you. And if I were going to accuse someone of stealing my car who didn't, I wouldn't pick a man who looks like a gladiator. That dude could probably tear me apart with his bare hands."

"If I find out you know this guy, that you could've led me right to him but didn't, it won't take a gladiator," Amarok said.

Dax's jaw dropped. "You threatening me?"

"That's my plan A." Amarok was too exhausted to be diplomatic.

"What kind of cop are you?" he asked, rallying.

"The kind who cares about only one thing — and that's getting my fiancée back." Amarok handed him his card. "Call me if you change your mind about what you had to say, or if you remember anything else."

Amarok started his truck as soon as he climbed in. He was afraid if he didn't keep pushing himself, if he sat there for even a few seconds, he'd succumb to the bone-deep weariness that was slowly dragging him down.

Makita made a questioning sound, not quite a growl or a bark.

"I'm all right," he muttered.

153

Emmett couldn't stand being at the abandoned ranch knowing he had a pregnant woman in the cooler — one who thought she was going to be turned over to a serial killer, no less. He kept walking down the dim corridor to tell her what Terry said — that she was wrong about Bishop — but he never actually opened the slot in the door to do it. He was afraid she'd quickly convince him of the opposite. And he didn't need that, didn't need her getting into his head. He'd already decided what he was going to do — he was going to see this through. He couldn't blow it. Now that Terry had lost his job, the shit was really going to hit the fan with Bridget.

To escape his troubled conscience, he went out to check on the dogs. He had to do something besides *think*.

The henhouse where he was keeping them was one of several long, rectangular buildings made of corrugated metal and filled with stacked wire cages. A damaged and rusty conveyor belt ran along each row to feed the birds that had once been inside, and the chicken shit dropped down and piled up underneath.

This type of henhouse reminded him of

prison. It didn't look like any kind of life, even for a chicken. And it stunk worse than the defunct processing plant.

The dogs were penned in one corner. When he'd cut the slot in the door of the cooler so he could provide Dr. Talbot with food and added a toilet and bed, he'd also scooped the chicken shit to one side and fenced off an area for the dogs in which he spread a ton of bagged mulch around so they wouldn't get filthy.

They barked and began to jump and whine when they saw him.

Emmett took the time to pet and scratch each one before feeding them and making sure their numerous bowls had clean water. He liked dogs more than he did humans, so after bagging the poop and tossing the loaded bombs into the far corner he took his favorite dog out to walk the perimeter of the property.

No one seemed to be snooping around.

He didn't feel as though he needed to worry about being discovered, but he couldn't bring himself to go back into the processing plant quite yet. He needed a longer break. Although he was afraid Evelyn might go into labor while he was gone, that was part of the reason he couldn't make himself stay. He couldn't tolerate the constant threat.

There was nothing he could do to help her even if she *did* have the baby early. He wasn't about to incriminate himself and serve more time in prison, so he figured he might as well return the dog to the pen and go have a drink.

9

Anchorage, AK — Wednesday, 10:40 p.m.
AKDT

At least she knew *where* to strike. Evelyn had gone to med school. If she could sever one of her captor's carotid arteries, it would cut off half the blood oxygenating his brain and render him unconscious in about sixty seconds. That sounded extreme, even to her, desperate as she felt, but if she had just one shot, she needed to make it good. That was the only way she'd be able to get out of her small prison.

The only problem was the weapon she'd be working with. A sharpened wire had no width. It would be easy to miss the carotid, especially if they were struggling with each other or he suddenly put up his hand to block her.

Even if she stabbed him in the perfect place and made a run for it, she'd have only ten minutes or so to get help before he

157

bled out.

Ten minutes wouldn't be enough; she probably wouldn't be able to save him.

Could she live with that — add yet another nightmare to the collection in her brain?

She'd have to; she didn't see any other choice. She knew how Bishop felt toward her, what he would do. Her baby's survival, and her own, depended on escaping before he arrived.

But getting close enough to the man he'd hired wouldn't be easy. She had to do more than moan and writhe to convince him she was in labor. She needed to make her Goliath of a captor believe she was on the verge of giving birth the second he saw her — believe it so strongly that he'd rush into the room without a moment's hesitation. Only if he was completely unprepared and totally surprised would she be able to stab him, especially in such a targeted place.

What would alarm him to that degree?

Blood, she decided. If anything was going to draw him to her side that would be it.

Fortunately, blood was one of the few things she still had access to. She also had a water bottle that was half-full. If she cut herself, squeezed the blood that oozed out into the water and poured the mixture onto the floor as well as the back of her beige dress, she could make it look as though her water had broken. Then she could curl into a ball facing away from the door. And when he brought her breakfast and she didn't come to take the tray, he'd bend down to see what was going on and spot her "suffering" on the bed.

She just had to be careful to put the bloody puddle in a place where it would look as natural as possible, she told herself, and the easiest way to do that would be to put the bottle between her legs before unscrewing the cap. Then the solution would fall naturally and she'd have bloodstains on her legs and feet, which would look even more authentic.

The question now was . . . when should she make her move? She was so frightened it was tempting to delay, hoping against hope that something would change. That he'd hear and respond to her entreaties. That his conscience would finally get the better of him. That Amarok would find and free her.

But Bishop could arrive at any moment. She'd be a fool to wait. . . .

Now. The time was now.

She took several deep breaths, seeking strength and clarity. Then she picked up the shiv.

Steeling herself not to flinch or cry out, she cut one finger after another until there was enough blood in that bottle to make it a nice watery red.

Hilltop, AK — Thursday, 12:30 a.m. AKDT
It was finally growing dark, but it would stay dark for only four hours. Nights were short this time of year, and farther north shorter still. Not too far from Fairbanks, night *never* came, not in June, especially as they approached the summer solstice.

Amarok hated to see the sun sink below the horizon. It reminded him that time was passing fast, *too* fast, and he hadn't yet found Evelyn. The darkness also made it more difficult to stay awake while he drove.

After speaking to Dax O'Leary, he'd gone to Roxanne's. Fortunately, there'd been several dancers and a few patrons who remembered the "big guy with the scar." The unknown man had stood out, not only because of the damage to his face but also because of his size and build.

Amarok hadn't had a chance to speak to the bouncer who'd been there the night the van was stolen, however. A different one was on duty, so the manager had provided Greg's phone number.

Amarok had already tried to call him. It'd

been after eleven by then, but sheer desperation overruled any qualms about disturbing someone in the middle of the night.

Greg had finally answered but only to say he remembered seeing the guy but didn't know who he was or where he was from.

After leaving the club, Amarok had gone to the Anchorage Police Department to see if they'd been able to learn anything about the carpet-cleaning van. He'd been hoping they'd found it, that something about where it had been dumped would arm him with new information. If it was possible to glean DNA evidence or fingerprints from the vehicle, he could probably find out the man's name and track him via his mobile phone or credit cards or, barring that, his friends and associates.

It could make a big difference in finding Evelyn.

But the stolen van hadn't been located. The only thing Amarok learned was what the investigating detective — there was only one specializing in car thefts — could tell him when he called her at home. She'd said she believed the van was taken while the bouncer was inside, handling a minor disturbance in which a guy got drunk, tried to start a fight and had to be escorted off the premises. No one saw the man with the scar after that, and when Dax walked out of the joint over an hour later the van was gone.

Amarok could only hope it would be found. He'd tried driving through the neighborhoods surrounding Roxanne's, looking for it. But stumbling across it like that, in a completely random way, was highly unlikely.

Instead of wasting more time, he'd headed home. He'd already checked his answering machine remotely — there weren't any messages from Evelyn or whoever had abducted her. He needed a fresh lead and planned to search through the boxes she had archived above their garage to review the files of her previous patients to see if details he'd found so far lined up with anyone she'd worked with in Boston.

Later, when it wasn't quite so early in Boston, he had some calls to make, too. The first one needed to be to her family. He had to tell them what was going on before they heard about it in the news.

As he started the descent into Hilltop, his radio crackled to life.

"Amarok, you copy?"

Suddenly realizing that he'd been driving while half-asleep, he blinked as Makita barked, and, with a fresh jolt of adrenaline, snatched up the handpiece. "Right here, Phil. What's up?"

It was getting late, but Phil had stayed at the trooper post in case Evelyn tried to call — or someone else tried to contact him with information. "Maybe nothing."

Amarok was almost as relieved by those two words as he was disappointed. Although he craved a break in the case, he'd been terrified that Phil was about to tell him Evelyn's body had been discovered — and it showed signs of torture and mutilation, which would be even worse than simply finding her dead. "What is it?" he asked.

"I just received a call from someone named Dax O'Leary."

"That's the owner of the carpet-cleaning van that was stolen. I spoke to him a couple of hours ago. Why'd he call?"

"He was so drunk he was slurring his words. It was tough to understand him, but I'm pretty sure he said to tell you that the 'gladiator' you were talking about has shown up at a place called The Landing Strip."

Amarok's heart leapt into his throat. *The gladiator?* "You said Dax *just* called?"

"That's right. We barely hung up."

"What's the address of The Landing Strip?"

"As you might guess, it's near the airport.

He told me that much. Let me look it up."

By the time Amarok had memorized the address, he'd already turned around and was racing back to Anchorage.

Too bad Dax hadn't spotted the guy earlier. Then he wouldn't have an hour's drive ahead of him. Given the opportunity Dax had just handed him, that sounded like an eternity. He prayed it wouldn't be too late by the time he arrived.

"Call Anchorage PD," he told Phil. "Explain to them what's going on and have them send someone to the club right away."

"I'm on it," he said.

Minneapolis, MN — Thursday, 4:30 a.m. CST
Escaping was far easier than Lyman had expected. But planning made the difference between success and failure on almost everything. He'd spent months befriending Terry, listening to his marriage troubles, his financial woes, his complaints about his job and so on. Making him feel important was what made it possible to pull this off. He could never have done it alone. He'd known that from the beginning. And, tonight, everything was falling neatly into place.

It helped that he'd dressed quietly and put his burner phone, fake ID and several twenties into his pocket while everyone else

164

was sleeping, except for the security guard and the two nurses who worked the closest station this time of night. The security guard who roamed the halls was vigilant about monitoring all activity, especially after bed check, but she adhered to routine a bit *too* strictly. She always ate her lunch at the same time, which took her out of circulation at a predictable point in her shift. She also sat and talked to the two nurses while she ate, which distracted them.

Why wouldn't she feel safe to do that? Lyman asked himself. All was quiet. Nothing had happened around the wards to indicate that this night would be different from any other.

Ironically, the only person who saw him go was Terry. Terry was mopping the hall down the way and happened to glance up as Lyman stepped out of his room. His eyes widened, but he quickly put his head back down. He'd already warned Lyman where all the security cameras were located and told him how to navigate the blind spots in the building so he could reach the door without being picked up on video.

Lyman didn't need him to do anything else.

Normally, opening the back door would set off the emergency alarm, but thanks to

Terry hacking into the main security system, the only thing Lyman heard was the quiet whoosh of air as it closed behind him.

He turned to make sure it latched tightly before hurrying away. Worst-case scenario, he'd call for a taxi. He just didn't want to do that anywhere near Beacon Point Mental Hospital. Although he was afraid this would be the most difficult part of his plan — he had to drag his left leg these days, had such an awkward gait that it took forever to get anywhere — he felt it was more important to leave without a trace than to move quickly. He couldn't go too far until after the banks opened in the morning, anyway.

Fortunately, the embrace of the cool night air and the thrill of freedom made it possible for him to walk almost three miles. At that point, he called a taxi and pulled up the hood of the sweatshirt he was wearing so the driver wouldn't be able to see that part of his face was paralyzed.

He had a couple of things he had to do before he left for Alaska. He had to go to his safety-deposit box and get his ATM card so he could withdraw the last of the money he had in savings. Then he had to visit a store where he could purchase a Visa card with which to charge his flight. But once the bank opened, that wouldn't take long, and, after he reached the airport and boarded his plane, he'd be looking at a five-hour flight.

Only those small hurdles now stood between him and Evelyn.

Normal people took for granted the ease with which such mundane things were handled, day in and day out.

But Lyman wasn't normal.

Stroke or no stroke, he never had been.

Anchorage, AK — Thursday, 1:30 a.m. AKDT
When Amarok found three cop cars idling at various angles in the parking lot of The Landing Strip, lights flashing, he came to a skidding stop close by and jumped out, leaving the door open for Makita to follow him. "Did you get him?" he asked the cop who rolled down his window.

His heart was pumping like the pistons of an engine. As tired as he'd been before, he was wide-awake now, hadn't felt a moment's fatigue during the entire rush to return. He had only one thought in mind: *Get Evelyn back.*

Maybe that was why the blow was especially severe when the officer looked up at him and shook his head. " 'Fraid not."

The pain in Amarok's injured hand, which he'd scarcely felt since Phil's call, began to

throb so badly it made him slightly nauseous. "What do you mean? I had someone,
Phil Robbins, call you an hour ago. Don't
tell me you just got here."

"We got here about thirty minutes ago,
but by then he was already gone."

Amarok could've sworn someone had just
dropped an anvil on his chest. "What?
Why?"

"I don't know. He just wasn't here."

An officer walked out of the building with
Dax O'Leary.

"There you are!" Dax exclaimed, and,
staggering slightly, walked over. "Wow,
that's a big malamute. How is he with
strangers?"

Amarok was so used to having Makita
with him in Hilltop the thought hadn't even
crossed his mind that the dog's presence
might make anyone nervous. "He doesn't
do anything I tell him not to."

"That's good. But what the hell took you
so long?"

"I was almost an hour away. I came as
soon as I could." He motioned to the other
police officers. "They got here sooner."

"Yeah, but not soon enough. After I called
you and walked back into the club, that
dude spotted me, and the jig was up. He
made a beeline for the door."

"Did you follow him? Catch a glimpse of the vehicle he was driving? Was it your van?"

"I don't know," Dax said. "I only followed as far as the door. I was afraid to step outside. I thought he might be waiting to ambush me, and I didn't want to get into a fight."

Amarok squeezed his eyes closed. No way could this be happening. The abduction suspect had been *right* within their grasp and they'd let him slip away? What little chance Evelyn had could've slipped away with him! "Please tell me someone here recognized him, knows who he is and where he might live."

"No." The officer who'd been walking with Dax spoke up. "I just went through the whole place, asking everyone. There wasn't one person who recognized him, except this guy." He hitched his thumb over his shoulder at Dax.

"What are the chances?" Amarok mumbled to himself, more dispirited than he'd ever been in his life.

"That's what I had to ask myself!" Dax's voice was unnecessarily loud. "I mean, talk about a coincidence, right? I was in the middle of taking a drink when I spotted him and just about spewed it on the table."

Dax couldn't have made the call and left

discreetly? Why did he have to go back in? Amarok wondered. Dax *had* to know that if the guy saw him he'd get spooked, especially if he was the one who'd stolen the van.

But Amarok didn't ask. What was the point? The damage was done. Obviously, Dax, who wasn't the smartest guy in the world to begin with, was drunk. He also didn't have as much at stake. Sure, he'd lost an old van and his only mode of transportation, but he didn't seem overly concerned about it. He hadn't had to pay for it in the first place.

"I'm thinking we should head to the other clubs in town, maybe hit a few of the bars, too," an officer by the name of K. Mc-Gowen said. "See if he went somewhere else."

Amarok kept picturing Evelyn as he'd seen her when he kissed her good-bye before leaving for work two days ago. If her abductor was out and about, what did that mean for her? Had he already killed her and disposed of her body? Was he now looking for someone else? "He won't be at any of those places," he said dully.

Officer McGowen blinked several times. "How do you know?"

"He'd be stupid to take the risk."

"He took the risk of coming here," Dax

170

pointed out, obviously feeling important since he'd had the power to evoke such an immediate and keen response from the police.

"Because he didn't expect to see you. But since he did, he'll realize the danger of running into you again — that this is a much smaller town than it appears — and be more cautious in the future."

"Well, damn," Dax grumbled. "You act as though it was my fault he got away. I'm the one who called you."

Amarok rubbed his face with both hands. He didn't have the emotional reserves he usually did. He didn't have any reserves at all. "If you ever see him again, let us know where he is and then get out before he can spot you, okay?"

"How was *I* supposed to know he'd recognize me?" he cried, stung by the criticism.

Amarok gave him a level look. "He stole your car, which meant he might've seen you park it. If he was smart, he'd be keeping an eye on the parking lot, looking for someone who was just going in, because that would mean they wouldn't be coming out right away."

"We don't know that for sure," Dax grumbled.

"Why take the chance, you idiot?"

171

McGowen put a hand on Amarok's shoulder. "Take it easy. We'll keep looking for him, let you know if we find anything."

Amarok nodded. The lump swelling in his throat kept him from saying more. The fatigue that had been held at bay by the brief but powerful belief that this nightmare might soon be over was crashing down on him like a fifty-foot wave.

He had to get home and go through Evelyn's files. That was all he was left with; there was no time to stick around here and rail at anyone or lick his wounds.

But when he swayed while trying to walk back to his truck and nearly lost his footing, McGowen came jogging up behind him.

"Hey, you're not getting behind the wheel right now, are you?" he asked tentatively.

"What do *you* think?" he asked. Wasn't it obvious? He had his keys out. . . .

The cop's eyebrows jerked together. "Looks that way to me. But it also looks as though you've been drinking, so —"

"Drinking?" Amarok echoed in shock.

"I bet it's lack of sleep," Dax spoke up, also hurrying over. "Like I told you before he got here, he's kinda ragged around the edges. And did you see his hand? Look how it's swelling! My brother told me he went berserk in his truck earlier, punching every-

172

thing. That hand's probably broken."

"I suggest you keep your mouth shut before I show you that I can still use it," Amarok bit out. He knew better than to behave like an asshole, but the retort was triggered by his frustration and exhaustion. He'd lost all restraint.

Hearing that, McGowen scowled. "Why don't you get in the back of my cruiser? I'll drive you over to the hospital."

Amarok started walking again. "I'm not going to the hospital. I'm not going anywhere until I find Evelyn."

McGowen hurried to catch up. "Your hand should be X-rayed."

"So? It's *my* hand. I'll deal with it."

"That wasn't a request, Sergeant." McGowen caught him by the arm and tried to stop him. His blue eyes were steely, as though he meant business. But Amarok didn't care. He was too far gone to care about anything anyone could do to *him*. And Makita didn't like anyone interfering with him. Unwilling to allow Amarok to be threatened, he growled, showing his teeth, and McGowen immediately let go.

"Tell your dog to stand down," he said, but Amarok simply flipped him off, called Mikita so they could climb into his truck and spewed gravel as he took off.

173

Fortunately, no one came after him.
Maybe they knew it would only make matters worse.

10

Anchorage, AK — Thursday, 9:00 a.m. AKDT
Evelyn shivered with fear and revulsion. She'd staged the bloody water. Had it all over her legs and dress. When she turned over, she could see the small puddle she'd made on the floor as well as the drops that led to her cot. She'd smeared some of those drops with her bare feet as she pretended to limp to the bed.

The scene looked convincing. Almost *too* convincing. That was part of the reason she was having such a severe reaction to what she planned to do. She believed it might actually work — at least well enough to draw her captor into the room, which meant, for better or for worse, one of them probably wouldn't be leaving this cell.

With time, she calmed down a little, but her hand began to sweat on the shiv she was hiding. Several hours must've passed since he'd brought her dinner — maybe as many

175

as . . . twelve? She felt weak and a little dizzy. And after being on edge for so long, she was getting sleepy in spite of her fear.

But she had to remain focused, determined.

He'll be coming soon, she told herself.

Once again, she prayed that Amarok would appear and rescue her. She knew he'd move heaven and earth to find her, but he didn't come. The only thing she heard was the heat as it kicked on with a soft rush of forced air.

Rocking back and forth, she stared at the white wall in front of her. *Hang in there. You* ***have*** *to hang in there.* She was doing this to save her child. But she was almost as afraid of her captor's arrival as she was of what would happen if she continued to wait.

If he hit her or kicked her in the stomach —

The sound of the bolt acted like an electric shock and sent her heart rate skyrocketing. *Oh God! This is it!* There was no turning back now, no changing her mind.

Clenching her jaw, she began to moan as she rocked. That part wasn't difficult. It wasn't hard to conjure the tears that streamed down her face, either. She was shaking all over.

At first, she heard nothing besides her own

176

moans. She imagined him bending down and peering through the slot. He had the same limitations she did when trying to look out, but she was fairly certain he could see her from his vantage point. She was far enough from the door.

"What the fuck?" he cried, immediately enraged.

She heard some rattling, as though the cooler had been locked on the outside with a chain and padlock, before the door came open.

Her shaking grew worse as he walked in. Striking upwards was always harder than striking down; she didn't have the benefit of leverage.

Could she do this?

She was no longer confident she'd have the strength to lift her arm, let alone plunge the shiv into his neck.

All the muscles to be found there flashed through her mind at once — the sternocleidomastoid, the omohyoid, the sternohyoid and so many others. It was almost as if she were back in anatomy class staring down at a cadaver. She could cut through any of the muscles. She believed she could even cut through the hyoid bone. If she hit his trachea, his jugular or one of his carotid arteries, she might have a shot at disabling him enough for her to get away. She just couldn't hit his mandible. If she did, he'd simply grab her hand, get hold of the shiv and . . . what? Kill her with it?

Although he hadn't seemed particularly violent, he *was* an ex-con. Who knew what he was capable of?

"No way!" he shouted. "This *can't* be happening!"

He stood over her; she could see his giant shadow on the wall.

Holding the shiv that much tighter, she continued to cry and shake. She didn't think she could speak. But nothing she could say would convince him if what he saw didn't.

"Hey, damn it! What's going on? Can't you hear me?" He bent down to grab her shoulder, trying to turn her so that she'd have to look at him.

In that moment, she was tempted to simply grovel and beg for him to let her go. But she couldn't be sure he'd have any sympathy. And she couldn't gamble with the only chance she had to escape. Lyman Bishop could be on his way right now, and she wasn't going to allow herself or her daughter to become a victim of his.

"Is the baby coming *now*?" he asked.

That last word, "now," galvanized her into

action. Rolling toward him as fast as she could, she caught only a brief glimpse of his face — a stranger's face with a scar — before bringing her hand up and shoving her shiv into his neck, right in the hollow under his ear.

She'd missed his jaw. *Thank God!*

His eyes flew so wide open they almost bugged out of his head. His mouth moved, but only a rasping gasp came out.

He reached for the weapon she'd created, but she didn't leave it in his neck. She pulled it out and shoved it in again and again.

She couldn't stop.

Why wasn't he crumbling to the floor?

She cried out with each thrust, a desperate, animalistic cry, and the strength she'd been lacking came flooding back.

Finally, he managed to overcome the shock and pain and catch hold of the shiv, so she let it go and dashed around him. The door stood open, beckoning her to freedom, and all she could think about was Amarok in Hilltop, searching for her to no avail, worried sick about her and their unborn child.

I'm coming.

She'd reached the open doorway.

She was going to survive.

She was *so* close.

Although she tried to slam the door behind her, something was in the way. It bounced back, but she didn't dare stay long enough to figure out why.

The building outside the cooler smelled of rotten eggs and nearly turned her stomach. She could barely keep the bile down. It wasn't only the smell — she'd just stabbed a man!

She'd never forget the feel of that sharpened wire sinking into his flesh or the feel of the warm blood that spurted out onto her face.

But none of that mattered, she told herself as she looked frantically for a way out. This guy, whoever he was, shouldn't have taken her captive in the first place. What she'd had to do was *his* fault.

Until she reached the makeshift living room, which was down a short hallway, she believed she was going to escape. But the first door she rushed to was boarded up on the outside.

What kind of place was this? A factory?

The musty smell in the air wasn't industrial.

An out-of-business store?

Hard to tell, and the dim light didn't help. "Shit! Shit, shit, shit!" She *had* to get out. A sudden sound made her whirl around.

He was staggering toward her with blood running down his neck and her shiv in one hand. The purposeful gleam in his bloodshot eyes made it clear he meant to use it.

She tried to run, to dodge him, but it was no use. Her legs were so unsteady, she ran into the sharp edge of a table. She caught herself so she didn't fall, but before she could get around the couch she felt his hand fist in her hair and drag her down.

Emmett could barely breathe, and his T-shirt was soaked with blood by the time he had Evelyn Talbot locked in the cooler again. The shiv he'd dropped in the break room when he grabbed her was only a thick wire. That couldn't have done *too* much damage, he thought.

But only seconds later, he changed his mind. He couldn't recover, had no idea how much blood he'd lost. He had to get to an ER.

Intending to get help, he dug his cell phone out of his pocket. But then he realized, somewhat belatedly since he wasn't thinking clearly, that he couldn't call for an ambulance, couldn't bring anyone *here,* not unless he wanted to get patched up at the hospital only to be taken to jail.

He'd have to drive himself to the closest

med clinic and lie to the staff that someone had jumped him for his wallet. They'd probably still call the police. The type of injuries he'd sustained had to be reported. But as far as the police would know, he hadn't done anything wrong. They'd get the same story plus a made-up description of his attacker. Without evidence to contradict his story, they'd be off to hunt down an imaginary perp and leave him there.

That was the way it *should* play out — as long as they didn't run the license plate on the van he'd stolen.

"Let me go!" Evelyn was raving, going completely all-out crazy. He could hear her desperation in the reedy thinness of her voice.

But he didn't feel any pity. Not after what she'd done to *him.* He'd been so worried that she'd go into labor, so afraid that the baby would die, and she'd used his fear against him.

The bitch was smart. He'd been careful, thought of everything, and yet he'd fallen right into her trap.

He should've told her to shut up. She had him so angry he could kill her. But he didn't have the voice to yell — or the air. His breathing was so ragged he was getting dizzy.

Using the walls for support, he tried to make his way to the empty store in front, but his legs didn't want to work, didn't want to bear his weight. And as he moved, the dizziness grew much worse — until he was afraid he'd black out.

"What . . . the hell's . . . happening?" he gasped.

Barely clinging to consciousness, he tried to take another step. Lyman Bishop was on his way. All Emmett had to do was hold on until he got paid. Then he could blow this joint, be done with the whole sordid mess. Let Lyman Bishop do what he would with the pregnant bitch. She was as vicious as the psychopaths she studied.

Holding one hand to his throat in an attempt to staunch the bleeding, he managed to turn around long enough to double-check that he'd locked the cooler.

Yes, he had. Thank goodness. He could see the closed lock hanging there. He didn't want to worry about Evelyn Talbot escaping while he was in such a mess.

That she wasn't going anywhere should've brought him some relief, except he was feeling so shitty he wasn't sure *anything* would help.

Concentrate! He had to focus if he was ever going to reach the van. And he *would*

183

reach it. He'd get paid despite what had almost happened. His sister needed Terry's half of the money in order to move out on her own. That was part of the reason Emmett had decided to see this through. Terry didn't know she was planning to leave him, of course, but that was what she'd told Emmett in her last text. So what else could he do? She was miserable, and his loyalties would always remain with her. Blood was thicker than water, as they say — and that included cellmates.

He bumped into the walls on either side of him until the short hallway ended and he reached the salesroom. He was tempted to sit down until the room quit spinning and he could catch his breath, but he had a feeling he should keep moving, get to a doctor while he could still drive.

He stepped over the discarded egg crates and other debris he'd been navigating all week to reach the front door.

The wind hit his face as he wrenched it open. He could see a hint of the blue van, sitting in the carport beneath overgrown vines where it was hidden from the road.

But when he tried to step toward it, his knees gave out and he fell with a sickening thud.

Startled by his inability to control his

body, he stared up at the building overhang above.

He wasn't going to make it, he realized. After everything he'd been through — doing hard time in state prison, surviving fights with his worst enemies — he was going to die because of a pregnant *woman*?

No. He couldn't believe it. But his ears began to ring and his vision dimmed until the darkness on all sides of him gathered into one tiny pinprick of light.

Which suddenly winked out.

The disappointment was so acute Evelyn couldn't quit sobbing. Her chest heaved as she beat on the door. She was acting like a child, but she didn't care. She'd come *so* close to escaping with her life and her baby's life!

Now all the courage she'd screwed up, the hope that had driven her, the painful effort of creating the lethal shiv, the hours and hours of terrified waiting . . .

It was all for nothing.

At least he hadn't killed her. That thought eventually lessened her despair. He could've done much worse than toss her back inside the cooler and lock the door, but she could hardly count that as a kindness when Lyman Bishop was on his way. She'd rather be murdered outright than become Bishop's next zombielike slave.

"Let me out!" she called again, but she'd been yelling for so long her voice was too tired and hoarse to be heard.

Drained of the energy she needed to maintain the onslaught, she sank to the floor.

What was she going to do now?

She wiped the blood from her face as she gazed at the blood spatter on the wall. The oatmeal her captor had brought was spilled all over the floor. The banana had been kicked under her cot. And the tray was bent. Apparently, that was what had been in the way when she'd tried to close the door.

It had all come down to a food tray. . . .

And now she didn't have anything to drink. She'd used the last of her water to deceive him and, if he'd tried to bring her more, it had ended up on the outside of the cooler and not here, where she needed it.

"Heaven help me," she muttered. Too weak and discouraged to even get to her feet, she crawled over to the bed and climbed into it. Despite the blood and the water all over everything, this thin mattress was the softest place to be, and she needed what small comfort it and the blanket could provide.

The pictures she'd reviewed from Bishop's file when he first arrived at Hanover House paraded before her mind's eye. They made her sick. So did what he'd done to his own sister.

Evelyn closed her eyes in an attempt to block out those images.

She couldn't face her own future, couldn't contemplate what she was looking at next.

11

"What are you doing calling me?" Terry asked, his voice a harsh whisper.

Adjusting to the muggy heat of the Midwest summer, Lyman Bishop removed the sweatshirt he'd worn earlier and leaned back on the park bench. It was so nice to feel the sun on his face and to know he'd never have to encounter another nurse or doctor from Beacon Point Mental Hospital. "I made it to the bank and withdrew the money, but I couldn't get a flight out until Saturday morning. Even then, the ticket was *outrageously* expensive."

"Last-minute plane fares usually are."

"I should've had you make the reservation for me. I bet it would've saved three hundred dollars."

"Hey, I fronted you too much dough already trying to get your damaged ass out of that place. What do you think, I'm made

188

of money?"

Bishop stiffened. Terry's mood certainly hadn't improved since last night. "It's an unnecessary loss. That's all. I'm not finding fault with you; I just hate waste."

"Doesn't everyone? Welcome to the real world, buddy. I guess now that you're no longer a big cancer researcher you gotta live like the rest of us."

Lyman grimaced. How could Terry say that after what he'd been through? Sometimes he didn't like the janitor very much — and yet Terry had been just about the best friend Lyman had ever had. He doubted anyone else would've helped him get out of Beacon Point. The orderlies and other medical staff had treated him like some kind of leper. One, in particular, always mentioned the lobotomies and said it was poetic justice that he'd lost his mind.

"I still have the intellect that made me a cancer researcher in the first place," he pointed out, which was more than he could say for Terry. What had Terry accomplished? Nothing. He wasn't very smart. He didn't know that his wife was going to leave him, even though, judging from what Lyman had heard of their arguments, he could tell that she was halfway out the door.

"I'm happy for you," Terry said sarcasti-

189

cally. "But I can't sit around and chitchat. Bridget will be home with the kids any minute. I've got to figure out a way to tell her I lost my job without it turning into another knock-down, drag-out."

"Oh. Okay. No problem. I just thought that maybe, since I'm here for the day anyway, you'd want to meet me and get your money. I was hoping it might help to have a wad of cash on hand when you talked to Bridget. That's why I called."

"You think we should meet up?" He sounded more interested. "I thought you said that would be too risky."

"It won't be if we can find a secluded spot. We wouldn't want anyone to see us together, but —"

"That won't be a problem," he broke in. "I'll leave a note for Bridget, tell her I had to run a quick errand. Where are you? Where should we meet?"

Bishop gazed complacently at the traffic that surrounded him in St. Paul. "Have you heard of Swede Hollow?"

"No."

"It's a ravine just off Seventh Street, near the old Hamm's Brewery."

"I know where that is. . . ."

"Then you can find it easily enough. Pick me up at the Metropolitan State University off Seventh, which is right by there, too, and I'll pay you. Then you can take me to the airport."

"I thought you said your flight doesn't leave until Saturday morning."

"It doesn't, but I don't want to worry about getting a room and another ride. I'll wait there."

"Okay, but why are we going somewhere so close to downtown? Won't there be scads of people?"

"Swede Hollow is very secluded. Did you know it used to be a shantytown until the 1950s, when the city knocked it down and kicked out the squatters? Hardly anyone even knew it existed, but there'd been people living down there without any electricity or water for over a hundred years."

"No. How do *you* know all that?"

"Oh, an article I once read." Lyman saw no need to tell him that he'd buried a body in the park once, a woman by the name of Starr Hoffman, who'd never been found. Not only was it quiet and wooded, it was also close to where he used to live. He'd always liked the place, mostly because of Starr, a student at the university who'd been so sweet and kind to everyone, including him, until he tried asking her out.

"Whatever. Listen, I'll be there in twenty

minutes."

"I'll be waiting." Lyman disconnected and stretched out his arms along the top of the bench, enjoying the fresh air until it was time to go meet Terry.

He arrived at MSU first, because he hadn't been far away to begin with. But he was surprised when Terry drove up shortly after, even sooner than expected, and rolled down his window.

"Why are you wearing *that*?" he asked without so much as a hello, indicating the sweatshirt Lyman had put back on since leaving the park. "Aren't you sweltering in this heat?"

Lyman waited for Terry to unlock the door and got in. "Being partially paralyzed makes me distinctive. I'd rather not draw attention to myself."

Terry snorted. "You will, though, wearing a sweatshirt in June."

"It's dark in color. No one has said a word."

"Fine. Go ahead and suffer," he said. "So . . . you want me to go *into* the hollow? How do I get there?"

"Through the improvement arches," he said as Terry pulled out of the university on Seventh.

"You've got my money, right?"

192

"Of course. But if you're in that much of a hurry, just stop here."

"On the street?"

"Why not? I'd like to take a look at the ravine. From what I remember, it's very steep."

Terry pulled to the side of the road, but he made no move to get out. "I don't care about seeing the ravine. Just pay me. Then you'll have to find your own way to the airport. I need to get back to Bridget."

Lyman opened the sack he'd been carrying with him. "Okay, but make sure there's no one looking."

As soon as Terry swiveled his head to check, Lyman pulled out the butcher knife he'd purchased that morning and plunged it into Terry's heart.

"W-why?" Terry gasped, his jaw sagging in stunned disbelief as he gazed down at the handle protruding from his chest.

"You should've done your homework," Lyman replied. "You would've known I don't have any money. My legal defense took almost everything I had. And I can't have you and Emmett going to the police, telling them you know where Evelyn Talbot is."

A desperate, choking gurgle was the only reply Terry could make. Which was fine with Lyman.

"It sounds like Emmett found the perfect place. I might want to stay there a while. But don't take it personally," he added. "It's me. I'm a fastidious person, can't leave any loose ends."

"Emmett will . . . k-kill you . . . for this," Terry somehow managed to say as his body began to convulse.

"Not if I kill him first." Lyman pulled the knife out and wiped it clean with some paper towels he'd also purchased and put it all back in the sack. Then he got out, walked around to the driver's side and opened the door.

The knowledge that he was absolutely powerless registered on Terry's face, along with the pain and fear. He clutched his chest as blood spread over his shirt like a blooming flower, and he tried to get out of the car. Perhaps he intended to flag down a passing motorist. There were plenty of other vehicles flowing past, all oblivious to what was occurring right in front of their eyes.

Bishop blocked him in, standing casually as though he were merely talking to a friend who'd dropped him off. One person honked; the driver didn't like that they were partway in the road, but after flipping the bird, he simply went around.

"I guess I haven't lost my touch," Bishop

194

said when Terry quit moving and stared sightlessly through the windshield. "Surprise provides *such* an advantage."

Whistling as he reached in to put the transmission in Drive, he closed the door, pulled his hood back up and started to walk away as though he'd had no part in sending the car rolling over into the ravine.

When it crashed a few seconds later, the noise drew some attention, but the few who heard it were so shocked and so clueless as to what could've happened that Lyman was stepping inside a taxi on Payne Avenue and heading to the airport before a crowd could even form.

Sometimes doing things right in the middle of the day, and in plain sight, raised far less suspicion.

Hilltop, AK — Thursday, 11:40 a.m. AKDT
Amarok had spent the time since he'd been back from Anchorage pulling Evelyn's old files down from the garage and searching through them. He heard a knock at the front door while he was just getting another box. Makita started to bark, but he didn't want to take the time to answer it. He wouldn't have, if his visitor hadn't continued to knock.

"Come on, Amarok!" Phil yelled from

outside. "Open up!"

With far more irritation than he had a right to feel, Amarok trudged back through the house, dropped the box he was carrying in the living room, told Makita to shut up and sit down and picked up Evelyn's cat, so that Sigmund wouldn't get outside as he wrenched open the door. "I'm busy. What is it?"

"I have a surprise for you. Can you come on over to the Moosehead?"

"No." He closed the door and put the cat down, but he didn't lock it, so Phil let himself in and followed Amarok into the living room.

"Finding anything?" He gestured at the boxes Amarok had searched so far, looking for a mug shot of a guy with a scar over his eye.

"No."

"Well, I hate to take you away from this. But it can wait thirty minutes or so, can't it?"

"I'm afraid not," Amarok insisted. "I have to do everything I possibly can, and I have to do it right away."

Phil propped his hands on his hips. "Amarok, you're demanding too much of yourself. You're not superhuman. Look at you — you can barely stay on your feet."

"I'm fine," he insisted gruffly. "I wouldn't be able to sleep, even if I tried."

"I doubt that's true. You're about to keel over right in front of my eyes, so why don't you let us help?"

He peeled the lid off the new box. "Who's 'us'?"

Phil put the lid back on so that Amarok would have to look up at him. "You'll see."

Amarok's eyes were burning, but he resisted the temptation to rub them. He didn't want to give Phil any more fuel for his side of the argument. "Fine," he said. "But whatever it is, you'd better make it quick."

As Phil pulled him out of the house, Amarok whistled for Makita behind him, but Phil wouldn't let him get into his own truck. "You're not driving anymore, buddy," he said, and all but shoved Amarok into the passenger seat of his new SUV before letting Makita in the backseat.

"Then hurry." Taking any time away from his search made Amarok feel he was letting Evelyn down.

When they pulled into the Moosehead, the parking lot was full, even though it was mid-morning — a time when Shorty rarely opened, especially on weekdays. "What's going on?" he asked.

"I've arranged a search party."

It took a second for that to register. Amarok was crashing hard after the caffeine pills he'd taken in order to drive safely back from Anchorage and remain functional since. "Where are you going to search?"

"Both here and in Anchorage. We'll be looking for any sign of the man with the scar — or anyone who's seen him, the van or Evelyn — and we'll cover as much ground as we can for as long as we can keep our volunteers."

The more people who were looking, the better chance Evelyn had. Amarok couldn't believe he hadn't thought of gathering so much help himself. It was proof that he was considering this more of a personal problem than a crime. "That's a good idea," he said, conceding.

Phil gestured at all the cars. "When I put out the call, I had no idea we'd get this level of response. I doubt there's a single person who knows you who isn't inside the bar right now. Some have even closed their shops and businesses. We're serious about this."

Amarok gazed at the jumble of vehicles, so many of which he recognized. He'd grown up with these people and, when his father had moved to Anchorage, they'd become his surrogate family. That was never

198

more apparent than now. "But some of them don't even like Evelyn," he said.

"Granted, there are those who aren't happy that she brought a prison like Hanover House to the area. But they aren't doing it for her," he said softly. "They're doing it for you. You've always been there for us. Now we're going to be there for you."

The support softened the anger that had been driving Amarok so far. The community was coming together right when he needed them most, and that meant a great deal. Maybe it would make all the difference. Maybe they'd find Evelyn — or the stolen van so that *he* could find Evelyn.

He thanked Phil, who'd had more sleep than he'd had since Evelyn went missing but still not a great deal, and managed to get through the next thirty minutes, during which he created two different searches, one for Anchorage and a smaller one for Hilltop. He appointed search captains, explained how to make a grid and walk shoulder to shoulder through any wilderness area with avalanche probes or other poles to poke through the undergrowth.

Although he did it all mechanically, trying to distance himself from the raw emotion he felt, that all changed when the Ledstetters walked in. He thought they might be coming to cause trouble but soon felt terrible for ever doubting them. They got in line to take an assignment just like everyone else.

Amarok waited until Davie and Junior were heading toward the door to intercept them. "You don't have to do this," he said.

Davie exchanged a look with Junior. "If we can save you from suffering the way we have, we'd like to help," he said, and Amarok's throat tightened as Davie gave him a bear hug with a couple of quick thumps on the back.

12

The call to the Talbot family wasn't one Amarok was looking forward to. He sat at his desk, his eyes so dry he could barely move them, hoping Phil would bring word that the searchers had found something. He clung fiercely to the belief that Evelyn was still alive — and wanted to wait to reach out to her family until he had more information. But the volunteers had just started. He'd been out there with them, making sure the search commenced as quickly as possible, but getting them going had still taken much longer than he'd anticipated.

He couldn't put off notifying her folks any longer. Evelyn's disappearance hadn't hit the news yet, but it was only a matter of time. Penny had called to let him know that Ted Bell, a beat reporter from Anchorage, had been trying to reach Evelyn all morning and was growing suspicious because

201

Penny kept putting him off. No doubt he'd heard Evelyn's name in the chatter on his police scanner last night, when Officer McGowen and the others had been called out to the strip joint, and that had started him digging.

With a sigh, Amarok stared across the room at Makita, who was lying on his dog bed, as he picked up the phone. The Talbots hated that their daughter lived so far away. They wanted her back in Boston, which was why he wasn't very confident they were happy she was marrying him. Knowing how they felt made delivering the news he had to give them that much harder. They'd no longer believe he could take care of her.

He rested his head on one fist while he listened to the phone begin to ring. Why *didn't* he do more to protect her while he had the chance? How could he have let this happen?

He knew those questions weren't entirely reasonable. He'd had no idea that something might go wrong, no warning, but he couldn't help asking himself why he hadn't been more cautious, just in case. Since Jasper had been caught, he'd relaxed *too* much.

"Hello?" Evelyn's mother sounded excited but slightly harried at the same time.

Standing in preparation for the punch this

conversation was sure to pack, he cleared his throat. "Lara, it's Amarok."

"Oh, I'm so glad you called!" she said. "Is Evelyn there with you?"

He winced. "No, she's not. I'm afraid —"

"Oh darn!" she broke in, obviously not hearing anything besides *no, she's not.* "I just tried to reach her at the prison but couldn't get her, and she's not answering at home. Where is she?"

Amarok hesitated. "Lara, I —"

Apparently, she wasn't truly committed to the question, because she didn't give him a chance to finish what he was about to say before continuing, "I need to reach her. Brianne's in labor. I'm heading over to the hospital right now."

Amarok had been up for so long, he felt as though he were ten feet underwater and everything was coming at him through the distortion of that medium. For a moment, he even wondered if he might be hallucinating. He'd never been awake for so many days at one time. It was scrambling his perception, his thoughts and, most of all, his emotions.

He pulled the phone away so he could look at it just to be sure it was solid and real.

"Hello?" she said impatiently. "Did you

hear what I said?"

He pulled the receiver back. "I did."

"You're probably calling to talk about the wedding, and I can't wait to hear all about it. I know you were supposed to meet with the people from that Moosehead place to get a price on food. Evelyn insists that you two are paying for the reception there, that she's too old for us to foot the bill. But that's nonsense. She's our girl, and we're going to give her a proper wedding. Never mind that there will be two receptions. They're both on us. We're the ones who requested a second event in Boston, and you're having to take time off work and travel all the way across the country."

Someone spoke in the background. Amarok could only suppose it was Grant, Evelyn's father.

She covered the phone. "I know, I know! I'll be right there." She came back on the line. "Grant's starting the car. I have to go if I don't want to miss the birth of my first grandchild. Can you tell Evelyn about Brianne? I'll update her from the hospital, if I can. I'll have my mobile with me, but when I went to visit my friend who had her knee replaced in that same hospital a few months ago, I couldn't get any reception. I don't have the foggiest idea why. There's too much equipment in that place or something. Grant doesn't believe me, but that's what I think it is. Anyway, I wanted to get word about the baby to Evelyn before I left, just in case I can't reach her from the hospital."

Amarok was speechless. Brianne's baby was coming *now*? He couldn't tell Lara that Evelyn had been abducted for the second time in her life. After what the Talbots had been through before, it was their worst nightmare. The moment he said a word, what they'd endured more than two decades earlier — the knowledge of how Evelyn had suffered — would come back to them, and it would ruin this moment, which was supposed to be special and belong exclusively to Brianne.

Lara didn't give him a chance to go into it, anyway. She said a fast good-bye and hung up.

He was still holding the phone, wondering if he should've told her, regardless, when the door banged open and Shorty's sister, Molly, marched in, carrying a white sack that smelled like food. "I saw your truck out front."

"I was just leaving." He put the phone down and started to go around his desk when she stopped him.

205

"Oh no you don't. You're not getting away from me *that* easily. I know you're going through hell, Benjamin Murphy, and I feel sorry for you. God knows I do. But you're not doing Evelyn any favors by running yourself into the ground. She needs you to be sharp." She tapped her head with her finger. "To think clearly. To make the hours you *do* work more effective. And in order to do that, you have to eat."

He tried to wave her away. He still had all those boxes waiting for him at home. "I'll grab something at the house," he said, but she wouldn't budge from the doorway.

She held up the sack. "You're going to eat *now,* so you might as well sit down. I've brought you some of my homemade chili. I know you like it. You order it all the time. So don't give me any trouble."

To be honest, Amarok was more tired than he was hungry. He'd ignored the complaints of his empty stomach for so long the hunger pains had gone away.

Still, he figured he wasn't going to get an easier meal. So he took the sack, returned to his desk and wolfed it down in a matter of minutes. "Thank you." Finished, he tossed the empty bowl and plastic spoon in the wastebasket and tried again to leave.

"Not yet," she said. "Now you're going to

sleep for a few hours. And I'll sit at your desk and watch that phone like a hawk, ready to snap it up on the first ring. If anyone tries to call that has anything to do with the investigation, I'll wake you. You have my word."

"Molly —"

"Don't Molly me," she said, reacting to the *no* in his voice. "I've been taking care of that stubborn brother of mine long enough to know how to handle a muleheaded man. You trust me to stay vigilant and get you right away, don't you?"

"Of course, but —"

"Uh uh uh! Then don't argue." She motioned to the couch. "Just lie down right there."

"Molly, really. I appreciate what you're trying to do. But there's no way I can rest right now. I'll grab a nap once I go through Evelyn's old files, okay? That can't take too long."

"It'll take a lot longer than it should if you're in this condition."

"I'm not as bad off as I look."

"Well, that's good to hear, because you look like death warmed over."

"I'll take a nap later this afternoon." He tried to circumvent her, but she grabbed hold of him.

"No," she insisted. "I'm not buying that. Either you lie down right here and rest, or I'll call Shorty and he'll bring some of the men to hog-tie you."

Amarok gaped at her. "You can't be serious."

Her eyebrows, which looked like they'd been drawn in with a dark pencil, slid up menacingly. "I am absolutely serious. You wouldn't want to take valuable time away from those who are searching so hard to find Evelyn, now, would you?"

No. He didn't want to do that, especially when even Makita seemed to agree with her. The dog merely lifted his head at the exchange and then put it down again.

Amarok realized he could continue to fight, waste time and resources he needed being stubborn and stupid, or he could get some rest while his friends and loved ones were doing all they could to help him.

He glanced over at the couch. He hated to succumb to his exhaustion, preferred to keep fighting. But he was afraid he'd miss something important if he didn't rest at least enough to bring his brain out of this fog. "Okay," he said, relenting.

"That's what I want to hear. There you go," she said, and gave him a little push in the right direction, like a mother might give to her sleepy boy.

Amarok would've smiled at that. He was six foot two, hardly little. But he was too upset to enjoy the humor of it.

Giving himself permission to sleep for an hour, just enough to provide his mind and body with a quick break, he lay down on the couch and drifted off so quickly he didn't even know when Molly draped a blanket over him until the phone rang and he felt her jiggling his shoulder.

Anchorage, AK — Thursday, 4:30 p.m. AKDT
"What's wrong with you?"

When he heard that question, Jasper peered out through the bars of his cell to find the man in the cage across from him watching him closely. A new inmate who'd arrived only two months ago, Roland Holmes was like a praying mantis. He blended in, waited for what he wanted to come to him — and then he could be lethal.

Jasper was cautious around him. Unlike the many braggarts he'd encountered since coming to Hanover House, Roland never said much about himself or his crimes, never talked about the killing that'd gotten him incarcerated.

But Jasper had heard what the others had to say about him. He'd bludgeoned his old

209

man to death when he was only fifteen. The judge had gone easy on him because his father had been such an abusive prick, but Roland hadn't stopped there. He'd killed three inmates while he was in prison — for attempting to gang-rape him, unless that was just a rumor that enhanced the story — and when he got out at thirty-four he killed his mother's new husband because the dude wouldn't allow him to see her for fear he was too "dangerous."

The inmates respected him. Truth be told, Jasper did, too. But he tried not to show it. Roland hated men who raped and tortured women — and if he learned you'd ever harmed a child, you were as good as dead. Jasper had once heard him mutter that going after such easy and innocent prey was like killing a household cat instead of having the balls to try for bigger game and that put whoever made such a mistake in the same category as his father.

But he didn't understand. Jasper didn't go after women because he was afraid of men. He had no sexual interest in men, gained no pleasure at the thought of torturing or killing them — not unless they were all he had to choose from.

Anyway, even Evelyn seemed to respect Roland, probably because he'd contacted her from wherever he was serving time before this and asked to come to Hanover House. Told her he wanted to know why he did what he did, why he didn't fear the consequences as he should and why he couldn't cope more effectively with his impulses.

"Nothing's wrong with me." Jasper wanted to tell Roland to mind his own business, but no one talked to Roland that way. If he did, Roland would simply bide his time until the perfect moment — and then he'd use a shiv. That was exactly the kind of excuse Roland was looking for from a man he'd already marked as having "broken the rules of engagement."

"You've been pacing like an angry cat."

Why was he always thinking of cats? "So? I'm anxious. You've never been anxious?"

"Not without cause. You didn't have anything to do with Dr. Talbot's abduction, did you?"

It would be a death sentence to say yes and Jasper knew it. "No."

"You're sure? Because she's pregnant. You know that."

Of course he knew that. How could he miss it? No doubt she loved that he had a front-row seat to her pregnancy because it symbolized her happiness and everything

211

he'd tried to take away from her. "I'm fully aware of that fact."

"I'm glad, because I'd hate to have a problem between us."

Jasper felt hatred begin to uncoil like a venomous snake in the pit of his stomach. There was going to come a time when he and Roland had a serious disagreement. He could feel it in his bones. He'd tried to stand clear, but if Roland was going to pick a fight in spite of that, Jasper would gladly accept the challenge. "Like I said, I had nothing to do with it. That's the thing. If *I* had nothing to do with it, who did?"

Roland flicked something out of his teeth. "I guess we'll just have to wait and see if Sergeant Murphy can figure it out."

"I guess so," Jasper said, but it had been two and a half days since Evelyn went missing. What were the chances she was even alive at this point?

The thought of her being killed by someone else bothered him tremendously. If she was dead, she'd won for good. He'd never be able to even the score.

So he had no intention of sitting back and waiting for Amarok. He'd already started a little investigation of his own. He just wished the wheels he'd put in motion would turn faster.

Hilltop, AK — Thursday, 5:30 p.m. AKDT

"*Who* are you?" Amarok had been out of action for three hours — far longer than he'd wanted to be, but once he'd closed his eyes he hadn't heard a thing, hadn't even dreamed. He'd slept so deeply he would've liked to continue floating in oblivion for a week or more. But he didn't feel rested. He was so groggy he could hardly comprehend what the female voice on the other end of the line was trying to tell him.

"My name's Chastity Sturdevant. I live in Cedar Rapids, Iowa."

He could hear the midwestern accent. "And you're calling me, *why?*"

"Because Jasper Moore asked me to."

"The Jasper Moore who's a serial killer and a psychopath? The one who's locked up at Hanover House right now?"

"He's not as bad as you're making him sound," she said.

"Then you're *seriously* deluded." Amarok was too tired to be diplomatic.

"That's what *you* think, I guess. Anyway, Jasper and I have been writing each other for a while now. We're . . . um . . . friends."

Her hesitation defining the relationship suggested they were more. What she didn't understand was that at least a dozen other women probably thought he was falling in

213

love with *them.* "I don't understand why he'd give you my number."

"He didn't. I had to look it up. But in the e-mail I received from him, he asked me to drive over and give you a call if I couldn't find that zombie-making bastard."

"Find *who*?" he asked, coming to his feet.

"Lyman Bishop!"

Amarok felt the hair on the back of his neck stand up. "You're in Minnesota?"

"Yeah. Took me four hours to get here, and it's all for nothing. I just left Beacon Point Mental Hospital. He's not there."

"That's not true," Amarok argued. "I've checked myself."

"Then you'd better check again, because I just tried to visit him and they told me he was no longer a patient."

"That's because they can't give out any information. They can't even let on that he's a patient."

"You don't understand. I slipped past the security desk at the door and went up in the elevator. I asked a nurse at some nurses' station where my 'father' was — said he was supposed to be on the third floor, but I couldn't find him — and she looked in her computer. She said she didn't show him as a patient anymore."

"Where did he go?"

"How am I supposed to know? The nurse had no idea."

"That can't be true," Amarok insisted, but the doubt she'd placed in his mind was quickly turning his stomach to acid.

"If you say so. I don't even know the dude, so *I* don't care. I was just helping out my boyfriend. Anyway, I've gotta go. I have another long drive ahead of me."

There was a snapping sound that led him to believe she was chewing gum. "How old are you?" he asked before she could hang up.

"Eighteen."

She said that with a touch of belligerence, as if she was also saying, *I'm old enough to do what the hell I want.*

"If you're smart you'll stay away from Jasper and anyone like him," Amarok said. "You've heard what he did to his high school girlfriend, haven't you?"

"He hates Evelyn," she said with a shrug in her voice. "He would never do that to *me.*"

"Don't be stupid. He would if he had the chance," Amarok said, and disconnected.

"What is it?" Molly was still there, watching him closely. "Anything that could help Evelyn?"

"Depends." If Lyman Bishop was involved

in Evelyn's abduction, maybe Amarok could track him in some way. Lyman didn't have any family to speak of and probably very few friends, but everyone needed money. He might be able to trace him through bank or credit card transactions.

Amarok looked up the number for Beacon Point and called them. It took twenty minutes of wrangling with different nurses and supervisors, but eventually he learned what "Chastity" had been trying to tell him: Lyman Bishop wasn't at Beacon Point anymore — and no one could say where he'd gone.

Anchorage, AK — Thursday, 11:00 p.m. AKDT

Evelyn had made her situation even worse!

Now she was going to die in this cooler — the long, slow way. It had been hours and hours since she'd stabbed the muscular man with the scar over his eye, and no one had come. She'd had no water, no food, hadn't heard a sound.

Had she killed him? Or had he taken off without telling anyone where to find her?

If he were around, she would've expected some sort of reprisal, unless neglecting her and letting her die of thirst or starvation was it.

When she couldn't bear to look at her surroundings any longer, she summoned the energy to get to her feet and dip her jacket in the toilet water so she could clean herself up. She wiped down the walls next. Being stranded in such a terrifying situation was difficult enough; she didn't need to see those red droplets every time she opened her eyes, didn't need to feel the blood drying on her face and arms.

Once both she and the walls were clean, she began to feel slightly better, despite the hunger pangs in her stomach, and used the plastic bowl that had once held oatmeal to scoop more water out of the toilet so she could rinse the floor. She pushed the blood, oatmeal and water mixture to the drain with her feet. Then she scrubbed the blood out of her blanket, rinsed out her jacket and used it to clean what she could of the mattress.

While she waited for everything to dry, she sat on the floor near the door and thought about her mother, father and only sibling. Her mother, who'd suffered from depression for years, had improved so much since Jasper had been caught. Her whole family had turned a corner and begun to heal, *really* heal, for the first time since Jasper attacked her more than two decades ago. She hated to imagine them hearing that she was missing again — hated what it would do to them.

Her sister was even more pregnant than she was, due any day. Evelyn had promised Brianne she'd fly home when Brianne had her baby and spend a couple of weeks, so everyone was expecting to see her soon.

As a family, they had so much to look forward to. New babies — her parents' first grandchildren. A wedding. Although Brianne's boyfriend had left her for someone else before either one of them knew about the baby and she'd been devastated by the rejection, she'd managed to rebound, slowly, over time. Until this happened, everything had been looking up. Now her family might get word of her abduction or, worse, her death — which also meant the death of her baby — in the same week or month they welcomed their first grandchild into the world.

She wished there were some way to leave them a message, to tell them that she wanted them to be happy eventually no matter what happened. She felt terrible knowing her choices had made things so hard for them, especially because she didn't see where she could've handled her life any differently. If she hadn't gone into psychiatry and focused on psychopathy, she would never have met Amarok. And it was him, as well as her knowledge and determination, who'd saved her from Jasper. Since she'd ultimately won that battle, maybe she'd bought herself some extra time she wouldn't have had otherwise.

She hoped they'd be able to look at her life and death that way.

She wiped the tear that threatened to drip off her chin and leaned her head against the wall. She'd never dreamed she'd wish to see Lyman Bishop, but he could easily be the only person in the world who knew where she was.

And if he didn't get here soon, she'd have no chance at all.

13

Anchorage, AK — Friday 11:00 a.m. AKDT

Evelyn's head pounded as she sat on the floor and stared into the toilet. Could she drink the water?

When she'd first been put in here, she'd thought she could never do it, not after what she'd been through before. She'd become somewhat of a germophobe since Jasper, particularly careful with her food. Her water was always rigorously filtered, her food never more than a day old. Everything, even her clothes, was washed in water that came through the same filter as the water she drank, and while Amarok loved a big, juicy steak, most of the time she couldn't stomach the thought of red meat. Occasionally, she'd crave a burger, but other times the smell alone turned her stomach, and it had been that way ever since Jasper had tried to force her to eat the roasted limb of one of her best friends.

The only thing that'd made healing possible was that she'd refused what he gave her, spat it out and retched every time he tried to shove it back in her mouth. He'd beaten her senseless for defying him. But she never gave in, and she felt that stubbornness was part of the reason he'd never forgotten her. There'd been some things he couldn't force her to do, no matter what the cost, and he both admired and hated her for it. From what he'd said since, she was the only woman he hadn't been able to break.

She pictured him sitting in his cell at Hanover House and wondered what he was thinking about her sudden disappearance. He was probably jealous and angry that someone else had managed to accomplish what he'd tried to do last winter. He was unrealistic enough to believe he was going to get out of Hanover House one day and have another chance. Grandiose sense of self was a common characteristic among psychopaths. . . .

Having him at Hanover House, where she worked and could speak to him at will, had also helped her put him and her ordeal into perspective. When he was at large, her mind had played tricks on her, had used her fear to imbue him with almost supernatural

221

capabilities — the ability to be in two places at once, the ability to see through walls, to read her mind, et cetera. Every night after work, she'd have to check all the closets, behind every door, even small spaces where someone his size wouldn't fit. And if she was alone, she'd tense at every sound, even the familiar ones.

It'd been highly therapeutic to see the human reality of the man who'd haunted her for so long — and understand that he was just a pitiful, manipulative individual with no love for anyone but himself and no conscience, either. He wasn't special. As a matter of fact, he wasn't all that different from the other psychopaths she'd studied. Maybe, like Lyman Bishop, he was smarter.

She rubbed her temples, trying to ease the pounding behind her eyes, before drawing her mind back to the water. *Drink it. You have to drink it.* If she didn't, she could start having contractions. And if she went into labor at only six months . . .

Hoping to get her baby to kick, she put a hand to her belly and pressed. She hadn't noticed any movement since she'd stabbed the muscular behemoth who'd kidnapped her. The thought that the stress of such a long night, waiting on pins and needles for her moment, and the subsequent deluge of adrenaline when that moment arrived might have been too much for her child scared her in a way nothing else could. The grief and the sense of loss she would experience if her baby was stillborn, especially in this godforsaken place, without the proper medical help and without Amarok . . .

She blinked rapidly, fighting tears as she frowned at her reflection. *Why are you being so stubborn? Do it for your child,* she told herself. But if she knew for sure it would help, she would've done it already. Problem was she could also throw herself into early labor or lose the baby if she got E. coli or some other bacterial infection.

Which way would her child have a better chance?

She squeezed her forehead, trying to decide. She was already experiencing the classic signs of dehydration — the headache, the dry mouth, the dizziness and the sleepiness. There were worse symptoms, ones that affected blood pressure, which were especially risky while pregnant.

She'd have to drink the toilet water and hope for the best, she decided, and formed her hands into a cup.

Anchorage, AK — Saturday, 3:30 p.m. AKDT
Bishop was surprised when he called Em-

mett's cell phone and Emmett didn't pick up. He'd just landed in Anchorage, but he wanted to pretend as though he were having trouble getting out of Minneapolis, so that Emmett wouldn't be expecting him.

He left a message saying he wouldn't arrive until tomorrow, to please stay and not leave Evelyn until he could get there. The last thing Lyman needed was for Emmett to decide he'd waited long enough and take off, as he'd threatened, only to return when Lyman was there, expecting his money. That would shift the element of surprise and all the advantage it brought to the other side of the equation.

Emmett was so much less predictable, so much less tractable, than Terry had been. Lyman worried about that while waiting for the owner of a car he'd rented via a private website to meet him at the airport. He could've used one of the big rental car companies — they were more convenient — but he couldn't take the risk. These days so many of them had GPS trackers. And he couldn't get in a taxi. He was going to need a vehicle to get groceries and other supplies. He might even need a trunk to dispose of Emmett's body. Lyman wasn't foolish enough to think he'd have the strength and coordination necessary to dig a grave, not when he was having trouble walking.

There had to be someplace on the property to conceal the corpse, however. Possibly under all the chicken shit Emmett had complained about finding when he first rented the place. If it already stunk to high heaven, as Emmett claimed, and the ranch was as remote as it had appeared when Lyman looked it up on Google Earth via the laptop Terry brought to the hospital, he just might get away with it.

The address Emmett had provided wasn't difficult to locate. A high chain-link fence enclosed the property, and the gate was padlocked, making it clear the ranch was no longer in business.

Weeds grew rampant in the small plot of grass and shrubs that had once created a more attractive entrance to the store at the front of the processing plant, and an air of general neglect hovered over everything.

Lyman drove past without stopping. He liked what he saw. The pictures he'd viewed on the Internet seemed both recent and accurate, but he wanted to take a closer look and he could do that more quietly on foot.

Once he hid his car down the road, he got the sack of tools and other items he'd bought from the hardware store after he landed and used a pair of bolt cutters to remove the padlock on the front gate.

As soon as he slipped inside, he could see the blue van in the carport, which came as a relief. Emmett had kept his word. He was still here. *Thank goodness!*

There were other things to be grateful for, too. Not only had Emmett found the perfect location, he'd been a plumber at one time, able to see to the necessary adjustments, like making sure the cooler was properly ventilated and had a flushing toilet.

Bishop hid the bolt cutters in the weeds and avoided the front of the building, where he could be seen through the many windows of the storefront, and walked slowly around to the back.

Sure enough, Emmett had only one way of getting in or out of the building, just as he'd said. When the chicken ranch went out of business, the owner had boarded up the back door to discourage vagrants from breaking in, and Emmett had said it was unwise to remove those boards, adding that more security was better than less.

Lyman had to agree, although it did make what he had in mind for Emmett a bit more difficult.

He decided to find the henhouse where Emmett was keeping the dogs and bang on the walls to rile them up. When Emmett came out to see what was going on, he'd step up behind him and stab him in the back. Then he'd drag his body inside the coop and, when the dogs got hungry enough, maybe they'd take care of the disposal part of the process.

Done. Easy.

Except that riling up the dogs didn't bring Emmett out as expected.

Was he sleeping? Getting high? What was going on?

Returning to the plant, Bishop circled slowly and quietly around to the front. Other than making sure anyone standing inside the store couldn't see him, he hadn't paid much attention to it. *Southwick Family Egg Ranch* was painted in cheerful colors on the large front window, but it was dark inside and, Bishop supposed, empty.

He got the knife out of the bag he carried and set the bag aside. He hoped to determine where Emmett was and what he was doing, but after he got halfway to the store he decided not to go any closer. It was too easy to see out and too difficult to see in.

After pulling his cell phone from his pocket, he dialed Emmett's number. He didn't plan to speak if Emmett answered; he just wanted to wake him so that he would have better luck luring him to the henhouse.

Except Emmett didn't pick up.

Bishop could hear his phone ringing. . . .

The weird thing was . . . the sound was coming from only fifteen feet or so away. How could that be?

The unanswered call went to Emmett's voicemail, so Bishop hung up and waited some more. If Emmett was outside and near the store, what was he doing? Was he on to Bishop? Had he heard about Terry and found it suspicious?

Maybe Emmett was planning to kill Bishop and was waiting and watching.

No. He would've silenced his phone, wouldn't have let it give him away as it had just done.

Bishop waited, listening for footsteps or movement, but heard nothing. Finally, he grew so curious he couldn't stop himself from creeping up to where he'd heard the ring — and nearly stumbled on Emmett, who was lying partly in the weeds and partly on the sidewalk outside the store, staring straight up, in full rigor mortis.

"Well, well, well!" he said. "What happened here?"

Emmett had obviously been hurt. There was blood everywhere.

He knelt to take a look at the wound in his neck. It appeared as though he'd been stabbed. But . . . by whom?

Lyman saw no one else, heard no sound except the flies buzzing around the body. The trail of blood that came from the store seemed to tell a story, however. Had Emmett attacked Evelyn — who then retaliated?

If so, how had she overcome such a big, strong man?

Bishop didn't care that she'd killed Emmett. She'd done him a favor there. But, terrified she'd gotten away, he gripped his chest as his heart began to pound. *Damn her!* What would he do if she was gone?

He pushed on the door to the store. It was unlocked.

A thick layer of dust covered the counters and the shelves, and the sales register had been removed, leaving a gaping hole in the wooden counter where it had been bolted down. He had to wade through the cardboard, busted egg crates, cans, fast-food wrappers and other garbage that littered the floor in order to get to the back, but he had no trouble finding the cooler. A trail of blood led him right to it.

The strange thing was . . . it was chained and locked.

Trying to overcome the panic charging through him, he drew a deep breath and slid the bolt, ready to lift the covering on the slot Emmett had cut into the door.

Please, be there. Bending, Bishop looked inside.

Evelyn felt a tremendous sense of relief when she heard the slide of the bolt. But that relief was short-lived. She knew her situation hadn't improved when she scrambled to the door and saw Lyman Bishop's beady eyes peering in at her.

"Wow! This is my lucky day, after all," he said. "I thought you'd escaped."

Evelyn wished that were the case. Actually, "wished" wasn't nearly a strong enough word.

"Water," she said simply. Although she'd forced down some toilet water — without getting sick — since she'd last seen Emmett, it wasn't nearly enough.

"What did you say?"

He had to have heard her. He just hadn't expected such a simple response — a response with no surprise at seeing him, no comment on his ability to get around or think despite the dire predictions after his hemorrhage and no pleading for her freedom.

Summoning what strength she had left, she raised her voice. "Water! I need water.

Now. And some food."

He didn't move. "Emmett wasn't bringing you anything to eat or drink?"

"I haven't seen him" — she swallowed against a dry throat — "for a while. I can't say for how long. I have no way of reckoning time in here."

"I'd have to guess it's been a day, maybe a day and a half. He's in full rigor, and that usually goes away after twenty-four hours."

"You should know," she said simply.

"Know what?"

A serial killer who'd buried so many victims had to be familiar with rigor mortis. But she let it go. She was too sick to argue.

"What happened to him?" he asked.

"No clue," she lied.

"That's interesting." He disappeared from the slot and she heard movement. When he returned, he showed her the shiv she'd made. "Because no one in the outside world would use this type of weapon."

She said nothing at the sight of her bloody shiv, merely slumped against the same wall as the door so he couldn't see her any longer and closed her eyes. She'd killed the guy who'd kidnapped her.

Emmett. Bishop had called him Emmett. Until now she hadn't even known his name! But she was surprised by how little she cared. If she had ahold of that shiv, she'd kill Bishop, too. She'd kill anyone who tried to stop her from getting out of this damn cell.

"Evelyn?"

She didn't bother answering.

"Hello? Where'd you go?"

Let him open the door to look. She wasn't going to make anything easy for him.

"How's the baby? Is everything okay there?"

"She's going to die without clean water. Is that what you want?" She guessed he did. To most of the dangerous men she'd met, a fetus would be a nuisance at best and a method to inflict maximum pain and torture on her at worst.

Was that what Bishop had in store? she wondered. Was he planning to cut her baby from her womb and kill the child in front of her, as Jasper would do?

"Of course that's not what I want," he said as though he was shocked she'd even suggest it. "I'm *excited* about the baby. This might be the only child I ever have."

Only child *he* ever had? What did he mean by *that*? She had no clue, but she wasn't about to ask. In this moment, all she cared about was getting something she could trust to drink. "Then get me some fucking water," she said.

Hilltop, AK — Saturday, 4:30 p.m. AKDT

Jasper studied the screen. They weren't allowed much computer time. The inmates faced stiff competition for such luxuries. Most had to earn it by participating in various studies, which he'd so far refused to do. He wouldn't permit Evelyn to examine him like some kind of lab rat. The only satisfaction he had left was denying her.

She pretended she didn't care that he refused, told him he'd eventually succumb to boredom and crave the benefits badly enough to change his mind.

Sometimes he worried that she'd turn out to be right. He did require a great deal of stimulation — someone who killed for fun was always searching for *some* kind of high. There were moments when he wondered if seeking that adrenaline rush was the only reason he'd done what he'd done.

But he didn't wonder enough to give in. As long as he had money on his books, he could pay for the privileges he didn't earn. So far, the women he corresponded with on the outside had taken pretty good care of him. The funds they sent enabled him to live passably well, for a prisoner — better than most, thanks to his notoriety and good looks.

He clicked away from the Internet to

233

check his e-mail again. He was hoping to receive word from Chastity Sturdevant. She was too young to be able to offer him the resources some of the other women he was involved with could. She'd graduated from high school only two weeks ago, didn't have a job. But she brought other assets to the table. She was far more attractive than the typical "desperate prison groupie" — hot and young enough that she made the other inmates jealous, which was fun. Jasper enjoyed being admired. That she also lived so close to Minneapolis and could drive to Beacon Point Mental Hospital had just been lucky.

No new messages. *Damn!* Where was she? She should've been there by now. Was Bishop still at the hospital? And, if not, did she call Sergeant Murphy as he'd told her to do?

He'd kill her one day if she didn't.

He glanced at the clock on the wall of the small prison library. Only five minutes left. If she didn't check in with him soon, he'd have to wait until he could afford more computer time, which could be several days. There were people who had a cell phone in this prison, but the bribe to be able to use it was much too expensive. He hadn't realized he would have such a need, so he hadn't saved for it.

"Hurry the hell up!" He was speaking to Chastity even though she wasn't there, but the inmate sitting next to him looked over.

"You talking to *me?*"

"What do *you* think?" Jasper gave him a withering *mind your own business or I'll tear your throat out* glare, and his neighbor made the right decision by returning his attention to his own computer.

With a sigh, Jasper once again clicked away from his in-box and returned to the Internet. While waiting for some word from Chastity, he'd been searching for anything that might signify Bishop was on the loose — any news of the escape or release of the Zombie Maker, any report of someone claiming to have been attacked by a man wielding an ice pick, any indication that Beth Bishop, Lyman's sister, had gone missing from her own institution.

All of those searches came up empty.

As the rest of his computer time wound down and there was still no word from Chastity, he nearly put his fist through the screen. *Damn her!* He'd told her to get back to him as soon as possible. What was she waiting for? She could check her e-mail and respond on her phone. Except she had no way of knowing he'd managed to trade a picture of her, as well as her address, for another inmate's library privileges.

Racking his brain for some other way to discover if Lyman Bishop was no longer where he was supposed to be, he tried using the words "convicted cancer researcher," "ice-pick murderer" and "ice-pick lobotomy" to bring up more information on him.

Those searches generated so many links he couldn't get through them all in time, but he checked the dates. They were years or months old.

A prison guard, a CO by the name of M. Cadiz, signaled that it was time to return to his cell, but Jasper didn't budge. He stayed where he was and typed in "Beacon Point Mental Hospital." He hadn't tried that because it seemed like such a long shot. He knew it would generate all kinds of information on the hospital itself, not necessarily its patients.

But just as Officer Cadiz started to walk over, he spotted a recent article titled: "Beacon Point Mental Hospital Janitor Dead in Swede Hollow."

"Just a sec," he told the CO, and clicked on it.

Terry Lovett, a janitor at Beacon Point Mental Hospital, was found dead in his car after driving off Seventh Street into Swede

Hollow yesterday afternoon. Four teenage boys were in the park, not far from the scene of the crash. Fortunately, no one else was hurt.

"It was weird," said one of the boys, age sixteen. "We were hanging out, talking after school, and suddenly this car comes plunging down the ravine. It crashed about twenty feet from us. We wanted to see if the driver was okay, but we didn't dare go too close. We thought it might burst into flames."

Lovett was found unresponsive behind the wheel and died before reaching the hospital. Initial reports indicate possible suicide. Not only had Lovett been fired from his job earlier in the day, he also was deeply in debt and, according to two different neighbors, he wasn't getting along with his wife. But his parents and siblings insist he would never take his own life. At their prodding, police have ordered an autopsy to confirm the cause of death.

"You gotta move." M. Cadiz stood at his shoulder, Taser out and ready to fire. "Now."

Jasper knew he might get tased, but he couldn't leave quite yet. He held up his hand. "Hang on. Please."

"Please? You're saying please to me? You tried to spit in my eye yesterday. Hell, no. You're not going to get one extra second."

Ignoring his response, Jasper quickly

typed: "Terry Lovett" into the search bar. He hoped the autopsy had been completed and the cause of death had been firmly established. Otherwise, he'd have to wait for more information on that, too.

Chances were Lovett's death had nothing to do with Bishop, but this incident was the only thing pertaining to Beacon Point that was at all recent, so Jasper wasn't going to rule it out until he knew for sure that he should. If Bishop had escaped Beacon Point, he'd have to do it some way and there would be ripples, small evidences that something was up.

"Get off the computer, or I'll zap you," Officer Cadiz said. "Consider this your only warning."

Jasper glanced up at him. He couldn't go back to his cell right now. He'd just spotted a link that indicated the autopsy had been finished, which spoke volumes in and of itself. Generally, autopsies could take days, sometimes weeks, depending on the backlog. The authorities had to be worried about *something* for it to have been done within two days.

"Inmate Moore?" Cadiz prodded.

"Quit being an asshole," Jasper growled.

His response shocked Cadiz enough that he gaped at him instead of pulling the trigger. The guards here at Hanover House didn't like to pick fights. They were dealing with hardened criminals, knew they lacked the same killer instinct and wouldn't come out on top if they went too hard on the more determined inmates, and they understood Jasper was one of those.

Cadiz's hesitancy gave Jasper enough time to click the link and scan the article.

Jasper came to his feet just as Officer Cadiz had worked up the courage to act on his threat. He yelled, "Taser, Taser, Taser!" and fired.

There was a clicking sound as the hooks hit him and fifty thousand volts of electricity locked up his body. He couldn't move a single muscle and would've fallen if Officer McKim hadn't responded to what was happening from the other side of the room and hurried over to catch him.

The intense, biting pain infuriated Jasper. But he had what he wanted. Terry Lovett hadn't committed suicide. He'd been killed by a knife to the chest.

As soon as the clicking stopped, so did the pain. Jasper's muscles felt stiff, as though he'd been through an exhausting workout, but he could move again. He proved that by flipping off Cadiz.

"What, you didn't get enough?" Cadiz

cried. "How about another shot?"

"You made your point," McKim warned, his voice a low rumble. "You've already shown him who's in charge. Don't get carried away."

Gritting his teeth as they dragged him to his cell, Jasper swore under his breath that he'd find a way to get even. He never forgot an insult or injury. But he couldn't retaliate now, so he remained focused on his original goal. Had those extra few seconds on the computer been worth it? Did what he'd found mean anything?

Possibly. Terry Lovett had been killed after Evelyn was kidnapped. That suggested that maybe it wasn't connected. But a murder was also an anomaly, something that didn't typically happen at Beacon Point, and it had occurred in the same week.

That had to be more than a coincidence.

14

Amarok had spent Friday and all of today supporting the search parties, who were finished with Hilltop but were still in Anchorage, and trying to find a way to track Lyman Bishop. He'd called the Minneapolis Police Department to enlist their help. They claimed the hospital hadn't contacted them about Bishop's disappearance until Terry Lovett was found dead, but they *did* confirm that Bishop was gone and had been since early Thursday morning.

They'd also checked Bishop's bank accounts and had called Amarok back to say that, sure enough, Bishop wasn't simply lost and wandering through the streets without knowledge of where he was at or what he was doing. He'd withdrawn all the money from his savings at a bank five miles from the hospital. They were currently trying to get video footage from the bank to see if he

241

could both walk and talk normally, so they'd all have a better picture of what they were looking for when they sent out the BOLO, or "Be on the Lookout."

Amarok was waiting for that, as well as some word on that scarred man and who he might be. He'd figured out how to make a copy of the video footage he'd seen at Quigley's Quick Stop, which he'd sent to the detective in Minneapolis yesterday morning — along with a request that he check with Beacon Point to see if the man driving that stolen van was a current or former patient or employee.

God forbid Bishop had a more distant relationship with the man than that. The more distantly related he was, the harder it would be to figure out who he was and where he was now.

When his phone rang, Amarok was so deeply immersed in composing another e-mail to Detective Lewis in Minnesota, the same detective who'd taken over the case once his predecessor had been fired for planting the panty evidence, that he startled.

Makita scrambled up and barked before Amarok grabbed the receiver.

"Hello?"

"Sergeant Amarok?"

"Yes?"

"This is Dr. Ricardo at Hanover House."

"Have you heard anything?" he asked.

"Not from Dr. Talbot, if that's what you mean. And, to my knowledge, neither has anyone else here. But Jasper Moore has been raising hell, demanding to speak with you."

Makita curled up on his bed as Amarok went back to his e-mail imploring Detective Lewis to move faster. He needed to see if Lyman Bishop had made a flight reservation. "What does he want?" he asked, still slightly distracted.

"From what the warden said, he won't speak to anyone except you. I told Ferris to tell him you're too busy right now. I won't allow him to sabotage your investigation by demanding your attention when it should be elsewhere, but he insists it's *about* the investigation. He seems to think he can help. So . . . I figured I'd let you know so *you* could make the decision."

"Jasper is trying to help *me*?" The irony was almost too good.

"Yes. He may not love Evelyn the way you do, but he *is* fixated on her, and I bet he'd be devastated if she was suddenly removed from his life, especially now that he's here and can't prey on anyone else."

Amarok wasn't going to pretend he could

understand the psychology behind a guy wanting to kill Evelyn so badly he'd be destroyed if someone else got to her first.

But he also wasn't going to ignore or turn away anything that could potentially help him find her, especially because Jasper had been right about Bishop. Lyman was definitely up to something, and Jasper could predict how he might act far better than Amarok could. "I'll be right over," he said.

Anchorage, AK — Saturday, 5:15 p.m. AKDT
After giving Evelyn a peanut butter and jelly sandwich — why Emmett couldn't have arranged for better food Bishop didn't know, but that was about all there was in the staff room — and several bottles of water, Lyman returned to the front of the store, where Emmett's corpse was lying in the weeds. He had to do something about him. Fortunately, he didn't think it would be too difficult.

He put on the pair of latex cleaning gloves he'd purchased when he stopped by the hardware store for the bolt cutters and other supplies. Then he reached into Emmett's pocket and took out the keys to the store and the van, his money and his cell phone. He considered sending all of Emmett's contacts a message that he was going to be out of town for a few days in order to buy some time before everyone started searching for him.

But the phone was locked. All he could do was destroy it so that anyone who might come looking for him wouldn't be able to track it. Lyman guessed that Terry's wife, at the very least, would try to reach her brother. She might have done so already, given the fact that Terry was dead and she had a funeral to plan. But even if she'd called the police, they wouldn't have started looking for Emmett yet. He couldn't have been dead more than a day and a half.

Lyman stood as he slipped Emmett's cash — seventy-eight dollars — into his own pocket. That was a nice little windfall. He wished he'd thought to empty Terry's pockets, too, but it was better that he hadn't. Anyone who investigated the wreck in the ravine would be less likely to believe it was a suicide if Terry's belongings were missing. His wife kept him on such a short leash, he probably never had more than ten or twenty bucks in his wallet, so it wasn't as though Lyman had missed much of an opportunity.

He stretched his neck. It'd been a rigorous few days for someone accustomed to lying in a hospital bed. He'd never been so exhausted in his life. No amount of therapy could've prepared him for this. He was becoming weaker and more uncoordinated as the day wore on.

But that didn't matter. He had to get Emmett's body into the henhouse. Just because someone hadn't discovered it yet didn't mean they wouldn't. Once rigor disappeared, the amount of decomposition would make for a much nastier, messier job, anyway.

He looked around the ranch until he found a pallet and a hand truck that had probably been used to move cases of eggs. After fitting the pallet onto the end of the hand truck to create a wide base, he rolled Emmett's body onto it.

It took more effort than he'd thought it would. A dead man was so heavy. Lyman had to stop time and again to rest, at which point more blood and other bodily fluids would leak out of the body.

Apparently, it'd been warm enough to speed decomposition. But he finally managed to move the corpse around back.

When he heard the dogs barking as he approached that particular henhouse, he changed his mind about putting Emmett in there. While he liked the idea of the dogs eating the corpse so he wouldn't have to worry about someone discovering it, he'd been bitten before, as a child, and he was afraid he'd get bitten again if he threw open those doors and went in with a bloody body.

So he put Emmett in another henhouse and covered him with manure. Only once he could move cautiously and wasn't weighed down with a hand truck and 240 pounds of deadweight did he approach the dogs. He fed them from the sack of food Emmett had left sitting outside and, while they were busy gulping down their dinner, filled their water bowls before making sure they couldn't get out and hobbled back to the plant.

He was dying to rest, but he had yet to clean up the blood on the sidewalk outside the store. He also had to decide what to do about the van. He couldn't afford to keep the car he'd rented, but it was dangerous to drive a stolen vehicle. He could easily attract the kind of interest he most needed to avoid.

Still, he decided he'd keep it, for now. He wouldn't take it out of its vine-covered hiding place unless he absolutely had to, and he'd trade the license plates with those of another vehicle — one of equal age so the number sequence wouldn't be a red flag to law enforcement — while he had the rental car and could easily move from place to place without fear of being pulled over. Maybe he'd paint the van, too. It wasn't as if he had to do a *good* job. Someone had already blacked out the name of the company. He just had to make sure the rest of the carpet-cleaning logo wasn't visible, and he could do that with a can of black spray paint.

Heck, why not spray the whole thing? No one would think twice about such a poor paint job, not on a clunker like that.

The van issue settled in his mind, he summoned a little more energy to clean the blood from the entryway of the store so that the owner of the property, if she happened to stop by, wouldn't see anything suspicious. Once that mess was gone and he'd settled in, he'd call the owner and tell her that Emmett Virtanen had quit and he was taking over with the temporary dog shelter. Then he should be safe — for a while. As much as he wished he could stay indefinitely, he'd have to find somewhere else eventually. He needed to move to a place that wasn't up for sale.

But that would be much easier after Evelyn had the baby. Only then could he safely cut into her brain without risking the loss of the child, and he *definitely* didn't want to lose the child. That Evelyn was pregnant added a whole new dimension to what he had planned. If he raised her baby from birth, the child would never know it had had another father, especially if Evelyn wasn't capable of remembering or articulating that information.

Even if he lost Evelyn, even if she didn't survive the "adjustment" she would require in order to be happy living with him, he'd have her child waiting in the wings, would never be alone again. And he wouldn't have to disable the child's brain in order to gain the control he craved — he'd only have to shape it.

Hilltop, AK — Saturday, 5:30 p.m. AKDT
Amarok had Jasper's chains removed, but this time it wasn't because he hoped it might provide him with an opportunity to vent his rage over the past. He'd done it because Jasper had been right. From the beginning, Jasper had suggested Lyman Bishop might be behind Evelyn's abduction, and if it hadn't been for Jasper asking his girlfriend to drive over to Beacon Point, Amarok would still be searching through Evelyn's files right now, looking for that one piece of evidence that would give his investigation some direction. And he'd be wasting his time, because what he sought

couldn't be found there.

He couldn't say he *respected* Jasper. He would always hold him in the greatest contempt. What he'd done to Evelyn and other human beings was unforgivable, especially because he'd do the same again, if he got the chance. But Amarok had to acknowledge that Jasper was both intelligent and capable, in many regards, and he was grateful to him in this one instance. If Bishop had yet to come to Alaska from Minneapolis, there was a possibility Evelyn was alive and well, and that hope — the hope that he might get her and their child back safely — was worth everything to him.

"Your girlfriend called me," Amarok said without preamble. He assumed Jasper had brought him to Hanover House to tell him what Chastity had found, so Amarok wasn't planning to waste a lot of time with this. He'd only taken the meeting in case she'd mentioned something to Jasper she hadn't thought to tell him — or Jasper had made more of it. "I know Bishop is gone from Beacon Point, if that's what this is about."

"He *is*? That clever son of a bitch." Jasper shook his head in apparent wonder.

So he hadn't *had any communication from Chastity?* "You didn't know?"

Jasper's mouth twisted into a wry grin.

250

"No. I got tased trying to wait for Chastity's e-mail at the library."

Amarok shrugged. "That sucks, man, but I don't feel sorry for you. Not after the pain you've inflicted on other people. If it helps, I've been tased before."

"As part of your training. That's different."

"How?"

"You volunteered. You don't hate the bastards who did it to you."

The promise in those words reminded Amarok that he and Jasper weren't on the same team, even now. "Maybe they enjoyed it. You would, right?"

He laughed softly. "Cadiz is too big a pussy to enjoy it. He nearly wet his pants he was shaking so badly."

"I hope you didn't call me over here to bitch about how you're being treated. Evelyn needs me."

"How sweet," he said, his voice dripping with irony. "I just wanted to tell you that you have a very small window in which to find her."

"I'm well aware of that."

"So have you been able to track Bishop?"

"Not exactly. But I know he withdrew all the money he had in savings on Thursday morning."

251

"Interesting. You understand what that means. . . ."

"Of course. He's on his way. But he still has to get here. I'm praying the logistics will buy me some time."

"Praying?" Jasper rolled his eyes as if that were the stupidest thing he'd ever heard.

"I can see why you might not care to believe in a higher power. True justice would suck for someone like you, wouldn't it?"

"*True* justice would suck for any of us. Anyway, forget about praying. Getting your ass in gear and finding out what you can about Terry Lovett would be a better idea."

Amarok was in such a hurry he'd already started to leave, but hearing that, he paused with his hand lifted to knock so the CO on the other side would let him out. "Who's Terry Lovett?"

"A janitor from Beacon Point."

"And?"

Jasper rolled his eyes. "Do I have to do *all* your work for you?"

Amarok arched his eyebrows. "Quit grandstanding and answer the question."

"I like you, you know that? I can see why Evelyn likes you, too. Those blue eyes, that nice body. You got a big dick for her? Or was mine the biggest she ever had?"

"From what she's told me, she wasn't

overly impressed with yours." He lifted his little finger. "But I'm done playing games, dude. If you want to pretend you're somehow in control here, or that you're smarter than me, you can have those delusions back in your cell."

A dark expression descended on Jasper's face. "I'm bigger than that."

"I don't give a shit," Amarok said. "Are you going to answer the question or not?"

"Lovett was murdered this week, probably the same day Lyman Bishop escaped."

"Hm. So you're thinking Lovett might've helped him and Bishop killed him to keep him silent."

"That's exactly what I'm thinking, especially because he made it look like a suicide. Imagine that. If it had gone down the way it had been planned, maybe I wouldn't have connected the two incidents."

Jasper had a point. "Go on," Amarok said.

"It was only because his family insisted on an autopsy that it came out he'd been stabbed in the chest before driving his car into a ravine."

"If Lovett died the same day Bishop escaped, the autopsy findings wouldn't be published this soon."

"Except they have been. Maybe the reporter is sleeping with the coroner. Who knows?"

"How do you know all of this?" Amarok asked.

"I did a Google search," he replied with a cocky shrug. "Beacon Point Mental Hospital. Look it up. I'm guessing it's the only time something like this has happened since the hospital opened its doors. It'd be quite a coincidence if a convicted felon escaped from Beacon Point the same day a janitor from the same place was murdered, don't you think?"

Amarok didn't want to give him *too* much credit, not when he was acting so smug. "I think it's worth looking into."

"If you need any more help, you know where to find me!" Jasper called after him.

Ignoring that last salvo, Amarok had the guard let him out and nearly bumped into Dr. Ricardo, who was charging down the hall.

"I heard you'd arrived," he said as the CO who'd been waiting to escort Jasper back to his cell ducked into the room behind them.

Amarok nodded by way of greeting. "Yes, but I'm already leaving."

When Amarok circumvented Ricardo, the neurologist turned and started jogging to keep up. "Was it worth the trip, at least?"

"If what Jasper is telling me is true, yes.

254

Thanks for the call."

"You bet, but" — he stepped in front of Amarok — "before you leave . . ."

Amarok couldn't wait to find out more about the janitor who'd been murdered in Minnesota. Maybe he'd left something behind that would indicate where Bishop was going, what he had planned. "What is it?"

"I think you should see something."

Amarok didn't want to be interrupted. Not now. "*What?* Does it have anything to do with Evelyn's disappearance?"

"It might. Since you're here, why don't you take a look?"

15

Hilltop, AK — Saturday, 6:00 p.m. AKDT

"It's very faint," Dr. Ricardo said. "Can you see it?"

Amarok *could* see it, but he couldn't believe anyone had noticed it. "Who found this?"

"Penny. After you told her that Dr. Talbot had to have been meeting someone for the day she went missing to play out as it did, she's been going through *everything*. The mail Evelyn has received. Her files, in case she jotted something on the jacket of one. The bits of paper that we sometimes leave in the labs. The message pads we keep in the interview rooms. Whatever she can think of."

"She thought to check the conference room?" he asked incredulously. At first glance, the room appeared as clean as it was empty, the pad next to the phone blank. He'd looked the day Evelyn had gone missing, and nothing had changed since.

"Not at first. Penny came in here to make sure it was set up for Monday's staff meeting and remembered that Evelyn had been working in this room lately. This big table gives us space to spread out our files, which is why we all like it. Anyway, Penny noticed the pad, checked it and saw the imprint of the writing, at which point she hurried to get me. She thinks it might be something Evelyn jotted down."

Amarok bent over to peer closely at what Penny had discovered. The lines were too faint to be able to make out the words or confirm that Evelyn had written them. But there was that possibility. "Do we know where the sheet on top of this one could have gone?"

"Sadly, I'm guessing whoever wrote on this pad last took it or threw it away. Penny's down in Janitorial and Maintenance right now, asking where the garbage goes once it's taken from here. I know a lot of it is eventually recycled or incinerated, but I'm hoping that hasn't happened yet."

Amarok straightened. "So am I. Stay here and don't let anyone touch this," he said, and ran down to his truck to get his forensics kit so he could use his high-res digital camera and oblique lighting to photograph the pad.

Once he'd taken multiple shots from different angles for future reference, he had Ricardo find him a soft lead pencil, which he rubbed gently over the indentations on the page.

Almost like magic, the writing appeared — a name and a number.

"No way," Amarok murmured.

"That's Evelyn's writing!" Ricardo said. "I recognize it myself." He bent closer. "But who's Alistair?"

Amarok shoved a hand through his hair as he gaped at the name. "My mother."

Anchorage, AK — Sunday 9:00 a.m. AKDT
Lyman Bishop was the opposite of the man Evelyn had killed. He wasn't particularly young, he wasn't fit or strong and instead of delivering her food in a no-nonsense manner, without even speaking to her or looking at her, if he could avoid it, he left the slot open and pulled up a chair to the other side of the door so he could talk to her. She could tell he'd been waiting for this moment and was now relishing the fact that he'd succeeded not only in surviving and escaping but also in kidnapping her.

"How have you been, anyway?" he asked as though they were good friends who hadn't seen each other in some time, sitting out on a porch somewhere.

She'd never witnessed a greater disconnect in anyone else, never known anyone less self-aware, even Jasper.

Instead of trying to point out the obvious, she said nothing, just kept shoveling down her oatmeal. This time she hadn't been provided with any fruit, which was something he'd apologized for when he handed her the tray. He'd said he needed to go out and get some groceries, that "Emmett" hadn't done a very good job of stocking the cupboards, but "beggars couldn't be choosers." He'd had to work with who he had to work with, he'd said.

"You're not going to talk to me?" he asked when the silence stretched out.

She took some small pleasure in his disappointment.

There was a brief silence before he said, "Of course. You're hungry. Go ahead. *I'll* do the talking. I'm sure you're curious to hear about everything that's happened to me since we last met."

She swallowed another spoonful of oatmeal. "No, not really. I don't care about you at all." She knew she'd be smarter to bridle her tongue, but she didn't have the emotional wherewithal. That the effort she'd put into getting away had failed, that going that far hadn't improved her situation and she didn't see any other avenue of escape, had devastated her, left her feeling miserable and defeated.

"Come on," he said, as though he was making an honest effort to mollify her. "I understand why you're mad, but there's no need for all of this hostility. It'll only make matters worse. The sooner you accept your new situation, the better off we'll be."

"You expect me to *accept* this?" She indicated the four walls of her prison.

"Why not? You kept me in a space about the same size — and with other men who would've torn me to pieces if they could get their hands on me."

"You deserved your prison sentence. I don't."

Lyman tsked. "None of us are perfect. Besides, nothing's going to change."

"Go to hell." Taking her food, she crossed over to sit against the same wall as the door so he couldn't see her, which she knew would bother him.

"I never dreamed you'd be such a bad sport," he said as if she'd hurt his feelings. "We'll have to rectify that."

"With an ice pick?" she asked bitterly.

This time he was the one who paused

before answering. "If that's what it takes."

"I'll *never* allow you to touch me. I'll *die* first!"

"You'll die eventually, yes. When I'm done with you. But not before you have the baby. And you'll treat me with respect while I allow you to live, or I might decide to take certain risks I was hoping to avoid until later."

The calmness with which he spoke contrasted sharply with the meaning of his words. That, as well as mention of the baby, made it impossible for her to continue eating. She had to keep up her strength for her child, had to take advantage of every meal. But if she swallowed one more bite, she'd throw up.

Setting her bowl aside, she drew her knees into her stomach. "What are you talking about?"

"I'm talking about the rules. Should we go over them now? Or would you like to have a pleasant morning together as I'd planned?"

A *pleasant* morning? Was he completely out of touch with reality? Or was he purposely ignoring the fact that she wasn't here because she wanted to be, that she was being held against her will? "What is it you want from me?" she asked.

"The only thing I've ever wanted from anybody. Love," he replied simply.

"You think any woman could love you while you're keeping her locked up like this?"

"I plan to let you out."

"When?"

"After you have the baby."

She swallowed against a dry throat. "You keep talking about the baby. . . ."

"Aren't you glad I'm taking the child into account? I would think you'd be grateful."

Evelyn drew a shaky breath. "I'll do whatever you want, for however long you want, if only you'll take my baby and leave her at a fire station with a note for Amarok."

He sighed dramatically. "Please, don't. This doesn't become you, you know."

She clenched her jaw. "*What* doesn't become me?"

"Lying. No matter what you've been to me in the past, I always felt I could rely on you for the truth."

Because she'd always stood by what she believed, even though, once the information about the planted evidence came to light, everyone else rushed to apologize to him for getting it wrong. But she wouldn't have known he was guilty, either, had she not studied so many psychopaths. Especially because Bishop was a bit of an anomaly. Most psychopaths — the kind who committed violent crimes and were actually caught — weren't highly educated, didn't have illustrious careers.

"It *is* the truth!" She *had* to convince him. That was the only way her child would have a chance. Not only would she do anything to save her baby, she also felt she owed it to Amarok to be sure that much of what they had survived.

"You may feel that way now, but as soon as I complied, you'd change your mind. I'm more confident in my own plan."

"Which is . . ."

"You're not in the mood to hear it." He sounded irritable. "So go ahead and feel sorry for yourself. I'm going to go shopping and do a few other things while I still have a rental car."

"You'd better let me go," she said.

"Or . . ."

She hated the cocky lilt to his voice. "Amarok will find you, and if you've hurt me or his baby, he'll make you pay."

"I've dreamed about this moment for so long. And now you're ruining it. You're obviously *not* a very nice person."

"I'm supposed to be happy about what

you're doing to me?"

"If you're smart, you'll make the most of it. I don't like the way you're making me feel. I won't allow it. You'll see."

With that ominous ending, the slot closed, the bolt slid home and she slumped against the wall, sickened at the sight of what remained of her oatmeal.

Hilltop, AK — Sunday, 11:30 a.m. AKDT
Sure enough, the phone number on that pad in the conference room at Hanover House wasn't his mother's. He'd spent all night trying to trace it. It belonged to a burner phone, which was now defunct. Amarok had guessed it would be. Although he never called his mom these days, she did occasionally call him, and that wasn't the number she used. She could've been on someone else's phone, of course — her husband's or even a friend's — but since they were estranged, that was unlikely. Difficult phone calls required more privacy, and their discussions were never easy.

As soon as Amarok had seen his mother's name and that unfamiliar number written in Evelyn's hand, he'd known: This was how Bishop had pulled it off. This was how he'd drawn Evelyn out of the prison in the middle of the day. This was the reason she hadn't told Amarok what she was doing. And this was the reason she didn't have the appointment on her calendar or scheduled with Penny. She'd thought she was meeting his mother for a private conversation about him or at least giving his mother an audience. Evelyn had asked him, on more than one occasion, if he felt he might regret his decision not to invite Alistair to their wedding, so he knew it was something she'd been concerned about. And because of the wedding, it was entirely believable that Alistair would try to go around him and connect with her.

"Son of a bitch," he muttered.

"Did you say something?" Phil sat up and so did Makita. Phil had been sleeping on the couch along the far wall since shortly after he came in to get the searchers started again today. Like Amarok, he was exhausted, but he wanted to be on hand to deal with the usual, like the poachers he'd intercepted last night, so that Amarok could focus strictly on finding Evelyn.

"It's nothing," Amarok said. "I'm sorry." He'd been making calls right and left, trying to track down the widow of the murdered janitor — no luck there so far — as well as trace the number he'd discovered on that second sheet of paper in the conference room of HH. None of it had disturbed Phil, so he wasn't thinking that a few words would suddenly jolt him out of his nap. "Go back to sleep."

Phil got up and walked over. "It's fine. I've got enough shut-eye for now. What is it? What have you found?"

"I know how Bishop got to Evelyn so cleanly and easily, without anyone being aware that something was up and without her feeling even a hint of suspicion or concern."

"How? It's not easy to pull one over on Evelyn! She was about the only person who *didn't* believe Bishop was innocent back when all of that came out about the evidence used to convict him. She trusted the detective who planted those panties, remember? Everyone was saying he did it for the sake of his career, to solve a high-profile case and move up the ranks, but she was convinced he'd done it to get Bishop off the streets, because he was dangerous."

"I remember." Amarok had been hoping she'd play along, for a change. They were going to release Bishop regardless of her opinion. He hadn't wanted her to risk her career, but as with everything else she felt passionately about, she hadn't been willing to back off.

"So what is it? What have you found?" Phil asked.

Amarok held up the paper he'd carefully removed from the message pad at HH. "He must've had someone call her, posing as my mother."

Phil blinked at what he was being shown. "Your *mother*?"

"Yeah."

"But . . . you don't have any contact with Alistair. Or has that changed?"

"It hasn't changed. But I'm getting married, and it'd be entirely believable to Evelyn that my mother would want to be a part of it all — that she would use the wedding as an excuse to try to put the past behind us."

Understanding began to dawn. "Got it. And Evelyn wouldn't recognize your mother's voice because she's had so little contact with her."

"I don't want my mother in my life. She hasn't had *any* contact with her."

"So Evelyn gets a call from someone claiming she's your mother and asking to talk."

"Yes. At which point she arranges a meeting at the house, early in the afternoon when she knows I won't be home."

"And she doesn't tell anyone about it

because she's not sure you'll like what she's doing. She just wants to hear your mother out, to see if there's any way to patch things up between you, because she thinks that's what will ultimately be best for you, too."

"Sounds like a psychiatrist, doesn't it?" Amarok asked wryly.

"I have to admit it does." Phil rolled his shoulders as if sleeping on the couch had given him a crick in his neck. "But how would Bishop know enough about *your* situation to think of that approach to begin with?"

"He was incarcerated at Hanover House for a while. You know how people talk."

The way he pursed his lips showed skepticism. "Do the inmates know your background?"

"I'm sure some of the guards do."

"How? Most of them are from Anchorage."

Makita walked over and rested his muzzle in Amarok's lap, and Amarok stroked him as he talked. "Quite a few hang out at the Moosehead after work, certainly enough to have heard people share just about anything. Bishop had to have come up with the information somehow."

"No . . ." Phil shook his head.

"No, what?"

"It wasn't at Hanover House or the Moosehead that he learned about the situation between you and your mother. It was that article."

"*What* article?" Amarok's mind had already shifted gears so he could launch into everything he had to do next.

"The one that uppity woman who came from New York City wrote for *People* magazine, remember?"

Amarok rocked back in his chair, which caused Makita to return to his bed. *Of course!* It had been big news when the man who'd tortured and nearly killed Evelyn Talbot was finally caught, which had thrust Amarok into the media circus, too, since he was the one to finally accomplish it. Everyone had been vying for the exclusive on the ending of the decades-long saga about the sixteen-year-old girl who turned into a psychiatrist driven to solve the mysteries of the psychopathic mind, thanks to the boy who'd once attacked her. Especially the big, national magazines.

Chloe Stokes, a top reporter for *People*, had stayed at The Shady Lady, the local motel, for over a week and had talked to just about everyone Amarok knew, including his father, once she went back to Anchorage to fly home. Amarok had thought she'd *never* leave Alaska. He'd tolerated her presence and her nosey questions, even played along to a degree, but only because Evelyn was so relieved to *finally* get some positive press for her work. To have people saying good things about her, that she got it right when everyone else missed the cues about Bishop, had been a welcome respite and stood in stark contrast to all the criticism she and her brainchild had endured since it opened — people saying that she was wasting government resources, that psychopaths could never be rehabilitated, that even if she was able to identify some differences in the brain between normal people and antisocial people, labeling someone as a psychopath and trying to extrapolate future behavior from that was a dangerous and touchy thing.

Ms. Stokes's article had helped them battle back in the arena of public opinion, but Amarok hadn't been happy that he'd been spotlighted in her final piece. She'd painted him as a lone, rugged lawman, raised by a man who was never the same after his wife abandoned him and headed for gentler climes, who turned out to be some sort of Alaskan superhero, standing guard over the whole town.

In a way, it had been flattering. He had to

admit that. But it had been even more embarrassing, something his friends made the most of by teasing him mercilessly the first several weeks after that issue hit newsstands.

After it was all over, he'd shoved it out of his mind. But he should've connected the dots immediately. Of course Bishop would keep an eye out for Evelyn's name in the press and read everything about her he could get his hands on. Chloe Stokes had handed him a golden ticket to kidnap Evelyn when she'd revealed so much about Amarok and his personal situation.

"You're right," he said. "It was the article."

"So what do we do now?"

"Try like hell to get hold of the widow of a guy by the name of Terry Lovett. It's three hours later in Minnesota, which puts it right smack in the middle of the afternoon for her, but she isn't picking up."

Phil scratched his head. "Apparently, I missed a lot while I was sleeping. Who's Terry Lovett?"

"A janitor at Beacon Point who was recently murdered."

"How does that tie into anything?"

"I'm not sure it does, but I plan on finding out if he helped Lyman Bishop escape — or had something to do with it."

Phil opened his mouth to say more. No doubt he was curious to learn how Amarok had learned about Terry. But Amarok raised his hand; he had to get back to work. "I'll tell you all about it if it amounts to anything. There's no need wasting the time if it doesn't."

"Okay." He started to walk over to his desk, only to turn back. "Amarok?"

Amarok glanced up from his computer, where he was rereading everything he'd found on Terry Lovett. He'd thought maybe the funeral was today and that was why he couldn't reach Bridget. They'd certainly rushed the autopsy. But since Terry was a murder victim, Amarok doubted his body would've been released so soon. "What?"

"Are you *sure* Bishop didn't involve your mother in the kidnap plot? That she wasn't the one who contacted Evelyn? I'd hate to think he held a gun to her head and made her place that call, but if he thought Evelyn might recognize your mother's voice, it's a possibility he went that far. He had eighteen months to plan her abduction, and he doesn't seem prone to making mistakes."

"The article mentioned that she moved to Seattle when she left my father, but it didn't give her address. How would Bishop find her?"

"It's not hard to find someone with such an unusual name. How many Alistair Wingates can there be?"

Amarok didn't care to acknowledge that, even to himself. "He was still at Beacon Point when Evelyn was kidnapped."

"But we know he had help. . . ."

"If the guy who's helping him was with my mother, he would've had her use her own phone, wouldn't have had to use a burner."

Phil still seemed reluctant to let it go, but, finally, he nodded. "Yeah. Okay. You're probably right."

"Besides, she would've called me if she'd had an encounter like that," Amarok added.

The door flew open and Heidi Perth Robbins walked in with dinner. The appearance of his wife distracted Phil. She was saying something about cooking enough for two, at which point Amarok should've smiled and thanked her, but he wasn't really listening. He couldn't quit thinking about the possibilities. Whoever was involved with Bishop may have figured out where his mother lived and gone to visit her. There was also the chance she hadn't called him about it because she couldn't. And maybe her murder hadn't been reported on the news because she and her husband were both dead and their bodies hadn't yet been discovered. After all, Jason, Amarok's twin brother, lived in Spokane these days. He probably didn't check in on their mother every day.

With a curse that made both Heidi and Phil stop talking and look over at him, Amarok picked up the phone. But he didn't get a chance to dial his mother; someone was already on the line.

"Amarok? How weird. I didn't even hear you say hello!"

It was Evelyn's mother. "I'm sorry. I . . . ah — How's everything with Brianne? Any news yet?" He hoped so. As far as he knew, she'd been in labor since Thursday night.

"It was a long, hard go. Her contractions didn't progress at first. So they gave her something, and she went into labor in earnest and finally delivered early this morning. We have a boy!" she announced.

16

Lyman Bishop knew from experience how easily having a disability could win trust and sympathy. He'd seen it happen with Beth. When she'd lived with him, he'd been admired and praised, mostly by his co-workers since he'd never had a wide circle of friends, for taking care of his mentally handicapped sister. Being Beth's guardian had made him look good, created a perfect cover for almost anything he wanted to do. And now he could see that his own handicap — the difficulty he had walking and the paralysis in his face — would serve the same purpose.

He mumbled that he was a war veteran with a head injury and other people held doors for him, smiled and even hurried to get him a cart at the grocery store or wave him on ahead of them at the checkout. And yet they didn't really *see* him or pay partic-

275

ular attention if they did, so there was little threat that he'd be distinctly remembered if someone were to ask about him. He was just one more pathetic figure they encountered while going about their daily routine, someone who meant nothing to them, other than the quick pat on the back they gave themselves for trying to be nice and the passing gratitude they felt for not being similarly afflicted.

He smiled at an attractive young woman who scrambled to get out of his way as he pushed his cart down the vegetable aisle. He loved food and wine, refused to be cheap when it came to either of those things. And now that he was out of Beacon Hill and could have something besides the institutional slop he'd been fed for the past eighteen months, food that would've been a disappointment to pigs, he planned to take full advantage of it. His new girlfriend, being so far along in her pregnancy, was going to need some good nutrition, too.

The memory of how Evelyn had treated him when he'd tried to talk to her this morning threatened to ruin his mood, but he refused to let it. He couldn't expect too much from her. Not at first. Being held against her will after being able to do just about anything she wanted must come as a terrible shock. She was a bright, accomplished woman and deserved a little more latitude than he'd offered his previous "girlfriends." Besides, he had no idea how Emmett had behaved with her. Maybe he'd been uncouth. He certainly hadn't been feeding her properly.

She'd get used to him, Bishop decided, would learn to love him the way Beth had — or at least to treat him as if she did, which was all the same to him — especially once she realized that he was willing to reward her when she behaved herself.

And if she refused to play nice?

He finished loading his cart with squash, watermelon, grapes, lettuce, corn on the cob and potatoes and headed off in search of the aisle that had a small section of kitchen implements. He needed a knife — he'd disposed of the one he'd used to kill Terry rather than draw attention by putting it in his luggage when he got on the plane. He also needed a new padlock for the front gate and an ordinary ice pick, the kind people used in their kitchens all the time, which meant purchasing one.

In a state where practically everyone else was packing a gun, that wouldn't raise any more eyebrows than seeing a forty-two-year-old man who was barely five eight, had already lost most of his hair and was carrying a few extra pounds around the middle shuffling along with a limp.

He smiled when he found what he was looking for. It was only $8.99, a small price to pay for a little insurance, especially because he already had plenty of sleeping pills.

Since he controlled Evelyn's food, he could ensure that she went to sleep whenever he decided it was necessary — and woke up *much* more manageable.

Anchorage, AK — Sunday 11:50 a.m. AKDT
Evelyn knew more about her surroundings than she'd known before. That was something, wasn't it? Maybe it was a small thing — a *very* small thing — but she had to find some tiny rainbow in what had transpired. She hadn't stabbed Emmett (thanks to Bishop, she now knew his name) for nothing. She'd gotten out of her cramped prison long enough to see where she was being kept and, as a consequence, had some inkling of the layout of the building.

She rolled over on her cot and gazed up at the smooth white walls. This had once been a cooler, as she'd guessed — a cooler in some type of processing plant. There was a staff room; she'd run in there when she'd been looking for a way out.

She'd been too frantic to take stock of what she saw at the time, not consciously, anyway. But now that she was once again locked up, she was determined to go over her memories and cement every detail in her mind. She had to believe she'd have another chance to escape, and then she could take advantage of what she'd learned to avoid making the same mistakes.

For instance, she'd have to remember *not* to go to the right. That was where Emmett had been staying and was most likely where Bishop would be staying now that Emmett was gone. Made sense, given it seemed to be the most hospitable area.

She'd caught a glimpse of a room without windows that had a big machine in it — it had smelled terrible, like rotten eggs — and another room with lots of windows and trash on the floor.

No, not all of it was trash, she decided as she closed her eyes and pictured it again. There'd been egg cartons. Lots of empty egg cartons. This place was most likely a plant that processed eggs, she decided. And the front part, with all the windows? That had to be a store that sold them, like a fruit stand a strawberry farmer put up on his own property.

The more she concentrated on piecing together what she'd seen and making sense of it, a commercial farm with egg-laying hens sounded plausible. And if that was the reality, she probably wasn't in a location that was *too* remote. An egg farm or ranch, or whatever they were called, wouldn't be right downtown but still sited fairly close to civilization. A cooler this size would hold a lot of eggs and yet the small store wasn't big enough to move a vast amount of product, which meant such a business would require a distribution method — trucks that carried cases of eggs to other retail outlets.

So she was likely on the outskirts of a place much bigger than Hilltop. Anchorage or Juneau. But since Anchorage was closer to Hilltop, if she had to bet, she'd bet on that one. Ted Stevens Anchorage International Airport was the largest and the busiest in the state and would make it easy for Bishop to relieve Emmett, since that had obviously been the plan.

The bad news was that there weren't any eggs in this cooler right now and all the trash she'd seen on the floor in the store, mixed with those egg crates, suggested the egg ranch was abandoned. Which meant little or no chance of a well-meaning customer or employee coming onto the property, stumbling upon what was going on and saving her.

She pressed her palm to her forehead. How was she supposed to cling to hope when it was all so hopeless? Bishop had completely blindsided her, had thought of everything. She couldn't even make another weapon, not now that she'd stabbed Emmett. Bishop would be watching for that. And if he caught her, he'd punish her.

She knew how he'd do it, too.

She was never getting out of here. She was only pretending it could happen, forcing herself to remember the details of the layout of the building to keep her mind off of what was *really* worrying her.

It'd been a while since she'd felt the baby move.

"Where are you?" she whispered to her child as she rubbed her belly in concern, and felt a single tear roll back into her hair.

Boston, MA — Sunday, 4:30 p.m. EST
Lara Talbot had to reach for a chair. She'd been so excited, so happy, for a change. Although Brianne wasn't married, as Lara would prefer, she had a good job as a hospital administrator, made fantastic money and would be thirty-eight in two months — plenty old enough to be able to

care for a child on her own. Several of Lara's more religious friends had expressed their disapproval that Brianne would have a baby out of wedlock, but Lara had decided not to let her younger daughter's single status ruin the enjoyment of having her first grandchild.

She'd had no idea she'd have much bigger things to worry about. . . .

"Not this again," she said as Amarok's words pierced through the euphoria she'd been feeling on the drive home from the hospital like a pin to a balloon.

She knew the sudden pain and fear in her voice had caught her husband's attention when Grant, who'd been hanging the car keys on a hook, whipped his head around to look at her.

"What is it, honey?" he asked, striding over to where she'd sagged onto a barstool at the granite-topped island in their kitchen. "It's not the baby, is it? Brianne and little Caden are okay. . . ."

"I can't do this again," she said simply, and handed the phone to him, at which point she headed straight for her bedroom and the anti-anxiety pills she kept in her nightstand. After Evelyn had been kidnapped the first time, they'd become a staple in her life — until the past eight months, when everything seemed as though it was going to be okay at last.

She sensed that Grant didn't know whether to follow her as he accepted her mobile, but she was glad he didn't. She heard him say, "Hello? Amarok?" just as she stepped into her bedroom and locked the door.

Hilltop, AK — Sunday, 12:40 p.m. AKDT
That call had been every bit as difficult as Amarok had anticipated. He didn't even have the chance to explain the entire situation to Lara before she disappeared and Grant came on the line.

Grant had listened quietly, hadn't railed or accused Amarok of not being diligent enough. He'd barely said a word, which had left Amarok trying to fill the silence — something he'd done awkwardly, at best. He'd promised Grant he was doing all he could to find Evelyn and heard himself saying all the same empty platitudes others had been saying to him — that she was a strong woman, that she'd weathered difficult situations before and would get through this, too, that the baby would be fine.

But Grant understood how bad it could get and what the real chances were. He'd been through this type of thing before. He'd gotten his daughter back, but that had been a miracle. He could hardly expect to have such luck again.

"What you told him, it's true," Phil said after Amarok had promised to keep them informed and hung up. "We *are* going to get Evelyn back safely."

Amarok had forgotten Phil was even in the room. He jerked his gaze away from the spot he'd been staring at — as if his eyes were laser beams and could drill holes through his desk — and nodded. He couldn't talk about it; he'd fall apart. And that was the *last* thing he could allow himself to do. He had to remain strong and clearheaded, for Evelyn's sake. In order to get through this, he could only think one step ahead, and his next step included another difficult call.

He wished Phil weren't watching as he dialed his mother's number. But as much as Amarok preferred a bit of privacy, he wasn't about to ask him to leave. Phil had been completely devoted to him and to keeping Hilltop safe since Amarok had chosen him as Village Public Safety Officer. He was proving his commitment now, by doing all he could to support and assist in Evelyn's investigation.

When his mother didn't answer right

away, Amarok's anxiety grew. Maybe Phil was right and she had been hurt. Although he didn't want anything to do with his mother, his feelings were a great deal more complex than he was willing to admit, even to Evelyn, which was probably why she'd kept pressing him about whether he *really* didn't care to invite Alistair to their wedding. Evelyn knew he had to be torn on some level; she was a mental health professional. And she was right. Alistair's death would only make his feelings where his mother was concerned more complicated.

He was about to hang up and call the Seattle police, to ask them to check on her, when he heard a breathless, "Hello?" as though she'd had to hurry to reach the phone.

"Alistair?" He hardly knew her, refused to call her Mom. He'd spoken to her only a handful of times since Jason had reached out to him on their eighteenth birthday, and there'd been no communication before that.

"Benjamin?"

That she used his given name only highlighted the fact that she'd missed his entire life, wasn't even familiar enough with what people called him to use it herself. "Yeah, it's me."

Now that he had her on the line, which

confirmed she was alive, he didn't know what to say next. *I'm just calling to make sure you're okay* wasn't something he felt comfortable with. That made it sound as though he cared a great deal, and since she hadn't cared enough about him to remain in contact after she walked away from him when he was only two years old, he wasn't willing to pretend she could so easily erase all of that.

"It's good to hear from you," she said softly.

He couldn't help bristling. It would've been good to hear from *her* while he'd been growing up without a mother, but he didn't say that. "I have a few questions I was hoping you could answer."

There was a slight pause, during which he could feel her tense. "Is this about the past? Because I've been hoping we could talk about that, that I could finally say I'm sorry for what I did. I know you're having a hard time believing it, but I loved you then, and I love you now."

She had a hell of a way of showing it, but saying so would only elicit the excuses she'd tried to give him before and make him angry. A mother didn't abandon her child if she had a choice. Period. "This isn't about the past," he said, ignoring everything else,

286

including the entreaty in her voice.

"What else could it be?" She sounded slightly bewildered. "Are you thinking of coming over this way? Because if you are, I'd *love* to see you."

"No. I don't have any travel plans."

"What about Boston? Jason said you're getting married next month."

"Evelyn and I were getting married here and having a second reception in Boston in the fall, after the baby arrives. But . . ." His throat tightened, threatening to squeeze off any sound.

He swallowed, trying to force down the lump that was nearly choking him. "But something's come up."

"What is it? Don't tell me you and Evelyn have broken the engagement. From what I hear, you're deeply in love and perfect for each other. And with a baby on the way . . ."

Apparently, Jason was telling their mother more than Amarok had realized, but Amarok should've guessed he would. Jason remained loyal to her, just as Amarok remained loyal to their father. "Evelyn's been kidnapped."

This was met with shocked silence. Then she said, "That's terrifying. Do you know who has her, where they've taken her or even *why* this happened?"

"She studies psychopaths for a living, that's why. And I think I know who, as well."

"Don't tell me Jasper Moore has escaped. . . ."

"No. Lyman Bishop."

"The *Zombie Maker*?"

He hadn't realized she'd be familiar with the media nickname. "Yes. You're aware of him?"

"I follow anything that has to do with Hilltop because . . . well, I know you'd probably be involved in some way."

He said nothing.

"I haven't seen anything on the news lately about him escaping," she added.

"The hospital didn't contact the police, didn't tell anyone."

"Why not? Don't they have a duty to do that?"

"No doubt they were hoping to avoid the bad publicity."

"But he's so dangerous!"

"They chose to believe he was too diminished to be harmful, I guess. One of their employees has been murdered, though, so I doubt he's *that* diminished."

"You think it was him?"

"It makes sense."

"Then they're going to come under fire."

"Yes. If the scandal hasn't hit the news

yet, it will soon. *You* haven't heard from anyone you don't know, have you? Maybe someone who mentioned Evelyn or asked where I live?"

"Are you talking about Lyman Bishop? What makes you believe he would ever try to contact *me*?"

"Because I'm fairly certain Evelyn thought she was meeting you at our house when she was abducted. She wrote your name and an odd number on a pad at Hanover House just before she went missing. You haven't called her, have you?"

"I haven't. I admit I've considered it on occasion. I've wanted to meet her, get to know her — beyond what I've read about her and seen on TV, I mean. But I was afraid it would only drive you further from me if I tried to enlist her help."

"What kind of help would you be hoping to get from her?" he asked, taken aback by this admission. "*She* can't explain why you did what you did."

Amarok had purposely not confronted Alistair with this before. He knew she couldn't come up with an excuse that would satisfy him, so there was no point. But he wasn't himself right now, was barely coping and knew things could still get a lot worse if Evelyn and his baby were dead.

"There's no good excuse," she said. "I admit that. I wanted out. That's all I remember. I couldn't take the darkness and the cold. I felt like I was going crazy. And I knew I'd never truly escape if I didn't make a clean getaway. I didn't want to be split between two places, especially when one of them was a small outpost in Alaska. It was selfish of me. I see that now."

"Really." What else could he say?

She didn't notice the sarcasm in his tone, evidently. Just went right on talking.

"I justified it by trying to make myself believe I was doing the right thing for everyone involved, that I was being fair to Hank by taking one boy and leaving him the other."

"What about *my* feelings?" Amarok asked.

"You were only two and you adored your father. I wanted to believe you'd be happy. I knew Hank would be a good father —"

"I *was* happy. But that doesn't mean I didn't need a mother!" he shouted, shocking himself as well as Phil, whose eyes widened at the outburst. Amarok never raised his voice.

Phil's eyebrows drew together in concern. "Maybe this isn't the best time to deal with the past," he murmured. He sounded worried and yet hesitant to intercede, but Amarok knew he was right. He'd let his control slip. It was the stress, the anxiety, the fatigue, the swollen and painful hand. Those things were coming down on him all at once, because he'd put everything he had, his whole heart, into loving Evelyn. The thought of someone harming her was agony for him.

"I'm sorry, Benjamin," his mother said.

He could tell she was crying and that only made him feel worse. "I can't deal with this on top of everything else," he said. "I've got to go."

He hung up before she could respond, and the phone rang almost the second he did. Thinking it might be one of the searchers or Terry Lovett's wife, returning his call and answering his message, he picked it up right away. He preferred *not* to face Phil after that conversation with his mother, which revealed more than he ever had, much more than he was comfortable putting out there. "Hello?"

"Sergeant Murphy?"

It was a man's voice — deep, emphatic, confident. "Yes?"

"This is Ted Bell with the *Anchorage Daily News.*"

Not one of the searchers. Not Terry Lovett's wife. Just another fire to put out.

291

Could the hell he was going through get any worse? "What can I do for you, Ted?"

Although Amarok's voice was clipped, Ted proved unflappable. "I hear you have a problem out that way," he replied smoothly.

Amarok rested his forehead on his fist. Thank God he'd told Evelyn's parents.

17

Jasper could feel Roland's eyes on him but refused to look over. Winters in Alaska were so damn long they didn't get much yard time. In such a cold climate, it was too expensive for the government to provide the necessary outerwear — that was what the guards said — but Jasper knew it had more to do with the difficulty of policing a large group of inmates in the dark, especially those housed at *this* facility. And in Alaska during the winter, it was almost always dark. Since he planned on making the most of summer and the added rec time they received because of the longer days, he wasn't about to let Roland or anyone else cause a problem for which he could be thrown in the hole.

What was it with Roland? he wondered as he took in all the men who were playing basketball or chess or just working out. Roland's interest in Jasper seemed to have grown since Evelyn disappeared. It was almost as though he resented Jasper for slitting Evelyn's throat, even though he'd done it more than twenty years ago, and wanted to make him pay for it. But Roland wasn't anything to Evelyn, had barely come to know her.

Or maybe it was something else entirely. Maybe now that he'd been at Hanover House for a couple of months, he'd grown comfortable enough to become bored. He was a patient man, evidently, liked to wait and watch and think things through. Could be he'd had it in for Jasper from the beginning, ever since he learned Jasper's history, but was only starting to make his move.

Jasper had worked in corrections; he knew some inmates were like that. They felt it was their responsibility to mete out punishment to those they considered worse than themselves — as if that changed what *they* were.

When Roland didn't shift his attention after a reasonable length of time, Jasper *had* to return his gaze. In prison, staring was almost as bad as shoving. If he didn't respond, Roland would know he was reluctant to become enemies, and then he'd be *forced* to put Roland in his place.

Otherwise, he'd become Roland's bitch, and Jasper couldn't let that happen. If he lost status at Hanover House, he'd be far more vulnerable than he was now. Everyone in this place preyed on the weak.

Making sure he gave no sign of the intimidation he was feeling, he glared back so Roland would know he wouldn't go down without a fight. He hoped that would be enough and Roland would go pick on someone else. He was one of the very few who'd ever made Jasper feel unsure of his own ability to come out on top.

He was just so damn confident. . . .

Roland didn't back off, however. He smiled as though Jasper's response amused him and sauntered over, going so far as to sit at the cement-like table where Jasper had his legs outstretched and his face turned up toward the sun.

"Enjoying yourself today?" he asked.

"I was until you decided to be a prick," Jasper replied.

Roland chuckled.

"You think that's funny?"

"No. What *I* think would be funny is to see how you behave when I have my knife at your throat and my dick up your ass."

Watching him warily, Jasper sat up straight. "What have I ever done to you?"

"You don't get it, do you?" He started scraping the dirt from beneath his fingernails. "I have a problem with men who victimize women and children. It's a fucked-up thing to do."

"What I've done or haven't done is none of your business," Jasper growled, but Roland didn't get angry in return.

"According to what I've read online, you've murdered at least thirty women. Some you raped and tortured for days or even weeks. That true?"

Jasper could hear his own blood roaring in his ears. He was tempted to lash out, to teach Roland he was no one who could be messed with. That was how he'd met every challenge in the past — by coming right back at whoever stood up to him, louder and fiercer. But he was no longer in the outside world where most people played by the rules. No longer had the advantage of being the only one willing to go to any lengths necessary. "Why do you ask?"

"Thirty's a lot."

"I'm not saying it was thirty."

"Well, we know there was at least one. Dr. Talbot has that scar on her neck to remind us. And you're the one who put it there."

Jasper could see where this was going. He just couldn't see how to derail it.

"Don't you ever wonder how they felt?" Roland asked when Jasper didn't respond.

"No." He didn't care. It wasn't about *them*. They didn't matter. It was about the pleasure having that much power brought *him*.

"Well, maybe you should."

"Are we going to have a problem, you and I?"

Roland didn't so much as blink. "You catch on quick."

Jasper narrowed his eyes. "You're not going to do anything to me, not if I get to you first."

"We'll see how well that works out for you." With another smile, he got up and walked away, and all through the rest of their time in the yard, Roland wouldn't quit staring at him. The other inmates were catching on to his interest, murmuring that he was Roland's next target and even placing bets as to who would survive in an incident between them.

If they were betting on Roland, they were betting on the wrong man, Jasper told himself. He never let *anyone* beat him.

Anchorage, AK — Sunday, 3:30 p.m. AKDT
Lyman Bishop hadn't had a second's trouble getting license plates for the van. He'd

297

taken the ones he needed to get rid of with him in the rental car and, on his way back from running errands, when he was no longer in a parking lot where there might be surveillance cameras, he drove down street after street until he found an old truck in a quiet neighborhood and made the swap.

No one else had been around; no one had seen him or tried to stop him. He doubted even the owner would notice the difference. License plates weren't something most people paid attention to, except cops. So once he got back to the chicken ranch, painted the van and put on the new plates, he'd return the rental car and be fairly safe.

As he drove back, he was looking forward to having a chance to rest and recover from all the activity and stress of the past few days — and getting to know Evelyn a bit better. He hoped she'd be friendlier when he spoke to her again. If she wasn't, if she was too stubborn for her own good, they would both lose out.

The show tune "Let the Memory Live Again" came on the radio, so he turned it up.

Boy, had it been a long time since he'd heard that song. He loved Broadway musicals! He and Beth used to sit and watch them over and over. They were a lot better than the negative crap on television these days. But there was something nostalgic about the lyrics of this particular song. It made him sort of melancholy to hear that line — *how did it go?* — about the memory of knowing happiness once upon a time.

He'd *never* known. Sometimes he not only felt estranged from those around him, he also felt estranged from the whole human race. What kind of a kid was so unlovable that even a mother wouldn't want him?

For the first time in ages, he thought of his mother. He'd believed he'd finally be happy after he gave her what she deserved for choosing her new husband over her children, but he'd never forget the look on her face when he stepped out of the bushes of her yard with that gun. It was almost as if she was glad to see him, but since he'd shot her right away, he had no idea what she was about to say.

Fortunately, his mood became less self-reflective as "Do You Hear the People Sing?" from *Les Misérables* came on. He was foolish for thinking of his mother. She didn't deserve the longing that sometimes sprang up.

He was tapping the steering wheel to the beat of the drums when the road curved to the right, but as he navigated that turn and the chicken ranch came into sight his heart jumped into his throat.

Everything wasn't as he'd left it. There was a white Explorer parked out front, and whoever had gotten out of it had somehow managed to open the gate he'd locked when he left — he distinctly remembered doing it — and gone inside.

Hilltop, AK — Sunday, 3:35 p.m. AKDT
Amarok was *so* torn. He wanted to fly to Minnesota and take the face close-up from the Quick Stop video around to each and every employee at Beacon Point himself. So much of police work involved reading body language and using his intuition about the people he met, whether they were being honest or not. But he was afraid to leave Alaska for fear the searchers would finally turn up something and he wouldn't be around to act on it.

He knew Evelyn was probably in Alaska somewhere, too, which also made it hard for him to leave. He didn't want to go any farther from her than he had to. He wished he could be in two places at once, but Detective Lewis insisted he was handling everything on his end as quickly as possible, and he had remained in close touch.

"The media is about to go crazy with

this," Amarok told Lewis on the phone.

"It's already been on the news here several times. And I'm being bombarded for updates on the case."

"It won't be long before an army of journalists flood into town. They'll be banging on the doors and windows at my trooper post, plus trying to stop me whenever they see me."

"That type of thing doesn't make our jobs any easier."

Amarok rubbed a hand over his face. "When you're as small as Hilltop, there aren't a lot of places to go in order to avoid them."

"Is there someone else you can refer them to so you can stay focused?"

He'd refer them to Shorty. Shorty could be tight-lipped when necessary; Phil couldn't. Phil was too kind and gregarious for his own good. "I'll muddle through."

"Maybe the media coverage will be a blessing. They've been running the video you sent me. I'm hoping it will help us identify him. So far, it's brought in quite a few dead ends, but I have a lot more leads to sift through."

"That video is pretty blurry."

"Still, there's an identifiable person in it."

"Maybe you're right. We need to ID him

fast. Evelyn has been gone for five days. Her chances dwindle with each passing second."

So did his hope of getting her back. . . .

"When's the last time you slept?" Lewis asked.

Amarok had slept in snatches — a couple of hours here and a couple of hours there when he simply couldn't go on — but he hadn't been resting *or* eating as he should. He could tell by the way his clothes fit him that he was already losing weight. He hadn't bothered to shave, either. For the first time since he was twenty-two, he had a beard.

The only *good* news was that the swelling in his hand had finally gone down. He was beginning to think he *hadn't* broken it. It hurt when he tried to use it, but it seemed to be healing. "I have no idea. It's not as though I'm keeping track."

"Well, I can tell you it's not enough."

Shorty, Molly and Phil had been saying the same thing. They were almost as distraught by what was happening to him as by what had happened to Evelyn. They'd already alerted his father to the fact that he wasn't taking care of himself. Hank had called him twice and begged him not to run himself into the ground. He was threatening to come to Hilltop and stay with him, to try to force the issue, but they all knew there wasn't anything Hank or anyone else could do.

"I don't want to talk about sleep, okay? I'm fairly certain this is the last day I'll have a search party at my disposal. They haven't found a thing — and that includes someone who's seen or recognized the man in the video I sent you. There might be a few who'd be willing to go out again tomorrow, but it's the start of a new week, and this is the fourth day they've been at it. People have to get back to their own lives at some point."

"I understand where they're at, and I understand the desperation you feel."

"Right," Amarok mumbled, but he didn't believe that anyone could truly understand. Not unless they'd been through something similar.

There was an awkward silence, as if Lewis could tell his comment had been deemed meaningless. Then he said, "Look. You have to trust others to help you. You can't do everything. I get that you don't know me very well, and you can't see everything I'm doing here in Minnesota, so you're afraid to rely on the fact that it's getting done."

"That's not —"

"I'm giving this case top priority, okay? Things don't happen in an instant just because we need them to. So relax and let me do my job. It's better to have two people on this than one, regardless of what your opinion is about how hard I'm going after it."

Lewis had a point, but Amarok was unwilling to concede. He'd convinced himself that the real answers, the ones that might actually net him something, were to be found in Minnesota, since the kidnapping had to have been planned while Bishop was at Beacon Point.

"Were you ever able to reach Terry Lovett's widow?" he asked Lewis. He didn't want to waste time with a pep talk, regardless of whether he needed it. "Because I can't get her to call me back no matter how many times I reach out to her."

"I got her on the phone just a few minutes ago."

"And?"

"She claims she's never heard of Lyman Bishop or Evelyn Talbot and she has no idea who'd want her husband dead."

"Did she say if Terry had been acting strange lately?"

"She wouldn't say much of anything, wouldn't give me more than two minutes of her time, but I'm not all that surprised, to be honest with you. She's just lost her husband."

"According to the article I read on Terry careening into that ravine, she wasn't getting along with him."

"Doesn't mean she'd want him dead."

"Then why won't she call me back?"

"Who knows?"

"Did you ask her if you could at least text her a photo of our suspect? See if she recognizes him?"

"I already sent it."

"And?"

"I haven't heard anything yet, but I sent it only an hour or so ago. I'll follow up as necessary. I'll attend the funeral, too, see if anyone suspicious shows up. Maybe I can talk to her a bit more when it's all over, bring a hard copy of the photo with me in case she doesn't respond to the text."

"When is the funeral?"

"On Friday."

Amarok came to his feet. "That's five days from now!"

"I know, but I can't *force* her to talk."

"Why wouldn't she *want* to? Maybe she had something to do with it."

"The murder of her husband?"

"And/or the kidnapping of Evelyn."

"I'd be really surprised if she did. From

what I'm getting from the neighbors, she's a regular mom with two kids, and she has no criminal history."

"They were having marriage problems, needed money, too. And we know Bishop withdrew the thirty-three hundred he had in savings."

"Doesn't necessarily mean anything. He'd need money to get to Alaska, too — although, as I've told you, his name doesn't show up on any of the flight manifests."

"You're monitoring the major carriers to see if that changes, right?"

"Of course."

Amarok rubbed his eyes. They knew Bridget Lovett was at her children's school when her husband was killed, so she hadn't been the one to stab him. Could she be involved in some other way? Or was she as clueless as to why her husband was now dead as she pretended to be? "She has to take a look at the photo I gleaned from the Quick Stop video. If she doesn't get back to you, I'll fly there myself and make sure she does."

"Wait a sec. Something just came in. Hang on. . . ."

Amarok dug some old trail mix out of his drawer and tossed a handful of nuts and raisins into his mouth while he waited for

Lewis to get back on the line. Makita trotted over because he knew Amarok kept doggy treats in the same drawer, and Amarok tossed him one.

"Sergeant Murphy?"

"Yes. What was it?"

"The surveillance video from the bank."

"Lyman's bank?"

"Yeah."

"Can you send it to me?"

"Already did."

Amarok waited for Lewis's e-mail to come in and clicked on the attachment as soon as it did. "He's getting around pretty damn good for a vegetable," he said, his eyes glued to the screen image of Bishop walking into the lobby and approaching a teller.

"I noticed that," Lewis responded.

Bishop had a limp. He looked heavier than before, too, but some of that could be attributed to the thick black sweatshirt he wore with the hood pulled up to obscure his face.

"Someone had to have helped him," Amarok said. "You need to ask Bridget Lovett if her husband bought anything like that sweatshirt recently."

"I'll keep trying to get her to talk to me."

Amarok froze the playback and enlarged the picture. What little he could see of

Bishop's face became so blurry it almost defeated the purpose, but he recognized those dark, lifeless eyes. "You bastard," he mumbled.

"I assume you're not talking to me," Lewis said dryly.

"*How* did he recover?"

"I wish I had that answer. No one saw this coming."

"So Bishop meets a janitor at Beacon Point, talks him into getting him street clothes and maybe a cell phone and letting him out."

"Then he stabs Lovett so he can't talk."

"But how does the man with the scar fit in?"

Lewis mulled it over for a few seconds. "He has to have a connection to Beacon Point."

"Or a connection to Terry Lovett."

Amarok knew Lewis agreed with him when he said, "Right. I'll keep working on the widow."

"Thanks."

As soon as Amarok hung up, he asked Phil if he'd look after Makita and Sigmund for a few days and went online to book a flight to Minneapolis first thing in the morning. As much as he hated to leave Alaska, he had to do it. He was convinced that the answers he needed to save Evelyn were in Minnesota.

18

Anchorage, AK — Sunday, 3:40 p.m. AKDT
"I hope you don't mind me stopping by. I
was in the area, so I thought I'd take the
opportunity to meet you."

Bishop wiped the sweat from his forehead.
He'd caught his landlady — Edna Southwick — with her keys out. She'd been just
about to go in through the store.

Or maybe she was coming out. . . .

He watched her closely, trying to determine how long she'd been on the property
and what she might've done before he arrived. Had she seen anything that might put
him at risk?

He didn't think so. She would've been far
more nervous if she had. He'd come upon
her just in time.

"I'm glad you did," he lied. "But it's a
good thing I arrived when I did, or it
would've been a wasted trip. Next time, I
hope you'll give me some notice."

"Of course."

When she glanced at her keys, still dangling from the lock, he got the impression she was hoping he'd invite her in, but he had no intention of doing that. He'd have to lead her to the staff room in order to sit down — it would seem strange if he let her into the store only to keep her standing in the garbage that littered the floor — and that meant she could easily see that the freezer had a slot in the door Emmett hadn't gotten permission to put there, as well as a chain and padlock on the handle so it couldn't be opened.

Bishop didn't want to have to come up with some way to explain those things. It was bad enough that, if he was reported missing and the police made a big deal about finding him, she might see his face splashed across her TV screen and recognize him.

"Are you finding that you have everything you need here?" she asked as she returned her keys to her purse. "This location isn't too remote, I hope?"

She looked like the TV actress Betty White — sweet and small, with white hair and a sweater over her turquoise shirt and matching slacks, even though it was plenty warm today. She took care of herself. He admired her for that. He could smell her lavender perfume, which brought back a vague recollection of his grandmother. Mrs. Southwick came off just as harmless as Grandma Henning. He'd always thought his life would've turned out very differently had his grandmother not died when he was six.

But, unlike Grandma Henning, Edna had shrewd eyes. He didn't believe for a second that she'd come by to "meet" him. She was checking on her property, that was all.

"I admit it isn't ideal," he heard himself say. "The smell can be a bit much at times. But, as we discussed on the phone, it's only for three or four months. I can get by."

"Where do you keep the dogs?"

"In one of the coops in back."

"If you have a moment, I'd really like to see them."

He hesitated. He wanted her to leave — to go and mind her own business. Emmett had paid the rent through the next three weeks. But Lyman knew the best way to make sure he wouldn't have any trouble with her in the future was to allay whatever curiosity, concern or worry had brought her here in the first place.

"Sure. I'm just getting started, so there are only a few. Emmett already found homes for the others," he said, covering for the fact that he had no idea how many dogs Emmett had told her he was sheltering.

"I'm surprised Emmett quit, especially so soon," she said. "From what I could tell, he was completely devoted to saving animals."

Bishop, doing all he could to minimize his limp, led her around the building instead of through it. After all, the back door was boarded up, and she had to be aware of that. "It came as a surprise to me, too, but his father just died. He had to go back to Montana, where he's from, to help his mother."

"Oh, I see. So . . . you're not going to replace him?"

"No. I'm here now, so I might as well stay. You wouldn't believe how hard it is to find good help."

"Oh yes I would." She rolled her eyes. "I'm sure you've noticed how my ex-manager left this place. I've been meaning to hire someone to get it cleaned up. That's part of the reason I was hoping to meet you in person today. I know you'd be more comfortable here if that happened, and it would help me sell the property, as well. I wanted to see if you might be interested in doing the cleanup yourself, in exchange for a reduction on the rent."

"Ah — no."

"I understand." She lifted one thin-skinned, blue-veined hand. "I can find someone else. I just don't know who to call. I've been so overwhelmed by all the things that have to be done when you lose a loved one it's been hard to think of anything else." Her eyes grew misty. "Bernie and I were together for fifty-four years — since I was sixteen. I almost don't know who I am without him."

"I'm sorry for your loss," Bishop mumbled. That was what he was supposed to say, but he was hardly sympathetic. She thought *she'd* had it rough? He was tempted to tell her what *he'd* been through, what his mother had done to him and Beth, the way he'd been bullied all through school, what the brain hemorrhage had cost him. But he knew he couldn't divulge anything about himself — nothing real, anyway.

"And then to find out we were so deeply in debt . . ." She shook her head. "He couldn't bear to tell me, I guess. Didn't want me to worry."

"It must've come as a blow." Bishop noticed some blood on the ground — probably from when he was wheeling Emmett's body around back — which was wet, thanks to the light rain they'd had this morning.

He made sure he retained eye contact with

his landlady so that *she* wouldn't notice it. He'd thought he'd done a better job of cleaning up than he had, but he'd been so tired and hadn't had a chance to come out and check his work. He'd been too eager to go buy what he needed to camouflage the stolen van — which he hoped she hadn't seen parked under the tangled vines shrouding the carport.

"It did. I inherited this ranch from my father. I should've stayed involved on the management end. But times were different back then. I was expected to stay at home and raise our kids, and that's what I did. I don't regret my choice. I love my four children."

"That's nice." Bishop made an attempt to sound sincere, but he wasn't sure if he was being successful.

"It's just that being thrust back into the business world after such a long break . . . I feel like a fish out of water," she said with a self-deprecating laugh.

She was obviously still mourning the death of her husband *and* their business. As a matter of fact, she was so caught up in her own personal anguish she hadn't been paying as much attention to the ranch as he imagined she would otherwise — lucky for him.

315

"I doubt *you* could've done anything to save it," he said flatly.

When her head jerked up, he knew his comment had sounded too harsh, too careless.

"Not to be insensitive," he added. "It's just . . . why beat yourself up for something you couldn't help? That's all. If your husband managed this place your entire married life, he must've done a decent job."

"Oh, I'm not saying he didn't!" she said. "He did all he could, of course. Small farms and ranches can't compete with the big boys anymore. That's all. I'm not *blaming* him. Just wishing I'd been more prepared for living without him."

"What about your children?" He conjured an interested expression. He wanted to keep her talking, keep her distracted. There could be something he'd missed, like the blood he'd noticed himself, that would make her take a second look. "They were never interested in getting involved in the family business?"

"No. Maybe if we'd had a boy it'd be a different story. But the girls all went to college in the Lower Forty-eight and only one came back. She's now married and works for a veterinarian."

The sky was darkening, promising more

rain. Bishop hoped that would motivate Mrs. Southwick to leave sooner than she might've done otherwise. "Some of the others could still return."

"I doubt they will. It's too hard to make a living here, unless you're a pilot, a roughneck in the oil fields or a hunting guide. About the only thing left is the tourism industry, and they'd tired of that by the time they got out of high school."

"There's the vet clinic, right?"

"Ada works there because she loves animals. She makes very little, but she doesn't have to earn a lot. Her husband's an ob/gyn and he has a thriving practice."

The dogs, who'd started barking as soon as they came around the building, began to whine and jump against the walls.

Bishop opened the door and, careful not to let them out, held it so that Mrs. Southwick could look in.

"There are just five left, huh? What are their names?"

Bishop tightened his jaw. She was too damn nosey. If she didn't watch herself, she'd be rotting right along with Emmett Virtanen in the coop closest to the fence on the far end.

He rattled off a few popular pet names and said he couldn't remember the last one, simply because he couldn't think of a fifth.

"How do you find homes for them?" she asked.

Bishop had reached his limit. He wasn't going to indulge her any longer. He shouldn't have to. He'd paid his rent. She had no reason to bother him. "Mrs. Southwick, I'm sorry, but I have groceries waiting in the car. Is there any way we could discuss this some other time? It's not as though I was expecting you, after all."

She blinked several times. "Of course. I'm sorry to have bothered you."

"No problem. It's been inconvenient," he admitted, "but I've been very accommodating. Wouldn't you say?"

"I'm not sure I'd say that at all," she mumbled, and hugged her purse to her chest as she began to march back to her car.

"You can't just drop in and expect me to be happy about it!" he called after her.

She turned, a look of wonder on her face. "This is *my* property!"

"I'm paying rent. I deserve a little privacy."

"It's too bad Emmett quit," she said. "I liked him a lot better than you."

That was the story of Bishop's life. No one liked him, and he couldn't figure out why. He had a right to draw some boundar-

318

ies, didn't he? Others did it all the time, and somehow they retained their friends. She was in his way, had interrupted his morning without any warning — so how was *he* in the wrong?

"I tried to be nice," he said as he followed her back around the plant.

"I've been through a harrowing ordeal the past six months. The least you could do is indulge me with a fifteen-minute visit. I was asking about the dogs because I was thinking of adopting one. I need something else in my life now that Bernie's gone. Sometimes, late at night, I think I might be losing my mind." Her voice broke, prompting him to say what everyone expected when someone started to cry.

"I'm sorry. I'm just . . . busy and . . . and stressed." What was more stressful than having a dead man in the coop in back and a kidnap victim locked in the cooler? He was doing something few people attempted and even fewer managed to pull off, right after recovering from a massive stroke. "With Emmett gone, I had to change my plans at the last minute. And I still haven't found a home for these dogs, even though I've got more coming. . . ."

At his conciliatory tone, her steps slowed. "Of course. I understand that I'm not the only one with problems." She seemed to be softening, making an attempt to see the situation from *his* point of view. He thought he just might have a chance to repair the damage he'd done.

But then she stepped on something — maybe a soft or muddy spot on the ground — that made her look down.

And when he followed her gaze, he saw what she saw: there was blood all over the hem of her turquoise pants.

Anchorage, AK — Sunday, 4:00 p.m. AKDT
If Evelyn had had the slightest inkling that Bishop was showing a visitor around the plant, any warning at all, she would've rushed the door. But she was busy trying to make another shiv when she heard a whoosh and the door swung open.

With her caught in the act of tearing apart her cot, it took her a guilty second to realize that Bishop wasn't paying attention, anyway. She saw only a flash of his balding head as she scrambled to her feet — not very fast now that she was so pregnant — and he tossed an older woman in with her before slamming the door.

With a mind to save them both, she ran past the woman, who was bleeding from the nose and mouth, and slammed herself up against the panel. She was hoping to catch Bishop before he locked it, maybe knock him down so she and whoever this other woman was might possibly overpower him or, short of that, get around him and try to escape.

But it was all for nothing. She only succeeded in hurting her shoulder. He'd obviously been prepared for her reaction and secured the door immediately.

"Damn it!" she cried in frustration.

A moan, coming from the floor where the other woman had fallen, grabbed her attention and kept her from pounding on the door.

"Who are you?" she asked as she bent to help her new cellmate over to the bed.

The woman was probably in her early seventies. She had white hair and fragile, birdlike bones, and she seemed dazed.

She blinked at Evelyn in apparent confusion. Then she put a hand to her head. "What happened?"

"I don't know," Evelyn replied. "I was hoping you'd be able to tell me."

Her expression grew more and more horrified as she looked around. "We're in the cooler!"

"Yes, I'm afraid so."

"But . . . why is there a bed in here? *And*

a toilet?"

Evelyn took her hand in an effort to soothe her. "I've been held captive here for I don't know how long. Several days."

Her eyes widened. "By the man who hit me?"

She was slowly piecing it all together. "If that was Lyman, the same man who just threw you in here, yes."

"No. It wasn't Lyman. I don't think I've ever heard that name. It was . . . it was my renter. His name is . . ." Probably too shocked and befuddled to recall his name, she let her words drift off as she touched her nose and held her hand out her to examine the blood.

"*What* was your renter's name?" Evelyn gently prodded.

"John Something," she decided.

An alias, no doubt. Of course Bishop would've picked a common name. "Let me guess . . . Smith?"

She didn't answer. "I came to see about a dog," she explained. "And to check on a few other things. There's a fertilizer company interested in buying the manure piled up in the coops. I could use the money, and it would help clean up the place, which I've been meaning to do ever since . . . ever since . . ."

She trailed off, starting again in a different place. "But I didn't get that far, had no chance to mention the fertilizer company before —" Her jaw dropped and she looked down at her pants. "This isn't my blood," she announced. "It was in the weeds. There was a whole puddle of it. As soon as I realized what I was standing in, that's when he hit me."

He hit her, but he didn't kill her. Why? Obviously, she knew too much, might've reported that blood, so he couldn't let her go.

But throwing her in with Evelyn? That was an interesting choice.

Evelyn feared he planned to practice up on his lobotomy skills. Maybe he'd lost confidence in his ability to operate after his brain hemorrhage.

"What's your name?" she asked.

"Edna Southwick."

Evelyn dumped water from one of her bottles on the sleeve of her own jacket so she could help Edna clean the blood from her face. "I'm Evelyn Talbot."

Her gaze dropped — and her eyes widened. "You're pregnant." She was stating the obvious, but Evelyn knew there was a lot to take in.

"Yes."

"When's the baby due?"

"In three months, if I can hold out that long."

The older woman's forehead furrowed with concern. "Aren't you terrified? Will you be out of here in time?"

"I don't know," she admitted.

Her pale blue eyes latched on to Evelyn's face. "What's going to happen to us?"

Evelyn considered telling her who Lyman Bishop was and what he'd done in the past. But Edna Southwick was hurt and scared and Evelyn didn't see any point in making it all worse. "We're going to do everything we can to survive and get back to the people who love us," she replied.

"You don't think the odds are in our favor."

Had she somehow revealed what she really felt? She'd been trying so hard not to.

Evelyn sat on the cot with her. "If it's any comfort, your odds are probably much better than mine."

"Why?"

"Because you aren't his intended target. You just inadvertently got in the way."

"Target?" she echoed. "What have I stumbled into?"

"It isn't anything good," Evelyn said with a sigh.

19

Minneapolis, MN — Monday 5:00 p.m. CST
Amarok wasn't going to give up. He'd flown three thousand miles to speak to Terry Lovett's widow. As soon as she realized he was with law enforcement, she'd refused to let him in or even give him an audience, but he planned to approach her friends, neighbors and family members. If the man he was looking for was involved with Terry, they had to know each other from somewhere, and Lewis had already established that it wasn't from work.

Although the afternoon sun glinted off the glass, so he couldn't actually see her, he sensed Bridget watching him from her front window as he crossed the street instead of getting into the rental car he'd parked at the curb in front of her house.

It took a moment for him to rouse someone, but eventually an obese man, using a cane, answered his knock.

Amarok identified himself as a police officer and took out the photo he'd brought with him. "Do you recognize this man?"

The gentleman scratched his thick beard growth as he considered the image. "Don't think so. I mean . . . he looks vaguely familiar, but the picture is so blurry . . ."

"I believe he was a friend of Terry Lovett's. Could that be where you've seen him? At your neighbor's house?"

"Naw. It's difficult for me to get out." He indicated his feet, which were so swollen it was a miracle he could still walk. "I pretty much keep to myself."

"You live alone, then?"

"It's just me and my mom."

"Where's your mom? Is there any chance I could speak with her?"

"Not right now. She's still at work."

Amarok made a note of their address. "When will she be home?"

"You're coming back?" He sounded surprised.

"If you don't mind . . ." Amarok planned to return regardless, but he was trying to be polite.

The skin hanging under the man's chin wagged as he shook his head. "No, of course not. I don't think she'll be able to help you, though. It's not like we have block parties in this crummy neighborhood. There was another officer going through here, so we heard that the neighbor's husband was murdered. Saw it on the news, too. And we feel bad about it. But we don't know her very well."

"Still, I'd like your mother to take a look at this photo. It's my job to be thorough."

"Okay," he said in a *suit yourself* voice.

After he left, Amarok went up the entire street, knocking on each and every door. Not everyone was home, but he made notes to indicate which houses required a second visit. By the time he'd made it back down to Bridget's, she was standing in her yard, glaring at him with her hands on her hips.

"What are you doing?" she snapped as he continued past.

"I told you. My fiancée has been kidnapped. I don't know if she's still alive, but even if she isn't I'm going to track down whoever took her, and this man" — he lifted the photo he'd tried to show her before — "could be him. I'm guessing he was involved with your late husband in some way. So until I find what I'm looking for, I'll talk to everyone you know."

"That's harassment! My husband just died. Why are you trying to make my life more difficult?"

Her husband had been murdered. He hadn't "just died," and yet her statement was passive, almost innocuous, as if no one were to blame. Inserting that kind of emotional distance was something he'd always associated with deception. Wouldn't an innocent person say, *My husband's just been killed?*

"I'm not harassing you or anyone else," Amarok said. "Just trying to save the life of the woman who's supposed to become my wife — and the life of our child. Evelyn's six months pregnant."

Bridget flinched at his mention of the baby but lifted her chin to a defiant angle only a second after. "Another detective already came by. He asked me and everyone else about the man in that blurry picture."

Some of the people Amarok had talked to so far had indicated the same thing, but others seemed totally unaware of the case, which just went to prove that Lewis hadn't been as dogged as Amarok. "If you know something, and you can save me the time and trouble of tracking down all your friends and relatives, I'd be extremely grateful."

With a dramatic sigh that suggested she was irritated by his persistence, she grabbed

328

the photo and stared at it. "I've never seen this man before in my life," she said, and handed it back.

Amarok made no reply. He simply accepted the photograph, pivoted and moved on to the house beyond hers.

"No one around here is going to recognize him!" she called out. "If he was a friend of my husband's, I'm the only one who would know that, and I'm telling you he wasn't."

"Then you won't mind me double-checking."

"You're wasting your time. That's all. What about your fiancée? She needs you to be doing more productive things."

"*I'll* decide what my fiancée needs from me. But thanks for the advice."

She started jogging to catch up with him and grabbed his arm to stop him. But when he shook her off, she threw up her hands and went back in her own house.

After another two hours spent canvassing the neighborhood, however, Amarok was afraid she was right. No one recognized the man.

He was standing on the corner, staring at the vehicle he'd parked in front of her house, wondering if there wasn't something better he could be doing with his time, after all, when he got a call on the mobile phone he'd purchased from Walmart as soon as he hit town. It was Detective Lewis.

"Who gave you this number?" he asked as soon as he answered. *He* hadn't done it; he'd thought it better if Lewis didn't know he was in town.

"Phil did. I just tried to call you at your trooper post."

If Phil had provided him with a way to contact Amarok, there had to be a compelling reason. "Do you have something?"

"I do, and I'd tell you what if I wasn't so pissed off," he said. "What are you doing in Minneapolis?"

"I'm tracking down the man who kidnapped my fiancée."

"Nothing I've said or done has convinced you that I'm doing my job?"

Lewis sounded put out, but Amarok didn't care. The detective wasn't as driven as Amarok was, wasn't as desperate to bring Evelyn home, and Amarok never completely trusted anyone else to do the things that were most important to him. "Don't be offended. I wouldn't trust *anyone.* This is Evelyn we're talking about."

"But you're wasting your time doing *my* work when you could be in Alaska doing yours."

Amarok covered a yawn. His body seemed

to have adjusted somewhat to "emergency" mode, and yet he couldn't seem to quit yawning. "Phil's got my back in Hilltop. He'll call if anything turns up."

"And if that happens, you'll be hours and hours away. You're okay with that?"

"I have to go where the investigation leads me. I don't have any choice."

"No choice? You could trust me, couldn't you? I'm doing my job! Maybe you'll believe me when I tell you I've found a possible connection between Terry Lovett and the man in the Quick Stop video."

Amarok gripped his phone that much tighter. "What is it?"

"You mentioned the guy who came to town was likely an ex-con, right?"

"That's what the tattoo on his hand signifies."

"I agree. Well, Terry Lovett also served time — eight years to be exact."

"Where?"

"Faribault — the biggest state prison in Minnesota. I'm heading there now to talk to the warden and other staff. If he was incarcerated there, and it was for any length of time, someone will remember him."

"How long will that take you?"

"It's an hour's drive. Depending on what I find, how many people I have to talk to, it could take most of the day."

Amarok had just opened his mouth to respond when he saw a blue Ford Focus stop in front of Terry Lovett's house. A young girl, about ten years old, climbed out. She was saying good-bye to the people still in the vehicle when Amarok told Lewis he'd call him back and hurried over.

"Hi there." He smiled at the woman behind the wheel as he flashed his badge. "I'm Sergeant Benjamin Murphy —"

"I haven't done anything wrong, have I?" she interrupted.

"No, of course not." He shifted so that the girl, who was watching him curiously, remained between him and the vehicle. "I'm working with Detective Lewis with the Minneapolis Police Department on an important case involving this man." He showed the woman the photograph. "You wouldn't happen to have seen him. . . ."

"No. I've never seen him before," she replied. "But I don't live in this neighborhood." She gestured at the girl who stood only a foot or so away from him. "Maybe Estelle will recognize him. I just picked her up after soccer practice. She lives here. Her mother and I carpool."

"Can I look?" Estelle asked.

He handed her the photo. "You bet."

She pushed her glasses up to the bridge of her nose, but she didn't have to study the photograph for any length of time. Her face brightened immediately. "I thought I recognized him. That's my uncle Emmett," she said proudly.

Amarok's heart began to race. "Your father's brother?"

"No, my mother's."

She'd barely gotten the words out when a shrill voice cried, "Estelle! Get in this house! *Right* now!"

They both turned to see Bridget Lovett standing on the stoop.

"I have to go," Estelle mumbled. Obviously frightened by her mother's reaction, she grabbed her backpack and hurried to do what she'd been told.

"Get off my property," Bridget said to Amarok, stabbing her pointing finger at the street. "She's a *kid*. I could sue you and the whole Minneapolis PD for talking to her without my permission."

"You go right ahead and do that," he said.

He wasn't worried. He now knew why Bridget had refused to cooperate: she was protecting her brother.

Anchorage — Monday, 5:30 p.m. AKDT
Lyman Bishop frowned at the laptop Em-

mett had left behind. Old and battered, with gym stickers all over the lid, it wasn't much to look at, but Emmett had brought it to Alaska so that he'd be able to watch movies on Netflix while he waited for Lyman. Emmett's life had been that simple. He couldn't go without entertainment for three or four days.

Nothing was simple for Lyman. It never had been but especially not now. After being unable to get out of bed for the past twenty-four hours, thanks to the physical exertion of escaping from Beacon Point, he'd finally fed his two captives (for the first time today, but he didn't think they deserved better treatment; he was very unhappy with them) and bellied up to the small breakfast bar in the staff room. He'd been so busy since he'd become a free man, taking care of one situation only to move on to the next, he hadn't had a chance to even think about what he'd left behind in Minnesota. After tossing his landlady in with Evelyn last night, he'd dragged himself over to the couch, where he'd curled into a ball to be able to endure the pain throbbing through his legs. Every muscle was protesting. But he was feeling a bit better, and he needed to know what was going on, what might be coming up from behind.

334

As soon as he entered Terry's name into Google, he learned that the police had ordered an autopsy on Terry's body and determined his death *wasn't* a suicide. That was unfortunate. He'd been hoping for a bit of luck, but he'd never been one to catch a break. And the more he dug, the worse the picture became. The authorities also knew he'd escaped from Beacon Point and were looking for him.

He shook his head. Now *everything* was messed up.

Lyman wished he had the energy to pace. There was so much anger pouring through him. He needed an outlet. But he wasn't about to stand up. He hadn't bounced back completely, was still having trouble controlling his left side. A second ago, he'd caught himself drooling like a baby — and groaned to think how he'd feel if Evelyn ever witnessed that. As if he didn't have enough going against him with the loss of his hair. He didn't want to look *totally* unappealing to her. He knew he'd enjoy having sex with her much more if he could verify she found him at least slightly attractive. Not to mention, at some point he'd need others to believe she was with him *voluntarily.*

Of course, her beauty would fade quickly enough. After the operation, Beth's looks had gone downhill almost right away. There was something about that loss of vitality and intelligence; it took a physical toll, too.

He scratched his head. What was he thinking? He couldn't worry about stuff like that right now. He had too many other things to deal with.

"How do I counteract it all?" he muttered, over and over again as he glared at the computer screen and the last article he'd pulled up. Edna Southwick had said three of her four children lived in the Lower 48, which was good. Being so far away, they were less likely to notice she was missing right away.

But the fourth child . . .

The fourth child could be a problem. It'd already been twenty-four hours.

Removing his glasses, he rubbed his eyes as he sagged against the back of the bar-stool and pictured the various scenarios he could potentially face. If the daughter who lived in Alaska came snooping around, looking for her mother, he could kill her. But that would only start her husband searching for her, and if Lyman killed *him* the chain would go on. Eventually, the police would show up with a search warrant and find the bodies.

He couldn't handle the problem of Edna

Southwick in that way. Initially, he'd thought he'd just keep her with Evelyn until the baby came. Edna had had four kids; he figured she could help Evelyn when it came time for the delivery, which would improve the odds of the child surviving.

But he hadn't really been thinking critically. Physical capacity wasn't the only thing he'd lost with the damn hemorrhage. He'd lost a lot of mental acuity, too.

He had to take Evelyn and leave this place, he decided. As much as he'd hoped to stay right here until the baby was born — in *so* many ways it was ideal — he couldn't. Law enforcement would eventually piece the whole thing together, would probably even realize that *he* was the one who'd kidnapped Evelyn and, for a time, kept her here. But with how easy it was to find work as a science editor or textbook ghostwriter, or even doing medical transcription, over the Internet, he could work from home, where it wouldn't be difficult to lay low. He could even have groceries and other supplies delivered to his house, wouldn't have to see *anyone.*

Which meant they wouldn't know where he'd gone. And they wouldn't be able to find him.

The only problem? Scouting out the

perfect situation and getting set up again could take days.

He could only hope there'd be enough time.

Hilltop, AK — Tuesday, 8:00 a.m. AKDT
Jasper was afraid to go into the showers. He'd been waiting for an ambush and, after what Roland said in the yard on Sunday afternoon, he knew that was where such a thing would most likely occur. There weren't enough hours in the day to allow all the inmates to shower separately — the government wasn't keen on spending the extra money on the number of showers that would require; it wasn't as though they were going to put one in every cell like some kind of motel — which left him vulnerable, especially because Roland was in the same cellblock. They'd been showering at the same time, three days a week, ever since Roland came to Hanover House, but Jasper had never been uneasy about it, not like this.

Although it would've been smarter for Roland to jump him when he wasn't expecting it, that wasn't Roland's style. He had that weird code of ethics, which he was always rattling on about to the other inmates — what he called a sense of fair play. He felt it only right to inform his intended target that

338

there would be trouble. He chose only his equals for opponents. And he never "sucker punched someone from behind," as he put it.

Jasper had none of those scruples. He'd launch a sneak attack on Roland in a heartbeat — would do much worse — if he ever got the chance. He knew, in the minds of the other inmates, that made him inferior to Roland in some way, but he didn't understand why. Roland was a fool to sacrifice the element of surprise. Why allow an opponent to get prepared?

Jasper saw no reason to give up *any* advantage. Ordinarily, advance notice would be enough to make it possible to prevail in any confrontation, since he now knew to keep his eyes open. But it wasn't that easy with Roland. The man had many watching out for him in this place. The other inmates seemed to see him as some kind of folk hero, and the guards liked him, too, which was the weird part. Jasper had never seen such broad-based support, especially because, unlike most of the other inmates, Roland hadn't cliqued up with any particular gang or group of friends. He remained aloof, his own man always, and measured everything according to that odd code of his.

"Getting nervous?"

Jasper didn't need to look over to know who'd asked the question. He could tell by the voice and couldn't help bristling at the taunt.

Turning, in his own sweet time, he looked over as casually as possible.

Sure enough, Roland was leaning up against the bars of his cell, watching Jasper. Roland had barely taken his eyes off Jasper since their encounter in the yard, had given him no privacy at all. Roland was *trying* to intimidate him, and Jasper understood that, hated that it was working, especially because Roland's interest drew so much attention. Not only were the other prisoners urging Roland to make his move, they also were rooting for him to succeed.

"Shut your mouth, or as soon as I get the chance, I'll shut it for you," Jasper growled. But he couldn't help watching the clock as it ticked inexorably toward eight thirty, when he'd be led to the showers along with everyone else in Cellblock D.

He could refuse to go. He was only *forced* to shower twice a week; the third was optional. But feigning sickness or lack of interest wouldn't ring true. He seized any opportunity to get out of his cell and had never begged off.

340

Besides, not heading to the showers like usual would only delay the inevitable. Such a move wouldn't be worth losing face over — a constant concern in prison, since falling to the bottom of the power pyramid could have even more dire consequences. He couldn't behave like the stupid kid in elementary school who tattled if someone was picking on him. He had to stand up and fight.

"You want to have sex with me that badly?" Jasper returned Roland's smile as if he wasn't concerned in the least.

Roland laughed softly. "Not me, no. If it were up to me, I'd beat you to a pulp and be done with it. I don't swing that way. But I have a friend who's expressed interest, and I don't see why I should deny him. After all, it's exactly what you deserve, and seeing you get what you deserve is the only reason I'm in this."

Jasper knew the man Roland was referring to. Rufus Moreno had created a small gang he called his family. He had a regular partner. Jasper had seen them making out in the yard many times. But Rufus was by no means exclusive. He loved to check out what he called fresh meat. "So what's your role? You're just gonna watch?"

His teeth flashed as his smile widened.

341

"I'm the one who's going to hold you down."

"You're an animal."

At this Roland's laugh grew loud enough to echo through the cavernous building, which started all the men around them laughing, too. "You can dish it out, but you can't take it? Is that it?"

Jasper began to pace. It wasn't a wise reaction. No doubt Roland could read his anxiety, but Roland already knew he had Jasper running scared, or he would've backed off by now. Nothing slipped past the man. And he didn't care about his own life, so that gave him an advantage over everyone who did. "I'll fight back," Jasper warned.

"You can try," he responded with a shrug.

"What, are you going to let all your friends pile on? Is that why you're so damn confident?"

"I'm not asking for any help. I won't need it."

"You think this is what Evelyn would want?" Jasper asked.

He bit off a hangnail and spat it on the floor. "I certainly don't think she'd mind. Do you?"

"She's not out for revenge. There's something different about my brain. She's hoping to study it."

"Then I'll save it for her — in a jar. It'll probably be a moot point, anyway. I doubt Evelyn's coming back, and if she doesn't, it's because of men like you."

So that was it. He was angry that Evelyn was gone, and he was taking it out on Jasper.

Jasper stopped pacing and grabbed hold of the bars of his cell. "You're a convicted murderer! You're not some defender of the innocent."

His eyebrows slid up at the outburst. "I've never killed anyone who didn't deserve it. Can you say the same?"

Jasper couldn't hold his temper any longer. He'd never been good at it in the first place. "I'm going to kill you!" he cried. "I'm going to kill you if it's the last thing I do!"

"You'll have the chance in a few minutes," Roland said.

The mail cart arrived. Jasper was breathing so hard he could feel his chest rising and falling as he jerked the mail from the hand of the inmate who came around to deliver it.

As usual, he had a stack of letters from women. He was too worked up to read them right now, figured he'd wait until he could enjoy them — if that time ever came. It was

343

entirely possible he'd never return from the shower.

"Hey!" Roland called, and grinned as he showed Jasper a handmade shiv, which he quickly put behind his back when the inmate pushing the mail cart stopped to look, too.

Jasper wished *he* had a weapon. He was feeling more and more at a disadvantage when it came to Roland. The most maddening part was that he couldn't figure out how Roland had managed to gain so much power and popularity in such a short time.

Intending to get to work sharpening his toothbrush — it was the only weapon he might have time to create in the few minutes he had left — he tossed his mail on the bed.

And that was when he saw it. He'd received a letter from Chastity.

Finally! At least now he'd get to learn, in her own words, what she'd found when she went to Beacon Point. Or maybe she'd tell him something Amarok had shared with her about the investigation he hadn't yet heard. He was and always had been the most interested in Evelyn, and this was as close to Evelyn as he could currently get.

But Chastity's letter said quite a bit more.

20

Minneapolis, MN — Tuesday, 11:10 a.m. CST
Amarok had the name of the guy who'd popped into the Quick Stop for a pack of cigarettes in that stolen carpet-cleaning van. It was Emmett Virtanen — a white male thirty-two years of age, six foot four inches tall and 240 pounds.

While sitting in a cheap motel room in St. Paul, Amarok studied the mug shot Detective Lewis sent via e-mail. According to Lewis, Virtanen had indeed served time at the Minnesota state prison in Faribault — eight years for second-degree burglary — with Terry Lovett. They'd been cellmates for over a year, and Terry had married Emmett's sister as soon as he got out, which was only a few months before Emmett was released, at which point Lovett became the stepfather to her two children, a boy of twelve and a ten-year-old girl, the girl being the one who'd inadvertently given her mother away when she identified him.

Amarok had been tempted to head back to Alaska immediately after he'd left Bridget's place last night, especially when he couldn't get her to open the door or answer any of his questions despite what he'd learned. He didn't like being gone when he had information that could lead to Evelyn.

But he wasn't foolish enough to believe it would happen that fast. Yes, they'd identified Emmett, but now they had to locate him. They'd both gone to his apartment this morning, only to find it dark and closed up. Although Lewis was working on it, they didn't yet have a search warrant. They couldn't go in, so Amarok had been busy since then contacting Emmett's other friends and associates — all of whom claimed they had no idea where he was.

Amarok hoped the warrant would come through so he could search the apartment while Lewis dealt with the service provider for Emmett's cell phone. Once they had his cell phone records, they should be able to locate Emmett whether he was in Minnesota or Alaska or anywhere else in the world.

How closely they could pinpoint his whereabouts depended on two factors, however. Whether his phone was on or off — on made it easier. And how many towers it had communicated with recently. Three towers allowed for triangulation, which would place the phone inside a two-mile radius. If that turned out to be in Alaska, Amarok would *definitely* want to be there, which was why he'd booked a flight out first thing in the morning.

Before he had to catch that plane and while he was waiting for the warrant, he planned to visit Beacon Point Mental Hospital to see Bishop's old room and talk to the staff there himself, just in case Lewis had missed something.

Let me know the second that warrant comes through, he wrote to Lewis. *I'm checking out of the motel now.*

Lewis had asked when he was heading back to Alaska, but Amarok hadn't answered that question. Lewis wouldn't be happy to hear he was going to Beacon Point — redoing work that had already been done — but if Amarok was here in town, he wasn't going to miss the opportunity to verify anything and everything he could.

He'd just checked out and put his bag in the trunk when his cell phone rang. Although he was hoping it was Lewis letting him know they now had what they needed, he recognized the number as belonging to someone else.

His father.

Amarok hesitated. He didn't really have time to talk right now. His entire focus was on saving Evelyn and their baby. It was all he could think about. But he figured he'd just be driving. He could give Hank a few minutes without it costing him anything.

"What's up?" he asked after he started the engine and the Bluetooth picked up.

"Your mother's called me twice in the past twenty-four hours."

He punched the Reverse button on the gearshift console but kept his foot on the brake pedal. "After thirty years you've heard from her twice in the same day?"

"I spoke to her one other time, when I was trying to get you to go to her fiftieth birthday shindig, remember?"

"Still. It must've been a shock to hear her voice."

"It was."

"I'm sorry."

"Why would *you* be sorry?" Hank asked.

"Because I'm sure it was our last telephone conversation that prompted her to reach out to you."

"That's probably true."

Amarok backed out of the parking space.

"Let me guess — she wants you to absolve her of any guilt?"

"Didn't say that, but . . . yes. Essentially, she'd like to be forgiven."

"You're not going to forgive her, though, are you?"

"I already have," he replied. "And I hope you'll do the same."

Amarok stomped on the brake. *"After what she did?"*

"People make mistakes, Amarok."

"Not like that one, they don't. And if they do, they don't get off with a, 'Whoops, I'm sorry,' so long after the fact."

"What good will it do to hold a grudge?"

Amarok didn't answer right away. He was busy logging the address for Beacon Point into his GPS.

"Amarok?"

Finished, he pulled out of the parking lot. "It won't do any good. But I'm not trying to punish her. I just don't need her in my life. I'm an adult now. It's too late."

"Why not accept whatever love she can offer whether you're an adult or not?"

"Because it'll be awkward, weird. Why would I put myself into such an uncomfortable situation?"

"For a lot of reasons."

"Name one."

There was a long pause. "Look, she's not a bad person. Sure, what she did wasn't fair to you. But I wasn't a perfect husband. Maybe some of what happened was my fault, too. I never mentioned your brother to you, either — not after they left."

Because he was afraid Amarok would start pleading to go live with his mother so he could be with his brother. *That* Amarok could forgive. Hank would gladly have been a part of Jason's life if only Alistair would've allowed it.

Amarok signaled for a left turn and slowed down. "Dad, you realize Evelyn is still missing, right? I don't give a rat's ass about anything except getting her back, so maybe we can talk about this later."

"Phil said the same thing when he gave me your number. But that's just it."

"What's 'just it'?"

"If you can't find Evelyn . . . If, for some reason, this ends badly, you're going to need all the love and support you can get. And your mother is ready and waiting for a second chance."

"I know you're worried about me, Dad. But if I don't get Evelyn back, there's nothing my mother can do to make it better."

There was a long silence. "Okay. But . . . I wanted you to know that it wouldn't be disloyal to me if you decide to welcome her back into your life. As a matter of fact, I'm in favor of it. You mean more to me than hating her. I'd let the devil in at the door if I thought it would be a good thing for you, especially right now, when you're going through so much."

"I'll be fine."

"You're still holding out hope?"

It didn't sound as though his father was very optimistic. "Of course. Evelyn's the woman I love."

"You need to be prepared, Amarok. It's been a week. What are the odds she's going to be okay?"

"Not great," he admitted. "But she's beaten the odds before, and I'm making progress on the investigation. It's just taking time."

Hank didn't say it, but Amarok knew what he had to be thinking: time was the one thing they probably didn't have.

"I'll let you go. I didn't call to upset you. Merely wanted to plant a seed."

"That you'd rather I reunite with my mother?"

"If you need her, yes. It's important to me that you have what you need."

"Well, in case you've been wondering, you've always been enough for me. Gotta go." He pressed the End Call button as he pulled into Beacon Point and tried to dismiss his father and mother from his mind. That situation would be there when he had time to deal with it. Evelyn needed him *now.*

He jogged to the building but forced himself to slow down once he reached the entrance.

Anchorage, AK — Tuesday, 8:20 a.m. AKDT
"You don't want to talk today?" Evelyn asked.

Lyman Bishop stood on the other side of the slot in the door. She could see his rounding paunch hanging over the brown belt holding up his baggy polyester pants — pants a much older man would typically wear. But, unlike before, when he'd been so gregarious, he didn't have much to say. He seemed sullen, upset. She was worried about what was going through his mind. He'd barely fed them yesterday. They'd received only one meal, and it hadn't been a large one. She had to draw him out, so he'd treat them better. Edna was so traumatized by what'd happened, she seemed almost childlike in her response to it, completely bewildered.

Evelyn had promised her, over and over

352

again, that everything would be okay. But it didn't seem to help. She kept saying things such as, "We'll never get out of here. If no one knows where we are, how will we ever get help?" And Evelyn would offer a soothing response only to have Edna repeat basically the same thing a few minutes later: "We'll never get out of here. We're going to die. He's going to *kill* us!"

Edna needed food, water and rest. The glassy look to her eyes had Evelyn concerned. But they had only the one small cot between them. Evelyn had taken off the mattress and the blanket so they could lie together on the floor, but with only their upper bodies on the padding, their hips had begun to ache almost immediately. They'd constantly shifted around, trying to get comfortable.

Evelyn guessed Edna had barely closed her eyes. She knew *she* hadn't slept for more than twenty minutes at a stretch. If this continued, they'd have to take turns napping on the bed just to remain sane. The floor wasn't a viable option.

"What is there to talk about?" Lyman handed in the piece of cardboard that now served as a food tray. It held two plastic bowls of scrambled eggs with sausage. When she'd tried to slam the door and accidentally hit the metal tray Emmett had used, it had been ruined, so they'd suffered a downgrade there, but the food looked better than when Emmett had been in charge.

"Did you make this?" she asked as she took it and handed it off to Edna, who was too afraid to come forward and retrieve it herself.

"Of course I made it. There isn't anyone else here, is there?"

Ignoring the obvious pique in his voice, she glanced over her shoulder to signal to Edna to remain silent — not that she felt Edna was about to jump in. Edna wasn't even eating, despite the food she'd put next to her. "Smells good."

"I used to be a fabulous cook." He spoke grudgingly, but she could tell he liked to talk, especially about himself, and especially in response to a compliment.

"What did you put in the eggs? Some onions and spinach with the sausage, maybe?"

He bent down to peer in at her. "Yes. I wanted to give the eggs a bit more flavor. And I figured you could use the vegetables."

"Good idea. But what I really need is a toothbrush. You wouldn't believe how terrible it is to go so long without brushing your teeth."

354

"You don't have a toothbrush?" he cried.

"No. Emmett never gave me one."

He sighed. "He was hard to deal with."

"Which is why I'm glad *you're* here." She held her breath, was afraid she'd gone too far with that statement. Psychopaths loved praise. She was pandering to his ego. But what she'd said was *so* farfetched it was hard to believe he wouldn't recognize it as the lie it was and call her out on her attempt to manipulate him.

To her amazement, he didn't. When he said, "I tried to tell you how lucky you were when I arrived," as if he'd totally bought in, she felt the tension gripping her chest lessen ever so slightly.

"Emmett wouldn't respond no matter what I needed," she complained. "But I told Edna *you're* not like that. You want us all to be happy together."

"I do," he said, his voice perking up.

"So you'll get me a toothbrush?"

"Of course. Dental hygiene is incredibly important. It affects your overall health. But Emmett was an uneducated fool, so he wouldn't know that."

"He wasn't as smart as you. That's for sure. Could I also get another pillow and blanket for Mrs. Southwick? She's having a hard time in here. It's an adjustment, as you

355

said before."

As nicely as she'd asked, she'd thought he'd want to continue playing the hero. She expected him to agree to such a simple request. But his expression darkened. "No. She's not getting anything."

Evelyn widened her eyes. "Why not?"

"Because she has no manners, that's why. She showed up here without even calling — and ruined everything!"

"I think it's *fortunate* she came by," Evelyn said, trying to soften his heart. "It's made me a lot happier to have some company, hasn't it?"

He seemed to consider her response. "Apparently so. I admit that at first I tried to look at it in a positive light, too. I thought she could help when it's time for you to have the baby. I'm worried about how that will go without a doctor. But I wasn't thinking clearly. It's not as if she can just disappear from everyday life."

"That's true," she said soothingly. She needed to keep him talking no matter what.

"People will be coming to look for her," he continued. "And, unlike you, she's connected to this ranch. After they search her house and maybe a few other places she frequents, they'll check here, too."

Evelyn furrowed her eyebrows. "Can't you

356

just say you haven't seen her? She told me no one else even knows she was planning to stop by."

It seemed as though he wanted to grab the easy solution she was trying to hand him. Now that Edna was with her, Evelyn didn't want him to move them somewhere else — because he was right. Edna's presence boosted their chances of being found.

But then he said, "And if they ask to look around?"

That would be the best of all eventualities for Evelyn, of course. Although she felt terrible that Edna was now facing the same deprivation, fear and outright danger, she couldn't help hoping the older woman's misfortune would have a silver lining — that they'd both be found. "You don't have to let them."

"If I refuse, they'll suspect something is up and come back with a search warrant, at which point they'll discover Emmett's body under all that chicken manure in the coop in back. And I doubt they'll believe me when I tell them it was *you* who killed him."

When she didn't deny her involvement, Edna whimpered on the bed. She had to be horrified by the conversation, as any normal person would be. Evelyn hadn't mentioned Emmett, hadn't told Edna what she'd had to do. Maybe that was a mistake; it was much harder to hear it stated so casually. But she couldn't explain or attempt to justify her actions right now. She had to make Bishop believe she was a confederate of sorts, appeal to his desire to be liked and admired — his desire to be *loved,* as tragic and depraved as lying to someone about that was — or they might never escape.

"I don't know if that's entirely true," she said, lowering her voice to a whisper so that only Bishop could hear. "She's just an old lady who's lost her husband and her business, doesn't have much else going on in her life. I don't get the impression she'll be missed."

Her heart pounded as she awaited Bishop's response. She desperately needed to sell him on the fact that there was nothing to worry about, so he'd relax and those who *would* miss Edna could have a chance of finding them.

"I can't take the risk," he said. "You and our baby mean too much to me."

Evelyn had to curve her fingernails into her palms to keep from reacting to that statement as violently as she was tempted to. He made it sound as though he could just that easily step into Amarok's shoes.

"So . . . what are you going to do?" She

was proud of herself when she managed to sound normal, interested, fine with having him claim her and her baby.

"I'm looking for another place for us to stay, of course. This one's out of the question — she ruined it."

He meant Edna.

"We can . . . we can figure out *some* way to stay, can't we?"

"Aren't you listening?" he said, obviously irritated. "No, we can't. And that's hugely inconvenient, especially when I need more time to recover and get on my feet."

He tried to peer around her to give Edna a nasty look. Clearly, he wanted to make sure Edna understood that all of this was *her* fault and no one else's. But Edna wasn't paying attention. She sat against the wall, huddled up in the blanket with her eyes closed, as though she couldn't bear to open them.

Evelyn bent closer to the slot. She wanted to ask Bishop what changing locations would mean for Edna, if Edna would be coming with them. But she was afraid of what Lyman would say — and that he wouldn't say it quietly. If she had to bet, he'd be happy to leave poor Edna moldering in the chicken shit with Emmett.

"Could you do me a favor?" she asked.

359

Acting surprised by the request — or probably just the intimacy of her voice, since she was trying to play on his mistaken belief that they would be a couple — he leaned closer, too. "What kind of favor?"

"Will you let me keep her with me as a helper for when I have the baby and then maybe as a nurse for the first few months? You had the right idea with that. We could really use her."

Evelyn held her breath as she awaited his reply. She had to think of *some* reason Edna needed to go with them. Although she couldn't be sure, she was fairly certain it was the only way to keep her alive. Because even if he didn't kill her outright, even if he just left her behind, locked in this damn cooler, it could be too late by the time someone found her.

He would never release her — *couldn't* release her. If he did, she might bring the police before he could get safely away.

"No," he said. "I don't like her. Besides, that will only make things more difficult for me."

And he, of course, was the only person who mattered. Psychopaths were the biggest assholes in the world.

Hilltop, AK — Tuesday, 8:30 a.m. AKDT
Jasper knew he was in trouble when he
couldn't get either of the COs escorting him
and the other inmates to even look at him.
"Hey, Cadiz!" he called. "Aren't you listening? I said, I need to talk to Sergeant Murphy." He'd stated that as soon as the door
to his cell had sprung open and he stepped
out of it. But Cadiz seemed to have cotton
in his ears. The same was true for CO Perez.

"What's wrong with you two?" he cried
when they pressed him to get walking with
a shooing motion of their hands. "I have
information on Dr. Talbot! I need to get to
the trooper as soon as possible."

Cadiz rolled his eyes. "Sure you do."

"It's true! I can tell him where she is —
or at least put him on the right track."

"Pretty convenient that you have this
information *now,*" someone else muttered.

"Suddenly he can help Sergeant Murphy
rescue the doc," another guy said, chuckling.

"As if he would, even if he could," a third
guy added.

"I would! I want her back as much as
anyone," he insisted, but when Cadiz
glanced back at Perez, who was bringing up
the rear — essentially asking what he should
do — Perez gave him a negative shake of
the head.

"What was that?" Jasper cried when he witnessed the exchange. "Why would you tell him no? You have no idea what I've learned!"

"We don't care what kind of bullshit you've come up with in order to save your ass. No one wants to miss watching you get what you have coming to you," yet another inmate said.

Jasper had been right to worry. Roland had something in store for him this morning. "If Dr. Talbot dies, it'll be *your* fault."

"You tried to kill her yourself!" someone cried. "On more than one occasion. So how do you expect us to believe you want to save her now?"

Jasper looked over his shoulder, searching for the man who'd been sneering at him all morning, and saw Roland walking in the midst of a knot of men directly in front of Perez. Everyone wanted to be by him. Even the guards were in his corner — the knowledge of which made Jasper uneasy. He couldn't figure how to wiggle out of this and regain the upper hand. For the first time in his life, he felt utterly powerless.

When Roland met his gaze, Jasper's knees went weak and his heart began to pound against his chest like a sledgehammer.

"Don't wet your pants," Roland crooned.

362

Holy shit! Jasper wasn't about to let himself get jumped. If something happened, the guards wouldn't intercede — at least not until they absolutely had to. They knew what was about to go down, yet they weren't doing anything to stop it.

"This is bullshit. I'm not going to the showers today," Jasper said, falling out of line.

Roland and his buddies passed by without another word, but Perez reached him a second later and lifted his Taser. "Keep moving."

"No. I don't have to. I'll take a shower on Thursday and Sunday."

"Sorry, but the rain has washed out the road, so we're a bit shorthanded this morning. I can't leave Cadiz in order to escort you back. Besides, you stink, and the other men are complaining about it. That means you're taking a shower *today.*"

He didn't stink, so no one could've complained. That was an excuse, a reason to force him into the showers, where Roland would be waiting for him.

"You don't seem so tough now!" someone called back to him, and, once again, there was laughter.

"Quit being a pussy," someone else snarled.

They'd *all* taken Roland's side, the bastards.

"Are you going to move, or do I have to fire this thing?" Perez asked.

Jasper lifted both hands in a defensive position. "Listen to me. You don't want any part of this. It's not right."

"You've brutally tortured and then murdered more than thirty women. You've even killed your own parents, for God's sake! And now you want to talk about what's *right*?"

Terror rose like bile, burning Jasper's throat. They felt justified in doing whatever they pleased because they considered it justice. "You need to stop and think! If you allow this to happen, you'll lose your job."

"No, I won't. I'm just making sure a filthy man takes a shower. That *is* my job."

Arguing was no good. It didn't matter what he said. They didn't believe he knew anything about Evelyn, thought he was simply trying to avoid a beating, which was the greatest irony he'd ever encountered, because he really *could* save her. At least, he thought he could — if what Chastity had sent him meant anything.

He turned and tried to make a run for it. He had no other choice.

Before he could take three steps, Perez hit

the button on his Taser and those hooks flew out like they had in the library, paralyzing him with an intense electric current. Then Perez dragged him to the showers, and once he was there two inmates stripped him naked.

Jasper had never felt more vulnerable than when he saw Roland waiting for him. That was the moment he knew he *really* wasn't getting out of this.

He took a swing at Roland — he wasn't going to wait, always be on the defensive — and fought as hard as he could. But after only a few minutes, Roland had his arm twisted behind his back until it felt as though it was being wrenched from the socket. He could only scream in pain — though he still noticed the slick feel of the shower wall when Roland forced him up against it.

"Well, well, what do we have here?" Rufus asked facetiously as he stepped through the steam gathering thick and hot around them.

Jasper couldn't see the guards anymore. They'd made themselves scarce so they could pretend they'd had no idea he was about to get assaulted.

"You motherfuckers! I'll make you all pay for this!" Jasper shouted, but no one seemed too concerned about his threats. He felt

Rufus's hairy chest press into his back, felt Rufus's breath, even hotter than the steam, curl over his cheek. "I love initiations," he murmured, and licked Jasper's ear.

"I know . . . I know where Dr. Talbot is," Jasper croaked. At this point, he didn't care if Evelyn made it back alive. He was merely trying to save his own skin.

Now they'll have *to believe me,* he thought. But no one did.

Or . . . maybe he *hadn't* actually brought those words to his lips. He didn't know, couldn't think straight, especially after he felt something he didn't want to feel against his backside and tried to kick Rufus to keep him away.

At that point, everyone who was hovering on the periphery of the circle seemed to crowd closer and a few even jumped in to hit or kick him, which triggered a free-for-all.

In one sense, that came as a relief to Jasper. They wouldn't all be standing around, watching him be raped, as Roland had planned. But with so much anger and testosterone the level of violence erupted so fast — like a match to a flame — and within seconds the situation turned into a regular old-fashioned beating.

Jasper felt blows coming from all sides —

366

fists, feet, knees, elbows. A vicious head butt caused him to see stars, but the agony turned to relief because he couldn't feel as much after that.

Roland tried to get the others to back off. Dimly, Jasper heard him yell that he could handle it, that it wasn't fair for everyone to pile on. But, for a change, no one listened to him, so he let go of Jasper and got out of the fray.

Even then Jasper couldn't escape. He was the carrion and they were the buzzards, feasting on his flesh.

The last thing he remembered was falling to the floor and staring up at the water spurting out of the showerheads as an inmate by the name of Lester, who had gold caps on his two front teeth, leaned over him, brandishing the shiv Roland had shown him earlier.

Maybe he was going to be stabbed before he could be raped, he thought, and then everything went dark.

21

Beacon Point was a bust. Amarok left frustrated that those in charge didn't seem to feel more responsible for Bishop getting out. Terry's boss, when he finally spoke to her, admitted that Terry had been a subpar worker. She said that was why she'd let him go, and she acted as though she'd done her part by giving him notice. But how could she and everyone else have missed the fact that one of their janitors was getting too friendly with a patient who was a known serial killer?

The security guard on duty that night had been fired since. Those in charge pointed to that as proof they'd done all they could in the aftermath. But the security guard wasn't the only one who hadn't done her job. Amarok *still* hadn't heard an acceptable reason as to why the hospital hadn't contacted the police immediately upon noticing Lyman's bed was empty. They claimed it was because they thought he was too impaired to harm anyone; they expected him to be found without any trouble and didn't want to send the whole community into a panic, especially one that was totally unnecessary.

But Amarok knew it was more about protecting their own asses. They were hoping to avoid the bad press; that was why they were *still* doing all they could to dodge the really difficult questions.

It was so hot and muggy that Amarok turned on the air-conditioning full blast the second he climbed back into his car. He'd been checking his phone ever since he arrived at the hospital, but he hadn't yet heard from Lewis.

What the hell was taking so long? They needed that search warrant. If Emmett had left behind a computer or even some receipts or notes, maybe they'd be able to figure out where he was staying.

He tried to call Lewis but got sent straight to voicemail. Although he was instructed to leave a message, he didn't.

"To hell with it. Some things have to be done regardless of the consequences," he mumbled as he put Emmett's address into his GPS.

369

"What can we do to get him to delay moving so that when someone comes looking for you they might actually have a chance of finding us?" Evelyn asked Edna. She wasn't necessarily expecting Edna to come up with the solution they needed. But she was trying to draw the older woman out, get her to think about surviving and then start *planning* on surviving, so she'd be more motivated to fight for her life.

As it was, Edna lacked any determination, seemed so damn fatalistic, as if she wanted to crawl into the corner and die, since she no longer had her husband, anyway. She'd been struggling to go on without him even before this happened, and that only made the situation more difficult for Evelyn. It was hard enough to keep her own spirits up and now she had to constantly encourage a stranger.

"We can't do anything," Edna replied. "No one's coming. I didn't tell anyone I was stopping here. This is probably the last place they'll look."

Evelyn rubbed her belly. Delivering the baby could potentially delay the move Lyman had in mind. At least, she hoped Bishop would be humane enough to wait for her to have the baby if she were to go into labor prematurely. But there were no guarantees. Because of that and the other risks, which were far worse, she couldn't bring herself to even hope for the baby to come early. "Even if we can't get him to stay any longer, maybe we could get him to tell us a little about where we will be going so we could somehow leave that information behind."

Edna gestured at the four walls. "How? Written in our own blood?" she asked, her voice shrill. She was clearly teetering on the edge of insanity.

Evelyn thought of what she'd done to get Emmett to believe she was having the baby so he'd come into the freezer. A couple of her fingers still hadn't finished healing. But she said nothing about that. She didn't want to remind Edna that she'd stabbed Emmett, knew that was part of the reason Edna was falling apart.

It was almost as though Edna regarded her as just another strange character — like all those encountered by Alice in Wonderland after she slid down the rabbit hole.

"If necessary, yes," Evelyn responded. "Or maybe we could escape during the drive. There're two of us now. It'll be harder for him to subdue us both." *If* Bishop planned to take Edna with them. He probably didn't,

371

but she saw no need to mention that.

Edna remained on the bed, slumped against the wall with the blanket wrapped around her. "There's nothing we can do," she said glumly.

Evelyn was tempted to grab her by the shoulders and shake her. She had to rally and soon. "Don't say that."

One age-spotted hand reached out from the blanket to touch the hem on her pants as if she still couldn't believe the stains she saw were blood. "It's true."

"Not necessarily. When your daughter can't get hold of you, she'll call the police."

"It could be a day or two before she even tries. She's *so* busy. It's not like we talk every single day."

Evelyn refused to be defeated. "They'll come eventually. And when they do —"

Edna wouldn't let her finish. "They'll ask that . . . that monster who hit me if he's seen me, and he'll say no."

"So?" Evelyn came right back at her, trying to rile her. "That won't be the end of it. When you don't turn up, they'll come back, question him more fully and get a search warrant."

"My father was a police officer. It could take a week or longer for it to escalate to that point. Meanwhile the man you call Lyman is already making plans to take us from here. We'll be long gone by then."

Evelyn didn't argue; Edna happened to be right. It wasn't as though a child had gone missing. Edna was a mature adult. For all anyone knew, she could've taken a long road trip to pull herself together after her husband's death — or gone to visit extended family in the Lower 48.

What would there be to rule that out? They'd find no signs of foul play at her house; she'd come to the ranch voluntarily. Unless someone had spotted her in the area or her car was discovered close by, the police wouldn't have any reason to suspect this location over any other. And that wasn't the worst of it. Edna didn't even have a cell phone the authorities could track. When Evelyn had revealed her shock at that discovery, she'd said she preferred landlines and didn't see any reason to adapt at this late date. As far as she was concerned, it'd be just another bill to pay.

"Regardless of how many days it'll take, we need to hold out as long as we can," Evelyn said to avoid agreeing or disagreeing.

Edna pulled the blanket tighter. "We'll be dead by the time they come."

The depression she'd suffered since her husband passed away was swallowing her whole. The difficulty of sleeping in shifts or somehow managing with only one narrow cot, one pillow and one blanket between them, wasn't helping. Neither was the lack of any kind of consistent meals. They were hungry or thirsty almost all the time.

After acting as though he was mad at Emmett for doing such a poor job of taking care of her, Lyman had done even worse. The food, when he brought it, tasted better. Evelyn had to give him that. But he was too preoccupied and freaked out by Edna's creating a new wrinkle in his plan to make sure he fed them regularly.

At least he'd brought them both toothbrushes. Evelyn had never realized what a luxury a toothbrush could be. They had to use bottled water and spit into the toilet or the drain, but being able to clean her mouth was a wonderful feeling.

With a sigh, she turned away from her cellmate and began to pace in the cramped space. "This is nothing compared to what I've been through before," she said, still trying to encourage Edna. "We're going to get out of here. I'm going to go back to my fiancé, and you're going to go back to your kids."

Edna said nothing. When Evelyn glanced over, she looked as though she were shrinking with her hollow cheeks, the dark smudges below her eyes and the way her head barely peeked out of that blanket.

Evelyn stopped pacing and went over to sit next to her on the cot. "Listen to me," she said, taking the other woman's frail, cold hands.

Edna's eyes shifted to Evelyn's face but only for a second before she flinched and went back to staring at the wall.

"We *are* going to get out of here," Evelyn repeated more emphatically. "And this is how we're going to do it."

When Edna looked over this time, Evelyn could tell she'd finally piqued her interest. "How?"

"We're going to use Bishop's own personality, his own needs, against him."

"What does that mean?"

"He wants to be liked, admired. He craves it like a drug. That's why he does what he does. He's been shunned and ridiculed his whole life, has a strong fear of abandonment and a great deal of resentment for the fact that other people don't recognize his genius. So he does what he does to punish the people around him and to make them stay at the same time. Sort of like . . . Dahmer with the men he killed, right?"

"Dahmer?" Edna said with a shudder.

"You're referring to the man who *ate* his victims?"

Evelyn immediately regretted what she'd blurted out. She didn't need to remind Edna of even more frightening people. "Never mind. The bottom line is this: when Bishop brings us food, we need to get him to talk, make him waste time, give him a false sense of security —"

A frown creased Edna's thin face, but, ignoring it, Evelyn forged on.

"And . . . and see if we can't get him to discuss his house hunting with us as if we're all friends and *want* to be here with him. That's his fantasy, what he'd like to believe. So let's play into it. He doesn't want to face that we hate him and would do anything to get away from him, so let's pretend we don't."

"How could he possibly believe that?"

"You'd be surprised at the delusions I've encountered in my work."

"But even if he tells us what he's found, how will we leave that information behind? We don't have any paper or pencil, and if we write on anything else — in blood, since that's all we've got — he'll see it."

"Not necessarily. We could write what we know on the bottom of this mattress. I doubt he'll think to flip it over."

Unless he decided to take it with them. Why would he leave it behind only to have to buy another one? But it was a chance — and it could be their only chance, which meant they had to take it, regardless.

A spark finally entered Edna's eyes and a bit of color showed in her cheeks. "Do you really think he'd reveal where he plans to take us?" she asked hopefully.

Evelyn held her breath for a second. She needed to fan the small flame she was attempting to build inside of Edna — and yet she couldn't outright *lie* to her. That wouldn't be fair and could cost her credibility later, possibly when she needed it most. "Have you ever heard the saying 'You miss every shot you don't take'?" she asked.

"No," Edna replied. "But I get the point."

"Then let's do all we can, take every opportunity. I'd rather decide my own fate, wouldn't you?"

When Edna squeezed her eyes closed, several tears escaped and ran unheeded down her cheeks, but she nodded.

Anchorage, AK — Tuesday, 3:45 p.m. AKDT
Lyman had driven Edna Southwick's SUV to a strip mall — one obscure enough that they weren't likely to have video surveillance and yet big enough that they had a

fairly busy parking lot where he could leave the SUV among plenty of others.

After he parked, he got out and went shopping, purposely staying in the store for over an hour so that anyone who'd seen him go in would be unlikely to still be there when he came out.

Once he did emerge, it was raining, which meant people were paying even less attention to what was going on around them as they rushed to avoid getting wet.

Relieved, he drew a deep breath and called an Uber to take him and his groceries back to the ranch.

He knew the police would find his landlady's Explorer eventually. When it didn't move after several days, an employee would likely report it. That could happen even sooner if the police turned to the media to help them find Edna and the make and model of her vehicle were heavily publicized, but Lyman hoped he'd have at least a few days before that. Even if the police came upon it right away, there was nothing inside it to lead them to the ranch. He'd checked. The SUV was registered to her home address. He had her purse in the staff room, so no one could stumble upon *that*. And he'd worn gloves so he wouldn't leave fingerprints when he drove. He'd even gone to the trouble of running her car through a car wash, getting the tires and hubcaps sparkling clean in the area set aside for cheapskates and fussbudgets who didn't want to pay the detail guys. He'd seen several forensics shows — while lying in bed day in and day out at Beacon Point — where some tiny weed or bug helped authorities track a vehicle to a particular crime scene, but that wasn't going to be what happened to him.

Common sense suggested he'd be gone before such extensive forensics could be performed, even if the investigation started right away. But it never hurt to be careful. He didn't want chicken shit in the tire treads to remind the authorities that there'd been a chicken ranch operating in the area not too long ago and bring them right to his door.

Getting rid of the Explorer without drawing any attention and knowing Edna was in the cooler, where she couldn't cause him any trouble, should have improved his mood. He'd overcome so many obstacles; he deserved a chance to enjoy his success. But it didn't look as though he was going to catch a break quite yet. He wasn't having any luck on the house hunting, which was cause for concern. He didn't want to stay in

Anchorage, where Emmett's body was and Edna's soon would be, which cut off Alaska's biggest housing market. Anchorage was too close to Hilltop and Amarok, anyway. He preferred Juneau, the capital. At about thirty thousand residents, it was still big enough that he wouldn't stand out. But there weren't a lot of houses for rent in Juneau, not during the summer when Alaska experienced an influx of seasonal labor, mostly young single people arriving to work on tourist excursions.

Maybe he'd have to go to Fairbanks. Similar in population to Juneau, it was the biggest city in the interior. But it was only 196 miles south of the Arctic Circle. The northern lights, which appeared an average of two hundred nights per year, according to what he'd read online, sounded lovely, but the chinook winds, which could bring rapid temperature changes in the winter, the dense wildfire smoke in summer and the ice fog, did not sound appealing.

"The average mean temperature is ten below, for crying out loud," he muttered as he frowned at the pictures he'd pulled up. It wasn't as though Minneapolis, his hometown, was warm during the winter, but it was never quite *that* cold. Fairbanks experienced one of the biggest temperature inversions on earth.

With a sigh, he searched for homes for rent, just to see what was available, and was pleasantly surprised to find several viable options. Some were in a town called North Pole, though, which came up in the same search. Once he realized that and weeded those out, he found one house, in particular, that looked promising. It was an older three-bedroom, two-bath with a single-car garage for eighteen hundred dollars per month on Nugget Road. A condo would be cheaper, but there weren't a lot of condos in Fairbanks and he couldn't risk having close neighbors. That was the beauty of Alaska — the population density was so low he had more privacy than anywhere else and freedom, too.

He supposed that made up for the cold.

Whistling "Don't Worry, Be Happy," which had been Beth's favorite song for years, he e-mailed the contact on the listing. But almost as soon as he hit Send, the desire to whistle vanished.

Someone was banging on the front of the building.

Anchorage, AK — Tuesday 4:00 p.m. AKDT
Ada Southwick-Rose shifted from foot to foot while she waited to see if her mother's

renter would answer her knock. It looked as though he was home. There was a van in the carport. But it had been painted with black spray paint and was pretty beat up, not the type of vehicle one saw on the road every day. She wasn't even sure it was drivable. Not only that, but he was taking a while.

Maybe he didn't want to be bothered. . . .

She felt uncomfortable disturbing a total stranger, but she was worried about her mother. Edna hadn't been home all day, and none of her friends knew where she was. It wasn't like her to be gone for long periods of time, especially since Ada's father had passed away. For one thing, her father had done all the driving, so her mother didn't feel comfortable behind the wheel.

She swatted at a mosquito buzzing around her head as she turned to gaze out across the property. Coming here was probably a waste of time, but her mother had been talking about getting a dog and had mentioned that her renter was using the ranch as a shelter. Ada thought it was possible Edna had stopped by to see what breeds he had. If he could cite the time that happened, it would at least help Ada trace her mother's footsteps. Edna might even have mentioned where she was going next —

"Can I help you?"

Startled by the sound, she whipped around to see a soft, balding man, shorter than she was, standing in the doorway. "Mr. Edmonson?"

It took half a beat for him to answer, just long enough for her to wonder if she'd gotten his name wrong. But that was the name on the lease she'd found on her mother's desk and he finally answered to it.

"Yes?"

"I'm, um, sorry to bother you. I was just . . . I was hoping that maybe you'd seen my mother?"

He blinked at her from behind thick-lensed eyeglasses with a tortoiseshell frame. "Your mother?"

"Yes. Edna Southwick? She owns this property."

"Oh, my landlady! No, I'm afraid not. I've only ever communicated with her over the phone."

"She didn't come to see the dogs?"

His expression remained neutral. "Was she supposed to?"

"She didn't say so specifically, but she was talking about adopting. She's been . . . struggling since my father died, so I tried to encourage her, told her I thought it was a great idea. My father was allergic, so they couldn't have a dog when he was alive. But now . . . a pet might be just the thing, you know? Mom could use the companionship."

"She hasn't mentioned it to me."

The worry that had been gnawing at the pit of Ada's stomach for the past several hours — after she'd hung out at her childhood home all morning, working on her computer, waiting for her mother, who never showed — grew worse. "Oh. Um, maybe the next time you talk to her, you can help convince her that a dog would be a good thing."

"Sure. I'll point that out," he said, but he seemed strangely indifferent, as if he didn't care one way or the other about finding homes for his dogs.

Ada had never met a less impassioned shelter owner. Because *she* loved dogs — owned three — she generally connected with others who did, too. But maybe it was that she'd dropped in on him unannounced and he wasn't pleased. He hadn't asked her in or mentioned letting her see the dogs in hopes she might get one for her mother.

And there was something else that struck her as a little odd. If he was having prospective pet owners come here, why didn't he at least sweep the floor? She could see trash and busted egg cartons at his feet. Apparently, he just waded through it. "Okay. Sorry for bothering you."

"No problem," he said.

She rubbed her arms. She should've brought a jacket. Thanks to the rain, it was unusually cold for June. But when she'd driven over to see why her mother wasn't answering the phone, she hadn't been planning to stay out all day. She'd just wanted to share the news she'd received yesterday afternoon — that she was expecting a baby. She felt it would lift Edna's spirits, give her something to look forward to, especially because, unlike her other grandchildren, this child would be geographically close to Edna so she could be more involved.

When Ada reached her car, she stopped and turned to look back. She assumed her mother's renter would've gone inside, but he hadn't. She found him still in the doorway, watching her with an expression that made her feel . . . uneasy.

It probably seemed weird to him that she was rambling around, looking for her mother. But Edna refused to get a cell phone and didn't have a computer. She wasn't open to new technology, wouldn't tackle the learning curve, so there was little that Ada could do to find her except go out and physically search.

She forced a smile as she waved and called her sister on Bluetooth the moment she drove away.

"Any word?" Nadine asked as soon as she answered.

"No. None."

"What do you think has happened to her?"

Ada felt like crying. "I don't know. I've looked everywhere. I've been to the grocery store, the gas station, her hairstylist, her dentist. I've called all her friends. No one has seen her."

"You sound like you're panicking."

"I am." She still couldn't shake the strange feeling she'd had while visiting the egg ranch.

"Then what I have to tell you isn't going to help."

Ada tightened her grip on the steering wheel. It was Nadine who'd been telling her to calm down, that everything would be fine in the end. And yet she could tell her sister was now as worried as she was. "What is it?"

"I spoke to the Merriweathers."

"The neighbors across the street from Mom? They came home?"

"Yeah."

"Why didn't they call me? I left a note."

"When I got hold of them, they'd just

walked through the door and were rushing to get their suitcases. They're leaving for California for two weeks. Scott said he was going to call you from the car. They were afraid they might miss their flight otherwise."

"But they took the time to talk to you?"

"They didn't have much to say, so it didn't take long."

Ada swallowed around the lump that was rising in her throat. "Have they seen Mom?"

"No. And they said her car hasn't been in the drive since Sunday."

22

Minneapolis, MN — Tuesday, 7:30 p.m. CST
Amarok had been hoping to come across some evidence of a woman in Emmett Virtanen's life. A photograph. A number on the fridge or counter. Makeup in the bathroom. Someone he might've talked to who'd know where he was and what he might be doing. Before she was kidnapped, a woman had called Evelyn, posing as his mother. If he could find her, maybe he could find *him.*

But there was nothing in Emmett's Spartan-like apartment that indicated he had a girlfriend. From what Amarok could tell, Emmett seemed to care only about his sister, his niece and nephew, weight lifting and working out. The pictures he had were of family, and his cupboards were filled with protein powder and supplements. Which made Amarok wonder if Bridget had been the woman to call Evelyn, pretending to be Alistair.

388

Someone had to have done it, and she was the most likely choice.

If only he could get her to talk. If he thought he had even a remote chance of that, he'd be knocking on her door again today. But her familial connection made her cooperation unlikely, especially if she was the female who'd impersonated his mother.

When he couldn't find anything to advance the investigation, the reality of what Evelyn was likely going through — if she was still alive — once again threatened to drown him in a sea of despair. As he searched, he kept remembering everything they'd been through together in the past three years — how skittish she'd been at first about even letting him touch her. Getting her to trust him enough to make love for the first time hadn't been easy. He'd actually given up, had thought it would *never* happen.

But all that had changed over time. The Evelyn he'd known most recently was emotionally healthy, happy, loving, even physically demonstrative. And she'd finally agreed to settle in Alaska with him and become his wife.

They'd been so happy.

If he got her back, would all of that be undone? What would she be like after what she'd been through this time? And what would it mean for their relationship and their child? Would she even want to stay with him? Be a mother?

He tried to block out those questions as he went through Emmett's car. It was sitting in what was probably his designated spot in the parking lot, unlocked. But there was nothing helpful there, so, hoping to find something he'd missed, he returned for a final walk-through of the apartment, only to be disappointed there, too.

He was just on his way out when Lewis arrived with the warrant and three other officers to help him perform the search.

"What are *you* doing here?" the detective demanded, shocked when Amarok met them at the front door.

"What do you think?" he asked.

"Wait, you didn't break in here. You realize that's a crime, not to mention you doing that would threaten the legitimacy of my investigation. I could have you arrested," he said, getting angrier as the possible ramifications sank in.

If he was charged, Amarok knew he could wind up suspended, or worse. Considering the situation, the DA would be unlikely to act on the charges, but there was always the risk that he would.

Amarok loved his job, had never been in trouble before, but every moment he waited for that warrant was another moment Evelyn had to endure whatever she was going through. Five or ten minutes, one or two hours, could be the difference between finding her alive and finding her dead. "You wanted me to sit around and wait?"

"That wasn't my choice to make! According to the law, it wasn't yours, either. Don't you care if what we find here is deemed inadmissible? Thrown out of court?"

"Hell yeah, I care. But I have to save my fiancée's *life*! We don't have the luxury of time — or of being too cautious."

Although Amarok knew the rules and, under any other circumstances, would've obeyed them, he refused to let proper procedure — or anything else — cost him Evelyn's life and the life of his unborn child.

Still, he'd put the detective in a terrible position, and he knew it.

Lewis turned to the officers behind him. "Please escort Sergeant Murphy off the premises."

"Nothing's here," Amarok told them as the men stepped forward. "So at least I can save you some time."

That he'd found no evidence made the whole inadmissible thing a moot point, but

Lewis was so angry he wouldn't let it go. "I'm done working with you!" he snapped. "Get your ass back to Alaska."

"Look, if there's a fall, I'll be the one to take it," Amarok said. "I'll freely admit that I broke in without your knowledge, that you had nothing to do with it. And if it costs me my job, so be it. I'll do whatever it takes to find Evelyn, and you'd do the same if it were the woman you loved."

Lewis scratched his neck as the other officers glanced at one another in indecision. It took a moment, but finally, the detective released an exaggerated sigh. "I probably would. We probably *all* would. Them too." He gestured at the men surrounding him. "That's why this is so hard. I sympathize, Amarok. I really do. But I can't let you break the law. How'd you get in, anyway?"

Amarok lifted his eyebrows as he turned to look at the broken window. "Do you really want to know?"

Lewis shook his head in exasperation. "No, I guess I don't." He pointed at the door. "Go."

Amarok didn't move. "What about Virtanen's car?"

"What about it?" he snapped.

"Did you include it in your warrant?"

"Of course. Along with his computer and

his mail, which the manager is bringing as we speak." He narrowed his eyes. "Why? Did you find a computer?"

"No. There's no computer and no laptop. And I didn't take anything else." He lifted his hands to prove he had nothing.

"You didn't search his car, too, did you?"

"I may have done that," he admitted. "But you'll be happy to know I didn't have to break in. It wasn't locked."

Virtanen must've taken an Uber or some other ride service to the airport, which made sense, since he'd been gone so long. His neighbors claimed they hadn't seen him for weeks.

"You didn't find anything there, either?" one of the other officers asked.

"No, it was clean. Just like this place."

"Get out!" Lewis said.

Amarok did as he was asked but turned back at the door. "What about the warrant for his phone records?"

"You heard me. Get out!" he yelled instead of answering.

Amarok narrowed his eyes. "You'd better call me as soon as you hear from the phone company."

"Or what?" the detective responded. "Now you're going to *threaten* me?"

"I'll do whatever it takes," he admitted.

393

"It's never smart to test a desperate man."

Lewis's face flushed red as he started forward, but one of the other officers grabbed his arm. "Hey. The guy's just trying to save his fiancée. And his unborn child. If there was no evidence here, or in the car, no harm, no foul, right?"

Lewis cast the guy a dirty look as he shook him off. "*You're* not in charge here. Do you remember what happened to the detective who worked the Lyman Bishop case before me? Do you know where he is now? He's working at a fucking pizza parlor!"

"We all know," one of the others said. "But this isn't the same."

"Yes it is. He was doing the wrong thing but for the right reason. That's exactly the same."

Amarok wasn't going to keep battling. Not now. Not when there wasn't anything to be gained. If Lewis had the phone records, he would've reacted differently when Amarok asked about them.

With a quick nod for the guy who'd stepped in to show him some empathy and had the balls to speak up, he walked out and let the door slam behind him.

He was striding angrily to his rental car when he saw a short, heavyset woman with bleached-blond hair, a ring through her nose and sleeve tattoos hurrying toward Virtanen's apartment carrying an armful of mail.

Grateful for the timing, he muttered, "Maybe there is a God," and intercepted her. "I'll take that from here," he said, pulling out his badge.

Since the police were there with a warrant, or maybe it was the authoritative way he'd spoken, she didn't hesitate to hand it over. "What's going on?" she asked, obviously flustered by the activity in her complex. "What has my tenant done?"

"We think he kidnapped a woman in Alaska," he admitted to keep her preoccupied and a bit off-kilter as he shuffled through the stack.

He was just being thorough by checking the mail and didn't really expect to find anything. These days, snail mail consisted mostly of solicitations and possibly a few bills. Even those came electronically for a large percentage of the population, what with the popularity of online banking.

The apartment manager was talking a mile a minute, expressing shock and horror at the seriousness of the crime for which they were investigating the tenant in Apartment #216, when he caught a glimpse of something that made him pause. It was a letter to a John Edmonson in care of Emmett Virtanen from someone — a woman, he assumed — named Edna Southwick. But it wasn't the name that jumped out at him. It was the return address.

She lived in Alaska.

Taking the letter, he handed the rest of the mail back to the woman who was still yapping about Emmett — that he'd seemed like such a nice man, that he always paid his rent on time, that he didn't bother his neighbors, that he kept his apartment clean and always parked in his designated spot.

"I'm afraid I'm in a hurry," he told her as he slipped the Alaska letter in his pocket. "Can you take the mail to Detective Lewis inside the apartment?"

He'd cut her off mid-sentence, but he didn't care. He needed to get out of there before Lewis caught wind of the fact that he'd beaten him to the mail, too.

"Oh. Of course," she said, obviously taken aback by the interruption as well as his brusque manner.

"Sorry I don't have the time to explain further," he said as he circumvented her.

"No problem!" she called after him. "I understand. You have a job to do. I hope you find the woman who's missing. What should I do if Mr. Virtanen comes back here? What if I see him?"

He stopped and returned to hand her his card. "Call me immediately."

Anchorage, AK — Tuesday, 4:40 p.m. AKDT
Evelyn was hungry again, but she had no idea if they'd get another meal anytime soon. She assumed he was scrambling to get them moved, that relocating had stolen his attention, and hoped he was struggling with the logistics and wouldn't be able to do it no matter how long he had to focus on that and leave them hungry. The moment they were taken away from here, their chances of being found went down dramatically.

It was her turn to sleep, so she was lying on the bed with her eyes closed. Her hand rested on her stomach just in case the baby moved. She wanted to feel it, needed the reassurance of a small kick or jab.

But she felt nothing. She couldn't drift off because of that. She was too miserable, too worried and too intent on listening for sounds outside the room that might indicate Lyman was going to bring them dinner. Not only did she want to put a stop to the hunger pangs in her stomach, and for Edna to be able to eat, too, she also craved the chance to talk to him, to get some idea of what was going on in his mind as well as in the world outside their prison.

Finally, with a sigh, she gave up trying to sleep and opened her eyes to find Edna watching her from where she was sitting in the corner, using the angles to help support her back. "Are you feeling okay?" she asked. "Do you need to lie down?"

Edna shook her head. "Aren't you worried about the baby?"

"Of course," Evelyn replied. "What mother wouldn't be?"

"What are you going to do if you go into labor while we're being held captive?"

"I'd rather not talk about it."

"You've said yourself that this is a high-risk pregnancy. With all the stress and what we're going through, it could happen anytime."

"Edna, *please.*"

She ignored that entreaty. "You have no idea how long he plans to keep you. Even if the baby survives, and you do, too, you can't raise a child in this situation."

"We're going to get out before I go into labor."

"I don't want to watch a baby die," she stated flatly.

Evelyn winced. "Don't — don't say things like that."

"I'm sorry. I just . . . I think I'm losing my mind. I can't cope with this. I can't bear it much longer."

"We don't have any choice," Evelyn said firmly. Edna wasn't bouncing back as Evelyn had hoped she would, and Evelyn desperately needed her to quit making matters worse. "We have to toughen up, do everything we can to encourage each other and stay alive."

"He's going to kill me. I'm useless to him. You'll be around longer, but it'll be a terrible existence." She lowered her voice. "In case you're wondering, I'd rather be me."

"We're *both* going to make it," Evelyn argued. "I've told you before, Amarok will find us. You'll see."

The slot opened, surprising them both by its suddenness, and Lyman pushed several bottles of water into the room. One burst open as it hit the floor; Evelyn hurried to retrieve it. He was being so sporadic with the food and water she didn't dare waste a drop, had no idea when they might get more. "Are you also bringing us something to eat?" she asked.

He bent to peer in at her. "I'm working on that!" he snapped as though it should be obvious. He'd been sulking ever since he'd tossed Edna into the cooler with her. He had such low frustration tolerance, and that seemed to be worse after his hemorrhage.

"Has something happened to upset you?" she asked.

"That's none of your business," he replied.

"I'm just being friendly. You want me to be friendly, don't you?"

He didn't answer. Leaving the slot open, he walked away.

Hearing his footsteps recede in the unique pattern of *step slide* that had become his gait, she ventured closer, trying to see more from inside the cooler than she'd been able to before. "It's light outside," she told Edna.

"That doesn't tell us much. It's light twenty hours a day this time of year," Edna responded.

"Yes, but it feels nice to see the sun. Would you like to take a look?"

She shook her head.

"Come on," Evelyn coaxed, motioning her over. "You can smell what he's cooking. Maybe you can help me identify it."

Reluctantly, the older woman crept closer, took one whiff and said, "Hamburgers."

"And onions," Evelyn said, closing her eyes as she breathed in the welcome scent.

"Maybe even with cheese," Edna added with a reluctant smile.

"I'm hoping for some nice, salty potato

chips to go along with that burger."

"A dill pickle would be nice. *You'd* probably like that, right?"

Evelyn laughed. "I'm not one for pickles, even now that I'm pregnant."

The moment they heard Lyman returning, Edna scrambled away. She wanted absolutely nothing to do with him, couldn't even bear to look at him. And that gave Evelyn no choice. She had to be the one to remain at the slot, had to get him to talk to her. Otherwise, they'd learn nothing.

"Here it is." Lyman shoved two large hamburgers with grilled onions through the slot. There were no potato chips or cheese, but two triangles of watermelon sat beside the burgers on their makeshift cardboard tray.

Evelyn took the food and handed it back to Edna. "Dinner looks amazing," she said. "Thank you."

He seemed gratified by her response. "I added soup mix to the meat. That'll make it more flavorful."

"I can't wait to try it. Are you having a burger, too?"

"I ate mine while making yours."

"I see. So . . . have you found another place for us to go?"

"As a matter of fact, I have."

401

Her stomach tightened. They couldn't leave here! "Where is it?" she asked. And if he'd found what he was looking for, why the heck was he in such a foul mood?

"In the interior."

"The interior?"

"That's what they call it, isn't it? It's inland."

"Do you mean Fairbanks?" There were other towns in Alaska's interior, but that was the largest.

He hesitated, obviously reluctant to get specific, but then he said it *was* Fairbanks, as if he couldn't see any danger in telling her that much.

Evelyn's heart sank when he confirmed it. That was so far away. "Why there?" she asked.

He bristled. "You have something against Fairbanks?"

"It's just . . . it's *so* cold."

"I know." He sounded a little less unhinged. "But we'll have a heater. We'll be fine."

"When will we be leaving?"

"As soon as I can get the darn paperwork so I can sign it and take possession. It's hard to rent a house these days."

"The owner probably expects you to see it first, right? And to meet you. Are you going up there?"

"I've been talking to a leasing company. They only care about the money. They want to know I'll be a good credit risk, so I'm working on that. It's tricky when you're using a fake ID."

That he might have to use his own Social Security number, which would help Amarok trace him, gave her hope. But then he added, "Terry assured me I'd be able to do whatever I wanted with the ID he got me, so . . . we'll see."

"Who's Terry?"

He suddenly whipped around as though someone were coming up behind him.

"What is it?" Evelyn asked.

"The dogs are barking," he said, and slammed the slot closed.

Evelyn looked back at Edna. "Do you think someone could be here?"

She seemed horrified instead of hopeful. "If there is, I pray it isn't my daughter."

Hilltop, AK — Tuesday, 4:45 p.m. AKDT
Jasper couldn't open his eyes. He'd been drifting in and out of consciousness while listening to a couple of disembodied voices and the steady, annoying beep of a machine. Where was he?

"He's coming around," a woman said as a

403

hand covered in latex lifted his arm. Whoever had spoken seemed intent upon doing something to him, but he couldn't tell what — taking his blood pressure? — and he didn't really care.

"Can you hear me, Inmate Moore?"

Inmate? He wasn't an inmate. He was a prison guard in Arizona, living with his nurse wife and her two girls, all of whom he hated. He'd spent a lot of time trying to decide how he'd eventually kill the older daughter, who got under his skin the worst. They'd had a pool, so drowning had seemed like his best alternative. But then he and his wife had broken up, and she'd been so nice about the whole thing — conceding on every issue — that he'd let her go, let them all go.

No, he'd let her go because he couldn't afford any trouble at that particular juncture in his life. He'd just been hired at —

Suddenly much more recent memories tumbled forward like a rockslide, and he realized that he'd momentarily forgotten the past eighteen months. He wasn't a prison guard anymore. He'd succeeded in getting on at Hanover House, where he'd worked for a time. But then, when the torture chamber he'd been building in his basement was complete and he'd finally made his

404

move on Evelyn Talbot, he'd been caught and prosecuted.

He *was* a prison inmate now, and unless he could devise a way to escape, which he hoped to do eventually, he was stuck behind bars until the day he died. All he had to look forward to, all he had to break the tedium, were his meetings with Evelyn and —

Evelyn! She was gone. Someone had taken her. That popped into his memory, too, as well as the fact that he'd been jumped in the showers.

Was he even alive? Or was this what happened after death?

He certainly hadn't expected to survive. The last thing he remembered was seeing that shiv — and then what?

Had he been stabbed?

He didn't know. Someone must've kicked him in the head. He was already down on the floor when he blacked out, and that was only a second after he realized he was about to be stabbed.

With extreme effort, he managed to open his eyes. He wasn't dead, not unless hell had hospital beds, doctors and nurses just like those in the land of the living.

He wanted to ask where he was and how long he'd been out, but he couldn't move his jaw. The best he could do was moan.

An older man with white hair, wearing scrubs and a mask, leaned over him. "Take it easy. You're really banged up."

Banged up? Hadn't he been knifed as well as beaten?

He tried to feel for any bandages on his stomach and chest, but the nurse on the other side of the bed caught his hand before he could move it much. "Don't touch anything. You could yank off your monitors or pull out your IV, and you wouldn't want that," she said. "That's how we're administering your pain meds."

Yeah, well, the pain meds weren't doing their job. He wished he could tell them that, too. He hurt *everywhere,* felt as though he'd been run over by a bus. "Where am I?" he croaked, but the question didn't come out as he'd intended. He heard only a bunch of unintelligible grunts.

What was going on? Why couldn't he talk?

"Shh. . . . You have a broken jaw. We had to wire your mouth shut. Don't try to speak," the nurse said.

But he had to communicate. He *had* to have answers, to at least learn if he was expected to survive. What else was wrong with him? Being stabbed could easily be worse than a broken jaw and yet she hadn't mentioned it.

He struggled to sit up, but the doctor forced him back. Then darkness encroached, and he closed his eyes again, wearily surrendering to it.

23

Minneapolis, MN — Tuesday, 7:50 p.m. CST
"*What* did you find?" Phil asked.

"It's a receipt," Amarok replied.

"That's what I thought you said. But for what?"

Amarok wished Edna Southwick had written an address or any other details on the receipt she'd sent to John Edmonson in care of Emmett Virtanen. But the only thing he'd found in the envelope he'd taken from Emmett's apartment manager was a preprinted receipt from a standard receipt book, like one would buy at an office supply store, with the words "June Rent" written on it and an amount — five hundred dollars. Who was John Edmonson? Was he Emmett? If so, what could Emmett have rented for only five hundred dollars? That figure didn't seem large enough for a house or an apartment.

Was it a storage locker?

God, he hoped not. He hated the thought

of what that would likely mean.

"We need to find out. Head over to the address I'm about to give you right away and speak to an Edna Southwick. Ask her how she knows Emmett Virtanen, what she rented to him and where it's located."

"Will do."

Amarok thought of Bridget's refusal to share any information with him or Lewis. "And just in case she's a friend or an extended family member, don't tell her why. Just say that we're looking for Emmett because we have a few questions we'd like to ask him about an accident we believe he witnessed."

"I'm happy to drive over there, Amarok, but if it's in Anchorage, wouldn't Anchorage PD be able to get there quicker? Are you planning to involve them?"

Amarok didn't want to let the investigation get out of his control. He couldn't afford to have someone mess it up now that he had a solid lead. "No. It'll only take you an hour or so." He gave Phil the address. "Head there now and call me as soon as you can."

"On my way."

After he disconnected, Amarok was tempted to call Lewis to see if Emmett's phone records had come through. He started to scroll for the number, but then he set his phone aside. The way things had gone at Virtanen's apartment, he needed to give Lewis some space. Calling wouldn't help. Lewis probably wouldn't answer and, even if he did, pressing him now might only guarantee that Lewis wouldn't work with him even after he cooled off.

This was when being in Minnesota instead of Alaska was difficult, Amarok decided. *He* wanted to be the one racing over to see what Edna Southwick knew. Once Phil had the address associated with the receipt, it might be possible to find Evelyn.

Amarok shoved a hand through his hair as he walked over to the window. Would she still be alive? And, if she was, would they be able to save her before Bishop subjected her to one of the lobotomies for which he was infamous?

If Bishop was already there in Alaska with her, if he'd arrived and joined Emmett, that didn't seem likely. A frontal lobotomy took just ten minutes.

Anchorage, AK — Tuesday, 5:15 p.m. AKDT
Ada watched anxiously as the police officers she'd summoned spoke to the same man she'd met at the door an hour or so earlier. They'd been reluctant to listen to her when

410

she called in, had tried to convince her that her mother was probably off on a vacation and would be back in a few days. But she'd been so adamant that something strange was going on with her mother's new tenant, they'd agreed to swing by the chicken ranch and talk to him.

Although Ada couldn't quite hear what was being said, she didn't care to go any closer. Something about the short, soft man with the thick glasses and the paralysis on the left side of his face gave her the heebie-jeebies. One officer actually had had the nerve to ask if she was afraid of him simply because he'd suffered a stroke or something and looked a little different.

She'd found the suggestion offensive. Why would that bother her? But she supposed they met all types and had to ask. Mr. Edmonson didn't appear threatening, and she'd admitted that to them.

Still, he had a disconcerting stare. The way he looked at her for so long without blinking made her uncomfortable.

Something was . . . off. That was the bottom line. After she'd left the first time she'd tried talking herself out of it, but she couldn't shake the uneasy feeling he gave her, even though he hadn't really done anything wrong, nothing she could point to.

It could be that she'd simply been watching too many true-crime shows and was imagining it all.

She wrung her hands, hoping she hadn't dragged the police out here for nothing. But the encounter ended too soon for her to believe otherwise.

She was waiting for them to return to where she'd parked and speak to her before they left when she caught sight of Mr. Edmonson just before he closed the door. He was glaring at her with such malevolence it stole her breath.

The lead police officer, Officer Daniels, saw her reaction and glanced back, but by then Mr. Edmonson was gone, and she knew Daniels probably wouldn't give a dirty look a whole lot of credence. No one had ever died from a dirty look. But her mother's tenant was obviously furious that she'd brought the police to his door.

"What did he say?" she asked.

Tall and thin, Daniels was somewhere in his thirties, with blond hair shaved close to his head and a bored expression. "Says he hasn't seen her."

"He *would* say that," she said. "That's what he told me, too. Did you ask if you could look around?"

"Of course."

"And?"

"He said no."

"So that means you're leaving?"

He frowned. "I've already explained this to you. We don't have any choice, not without a warrant, and your, um, intuition doesn't give me enough grounds to get one."

"But he knows something! He must. Why else would he have a problem with letting you look around?"

Daniels's partner, Officer Brown, who was about the same age but shorter and wider, with a pockmarked face, spread his hands wide. "Who knows? Maybe he's got drugs on the premises, or stolen property, and he's afraid we'll find it."

"It's a privacy thing," Daniels chimed in. "Could be he just wants to be left alone. Doesn't have to mean he's kidnapped or hurt your mother."

"A lot of people, even those who haven't done anything wrong, aren't comfortable with letting the police go through their house or yard," Brown agreed.

"So that's it?" she asked. "We all just . . . believe him, whether he's lying or not, and drive away?"

"If you'll come down and fill out the missing person report like we discussed, we'll follow up."

413

"And that's all you can do?"

Daniels sighed. "Look, we shouldn't have come out here until you'd done that, but you were so worried and so convinced, I didn't dare put it off for fear we'd miss something important."

Close to tears again, she gazed back at the building where she'd often gone to help her father as a little girl. Had something terrible happened here at the ranch, where she'd always felt so safe and happy?

The place no longer looked the same. Now that everything had been shut down, it looked sad, neglected and even a little sinister.

"I don't like him," she said, speaking of her mother's renter.

"I can see why," Officer Daniels admitted. "But not being particularly friendly to authority isn't a crime."

Ada felt sick inside as she opened her car door. "I'll follow you to the station," she said, as though she'd let it go with that.

But she knew she couldn't just sit back and wait for them to come to the rescue. By the time they realized what she already knew — that her mother would never go anywhere without saying something to her or one of her siblings — and began to investigate in earnest, it could be too late.

Lyman Bishop stood to the side of the window, watching to be sure Edna's bitch of a daughter left with the police. She was causing trouble, just as he'd feared she would. He had to get Evelyn to a place where she wouldn't be discovered, where he wasn't constantly having people coming to the door, asking if he'd seen his landlady.

But he didn't yet have the house in Fairbanks.

The taillights of the police cruiser disappeared from view as he tried to think beyond the adrenaline and anger pouring through him. What should he do? Where should he go?

He'd kill Edna, he decided, and dump her body in the chicken coop to rot with Emmett's. He could leave her alive and locked in the cooler, but it was less risky to get rid of her once and for all, and it would be much more satisfying. As far as he was concerned, she deserved it. Her daughter deserved whatever he could devise for her, too. But he wouldn't let himself be sidetracked by a desire for revenge.

He could exercise patience when necessary. He'd waited years to get even with his mother, hadn't he?

He shifted to get a better view of the road.

It appeared clear, but he couldn't take anything for granted. The police, or Ada, could turn around. They might even start surveillance. He'd seen one of the officers eyeing the van. The officer had seemed satisfied with what he saw. At first glance, it looked legit. But if he'd memorized the license plate and was planning to run it, he'd find it didn't belong to a van at all.

The possibility made Lyman paranoid. He'd seen the suspicious way Ada looked at him. She'd be back. But it would be too late. Once he was rid of Edna, he'd bind and gag Evelyn and take her away from this place. They'd sleep in the van until he could get the house in Fairbanks or find another one — which could mean performing the lobotomy much sooner than he'd planned. In his diminished state, it might be too hard to contain and control her without a secure place to keep her. But, with any luck, she *and* the baby would survive the procedure.

If it didn't, he'd just have to figure out a way to get her pregnant again. Now that he'd decided he wanted a child, he wouldn't settle for anything less. Finding a man who'd have sex with a woman who looked like Evelyn wouldn't be hard. Once he did the lobotomy, he'd be able to take her anywhere and pass her off as his wife or his sister, whichever served his purposes at the time. He could take her to a bar, invite someone to come home with them and keep at it until she was pregnant. If that didn't work — or he was afraid she'd be recognized — he could always buy sperm and use a turkey baster to artificially inseminate her as many times as it took.

Maybe he'd turn her into his own brood mare. . . .

That was an interesting thought, one he hadn't considered before. The idea of forcing her to give him several children, a large family, made him take heart. He couldn't have children with Beth. He'd gotten a little too experimental with her when they were both younger. Now that he'd matured, he'd be careful to keep Evelyn's reproductive organs intact.

Everything was going to be okay. . . .

Blowing out a sigh, he shook his hands to bring some feeling back into them. Ever since the hemorrhage, whenever he got upset or anxious his hands went numb. Changing his plans wasn't convenient, wasn't *easy*. But he didn't have any choice. He couldn't risk getting caught. He'd go to prison for sure the next time, and they'd never let him out.

Finally assured that both the police and

417

Edna's daughter were really gone, he limped back to the staff room and found the sleeping pills he'd saved at Beacon Point. Unfortunately, he'd just fed Evelyn and Edna. No way were they hungry right now, and they would have to be famished to eat everything he put in front of them even if it tasted weird. He also wanted it to be dark when he dragged Evelyn out to the van in case someone was watching the place.

It was decided, then. He'd starve Evelyn and Edna until tomorrow night, feed them a drug-laced dinner just before dark, and, once the medication kicked in, make his move.

Minneapolis, MN — Tuesday, 9:30 p.m. CST
Startled by the chime of his phone, Amarok came awake sitting up against the headboard of the bed in his motel room. He was still so anxious he didn't know how he'd managed to fall asleep, but, somehow, he'd nodded off. "Hello?"

"Amarok?"

He cleared his throat so he could speak clearly. It was Phil, all right — the call he'd been waiting for. Amarok hadn't recognized the number, but Phil didn't have a cell phone, which meant he had to use whatever phone he could. "Yeah?"

418

"I went to the address you gave me, but there's no one home."

Amarok rubbed his eyes, feeling groggy. A troubling dream of swimming underwater lingered in his mind. He'd been trying and trying to break the surface of a lake and couldn't quite make it.

Drawing in a deep breath, he sat up straight and moved to the edge of the bed. "Have you talked to the neighbors to see if they know anything about the woman who lives there? Where she might be? When she might be back?"

"I've talked to a few. That's why it took so long for me to call. But no one knows where she is. No one's seen her for several days."

Disappointment finally snapped Amarok out of the fog and brought reality into sharp focus. *"No!"* He came to his feet. "Are you kidding me?"

" 'Fraid not. The neighbor next door said the family across the street knows her best, but they aren't home, either."

"Is her car there?"

"No."

"Are you sure?"

"I was able to open the man door and take a peek into the garage. It's empty. I looked around the house as best I could without actually going in, too. Nothing seems to be

419

disturbed from what I could tell."

"Maybe the neighbor you spoke to can provide a list of places to look. Her hairdresser. Nail salon. Kids' houses. What have you."

"I asked for those things. She didn't have any answers and neither did anyone else."

"Can someone put us in touch with her family?"

"The neighbor on the other side just moved in a few months ago. He didn't even know her name. The others seem more familiar with her routine but not especially close to her. They knew her husband better. I guess he was the more outgoing of the two. But he died six months ago."

"Shit."

"So . . . what do you want me to do?"

Amarok looked out the clouded window, not seeing much. "It's only six thirty your time. Stay there in case she shows up tonight and call me if she does. Failing that, maybe the neighbor across the street will come home and be able to tell us more. We need her cell number, at the very least."

"Hate to tell you this, Amarok, but she doesn't have a cell. Doesn't care for technology. The lady three doors down told me that."

Amarok pinched his bottom lip as he

searched his mind for a fresh angle. He couldn't be stymied after getting this far. . . .

"You still there?" Phil prodded.

He dropped his hand. "Yeah. Just find some way to reach her, okay? Do whatever you have to." He was about to hang up when Phil caught him with a question.

"You don't think something's happened to her, do you? I mean, it's kind of weird that Emmett is connected to Evelyn's disappearance and now this lady goes missing, too. The neighbor who told me she doesn't have a cell phone also said that since her husband died she's been pretty depressed. Hasn't gone hardly anywhere."

"She could be out of town."

"Without stopping her mail?"

"Her mail is piling up?"

"I checked the mailbox out front. She hasn't gotten it for a few days."

Amarok hoped nothing had happened to her. Without the link she inadvertently provided to Emmett Virtanen, he might never find Evelyn. "Maybe it slipped her mind. Anything's possible," he insisted.

But that was the terrifying part. When dealing with someone such as Lyman Bishop — even an ex-con like Virtanen — there were no assurances.

Ada called her husband in Seattle as soon as she got home from the police station. She'd filled out a missing person report, but she didn't get the feeling anyone on the force was very gung ho to find out what'd happened to her mother. The officer she'd spoken to kept assuring her he'd look into it. But he was so casual in his approach. Since she could attest to the fact that there hadn't been a break-in — she'd been at the house for the better part of the day and hadn't noticed anything out of place — they seemed to believe she was getting worked up for nothing, that Edna had merely gone on a trip and neglected to tell her.

She wished *she* could believe that, but leaving town without notifying someone would be so unlike her mother.

"What's going on, babe? Any news?" Reed said the moment he picked up.

The genuine concern in his voice helped comfort her. He was on a business trip, so she'd been dealing with this on her own. "No news," she replied. "I just left the police station."

"Are they going to start looking for her?"

"They say they are."

"But . . ."

"The officer I spoke to was near the end

422

of his shift. Although he didn't come right out and say it, I got the impression he had some family thing to attend or something. He filed the report and told me if Mom's not back by tomorrow morning he'll go over to the house and take a look around. Maybe I should've sent them there instead of to the chicken ranch to begin with."

"Who knows? You did what you thought was best. And don't panic quite yet. Maybe he'll find proof your mother bought a plane ticket and flew off to Sacramento to visit Nadine or something."

Irritation bit deep. How could Reed even suggest that? Obviously, he wasn't as concerned as she was, because she'd already looked through her mother's office. If that kind of proof was there, she would've found it. "Reed, I've spoken to Nadine, and she's worried, too. Mom isn't there."

"What about your other sisters?"

"They haven't heard from her, either. And if she left Alaska hoping to surprise one of them, she would've arrived by now. It doesn't take three days to get to Oregon or California."

"Who said she's been gone three days?"

"The neighbor across the street. He claims she forgot, or didn't bother, to put down her garage door the last time she left, so he lowered it for her. That was Sunday. He hasn't seen her since."

"Did you tell the police?"

"Of course!"

"Could she have met someone?"

Officer Daniels had suggested the same thing. He'd said his aunt, at eighty-two, had eloped with a man his family had never met and they'd been happily married for the past decade. That was another reason she felt he wasn't taking her seriously. But her mother was still grieving. She would never do that. "My father died only six months ago."

"Your parents were together as long as you've known them, so you can't really say how she might act without him, honey. Loneliness can cause people to do a lot of things they wouldn't ordinarily do."

"I get that. But *how* would she meet someone? She doesn't own a computer, wouldn't know how to put up a dating profile even if she did."

"There are other ways to meet people."

"She would *never* hang out at a bar."

"She could've bumped into someone at the grocery store, the mall, the movies — anywhere. What about the guys she hires to shovel her walks in the winter?"

"College kids. And it's not winter."

"That doesn't mean anything. It's possible she *wouldn't* mention a romantic interest, especially because it hasn't been all that long since your dad died. She may be afraid of how you might react."

"You don't think she has . . . undiagnosed dementia, do you?"

"Your mother? No. She hasn't exhibited any of the signs."

"That's true." Ada raked her fingers through her hair. Maybe he and the police were right — she was getting worked up for nothing. No one had anything against her mother, no reason to harm her. And, as she'd already noted, nothing had been stolen from the house.

"Look, I don't mean to be a patronizing asshole," he said. "But you *are* pregnant."

She poured herself a tall glass of water. "What's that supposed to mean?"

"It means you have all kinds of hormones raging through your body, and they could be making you extra emotional."

He should know; he was an ob/gyn. "You don't think I should be worried."

"Not quite yet. You said yourself that you found nothing to indicate foul play at your mother's house."

"What about the renter?"

"What renter?"

"*Mom's* renter. At the chicken ranch." She'd mentioned him before, but her husband had probably been distracted.

"Was he still there when the police came?"

"Yes. . . ."

"Well, there you have it."

"What?"

"If he harmed your mother, I doubt he'd stick around to talk to the police."

Reed had a point. . . .

"Honey?"

"I'm listening."

"Should I pull out of this and fly home? Do you need me there with you?"

He was at a weeklong symposium he'd paid several thousand dollars to attend. She didn't want him to feel as though he had to cut it short, not if her fears weren't well founded. "No, it's too soon to make that determination. I'm just trying to figure this out."

"I can see why you're worried. But give the police a chance."

She couldn't help recalling the chilling stare she'd received from her mother's renter. But she had to admit there could be a lot of reasons for his less than friendly behavior. Maybe he was busy and didn't like being interrupted. Or, as the police had suggested, he could have something to hide

426

that had nothing to do with Edna. It could even be that the paralysis in his face made him appear to feel something he wasn't experiencing at all — and that wasn't anything he could help.

"Honey, are you listening to me?" Reed asked gently.

"Yes, of course. I guess you're right about most of it. But if I don't hear from her by tomorrow, I'm going back to take a look around."

"Whoa! Whatever you do, don't go back there alone."

"I won't," she said. But she wasn't about to take the police with her again. They couldn't do anything, not without a warrant, and unless she could point to something that would give them probable cause, they wouldn't be able to get one.

24

Anchorage, AK — Wednesday, 6:00 p.m. AKDT

Amarok was *so* glad to be home. He'd left Alaska only twice in his life and Evelyn had been the reason for both trips. The first time, he'd been trying to find Jasper Moore, so he'd flown to San Diego to visit Jasper's parents. He'd been hoping to get them to talk, at last, and he managed to get a little information — enough to indicate they could say more if only they would. But his visit was what had precipitated their murder. He still felt terrible about what'd happened to them after he left. Even though they'd been aiding and abetting a known killer and it was that killer who'd turned on them, Jasper was their son. Amarok could understand the denial that had led them to believe the lies he told.

The whole thing had been quite an experience. And now, only two years later, he was

428

going through something even worse.

His legs and back felt stiff as he carried his bag off the plane. He hated being cooped up, couldn't understand why anyone would want to live in a big city, teeming with traffic, people and pollution. He'd thought he'd be miserable crammed into a plane, but after a long layover in Denver and a flight delay of nearly three hours, he'd slept from the moment they took off until they landed. The flight attendant had finally awakened him after everyone else had deplaned.

As soon as he cleared the gangway, he pulled out the cell phone he'd bought in Minneapolis and called his trooper post.

Shorty answered on the first ring. "Trooper Murphy's office."

"Where's Phil?" Amarok asked without preamble.

"In Anchorage, where you told him to stay."

"He's still at Ms. Southwick's?"

"That's right. Slept in his truck last night and has stayed there waiting for her to show up ever since."

Phil was almost as loyal to him as Makita. "She never came home?"

"Nope."

"When's the last time you heard from him?"

"Thirty minutes or so ago. He was checking to see if I'd heard from you."

"What about the neighbors across the street? Has he been able to talk to them?"

"No. They won't be back for two weeks."

Amarok plugged one ear so he could hear above the airport PA system. "How do you know?"

"Phil spoke to the mail carrier when she came by. She told him their mail's being held until they get back from California."

Of all times for them to leave . . . "Can he get me a cell number for anyone in the household?"

"How would he?"

"By asking around. That's what police officers do." Amarok wasn't usually this short-tempered, but he'd never been in a situation that tested him to this degree.

"Amarok, from what Phil told me this isn't that kind of neighborhood. It's a street with a handful of houses sprinkled along it, some of which are a quarter mile apart. People who live spread out like that don't typically share a lot of information. They mind their own business."

"Fine. Is there a car in the neighbors' drive? If I could get a plate number I could run it through the DMV database."

"As soon as he gets here, I'll ask him if he thought of that."

"He's on his way back?"

"You expected him to stay longer? He's been gone for twenty-four hours. He's exhausted and he needs to feed Makita."

Amarok dropped his bag at his feet while he waited for the parking shuttle. "Makita's with him?"

"Yeah, the pup wanted to go."

"Makita *always* wants to go."

"I think he was a bit put out that you left him behind."

"Because I don't do that very often. What about Sigmund?" Evelyn's beloved cat never wanted to go anywhere besides a warm sofa.

"Molly's been taking care of him."

"I appreciate it."

"No problem. Are you on your way back here, then?"

"Not yet."

"Where are you going now?"

"Edna Southwick's."

"Why? I told you, Phil just left there."

"That's fine. I'll take over now."

"And do what?" Shorty asked.

"Look around."

"What more can you do?"

Amarok had already broken into one

431

house; he wasn't above breaking into another, not if it meant finding Evelyn. Hopefully, by the time he went to jail she'd be safe. "That all depends on how far I'm willing to go, doesn't it?"

"Amarok, be careful."

"I'm always careful, Shorty. You know that."

The owner of the Moosehead hesitated as if he wanted to offer more words of caution but ultimately thought better of it. "Okay, but before you go there's something else."

Amarok picked up his bag. He could see the bus coming. "Don't tell me you've heard from Detective Lewis."

"Not a word."

That didn't surprise Amarok. If Lewis had Virtanen's cell phone records, he was proceeding with the investigation on his own. Amarok hoped Lewis was including Anchorage PD, at least, so he'd have some boots on the ground in Alaska. "What is it, then?"

"Jasper Moore ran into a bit of bad luck while you were gone."

"What kind of bad luck?"

"Well deserved, if you ask me. Karma can be a bitch, as they say."

Amarok longed for a shower or something else to revive him. He felt rumpled and jet-lagged despite his recent nap. "I could use a few more details, Shorty."

"Some of the inmates at Hanover House jumped him in the showers. Beat him up pretty bad."

"Is he dead?"

"Not quite. But he came damn close. And it could be he's not out of the woods yet."

"Where is he now? At the hospital here in Anchorage?"

"No, the med center at the prison."

"If he's *that* bad off, why didn't they transport him?" They had the capability. They'd had to medevac a victim who'd been stabbed not long after HH opened, so they'd been known to do it, too.

"From what I understand, they almost did, but the doc on staff felt he could handle the situation. I mean, without endangering the public by putting a known serial killer in a room without bars. And it looks like he managed to save the bastard's life, because he's still breathing."

Jasper hadn't only killed strangers; he'd killed two people Amarok had known and cared about, two people from Hilltop whom Amarok, as the town's only police officer, had felt somewhat responsible for. And then there was his history with Evelyn, of course. Amarok would never forgive Jasper for that, either. "If I'm supposed to feel bad for him,

I don't."

"I didn't tell you because I thought you'd be concerned for *him*. His brain is swelling, so they're keeping him pretty sedated, but when he came to this morning, he kept asking for you."

"For *me*?"

"Well, they *think* that's what he wanted. His jaw's broken, so they wired it shut, which makes it awfully hard to understand him."

"Who told you this?"

"Dr. Ricardo called here an hour or so ago."

"What could Jasper want *now*?"

"He believes he can tell you where Evelyn is."

Amarok caught his breath. "How?"

"I have no clue. And neither does Ricardo."

Evelyn's old nemesis had to be lying, didn't he?

Yes. Amarok knew it. But then his mind flashed back to the way Jasper had guided the investigation to Lyman Bishop right from the start. "Does Ricardo believe him?"

"Not entirely. Given Moore's current state, he could be delusional. Or he could be playing games. You know how crafty he is, how much he craves attention. Ricardo said he might be trying to insert himself, to be part of everything, to feel important again."

"Not to mention, if he knows something and *really* wants to help, he could tell someone else."

"That's a big if."

"You're saying he won't, Shorty? Why not? Why does it have to be me?"

"Good question, but Ricardo had no answer for that, either."

The air brakes sounded on the arriving bus and the doors whooshed open. "He *can't* know anything," Amarok said skeptically. "I've been on the outside, doing everything possible to find her, and *I* still don't know where she's at."

"Yeah. It's probably BS."

"Has to be."

Those waiting for the parking shuttle with him began to climb on, so Amarok lifted his bag. He wasn't going to Hanover House. He was better off staying in Anchorage and following up on the lead he'd found via Emmett's mail. Edna Southwick was his best possible chance at finding Evelyn.

Or was she? Jasper Moore didn't have to care about Evelyn to want to save her. He was obsessed with her, which was turning out to be close to the same thing, or at least eerily similar.

And he *had* been right before.

With a curse, Amarok sank into a seat on the shuttle to the parking lot. He hated the amount of time it would take, but as soon as he reached his truck and left the airport he turned toward Hilltop. If Jasper was lying, if he was causing Amarok to waste such precious hours, it would be all Amarok could do not to kill the prick himself.

Hilltop, AK — Wednesday, 6:35 p.m. AKDT

When the nurse finally came back into the room to take his blood pressure, Jasper jerked his arm away. No one would listen to him, trust him, *believe* him. And if only they would, he could save Evelyn. "Is he coming?"

The nurse, with a scolding look at him for thwarting her attempt to do her job, propped her hands on her hips. "You know I can't understand a word you're saying. Now give me your arm."

"Amarok!" he cried. That, too, came out muddled since he couldn't open his mouth.

But Jasper knew she understood what he wanted when she said, "From what I understand, he's on his way, okay? Are you happy now? Will you let me get your blood pressure? Because I'd like to go home at some

436

point, and I've still got a lot of other things to do."

"So he'll be here soon?" he asked, allowing her to take his arm.

Although she didn't respond, didn't make any attempt to reassure him, he clung to the promise she'd already given him — *he's on his way* — as the blood pressure cuff tightened around his bicep.

"I think you're going to make it," she said as she recorded the reading on his chart and tore off the cuff.

He hadn't realized there'd been any question about his survival, not since he'd learned several hours ago that Officers Cadiz and Perez had finally stepped in to break up the fight, *before* Lester could thrust that shiv into his heart. He hadn't been raped or stabbed, but the doctor had him on so much medication he'd been drifting in and out of consciousness all day without much interaction with anyone, other than to plead with medical staff who happened to be in the room when he was awake to get Amarok.

"When will he be here?" he asked, pressing her again.

She sighed as she rolled up the blood pressure cuff. "You just don't give up, do you?"

"I can save Evelyn!" he insisted.

"Only about every other word you say makes any sense to me. Tell you what." She stuck the cuff back in its holder. "I'll bring you a piece of paper and a pen." She lifted a hand. "I know you're not supposed to have a pen, but I'm going to come back for it before I leave."

"You can trust me," he insisted.

She rolled her eyes. "I never would. But in your current condition, I can't imagine you could be too dangerous. You'd fall over if you even tried to stand. As a matter of fact, it won't be easy for you to write, but at least you can get across what it is you're dying to tell the sergeant. Maybe then you can relax. You're not doing yourself any favors by fighting sleep, you know. You took quite a beating."

He hated to think what life was going to be like once he was put back into general population — if he'd suffer a second attack. At a minimum, he'd be whispered about.

But he'd get even, with the inmates who attacked him and the COs who allowed it to happen.

Telling himself he'd worry about all of that later, when he was recovered, he fell back on the pillow. The nurse was right. It wouldn't be easy to use a pen in his condition. He was so weak. And he had so many

438

tubes going in and out of him. But at least he wouldn't have to force his eyelids open every time someone walked into the room or worry that he might miss the sergeant. "Okay."

He fought the drag of sleep, which threatened to pull him back under, as he waited for the nurse to return.

Just when he was summoning the energy to start yelling, because he thought either she'd forgotten him or she didn't care enough to follow through, she walked back into the room.

"Here you go." She set a sheet of paper and a pen on the rolling table, which she pulled across his lap.

"Thank you."

She raised his bed into a sitting position, told him he had about twenty minutes before she returned for the pen and bustled out.

Spots danced before his eyes as he hunched over, trying to see well enough to write. He knew what Amarok would ask. The sergeant would want to know why he should trust the information Jasper had to give him, so there was a lot Jasper needed to communicate. How Chastity had realized she might get more from talking to the other patients at Beacon Point than the doctors.

How the guy in the next room claims to have heard Bishop and the janitor discussing an abandoned warehouse in the industrial part of Anchorage in the days leading up to Bishop's escape. And, above all, how Evelyn's name had been used in that conversation.

But Jasper could manage to scrawl only a few words — even then he wasn't sure Amarok would be able to read them — before blacking out: *Old FedEx Warehouse in Anchorage.*

Anchorage, AK — Wednesday, 11:00 p.m. AKDT

It wasn't quite dark, but Ada felt this was the best time to visit the ranch. She could see well enough that she wouldn't need to rely too heavily on her flashlight. A beam dancing around outside the window could all too easily draw Edmonson's attention; she didn't want to turn it on unless she absolutely had to. And yet dusk provided her with *some* cover.

As she got out of the car, she couldn't help remembering her husband's warning not to come back alone. He'd repeated that warning when she'd spoken to him this morning, and, once again, she'd promised she wouldn't. But she still hadn't heard from

440

her mother. Neither had any of her sisters.

The police had gone out to her mother's house at six and found nothing to indicate trouble. She'd been at the vet clinic when they went — there'd been an emergency just before she got off, so she'd stayed to help — but she'd told them where to find the key, so they'd been able to go inside. Now that they'd looked through the house, they believed her that there was no evidence Edna had purchased a plane ticket or a cruise, could see for themselves that her makeup and luggage were still there. Now they were searching for her car.

Or so they said. Ada hadn't heard anything since they finished up at six thirty. She feared the officer who was investigating had simply gone home to his family after he left her mother's place and any further investigation would have to wait until morning.

What could she do? He wasn't approaching the situation with the same degree of alarm because it wasn't *his* mother who'd gone missing. That, more than anything else, was what convinced Ada she had to do all she could herself. If she found something suspicious here on the ranch — her mother's car, purse or some article of clothing — perhaps they'd take the situation more seriously. They might even be able to get a search warrant.

The thought that Edna might have been depressed enough to drive somewhere and commit suicide, so that Ada wouldn't have to be the one to find her, crossed Ada's mind, but she refused to accept the possibility. Her mother had been lost without her father, but she hadn't been *suicidal.* There *had* to be another explanation.

To put her mind at rest, she needed to make sure she had no reason to suspect the strange little man who'd rented her mother's chicken ranch, because the two encounters she'd had with him had already made her decidedly uneasy.

She looked both ways before crossing the street, but there wasn't another car or truck in the area, probably because there weren't any houses close by, either. Although that gave her enough confidence to creep around to the back, take a peek into the chicken coops and even the plant — if she deemed it safe — and return to her car without being spotted, it also meant she couldn't rely on help being close at hand, should she need it.

She had her cell phone with her, though. She could call the police if she got into trouble. And if they didn't arrive quickly enough? She'd brought a gun. She wasn't a particularly *good* shot, not like her husband, but she didn't think she'd need to be good — not if she was only feet away from her target.

Dressed in a pair of black jeans, a black turtleneck and black tennis shoes, she had her hair pulled into a ponytail, her husband's 9mm GLOCK jammed into her waistband — no way had she wanted to carry his much heavier rifle — her phone in her pocket and a flashlight in her right hand as she left her vehicle. Terrified that John Edmonson would hear the engine or spot the headlights if she got too close, she'd parked almost a quarter mile down the road. But she ran five miles every other day for exercise. She could get back to it fairly quickly, if escape became necessary. Surely, given the fact that he limped, she could outrun the man living on her parents' chicken ranch.

She jogged along the road, her feet falling in soft *put, put, puts* on the bare earth while her head swiveled from side to side as she watched for any activity.

There was no one around, nothing happening — until she startled a doe, grazing in the field to her left, with a fawn. Jerking their heads up, the deer bolted away, the sound of which nearly gave Ada a heart attack.

As soon as she spotted the perimeter fence, she slowed to a walk and checked behind her again. There was no guarantee John Edmonson was at home. He could have gone out for a beer or something else and, if that was the case, he could come up behind her.

Fortunately, that didn't happen. No one came.

The gate, when she reached it, was locked. It seemed odd to her that Mr. Edmonson was so concerned with security, but maybe she was judging him by her own husband, who felt he could handle anything. Or maybe he *was* up to something illegal, even if it had nothing to do with her mother. . . .

She stood on tiptoe, trying to see if the van she'd noticed before was still there. But the carport was off to one side and, with the gathering dusk and the vines that had all but overtaken the structure, she couldn't tell.

She did, however, see the dim glow of a light in the building, which told her Emmett was probably home.

She'd have to climb the fence in order to get onto the property, but she'd be foolhardy to do it here in front.

She circled around to the back, out of view of the windows, and although she managed to get up and over, she landed awkwardly on the other side, twisting an ankle and dropping her flashlight in the process.

She bit back a curse as she tested her foot to see if she could still put pressure on it. Her ankle hurt, but she could walk. Although that was good news, she was beginning to regret coming here. It seemed darker in back, due to all the trees blocking the last rays of the sun.

The pain of her awkward landing started to radiate all the way up her leg.

Ada winced as she squatted, feeling around for the flashlight in the dirt and weeds, and breathed a sigh of relief when she was able to come up with it. By some miracle, she hadn't shot herself climbing over the fence, but at one point the gun had bitten deep in her abdomen, which was why she'd landed wrong.

She adjusted the GLOCK and moved on.

The dogs began to bark as soon as she came close to the coop they were in. Although she'd anticipated their presence and their reaction, the noise seemed amplified, like she'd set off a blaring alarm in the otherwise silent night. But there were a lot of things that could cause dogs to bark — a skunk, a possum, a wolf, to name a few. They could even get into fights among themselves sometimes. She didn't feel as though having them react would necessarily give her presence away.

Still, she hoped Emmett was asleep or watching television and wouldn't notice the racket. Just in case, she had to move away from the dogs and keep to the shadows so that even if he did come out he wouldn't realize he had company.

She was hurrying along the back fence, moving from one long metal warehouse-like coop to the next and turning her flashlight on for only a few seconds here and there as she peered into each one, when she heard something more definite.

Was it footsteps? Movement? A voice?

With the dogs making a fuss, it was difficult to tell, but she was suddenly convinced she was no longer alone.

Shit! Heart pounding, she pressed her back up against the closest wall and peered around the corner every so often to see if she could spot Edmonson. She couldn't, and she couldn't hear anything, either. The dogs wouldn't settle down.

Closing her eyes, she waited, trying to breathe deeply enough to stave off the panic rising inside her. She prayed Edmonson

446

would check on his rescued animals, figure it was nothing to be concerned about and go back inside. For all of the anger and determination she'd felt only moments before, she *really* didn't want to confront him.

A loud thud made her jump. Was it one of the dogs trying to get out? The door being thrown open by Edmonson? *What?*

Once again, she tried to look but couldn't see anything from where she was hiding. It was getting darker by the second, which didn't help.

She eyed the fence, wondering if she should go ahead and climb over and run back to her car. She wanted to get out of there.

But it wouldn't be wise to try to escape right now. What if she was caught while scaling the fence? She wouldn't be able to use her phone or her gun.

She'd come this far; she had to ride it out.

Moving the flashlight to her left hand, she pulled the gun from her waistband. The solid weight of it in her palm gave her courage, even though it felt much heavier than it ever had before. But that courage quickly faded as various questions began to bombard her: Could she shoot another human being? Shoot Emmett?

And would she be justified if she did?

All the gray areas she hadn't considered when she'd been so intent on her purpose flashed through her mind. She was technically trespassing. How would she know if her mother's renter was a threat? If she shot him before he made that clear, she could kill an innocent man.

But if she didn't shoot him right away and he got close enough, he could potentially gain the upper hand.

She hoped the right answers would come to her when she needed them most. But uncertainty handicapped her even more than fear. Her palm was sweating on the handle of the GLOCK despite the recent rains and cool weather.

A dark figure moved across the property, limping, it appeared, toward the coop that contained the dogs, so she slipped around the building at her back and hurried down two more rows. But then something else occurred to her: What if Edmonson let the dogs out?

They could come running right to her!

She needed shelter, a place where they couldn't reach her, just in case. Then, after he went back inside, she'd get the hell out of there.

The chicken manure made her wrinkle her

nose as she unbolted the door to the last coop, but she ignored the stink and let herself in. She'd grown up with this smell; it wasn't anything new. At least now she couldn't be seen and the dogs couldn't tear her apart if he let them loose.

Closing the door blocked what little light remained, leaving her in total darkness. She had her flashlight, but she didn't want to turn it on. Now that Edmonson seemed close, she was too afraid the light could be spotted through the cracks at the corners of the building or around the roof. So she huddled not too far inside the door, blinking at nothing while waiting to see what would happen.

It seemed to take forever, but, finally, the dogs quieted.

As the tension left her body, she began to feel silly for being as frightened as she'd been. Where was all her bravado, her certainty that she could outrun a man like Edmonson? Even if she couldn't, given the fence, she had a gun, for crying out loud. If he had a weapon, too, she'd probably be justified in using it.

So far, there'd been no reason for her to get this worked up. There was nothing threatening about a man coming out to check on his dogs. As far as she knew, he hadn't done anything wrong.

Stop being a baby, she scolded herself. But she waited another fifteen minutes to give Edmonson plenty of time to get back inside the plant before making her move.

When she couldn't hear anything except the wind brushing against the corrugated walls of the building, she switched on her flashlight. The old wire cages that had once held four or five chickens each, and the machinery to feed them, were still there. So was the manure that had piled up underneath. The coop was big enough to easily hide her mother's car at one end, even with everything else intact, but she saw nothing to indicate Edna had been here.

She was about to let herself out when she saw a shovel leaning against the wall with what looked like fresh manure on the blade.

As she walked over to it, she noticed several spots of some dark substance just inside the door.

She bent to see what the substance could be. It was difficult to tell in the dirt. Probably motor oil, she decided. The odor of the chicken shit was so nasty she didn't want to stay any longer now that she felt it was safe to go.

But those drops made her hesitate. If there'd been no car in here, why would there be motor oil?

She followed the drips to the manure below the closest row of cages. Someone had been digging in it. It didn't have the same conical shape as the others. But . . . why? Why would anyone brave the smell in here, let alone play around in the chicken shit?

Moving closer, she lifted the beam of her flashlight a little higher. Then she dropped it as well as her gun and screamed.

A human hand was sticking out of the manure, and the skin was falling off.

451

25

Anchorage, AK — Wednesday, 11:30 p.m.
  AKDT

Evelyn could feel movement, a gentle and consistent rocking. She could also hear the steady thrum of tires. She was in a vehicle of some sort, lying on her side, the scratch of cheap carpet against her cheek. She couldn't see anything except darkness, and she couldn't move. Worse than anything, she couldn't think clearly.

What'd happened? How did she get here? And where was she going?

As her addled brain struggled to find answers, an image conjured before her mind's eye: Lyman Bishop opening the cooler door and coming inside.

Had she dreamed that?

It was possible, but since she was no longer inside the cooler, she didn't think so. She remembered desperately wanting to get up, to shove him out of the way — fight

452

him, if necessary — so she could get past him. The door had stood open; she'd *finally* had her chance to escape. But she hadn't been able to take advantage of the opportunity, hadn't been able to so much as lift her head. Then, like now, her body had been far too heavy.

He'd crouched beside her, lifted her eyelids and checked her pupils with a penlight, as a doctor would do, while she ordered herself to react, to strike him, to kick him, to do whatever she could to incapacitate him. *Now! This is your chance!* her brain had screamed. But it was all for nothing. She'd offered no more resistance than a sack of potatoes when he rolled her to one side so he could tie her hands.

Her hands were *still* tied, or so she believed. She couldn't tell, couldn't feel them at all.

Light from an approaching car or truck filled the space around her like the tide rolling in, only to roll right back out as the sound of the other engine receded.

Then she knew — and the realization hit hard.

She was back in the van Emmett had used to kidnap her. She recognized the name etched into the paint on the wall: *Billy, 2012.* She had no idea who Billy was or why that date had been significant to him, but focusing on him, wondering about him, helped her keep from screaming once her mind began to produce other, more disturbing images.

Edna. Bishop had been so angry when he'd brought their dinner he'd told her he was going to kill her bitch of a daughter, which had upset her so badly she'd refused to eat more than a few bites.

She'd finally fallen asleep just before Bishop came in — at least Evelyn assumed that was what'd happened. She had no recollection of anything after finishing her meal, not until she'd heard the door open and roused enough to see him moving toward her.

Whether Edna had been asleep or not, Bishop hadn't seemed concerned about her until the older woman rushed him, screaming like a banshee. Edna might've been able to get around him while he'd been preoccupied tying Evelyn's hands. That thought had struck Evelyn then as it did now and made her feel even worse. Edna had tried to fight him off for Evelyn's sake — and for the sake of Evelyn's unborn child. She hadn't only been thinking of herself and her daughter, or she would simply have run.

Tears welled up as Evelyn remembered

seeing the older woman hit the wall. The way she'd fallen . . .

Swallowing hard, Evelyn struggled to banish the memory. She'd prayed that Edna would rally or show some sign of life, but she'd given up hope when Bishop had gone over and started choking her. He'd been livid, sputtering and cursing and using his weight so that Edna had no chance of getting up or getting away.

Only when Evelyn called out — or groaned, since she wasn't capable of speaking coherently — had she been able to draw his attention back to her. Then he'd snapped out of his rage, become purposeful and efficient again and returned to finish tying her hands behind her back.

He must've gagged her at some point, too. Although she didn't remember that part, she could feel fabric biting into the sides of her mouth. To avoid having to cope with what was happening, she'd willingly surrendered to the dark void on the edge of her consciousness throughout the encounter.

She wished she could do the same now — give up and just drift away. But she had to fight to overcome the drug he must've given her, or what happened to her next would be even worse than what'd happened to Edna.

455

I'd rather be me, the older woman had said when discussing the future they each would likely face. Evelyn hadn't admitted it at the time, but she felt the same. She would rather die than become Lyman's next "Beth."

Music came on. Show tunes. Bishop seemed to like those. So did Evelyn. They were so familiar they calmed her fears, to a point, until he started singing along to "All I Ask of You" from *The Phantom of the Opera* and she got the impression he identified with Raoul instead of the Phantom. He didn't see himself as a monster.

Somehow, that knowledge made her face how terrible her situation really was. He'd taken her from the ranch before Amarok or anyone else could find her.

Now she had almost no chance at all.

Anchorage, AK — Thursday, 12:05 a.m. AKDT

The scream he heard at the chicken ranch went through Amarok like shards of glass.

After getting halfway to Hilltop, he'd suddenly whipped around and returned to Anchorage. Something about leaving had just felt *wrong,* and that sense of impending doom had grown worse with each passing mile. Convinced as he was that Edna Southwick was the key to solving Evelyn's disappearance, he'd decided he wasn't going to drop everything and hurry to Hanover House to see Jasper Moore. If it was that important, Jasper could share whatever he knew with someone else who could then pass on the information. Right now Evelyn needed him too much for Amarok to risk making any mistakes, and since he didn't know what would be a mistake, not at this juncture, he could only trust his gut.

When he'd reached Edna Southwick's home, there'd been no one there. Considering what he had planned, he'd been grateful for the privacy. He'd thought it might be hard to break in, that he might bump into Anchorage PD, if someone had called them about Edna, or that the noise would draw the attention of a neighbor.

But that didn't prove to be the case. As he circled the house, he'd noticed that one of the windows wasn't closed all the way, so he'd used his pocketknife to cut the screen, forced the pane up and crawled through. What took considerably more time was going through Ms. Southwick's office, searching for the rental agreement that corresponded to the receipt she'd mailed to Emmett.

He'd torn the whole room apart before

457

It wasn't long before she could feel a slick, sticky substance on her hands. She was bleeding, all right. But she didn't let that deter her. Her life — and her child's life — depended on how she handled the next few minutes. She just wished she were stronger. The drugs he must have slipped her left her feeling slow and lethargic, not to mention dim-witted.

Dim-witted? She stiffened. Had he already performed the lobotomy he planned to give her? He'd been waiting until after she had the baby, but with everything else that was going on — this sudden flight from the ranch — he could easily have changed his mind. Maybe she wasn't drugged. Maybe he'd cut into her brain while she was lying on the cooler floor so that she wouldn't become a problem.

She blinked rapidly, trying to tell whether there was any pain in her eye sockets. A lobotomy affected each individual differently. Some of the thirty-five hundred people who'd received a lobotomy at the hands of Dr. Walter Freeman back in the forties and fifties had lived relatively normal lives afterwards; others had not. Bishop's track record for his victims' survival was far worse, but still. If he'd drilled through her eye sockets, they would take a few days to realizing it wasn't there, after which he'd had to go through the rest of the house. That contract was the one thing he needed, the one thing he *had* to have, because he knew it *should* have the address that she hadn't bothered to copy on to the receipt.

At last, he'd found it in a stack of mail shoved into one of the drawers in the laundry room, of all places. But the second he'd seen John Edmonson's name, the five-hundred-dollar amount and the name of the property — Southwick Family Egg Ranch — he'd known he'd done the right thing.

This was where Emmett had taken Evelyn; he was sure of it.

Whether she was still there, however, remained to be seen.

The second he'd had the address, he'd rushed to his truck, jumped inside and sped off. But once he'd arrived at the ranch, he'd had to slow his approach considerably. Although he saw no vehicle on the premises, there was a light on in the building. He had no idea what was going on in there. He'd just been creeping up from behind, his gun at the ready, trying to get close enough to decide what he was dealing with and how he would handle it when he'd heard the scream.

Only it hadn't come from the plant, as he

would've expected.

It'd come from one of the long, narrow coops not far from where he'd hopped the fence.

Amarok arrived at that specific coop in a matter of seconds, but when he threw open the door and angled his gun and his flashlight inside, expecting to see Evelyn, he was surprised.

A young woman he didn't recognize was kneeling on the ground, trying to retrieve a handgun of her own. She grabbed it as he filled the entrance, and, for a moment, he thought she might shoot him. She pointed the muzzle at him but, thankfully, realized he was a police officer and dropped the weapon.

"I'm Sergeant Murphy," he said, lowering his gun, too. "Who are you? And what are you doing here?"

She didn't answer either question. Her hand shaking, she pointed at a pile of manure. "Th-there's a dead body," she said, and burst into tears.

Amarok was just bending down to pick up her flashlight, which had rolled away from her, the beam forming an eerie white circle on the wall, when he saw what had, apparently, made her scream.

Catching her by the arm, he helped her

up and pushed her behind him so she wouldn't have to see the gruesome sight any longer. Then he grabbed the shovel he found nearby and used it to uncover enough of the corpse that he could determine it *wasn't* a woman.

Thank God!

"Emmett Virtanen," he said.

What with the bloating, skin slippage and insect activity — Amarok was fairly certain the body had been here for several days — it was difficult to determine what this person had looked like. He'd only guessed it was Emmett because it wasn't Lyman Bishop and there were vague similarities between this corpse and the pictures he'd seen of Emmett in that grainy video from the Quick Stop.

"Who's that?"

"No one you'd ever want to meet."

"And the short, balding man with the limp? He's okay?"

Amarok felt his pulse leap. "The *limp*? Are you talking about Lyman Bishop?"

She turned bewildered eyes on him. "Isn't his name John Edmonson?"

"No. It's Lyman Bishop, and he's a serial killer from Minnesota, who I believe is currently in Alaska. He could even be on the property. You need to get out of here."

"Oh my God!" she whispered, covering her mouth. "I was right. He *is* dangerous. I could feel it. He made my skin crawl. You don't think he killed my mother, do you?"

"Your mother?"

"Edna Southwick. Aren't you here looking for her?"

She didn't give him a chance to answer before she added, "Please tell me we won't find her if . . . if we keep digging. Please!" Fresh tears filled her eyes as she surveyed the piles of manure, but when she started for the shovel as though she'd find out for herself, Amarok stopped her.

He couldn't promise that her mother wasn't dead. If Edna had had a run-in with Bishop, she could very likely be in a similar condition to Emmett. "We'll look when we can," he said. "But first, I have to see who's in the building. What's your name?"

"Ada."

"Give me your phone number, Ada."

She seemed too upset to be able to remember it. "My number?" she repeated, bewildered. *"Why?"*

Afraid Bishop or someone else would come up and surprise them, Amarok glanced at the doorway. "Because I need to get you off the property while there's still time — but I might also need to contact

461

you later if . . . if I learn anything about your mother."

She grabbed him, her fingers curling like talons into his arm. "I'm not going anywhere without you!"

In case she was in shock, he wasn't going to insist. He'd actually already reversed his decision, anyway. For all he knew, she'd bump into Lyman Bishop on the way to her car. He couldn't send her anywhere alone, not around here.

"Fine," he said. "You can stick with me until we both know it's safe. But whatever you do, stay behind me, don't make a sound and, if there's any trouble, run like hell."

Anchorage, AK — Thursday, 12:30 a.m. AKDT

When Evelyn came to, the vehicle wasn't moving anymore.

Everything was dark and silent.

She tried to lift herself up enough to see what was going on. If Bishop was gone, she might have the opportunity to escape. Now that Amarok had lost his best chance of finding her, she had to do *something*. The longer this went on, the less likely it was that she and her child would survive.

But she was still tied up and in such an awkward position she couldn't manage to

462

even get to her knees.

Winded by the effort, she slumped back to the carpet and tried to catch her breath, which wasn't easy due to the cloth jammed into her mouth, and strained to make out any sound around her.

She couldn't hear anything distinctive enough to tell her where she was — no car doors slamming or people talking. That made her believe she was out in the middle of nowhere, parked on the side of the road. Was he taking her to Fairbanks? If so, it was a six-and-a-half-hour drive from Anchorage. How far into it were they?

They couldn't be too far. It was still dark, and it didn't remain dark in Alaska for long, not this time of year.

"Bishop?" His name came out like "Be-op," but that was the best she could do with a gag in her mouth.

He didn't answer. Was he asleep in the driver's seat or out going to the bathroom, getting a room at a motel or something else?

She couldn't even begin to guess, but being outside the cooler, being somewhere that seemed so close to the rest of the world, made her feel as though she just might escape, if only she tried hard enough.

Closing her eyes, she concentrated on freeing her hands. She was relieved he hadn't used zip ties. He'd used old-fashioned rope instead, probably because he'd found it lying around the ranch.

"Come on, come on," she whispered to herself, pulling and straining against her bonds because she couldn't reach the knot, let alone untie it — not with numb fingers.

She had no idea of the injury she was causing to her wrists, but she didn't care. She didn't feel any pain; she was too filled with adrenaline, too driven by the thought that if she could only get free and figure out where Bishop was, she could hit him with something so she could take the van and get away.

Her heart was thumping so hard she could feel it banging against her chest.

Boom, boom, boom.

She tried to ignore it even though it seemed to reverberate around her, so loud anyone in the immediate vicinity could hear.

You can do it. Keep fighting. Pull. Twist. She felt like a rabbit caught in a snare, chewing off its own paw in order to escape, but she was willing to make that sacrifice. At this point, she was willing to make almost *any* sacrifice if it meant freedom.

To her surprise, her feet came loose but not her hands. Bishop must not have tied them as securely. She guessed he hadn't been as worried about her feet, but she prayed that one small mistake — his first, as far as she was concerned — would be his undoing.

Although it was plenty cool in the van, she was sweating by the time she kicked off the rope around her ankles. Were the restraints on her wrists loosening?

Or was that just wishful thinking?

She was still struggling when the driver's side door opened with a loud, rusty creak and the cabin light snapped on.

Clamping her ankles together as though they were still tied and rolling onto her hands to hide any bleeding, she held her breath.

The van swayed as Bishop climbed in. She had her eyes shut, so she couldn't see if he looked back at her, but she prayed he'd believe she was still unconscious if he did.

When the engine started, the radio came on. More show tunes. The engine and music snapping off so suddenly when he stopped was probably what had awakened her. Thank heaven *something* had.

He switched stations as they pulled onto the road and Elvis came on. He hummed along to "Burning Love" as she continued to try to pull her hands out of the rope he'd used to tie her.

heal and she'd likely have two black eyes even if she hadn't lost *all* ability to think and reason.

Fortunately, she couldn't feel any pain or soreness. But whether he'd given her a frontal lobotomy or not, she couldn't lie there and allow Bishop to take her even farther from Amarok. She had to use what faculties she had left to escape.

Her hands were swelling, further hampering her efforts.

She almost gave up — several times. But the harder she tried, the more she bled, and, in the end, it was the blood that made the difference because it acted as a lubricant.

When she finally managed to pull her hands free, she almost couldn't believe it. She hadn't untied the rope, but she'd stretched it just enough.

At first, having her hands free did nothing for her. They were too unwieldy — like trying to use two bricks. But that wasn't the worst of what she was experiencing. As full circulation returned, her fingers and hands began to feel as though they were on fire.

Resisting the urge to rip the gag out of her mouth first thing, she curled into herself, trying to endure the pain without so much as a whimper. She needed the ability to feel if she was going to find something in the back of the van to use as a weapon. The glow of the instrument panel didn't reach into the back and it was too dark to see much of anything. There was nothing she could do but wait it out.

Regaining feeling took longer than she would've expected. Or maybe it was just that every minute in the van felt like an hour. She couldn't accurately judge time when she was this frantic; she was too afraid they'd arrive at their destination and her opportunity would be lost.

Once she was capable, she again considered removing the gag. She was dying to do it, to be able to wet her mouth and breathe normally. But she resisted the urge, in case he happened to glance back at her.

Evelyn thought of coming up behind him with the rope he'd used to tie her, putting it around his neck and pulling until he was no longer a threat to anyone. She was just desperate and angry enough to do it.

Problem was the attempt could cause a wreck that would kill them *both*. And while she would've risked it, it wasn't only *her* life that hung in the balance. She planned to get her *and* her baby out of this.

Intent on grabbing a tire iron, an ax or something else she could use as a weapon instead, she slowly and quietly began to feel around her.

She found a sack of groceries.

And some bedding. That wouldn't help her escape, but she was even angrier that he'd had blankets and yet he hadn't used them to pad the van before tossing her inside. *Bastard.*

She also found a toolbox. But everything inside it was so small: nails and screws and a level. There were several other things she couldn't identify by touch alone, but she did manage to find a screwdriver and a hammer. Both could be lethal, under the right circumstances. She just wasn't in those circumstances. She preferred a weapon she could brandish that would keep him at a distance, preferred something that gave her much higher odds of success.

Too bad there was nothing. Since she had to take what she could get, she chose the screwdriver. With that as her weapon, she could thrust upwards at least. Without leverage, a hammer would be less effective. She'd have to pretend she was still unconscious until he opened the back to get her out and then ambush him.

Remembering how terrible a close encounter like that was — how nerve-racking the mere sound of Emmett entering the cooler had been, how hard it had been not

469

to freak out as he approached and give herself away, and how the adrenaline flowing through her body had threatened to turn her arms to rubber before she could even strike — made her nauseous.

But she had no choice. If she wanted to escape, she had to wait until Bishop was right next to her. It was just as it had been with her homemade shiv. Only this time there was even more at stake. Because if she tried to stab him with the screwdriver and somehow failed, Bishop would for sure give her a lobotomy, regardless of the baby.

This would be the end — one way or the other. Either she would escape or she'd become someone even *she* didn't recognize, if she survived at all.

26

Anchorage, AK — Thursday, 1:00 a.m. AKDT
Steeling himself for what he might find, Amarok crept toward the back of the processing plant, Edna Southwick's daughter close on his heels. After the gruesome sight of Emmett's decomposing body in the chicken coop, he felt certain Bishop had been here. He could *still* be here. There wasn't a vehicle on the premises — not one he'd seen — but that didn't necessarily mean anything. Bishop and Evelyn could be in the plant.

The alternate scenario — that something had spooked Bishop and he'd either killed Evelyn and driven off or taken her with him — was also a possibility, one that was too upsetting to contemplate.

And what about Ada's mother? Where had she gone?

Once again using his service pistol, a Gen4 GLOCK 22, Amarok motioned for

471

Ada to hang back a bit more as he approached the window. Although he typically preferred using his rifle, was more accustomed to it since it was better for the types of things he usually policed, that wasn't the case here. He had to rely on his sidearm. He missed Makita, too. Approaching danger without the superior eyes and nose of his dog made him feel slightly handicapped.

He'd called Phil as soon as he'd found the address for the chicken ranch at Edna Southwick's and asked him to return to Anchorage. If Phil had left right away, he and Makita should both arrive soon. But he couldn't stand around and wait. If Evelyn was on the premises and she was still alive, he wouldn't want Bishop to return before he could set her free.

"Do you see anything?" Ada whispered as he tried to peer into the room.

Although the light was on, a navy blue sheet covered the window, making it difficult to determine what, if anything, was going on inside. "No."

"So what are you going to do?"

He eyed the door that was boarded shut. It would take too much time to rip off the boards and enter from behind. Even if he could do it quickly, which he couldn't, the

472

noise would give his presence away.

But would it be any smarter to go in through the store? Breaking glass might be fast, but it wouldn't be any quieter.

Maybe it was unlocked. Since the gate had a padlock on it, which was why he'd had to climb over the fence in back, he doubted Bishop had left the plant open, but it was worth a try.

He gestured for Ada to remain silent as they slipped around to the side. He had to concentrate so he didn't miss something that could get one or both of them killed.

Fortunately, with it being light in the building and dark outside, he had a slight advantage, despite all the windows.

Although he'd made it clear she wasn't to talk, Ada murmured, "The van's gone."

"What van?" he asked.

"The one that was here before — in the carport."

"Was it a blue carpet-cleaning van?"

"No. It was spray-painted black."

That didn't rule out the carpet-cleaning van. Anyone could spray-paint a vehicle. That gave him hope everything was coming together as he peered into the store.

"See anyone?" she asked.

"No," he breathed. "Is there a way in where I don't have to break anything?"

"Yes." She pulled a key from her pocket.

"You have a key?" he said in surprise.

"I took it from my mother's house."

He gaped at her. "You were going to go in by yourself?"

"I don't know. I brought it just in case."

She could easily have landed right in Lyman's lap, which wouldn't have been a good place to find herself. But he didn't say anything. He was *glad* he'd bumped into her out here. Thanks to her, he was finally catching a break.

The front door opened almost silently, no jingle to announce their arrival. He supposed all of that, if it had once existed, had been disabled when the chicken ranch went out of business.

"You know the layout of the building?" he asked, keeping his voice low.

Her eyes were round and watchful as she nodded.

The light from the hallway filtered in well enough that he didn't need his flashlight to see the garbage at their feet. It didn't smell *good* in here, but at least he didn't catch the nauseating stench of decomposition. "What's up ahead?" He motioned to the doorway leading to the rest of the plant.

"There's a cooler and a bathroom to the right and a staff room with a small kitchenette to the left."

Bishop and Evelyn, if they were here, would probably be in the staff room, or so he thought until he saw the heavy chain dangling from the handle of the cooler.

He nudged Ada to get her attention and pointed toward it.

When she realized what he was trying to show her she covered her mouth and turned in that direction, but he shook his head. He had to clear the rest of the building first.

Fortunately, the place was small enough that wasn't a difficult task. He didn't find Bishop, Evelyn or Edna. But after seeing that ominous chain hanging from the handle of the cooler, and the slot that had been cut into the door, he knew she hadn't been kept in the staff room.

"He's gone," Ada said.

Yes. They were too late. Bishop wasn't just gone, he wasn't coming back. The place had been cleaned out.

"You'd better stay here," he told Ada as he moved toward the cooler.

Her throat worked as she struggled to swallow. "You think my mother's in there."

"I'm not sure who or what I'll find, but, knowing Bishop, it won't be pretty."

Her face creased with worry as she stopped at the end of the hall and hugged herself while he continued. He tried to think of her and how devastated she'd be if her mother was dead. But Evelyn could be inside the cooler, too. Maybe Bishop had decided to take his revenge and hit the road. It would be so much easier to travel without someone he had to care for or restrain, especially a woman who was about to have a baby in a few months.

He hauled in a deep breath and, bracing for the worst, peered into the opening.

A woman was lying on the floor of the cooler, but it wasn't Evelyn.

"Call an ambulance," he barked out.

"What do you see?" Ada's voice rose with the level of her panic.

"I think it's your mother."

"No!" she wailed, and came rushing in behind him.

He tried to catch her. He saw a trickle of blood rolling from Edna's head toward the drain in the center of the room and thought it was too late. He didn't want this to be the last memory Ada had of her mother. But she refused to be denied. Ripping herself out of his arms, she immediately dropped down beside Edna.

"Mom?" she cried, bursting into tears. *"Mom?"*

Amarok called the ambulance himself. He

476

thought he should be contacting the medical examiner, but he wasn't a doctor, so he wasn't going to make that decision. He was holding out hope and, a moment later, he was relieved he hadn't fully accepted Edna's death because everything changed when she moaned.

Between Anchorage and Fairbanks, AK —
Thursday, 1:30 a.m. AKDT
Lyman Bishop told himself that what'd happened in Anchorage didn't matter. He refused to even think about it. Put the past behind him, and everything upsetting, too — that was his motto. He was better off leaving the ranch and cutting ties with anything associated with Emmett Virtanen, anyway. Now that he was out and away from the corpse decomposing in the chicken coop, the dogs, which he had no idea how to take care of beyond giving them food and water, and he no longer had to worry about a nosey landlady, her daughter or the police circling like vultures, he was happier than he'd been in several days.

He was free! And even though he'd had to spend three hours and a significant chunk of money visiting the worst part of Anchorage in order to get an unregistered semi-automatic handgun before he left, it was

477

worth it. Now he'd be able to control Evelyn even if she woke up earlier than expected.

He glanced at the pistol sitting on the passenger seat, where he could easily grab it. He had plenty of reason to feel hopeful and relieved. But he wasn't quite sure where he was going. He didn't have the house in Fairbanks yet. The property management company had told him earlier that they were processing his paperwork, but perhaps going there would speed things up. If he appeared at the office tomorrow morning and showed them how well-mannered, educated and trustworthy he was, maybe it would make all the difference.

That kind of approach had worked before. He'd had a great deal of success with it in the past — one of the benefits of looking absolutely average, harmless and nondescript — so that was his new plan. The only problem was that he didn't quite know what he'd do with Evelyn while he was in their office and running other errands, making sure they'd have what they needed. He couldn't drug her again. She'd be wise to that now, would probably refuse to eat, even for the sake of her unborn baby.

He could keep her bound and gagged for a day or two, though. Although he couldn't imagine that would be good for a woman in her condition, either, he didn't have a lot of other options.

Quit dwelling on the negative. That never helped. He needed to remain optimistic. To march boldly forward. This was his chance to start over and, for the first time in his life, he was going to have a companion who was worthy of him.

He twisted around to look in the back of the van. It had been a long time since he'd been with a woman. He'd always had such a strong libido, missed sex more than anything else since the hemorrhage, so he'd spent a great deal of time thinking about it, wanting it, *craving* it. And Evelyn was still unconscious, completely incapacitated. If he acted now, he wouldn't have to worry about overcoming any kind of resistance. He'd also get to experience Evelyn as a whole person, see the intelligence in her eyes as she looked up at him — an opportunity he wouldn't have for long.

He checked his mirrors. No one else was on the road. There wasn't anything or anyone waiting for him in Fairbanks. And if she woke up? He had the gun. He could simply put the muzzle to her head and demand she lie still.

With all of that in his favor, why not pull

479

over and consummate his relationship with the mother of the child he would soon make his own?

Anchorage, AK — Thursday, 1:40 a.m. AKDT Makita kept rubbing up against Amarok's leg to show his excitement at their reunion. Amarok was equally relieved. He wasn't accustomed to being without his dog. But he was too focused on saving Evelyn to give Makita any real attention. Before the paramedics had arrived, Edna had roused enough to tell him — in a hoarse and broken whisper — that Bishop had probably taken Evelyn to Fairbanks. Apparently, she'd heard him say he was trying to rent a house there or something.

It was difficult to understand her, and she was too injured to provide any other information. He didn't know if Evelyn had also been hurt or if she still had the baby — only that she was alive.

Amarok wished he could've gotten a few more details, like how long ago Bishop had left with Evelyn or anything about the house he was renting. Any detail could help narrow his search. At this point, he couldn't even rule out a condominium, a duplex or a ranch house on a lot of land.

Fairbanks was 350 miles away. And it

wasn't nearly as small as Hilltop. Bishop could easily blend in there, making it difficult for Amarok to *ever* find him, especially if he wasn't using his real name, which he would never be stupid enough to do.

"Mom, please relax," he heard Ada say as he, Makita and Phil passed the paramedics, who were loading her mother into the ambulance. They'd pulled into the driveway after using a pair of bolt cutters to get onto the property, and Edna had roused again now that they were transporting her, kept mumbling incoherently and crying. "Don't try to talk anymore. Everything's going to be okay," Ada added.

Edna had bruising all around her neck. No one had said anything, but it was clear that Bishop had choked her and left her for dead. It was a miracle she'd survived, especially at her age, because she also had a head injury, which was still bleeding. If they hadn't found her when they did, who could say what might've happened? He admired her daughter for coming after her, in spite of the risk. Ada was a fighter. She reminded him of Evelyn.

"There's a body in one of the coops in back — the one on the end," he told Phil as Phil walked him to his truck. "Anchorage PD will be here soon. So will the medical

481

examiner. Stay to meet them. Then you're free to head home."

"Where are *you* going?"

"Fairbanks."

"Right now? It's the middle of the night! And it's a six- or seven-hour drive."

They'd reached his truck. Amarok opened the door and Makita jumped into the cab. "Assuming he waited until it was dark or almost dark to leave, Bishop has a two-or three-hour head start. Maybe longer, if he didn't wait until dark." He hoisted himself into the driver's seat. "It'll only get harder to find him later."

"It won't be easy now," Phil said, one hand on the open door. "In case you've forgotten, Fairbanks is a big city."

Certainly not to the rest of the world, but it was to them. "There can only be so many houses for rent."

"There could be a lot more than you think, especially if he was referring to the Fairbanks area and not Fairbanks proper. Or maybe he said Fairbanks but has since changed his mind. It's even possible that the old lady wasn't remembering correctly when she passed you that information. She has a nasty head wound."

"I've come this far. I can't lose Evelyn now."

"But without something else to go on, you'll just be spinning your wheels."

"I have to start looking."

"How?"

"I'll go to each rental listing until I find the van."

"And if he's already ditched the van?"

"He has Evelyn with him. Until he gets another place to put her, I doubt he'll have the mobility to do a whole lot."

"He could leave her in the van while stealing another car, and then come back for her."

Amarok jammed the key in the ignition. "He doesn't know I know he has the van. Why would he risk getting caught by trying to steal another one? He might not even have the skills. It was the dead guy in the chicken coop who stole the van, remember?"

Phil covered a yawn. "How do you know who stole the van?"

"Well, it wasn't Bishop. Bishop was still at Beacon Point when Evelyn was kidnapped."

A sheepish look crossed Phil's face. "Oh, right."

"And Bishop thought the old lady was dead when he left here, so he also doesn't know I know where he's going. He has no reason to change his mind."

Phil scratched his neck. "True. I'm so

tired I'm getting punchy. I don't know how you're still functioning."

Amarok thought of Evelyn and what she meant to him. He'd give anything for her and their unborn child, even his life. "When something happens to someone you love, you do what you have to do," he said, and closed the door.

Between Anchorage and Fairbanks, AK — Thursday, 1:45 a.m. AKDT

Evelyn felt the van come to a stop and tensed. Were they already in Fairbanks? It couldn't have been more than a few minutes since they'd pulled over before. But they *had* turned off the highway. She'd been able to tell because the tires had begun to make a different sound. They were rolling over dirt and rocks and not pavement.

Maybe Bishop had been picking up keys or something. She didn't have much concept of time. It seemed as though it had been a while since he'd complained about how difficult it was to rent a house these days, though. The property management company he'd referenced must've come through.

At least the wait was over. As terrified as she was for what was about to occur, she was also anxious to have it over with, to

484

finally reunite with Amarok — if possible.

The driver's side door creaked as it had before and, once again, the cabin light came on. She was so frightened by what might lie ahead she was beginning to sweat and tremble. The memory of stabbing Emmett was returning to her even though she was trying hard not to think about it, sending her adrenaline skyrocketing too soon. She couldn't even keep her eyes closed properly and feared Bishop would notice the effort she was putting into it.

Was he looking at her? It was taking him some time to get out of the front seat. She was dying to know why.

What was he doing? After hearing him rummage around in the passenger seat, she smelled cheap men's cologne. He'd put on so much she almost gagged.

He was getting ready for something. But what? It was still dark outside. Certainly, he wasn't meeting someone in the middle of the night. . . .

She curled her fingernails into her palms, waiting to see what would happen next.

He closed the driver's side door, but softly, as though he feared slamming it might wake her, and just when she'd assumed he'd left her and was about to get to her knees so she could look through the windshield — thinking she might be able to get out of the van while he was gone and sneak away without having to confront him — she heard him unlock the back.

He was coming for *her.*

She hated that she was still wearing the gag. She could hardly breathe through it, was getting winded even before she had to act. But without that in her mouth, he'd know something was up as soon as he saw her.

Calm down. Unless you want him to stick an ice pick through your eye sockets and scramble your brain tonight, you have to play this just *right.*

She also needed a measure of luck and a whole lot of nerve. She had the screwdriver in her right hand, was hiding it behind her as though her wrists were still tied, and she'd managed to adjust her position a bit. She was now lying on her side horizontally across the back of the van as though the movement of the vehicle had shifted her around. Rising up from a prone position, and in her condition, wasn't an easy thing to do, of course, but she'd done it before, with Emmett.

If only her aim could be as true . . .

At least she had a sturdier weapon.

But it was also duller and thicker. It would

486

take all her strength to jam it into his body.

"Evelyn?" Bishop's voice held no command. He wasn't trying to wake her; he was testing her to see if she was asleep.

She didn't react. She needed to draw him closer, get him to focus on hauling her out of the van all on his own. Only then would she have the chance to stab him, kick him out the back, crawl through to the front and take off, leaving him on the road.

He deserved to bleed out right there — deserved much worse, in fact, and she had no compunction about making it happen, not with her own life and her child's life in jeopardy.

But he didn't try to pull her out to take her inside of wherever they'd be staying next.

She heard his buckle jingle as he undid his pants.

Then he started to crawl inside with her.

27

Makita sat in the passenger seat, his eyes glued to the windshield as Amarok rocketed down the East Parks Highway toward Fairbanks. Amarok knew his dog could sense his focus, his anxiety, his own watchfulness, and was paying strict attention. In short, Makita understood they were working and he was eager to do his part.

"We aren't looking for any hunters tonight," Amarok told his dog. But he supposed that wasn't entirely true. Bishop was a hunter, of sorts. It was just that he hunted women instead of animals.

Amarok glanced at the cell phone on the seat beside him. He'd called Fairbanks PD before leaving Anchorage, told them a known serial killer with a kidnap victim was headed for their city and asked them to set up a roadblock on AK-3. He had no way of telling how far Bishop was ahead of him. But there was only one highway connecting Anchorage and Fairbanks. If Bishop hadn't already arrived, if he was still on the road, at least he couldn't branch off. If they stopped every motorist until early morning, when Amarok arrived, they might be able to sandwich Bishop between them.

That had been a good call, one that gave Amarok a degree of confidence that this might soon be over. But was there anyone else he should contact? What more could he do? He was getting used to being able to call anyone at any time, but he was back in Alaska now. There'd be some long stretches without service as he passed through the wilderness areas of the interior.

He considered checking in with Ada to see if her mom was going to pull through — and to see if Edna had been able to offer any more information on Evelyn — but he guessed they didn't know much yet. It took so long to be admitted to the hospital and for the doctors to do their thing.

Ada would've reached out to him if she had anything to report. They'd developed sort of a kinship during their brief encounter on the ranch. She'd just recovered her loved one, but she understood how desperately he was working to recover his.

"Makita, you're on my phone," he said once he started looking for it and couldn't see it.

The hyperfocused dog didn't budge, but Amarok managed to slide his hand underneath and come up with it.

He checked to make sure the ringer was back on — he'd silenced it when he went onto the ranch so it couldn't give him away — and realized that he'd already missed a call. He hadn't seen it when he spoke to Fairbanks PD, but there it was, and he recognized the caller.

Detective Lewis had tried to reach him.

So, the bastard had called him back, after all. Did Lewis have Emmett Virtanen's phone records at last? Or was he enraged because he'd somehow learned that Amarok had snatched that rental receipt out of Emmett's mail?

He pressed the voicemail icon and listened to Lewis's message.

Amarok, the phone records are in. It's pretty late here, so I'm heading home, but I wanted you to know I wasn't holding out on you, as you've probably been thinking.

Amarok *had* been thinking he was being stonewalled, so having Lewis call him out on it made him feel as though he'd been too much of an ass himself.

490

I still don't agree with what you did, Lewis continued. *But . . .* He sighed. *I understand why you did it. Anyway, I'm e-mailing you a map of the area in Anchorage where Emmett's phone was last used. I'm hoping you'll find an obvious place inside the boundaries I have marked where Evelyn might be — or at least be able to pinpoint the best places to look.*

It sounded as if he was about to hang up, but then he came back on the line.

I'm afraid there's one more thing. Emmett hasn't used his phone since last Thursday. I'm sorry. I know that doesn't bode well. If he's destroyed it so we can't track him, he could be pretty far from that location. Call me tomorrow so we can talk about this.

Emmett hadn't used his phone because he *couldn't* use his phone. Lyman had probably killed him the moment he arrived in Alaska. How he'd gotten the better of someone so much bigger and stronger Amarok couldn't even begin to guess. Maybe he had a gun and trust, or overconfidence, had left Emmett vulnerable. Amarok hadn't done enough with the body to determine how Emmett was killed. He hadn't had the time, hadn't wanted to destroy any evidence. Determining the cause of death was the medical examiner's job, anyway.

Makita seemed to be getting sleepy. He

491

yawned widely as Amarok returned Lewis's call. Amarok wasn't expecting the detective to pick up; he merely wanted to leave a message.

Before he could do that, however, he got a call himself.

Pulling the phone away from his ear to see who was trying to reach him, he cursed. This was a call he'd been dreading.

It was Brianne, Evelyn's sister. Evelyn's entire family was frantic. Evelyn had been missing for over a week. Her mother hadn't even been functional since receiving the news.

And now he had to tell them that he wasn't really much closer to finding her.

Between Anchorage and Fairbanks, AK — Thursday, 2:05 a.m. AKDT

Evelyn tried not to hold her breath as Bishop brushed the hair off her face. He'd left the back doors open when he climbed into the van with her, so, thanks to the cabin light, she knew he could see her quite well despite the darkness of the woods around them.

She had to make it appear as though she were sleeping peacefully. He would find it strange if her chest weren't rising and falling — or if her eyes were scrunched too tightly closed. But it was so difficult not to try to peek at what he was doing.

She longed to use the screwdriver she had hidden behind her back right away. She was in full fight-or-flight mode. But she could hear him and guessed he was positioned too close to the open doors. If she tried to stab him now, he'd just rear up in surprise and fall out, and then he'd be on her again before she could crawl into the front of the van and drive off.

No. She had to wait until he was fully committed to the rape he obviously had in mind. Only once he dropped his pants along with his defenses, was overcome with lust, would she have the opportunity to do enough damage to possibly save herself.

When she didn't move, didn't react to his touch or his voice, he said, "You are *so* elegant. I've never seen a more beautiful woman. I think I've loved you from first sight."

Love? The only person Bishop loved was himself, but he *did* crave attention, admiration and, of course, physical gratification.

Evelyn was so stiff she was afraid she'd give herself away before she could make a concerted effort to stab him.

"Let me touch you," he whispered. "What are you saying? You want me, too? Really? I

493

never knew."

The fantasy he was playing out was so confusing for a rape. He was approaching her gently, kindly. Luckily for her, Bishop didn't have a taste for violence unless he felt threatened or he was angry. She and her baby had that going for them. But she also knew he'd switch the second she offered any resistance. She'd seen him turn into Mr. Hyde with Edna. And she'd heard about his encounters with Beth.

Right now, he was enjoying pretending that this was consensual, as though they were lovers, which fit with the odd things he'd said about becoming the father of her baby.

When his hand covered her breast and squeezed, it was all she could do not to recoil. But she remained perfectly still. He was starting to get aroused; she could tell by the shallowness of his breathing. She needed that, needed the testosterone in his system to interfere with his thinking.

"You feel like a goddess," he whispered. "And it's been so long for me. All I did was dream about making love to you while I was away."

At some point, he'd realize her legs weren't tied. If he planned on mounting her, he'd expect to untie them first. She'd have to act as soon as his hands wandered low enough, but he wasn't in any hurry to get down to business. He seemed to relish the anticipation, wanted to make a whole production of it.

She kept telling herself to ignore the way his fingers were caressing her nipple, the overpowering scent of his cologne and the breathless quality of his voice, all of which acted on her nerves like nails going down a chalkboard. But she couldn't manage to lie still when he removed the gag and his wet, soft lips closed over hers, licking and sucking.

The second he slid his tongue into her mouth, she bit down as hard as she could, until she tasted blood, and brought the screwdriver around to stab him.

She wanted to feel the metal slide into his abdomen all the way to the hilt. Only then could she be somewhat assured that she'd hurt him as badly as she needed to. But she couldn't get it to go any deeper than an inch or so.

She must've hit a rib!

She drew back to thrust again; she had to act fast.

He slugged her in the jaw before she could. It was a knee-jerk reaction to the pain of her bite and her first thrust, both of which had happened at the same time, and not a particularly powerful blow. She didn't feel his *full* response until a second later, when the initial shock wore off and he realized she wasn't only awake but free of the ropes and fighting to achieve her freedom.

Using the leverage of his body, he rolled her onto her back and pinned her right hand to the floor, squeezing so tightly she had to release her weapon. Then he seemed to fumble for something he couldn't find — *A weapon of his own? Maybe a knife or a gun?* — buying her a few precious seconds before his hands closed around her throat.

He cursed at her as he began to squeeze, just like he had with Edna.

Unable to pry his hands away, Evelyn began to buck, knocking him off center just enough that he had to let go of her neck to stop himself from being thrown to one side.

She screamed for help the second she was capable, as loudly as possible, and she kept screaming and thrashing around, trying to reach the screwdriver again, or the hammer.

Even if she couldn't find a weapon, if she could just get around him and get out she could disappear into the thick stand of trees she'd glimpsed outside.

"Shut up, you *bitch*!" he cried, and slapped her so hard her ears rang.

The fight wasn't going well. She was losing, and she knew it. It was only a matter of time before he subdued her again. And then what would she do? She'd already sprung her surprise, knew she would never have another chance, not now that he understood how determined she was to get away.

"I've got a gun! Do you want me to kill your baby?" he yelled. "Kill *you*? Here I am offering to love you, to pleasure you. And this is what I get. Haven't I been good to you?" he railed, and, shaking her like a rag doll, started to choke her again.

Stars danced before Evelyn's eyes. He'd mentioned a gun. That had to be what he'd been searching for before. If only *she* could find it.

In order to do that, however, she had to get him off her.

Although she clawed at his hands, his arms and his face, it was no good. She was growing weaker, could feel herself losing consciousness.

And then, suddenly, the pressure eased. He grabbed something from the floor not far away — she was pretty sure it was indeed the gun he'd mentioned — and jumped off her.

She gasped for breath, filling her lungs with air. Her eyes were watering, and her limbs felt like rubber.

Why hadn't he shot her? Where had he gone?

It took several moments before she could think straight, which turned out to be a tragedy. Had she been able to gather her wits sooner, she might've had another chance to escape. But it wasn't until Bishop slammed the back doors, jumped into the driver's seat and revved the engine that she realized he'd been interrupted.

Someone else had come upon them. In her short-term memory, she could recall hearing voices: *Hey, what are you doing out here? What's going on?*

She screamed and banged on the walls of the van, but she was afraid whoever it was — *Hunters? The police? A nearby home or cabin owner?* — couldn't hear her.

And then the chance was gone.

She fell back, rolling into the opposite wall as Bishop put the transmission in gear, backed up so fast it caused the van to sway from side to side and took off, the tires bouncing over boulders and ruts as he drove relentlessly away.

Between Anchorage and Fairbanks, AK — Thursday, 2:20 a.m. AKDT

Bishop could feel something wet soaking

498

his shirt and knew it was blood. The bitch had *stabbed* him! He didn't know what she'd used. He'd been too frantic to pay attention to it in those rage-filled seconds immediately after. But he was hurting, and it was her fault. He'd also injured his lame leg in the mad scramble to reach the driver's seat and get out of the forest before those hunters, who were out spotlighting, no doubt — as if what they were doing was any more legal than what he was doing — could figure out he had a high-profile kidnap victim in his van.

Part of him worried he'd pop a tire driving out of the forest so recklessly. The van jounced and swayed, throwing him back and forth and making him gasp in pain, as he navigated the narrow dirt road to the highway, but it didn't take long to reach the pavement.

As soon as he did, he made sure he had the gun he'd grabbed as he got out of the back of the van and pressed the gas pedal down.

Evelyn, who'd been knocked about in the back, was still trying to right herself, so he checked his rearview mirror for headlights.

There was a pair coming up on him. They had their brights on, which suddenly dimmed.

He didn't think it was the hunters. They couldn't have been close enough to their vehicle when they came upon him to be able to jump in it and give chase so quickly.

Sure enough, the other car fell back and disappeared from view.

No one was coming after him, thank God. He was in the clear. Even if the hunters had reached their truck or car by now, they wouldn't be able to catch him. He doubted they'd be able to tell the police, or anyone else, either — not before they got back to the city. No way did they have cell service. They were in the middle of nowhere, not even halfway to Fairbanks.

Evelyn, however, was still a problem. She was no longer tied up and she had access to whatever she'd used to stab him. He hadn't had a chance to pick up whatever it was. He'd been too worried about reclaiming the gun.

Turning on the cabin light so he'd be able to see her, he checked his rearview mirror. After attempting, unsuccessfully, to get out the back and, he supposed, jump onto the road, which would probably have killed her, she was now trying to reach him *with a hammer*!

He jerked the wheel, throwing her off balance and knocking her down. But he had to

500

keep driving like a maniac to make sure she stayed down, and he was afraid it would cause him to wreck.

He had to pull over so he could tie her up again and check his wound, and he had to do it right away.

While he was at it, he'd knock her out with that hammer she was wielding and give her a lobotomy. She'd had plenty of chances to behave. It wasn't *his* fault he was going to cut into her brain while she was pregnant.

He gripped his side to slow the bleeding and ease the pain.

So much for trying to be nice.

She'd just caused him the last problem she'd ever be able to give him.

Between Anchorage and Fairbanks, AK — Thursday, 2:30 a.m. AKDT

When Brianne had called, it was just after six her time. Amarok assumed she'd wanted to talk to him before her mother got up. She was staying with her folks so they could help her take care of the newborn.

She'd said baby Caden was doing fine, and she seemed to be holding up herself. But she'd been understandably subdued and concerned, as he'd known she would be, about Evelyn — Lara too. Thanks to what was going on, Lara had fallen into a

501

deep depression. The doctor had her on a high dose of anti-anxiety meds and was giving her sleeping pills just so she could get through the nights.

Amarok felt terrible that he couldn't tell Evelyn's family he had everything under control. He wished he could. But he had no idea how this would end, and he had to be honest about that. He couldn't set them up, give them false expectations.

He studied the road ahead, searching for taillights. Every new vehicle he came upon offered him fresh hope, until he drew close enough to see that he hadn't yet found the van.

His eyes flicked to the clock on his dashboard. How much longer could it take? He wasn't getting to Fairbanks fast enough. What if Bishop was already there? What if he was too late?

Raking his fingers through his hair, Amarok struggled to fight off another wave of exhaustion. He wasn't at his best. He wasn't anywhere near his best. He couldn't even think clearly anymore.

But he had to keep going. This could be his only chance to recover Evelyn and, God willing, their child — if their child was still alive.

He picked up his phone to see if he had

cellular service.

He didn't. That wasn't unexpected, but he wished he could check in with Fairbanks PD, make sure they had their roadblock in place. Even if *he* couldn't catch up with Bishop, maybe *they'd* stop him and put an end to this nightmare.

He contemplated the call he'd received from Shorty after hanging up with Brianne. Shorty had been so eager to tell him that Jasper had given up his information and named a particular warehouse in the industrial part of Anchorage as the place where Evelyn would be. But Amarok couldn't imagine how that related to anything he'd learned himself, so he was glad he hadn't driven all the way to Hilltop. Had he gone to Hanover House instead of Edna Southwick's, it would've set him back by two or three hours. He would've missed finding Edna and receiving the much more valuable information she'd provided.

For all he knew, she'd passed away since, so those two or three hours could've made all the difference. Going to the prison instead might even have cost him the opportunity he had now of catching up with Bishop before Bishop disappeared into the three hundred thousand people who populated the city of Fairbanks.

Dawn was breaking. Amarok could see the sun rising over the tops of the mountains and was grateful for the light. Not only did it help him stay alert, but also if he *did* come upon Bishop, at least now he'd be able to see him and anything he might have in his hands.

That could make all the difference.

His mother entered his mind, his father's words regarding his mother, too, but he quickly banished any thought of them. He'd said it before, but what he was going through was bad enough without having to address the resentment he felt toward the woman who'd given him birth —

He slammed on his brakes.

Mikita half-slid off the seat, grunting.

"Sorry, buddy." He'd been pushing forward so fast, thinking he'd find Bishop on the road ahead and not pulled over on the side, that he almost missed the black van, only the back of which he could see, parked down a dirt road off to one side. It looked as though it had been spray-painted, that *this* was the van he'd been searching for, but he couldn't be sure. It was almost hidden by trees. Had the driver pulled any farther off the road, Amarok would've missed it. And had this happened any earlier, he wouldn't have been able to see

504

for the dark.

As it was, he'd flown past it before the sight registered.

Had he caught up with them? If so, he had no backup, no help from Fairbanks PD, since any roadblock they put up was still several hours away.

He had no cell service, so he couldn't alert anyone, either. And he had no idea what he'd be facing, whether Bishop had a gun or some other weapon.

But he was used to working alone.

After pulling into the trees a quarter mile or so beyond the van, he grabbed his rifle, climbed out and waited for Makita to jump down. "Let's go get Evelyn," he murmured softly, and motioned for his dog, who knew what to do from the countless times they'd had to creep up on hunters who were spotlighting, to follow him quietly and at a distance.

28

The metallic taste of blood filled Evelyn's mouth.

She'd dropped the hammer and stopped fighting a split second after Bishop waved a gun in her face, screaming he'd shoot her if she didn't shut up and hold still. But he was so upset that she'd stabbed him, so enraged that she would try to escape after all he'd done so that they could be together, as he put it, he lost control. Retying her hands and feet wasn't enough. He'd slapped her several times with his left hand before using the gun in his right to strike a much more savage blow, which was why she had blood running from her nose and her mouth.

He was bleeding, too, even though she hadn't been able to stab him very deeply. His shirt was soaked, and the red stain on his pants was growing ever larger. She could see it easily now that it was getting light.

"If I can't fix this — if I have to risk capture by going to a hospital, I'm going to kill you before I leave!" he gasped, yanking up his shirt to take a look at his own injury. "I would've been so good to you. But you won't meet me halfway."

Seeing the gaping wound in his soft, white belly made him flinch.

He fixated on it while Evelyn struggled to regain some of her faculties. Whatever drug he'd slipped her last night with dinner had worn off, but her head was still swimming from the aftereffects, what she'd witnessed with Edna, the lack of sleep and the beating.

"You were . . . trying to . . . rape me," she pointed out, speaking despite her swollen lip. She hoped appealing to logic would get him to see reason, help him to calm down. No matter what, he was far more educated than most of the psychopaths she'd studied. He had to understand what had provoked her, didn't he?

"No. I wasn't *raping* you," he snarled. "I was making love to you. You'll soon learn that there's a difference."

So that was how he rationalized it. She almost said so out loud but caught herself just in time. She didn't dare provoke him any further.

"What do you have to say to that, smarty-pants?" he demanded.

Apparently, he could tell she had a comeback on the tip of her tongue.

"You're not so clever," he spat when she remained silent.

As intelligent as he was, he sounded like he was no more than eight years old. But she'd seen that type of thing so often in her studies — grown men and women arrested at an early stage of development because of severe emotional trauma. By being abandoned by his mother, who chose her new husband over her children, Bishop had endured something that would be incredibly hurtful. He'd been left at the mall, of all places, with Beth, who'd been only ten at the time. And when they finally managed to get home via a city bus? They'd found the house empty, completely cleaned out. His mother had left not only the city but also the state, without giving them any way to find her.

It was no excuse for what he'd become, of course. A lot of people endured abandonment and abuse without becoming serial killers. But given his mother was one of his first victims, Evelyn felt safe in assuming his childhood had, indeed, warped his brain. Without what he'd been through, maybe he wouldn't have become what he was.

"Aren't you going to promise me that you'll behave from here on out? That you won't try to escape?" he taunted. "Well, don't bother. Now I know you're a liar, just like my mother. You don't know how to love anyone. I can't trust you."

Evelyn searched for words she could use to placate him. She'd made him no promises; any promise he remembered was a figment of his imagination. But he seemed to rewrite the script however he wanted it to go.

Still, she had to do *something* to buy time, didn't she? She had no more energy, no more strength with which to fight.

What was the point of continuing to fight, anyway? She'd already given it her best. What good would another hour or two do? Amarok wouldn't be able to find her that soon. They were out in the middle of nowhere, and Bishop was going to give her a transorbital lobotomy before they got back on the road.

Part of her wanted to take a bullet instead of allowing him to cut into her brain — except the sudden thought that, no matter what happened to her, by some miracle her baby might survive and be rescued one day, if only she stuck around long enough to finish carrying it, kept her from getting *too* reckless.

She could choose death over the life she'd have with Bishop for herself, but she couldn't make that choice for her child.

She struggled to speak despite a hoarse throat that hurt when she tried to talk. "Just . . . get it over with. Maybe if I don't have my brain, I won't want to puke every time you touch me."

He blinked, obviously shocked by the vitriol in her words. "You're vile! The worst kind of whore!" he cried, and disappeared for several seconds.

Evelyn closed her eyes as she heard him rummaging in the glove compartment. She wanted her last thought to be of Amarok, to be the memory of the love and fulfillment he'd provided.

As Bishop returned with the ice pick, she wished she could touch her belly, try to reassure her unborn child in some small way. Or say good-bye. "Will you promise me one thing?" she asked dully.

Taken aback by the calm in her voice, he hesitated. "What?"

"If I don't make it, will you try to save my child?"

He scowled at her. "Of course. I want it to live, too," he replied gruffly.

The van swayed as he climbed inside, and the terror Evelyn thought she'd vanquished rose inside her again. "Aren't you going to knock me out?"

"With what? The hammer you tried to use on me? That could do even more damage — damage I can't control as well."

"What did you give me before?"

"Some sleeping pills I took from Beacon Point — the ones they gave me every night. But they will take too long to kick in. I only need a few minutes." He straddled her, taking care to sit on her chest and not on the baby, as if he were doing her a big favor by having that much consideration.

She considered bucking him off. But he'd only begin to beat her again, and if he got too vicious she wouldn't survive. That meant the baby wouldn't, either.

Tears ran into the hair at her temples as she saw the sharp point of the ice pick coming toward her. And, even though she told herself not to, she couldn't help screaming.

*Between Anchorage and Fairbanks, AK —
Thursday, 2:43 a.m. AKDT*

Amarok didn't have time to plan anything that might draw Bishop away from the van or help him recover Evelyn without a dangerous confrontation. He'd barely reached the area where the van was parked when he saw Bishop get into the back of it and heard Evelyn cry out.

Was he raping her? *Killing* her? Hurting their baby?

Making a motion with his hand, he let Makita know to stay back.

The dog obeyed as Amarok rushed from the trees he'd been using to cover his approach. He didn't have much of a plan. There wasn't time to set up anything. He could only bang on the side of the vehicle to startle Bishop and, hopefully, draw his attention away from Evelyn.

"Come out with your hands up!" he yelled, his rifle raised to his shoulder as he edged around so that he could see inside the open doors in back.

Sure enough, Evelyn was there. Alive but tied up and bleeding.

Bishop fisted his hand in her hair and pulled her up and in front of him as he moved to the back bumper. "You come any closer, I'll blow her brains out," he warned, holding a gun to her head with his other hand.

Amarok's eyes narrowed until all he could see was his target. Could he shoot Bishop before Bishop could pull the trigger?

He was tempted to try. He was desperate to reach Evelyn, to put her out of danger. She looked crazed with fright. Blood ran from her right eye, her nose and her mouth.

"It's all over," he said to Bishop. "Even if you shoot her, you won't get away from here, so there's no point."

"Making sure *you* can't have her, that she gets what's coming to her, is all the point I need," he responded. "She destroyed my life, took away everything I cared about. Now put down the rifle. If you're lucky, I'll just shoot you and take off with her."

Could he pick Bishop off?

No. Bishop was prepared for that, was using Evelyn as a shield. And even if he weren't behind her, there was no guarantee they wouldn't fire simultaneously.

Amarok couldn't take the risk.

"I won't ask again," Bishop threatened.

Amarok's mind raced as he slowly lowered his weapon to the ground.

"No!" Evelyn cried as Bishop turned his gun on Amarok instead. But Amarok hadn't left himself *completely* defenseless. He'd just had to be sure that Bishop wouldn't squeeze the trigger while that gun was aimed at Evelyn.

With a quick whistle Amarok called his

dog, and Makita came leaping out of the trees. His growl was deep and threatening and the blur of his coat caught Bishop's attention, startling him.

Bishop reared back — and fired. Amarok felt a burning sensation in his shoulder as the sharp crack echoed through the forest, but Bishop wasn't going to get the chance to fire again. Makita had already dragged him out of the van and had ahold of his arm as they rolled around in the dirt.

Trained never to let go, the malamute had clamped on for all he was worth.

Dropping the gun since he could no longer hold it, Bishop screamed as Amarok gave Makita another command. Then the dog did let go of his arm — and lunged for his throat.

"That's it," Amarok said, encouraging Makita as he managed to retrieve his rifle and drag it over to the van.

"Call him off!" Bishop whimpered. "Please, he's going to kill me. Call him off!"

Amarok whistled to get Makita to stand down. But the second the dog pulled back, Bishop reached for the gun that had fallen out of the van when he did.

No. . . .

Putting the muzzle of his rifle right over the place where Bishop's heart would be, if he had one, Amarok grimaced against the agonizing pain in his shoulder and somehow managed to pull the trigger.

Between Anchorage and Fairbanks, AK —
Thursday, 2:47 a.m. AKDT
Evelyn couldn't believe it was over. Amarok had appeared out of nowhere and put a stop to everything. Bishop had barely scratched her eyelid with the ice pick, and that was because he'd jerked when he heard Amarok hit the side of the van. He hadn't had time to push it through the thin bone of her eye socket to reach her brain.

She was fine, would recover. She just didn't know if she could say the same about her baby. She couldn't feel any movement. Not a kick or a jab. Not so much as a flutter. The trauma she'd been through might've been too much for their child.

"Are you okay?" Amarok used his good hand to untie her.

She glanced over at Bishop, who was lying on his side, staring sightlessly under the vehicle.

"Don't look at him," Amarok said. "Look at me."

She couldn't hold back the tears as the ropes on her hands and feet came loose. She told herself there was no reason to cry,

515

but she couldn't help it. Her relief was that profound. "How'd you find me?" she asked, wiping the blood from her nose and mouth.

He didn't take the time to explain, just reached out to draw her closer.

She leaned against his chest, painfully aware that he'd been shot, grateful for the strong hand that cupped the back of her head as she broke down and wept.

"What'd he do to you?" he asked at length.

"I'll tell you everything," she said. "But not now. We need to get you to a hospital."

"I'll be fine," he insisted, but she got the impression he couldn't move his right arm anymore, and it looked as though he was about to pass out.

"Where's your truck?"

Letting go of her, he sank onto the bumper of the van and put his head between his knees. "A quarter of a mile down the road. Give me a minute. I can't walk that far quite yet." He drew a deep, audible breath. "I can't believe you're safe. I can't believe I've got you back."

When his eyes lifted to her swollen belly, she understood what he wanted to know but was afraid to ask. "I can't tell you anything about the baby," she said. "Only that Bishop didn't manage to rape me, or . . . or even hurt me."

"But . . ."

Apparently, he could hear the hesitation in her voice. "But I haven't felt any movement for the past couple of days. Bishop drugged me to get me out of the cooler and into this van, though. I'm not sure what effect that might've had on the baby."

"We'll get you to a doctor," he said more matter-of-factly, and she knew then that he was trying to be stoic, to hide his worry and concern for her benefit.

"Okay, but we're going to get *you* to a doctor first. We'll drive this bucket of bolts to your truck and come back for it and Bishop later."

"Two for the road," he joked. "Let's do it."

She felt Makita's wet nose on her hand and took a moment to scratch him behind the ears. "You mean three. We wouldn't be alive to tell the tale without Makita."

Amarok whistled and his dog jumped into the back of the van with him. Evelyn saw Makita licking his face as he leaned back to rest against the interior wall.

With a smile, she closed the doors. Then she got behind the wheel and, taking care to avoid hitting Bishop's body on the way out, drove them to the truck and then on to Anchorage.

Evelyn could feel the soft skin and hard sinew of Amarok's naked body pressed up against her own and refused to open her eyes. They'd spent all day yesterday at the hospital, getting patched up and reassuring their friends and families, so she was enjoying being at home with him, alone.

She didn't want to stir for fear it would wake him and he'd get up. It wasn't like him to lie around, not in the middle of the day. If he wasn't working, he generally had some project going. It was bad enough that Phil had been calling every few hours to report various things — that the Fairbanks Police Department had not only found Bishop's body and sent it to the medical examiner's office, they'd also impounded his van. That the corpse Amarok discovered at the egg ranch was, in fact, Emmett Virtanen. That Edna Southwick was going to pull through. And that her daughter had called to say she was relieved Evelyn was safe, too.

Evelyn had no idea how long it might be before they heard from Phil or someone else again and planned to relish these quiet few minutes.

"Hey," he murmured, kissing her head.

Apparently, she didn't have to worry about waking him. He was already awake and had been able to notice the subtle difference in her breathing or something else to alert him that she was, too. "Hey."

"You feeling okay?"

"Yeah. But I'm not ready to move quite yet."

"Me either. I like this too much."

"How's your arm?"

"Beginning to throb. I should take another pain pill."

"Oh no! Here I was scheming to keep you in bed with me for as long as possible and you need something." She started to roll away from him so she could get it, but he stopped her.

"Don't leave just yet. It's not too bad. I can tolerate a few more minutes."

He shifted onto his back, though, and brought her against him with his good arm.

"Being home is like a dream. I never thought I'd see this place again, ever be with *you* again," she said.

"Mmm." He let his eyes drift closed. "I wouldn't have let that happen. I would've chased Bishop to the ends of the earth, if possible."

"You did. Isn't Fairbanks pretty close to one end of the earth?"

"It's getting there, I guess."

She could hear the smile in his voice as

his fingers combed through her hair.

"Are we still getting married?" he asked.

"Why wouldn't we?"

He sobered. "Because of everything you've been through. Maybe you need more time."

"If we wait any longer, the baby will be here."

They'd performed an ultrasound at the hospital yesterday, and her doctor had told her the baby looked fine. They wouldn't know for sure, of course, until she was born, but their little girl seemed to have weathered the ordeal better than Evelyn had. "We could put it off for six months or another year."

"Do *you* want to wait?" she asked in surprise.

"I've never wanted to wait," he replied. "I'm trying to think of you."

She lifted up on her elbows to look down into his face. "Then we're not changing anything, because I want to marry you now more than ever."

His lips curved into a smile as she lowered her head to kiss him, but then the phone interrupted.

So that he wouldn't have to move any more than necessary, she got it off the night-stand and, assuming it would be Phil again, handed it to him.

"Hello?" she heard him say. "Lewis . . . Yeah. . . . What's up? . . . No kidding . . . I believe it. . . . I always thought that was the case. . . . Good thing she finally came clean . . ."

He and the detective from Minnesota — Evelyn recognized the name — chatted for a few minutes more and then Amarok hung up.

"What'd Lewis have to say?" she asked.

"Terry's wife was the one who called you, pretending to be my mother."

"She admitted it?"

"Lewis said once she found out that Bishop had killed her brother, she broke down and told him everything. I guess she and Emmett planned to double-cross Terry."

"In what way?"

"She planned to take his share of the money so she could leave him."

"*He* might've had something to say about that."

"I doubt it. Not with Emmett on her side."

Evelyn was glad they had closure on who'd called as Alistair, but she bit her lip as she replayed in her mind a different part of what Amarok had just said: *Once she found out that Bishop had killed her brother, she broke down and told him everything.*

"What is it?" Amarok asked, noticing her

sudden reticence.

She sat up, pulling the sheet with her. "I have something to tell you."

His face registered concern. "There's something else?"

She tucked her hair behind her ears as she nodded.

Wincing, he managed to sit up, too. "What is it?"

"Bishop didn't kill Emmett."

"How do you know?" he asked.

She drew a deep breath. "Because I did."

His eyes widened. "Are you serious?"

"Completely."

"How?"

She shook her head. "I don't want to talk about it. It's too upsetting. But . . . do you think I should let the police know? Does it matter if I killed Emmett or Bishop did?"

He studied her for several seconds. Then he reached up to caress her cheek. "No."

She caught his hand, holding it in place. "Are you sure?"

"I'm positive," he replied. "You did only what you had to do. And no one else needs to hear about it."

She struggled to swallow the lump that rose in her throat. "I love you."

"I love you, too," he said. "We're going to recover from this just like we've recovered

from everything else. I promise."

She sniffed and wiped her cheeks. "I know."

523

EPILOGUE

Hilltop, AK — Saturday, three weeks later, 10:30 p.m. AKDT

Amarok sat at the bar, the tie loosened on his tux as he nursed one final cold one. His wedding, which he'd believed might never happen, was over. Many of his and Evelyn's guests were drifting off, making it less crowded and more relaxed — like the Moosehead normally was. That they'd been able to go ahead and have the ceremony without a delay, after all they'd been through, was almost a miracle. But Evelyn had insisted she didn't want to wait. Amarok had been hesitant to put it off, too, what with the baby coming in a few weeks. Soon he'd be a father as well as a husband — just what he'd hoped for ever since he first fell in love with Evelyn.

This was a good day. He wasn't sure he'd ever had a better one.

"You going to have trouble getting used

to that thing?" Shorty joked, coming up on the other side of the bar and angling his head toward Amarok's left hand.

Amarok turned the simple gold band on his third finger. "Not at all. I like the feel of it."

"You like the meaning behind it."

He glanced over to see Evelyn talking to Molly in the corner, by where they'd served the cake. Fortunately, the swelling and bruising on her face were gone. "That too."

Shorty popped the top on another beer, this one for himself. "You're a lucky man. I guess I can tell you now that I didn't think you'd get her back alive."

Amarok shook his head as he remembered those dark days, knowing he'd never forget them. "I guess I can tell *you* now that I didn't, either."

Clinking his bottle against Amarok's, Shorty took a long pull before changing the subject. "I expected some of Evelyn's family to fly out for this. Kinda surprised that Brianne, at least, didn't make it."

"She's got to help look out for Evelyn's mother."

"Evelyn told me Lara . . . struggles. That hasn't improved?"

"It has. She's doing better these days, but Brianne's baby is only a month old. Didn't make sense to put him on a plane when we'll be going there in the fall for a second reception."

"Guess not," Shorty agreed. "I was just hoping to see her again, that's all. She doing okay?"

Amarok nodded. It had been a touchy situation to have Brianne as a guest in his home last fall, right after she'd learned she was pregnant and before Jasper was caught. "Better than she was when she was here before — I can tell you that," he said wryly.

Shorty chuckled. "It's still hard for me to believe she struck up a friendship with Jasper Moore while she was here. I shake my head whenever I remember seeing them dancing together."

"Yeah, well, he was Andy Smith then — a correctional officer at the prison. She wasn't the only one who was fooled."

"True." Shorty straightened. "What's up with him these days, anyway? He out of the infirmary yet?"

"He was just transferred back to his cell this week."

"So he's going to be okay."

"That depends on how well he gets along with the other inmates moving forward. He's not the type who makes friends easily — especially not now that the mask has come off."

"Deserves whatever he gets. That's my take."

"A lot of people would agree. But Evelyn's seen to it that they've suspended the guards who were responsible for him when it happened. They can't let that kind of shit occur."

"Yeah, I know."

Shorty wasn't one who stopped to chat for very long when he was working the bar. But with the wedding over, Amarok could tell he was warming up to the question he *really* wanted to ask.

After Shorty had put so much into making the wedding as nice as it had been, Amarok decided to save him the trouble of searching for the right lead-in. "I decided to invite her," he said, out of the blue.

Amarok knew he was right, that Shorty had wanted to ask about Alistair's appearance at the wedding, when Shorty didn't say, *Who?*

"Change of heart, huh?" he said instead.

"I don't know. Life just seems too short to carry that kind of resentment around."

"She kept her distance and left as soon as it was over. I think she's trying to respect your boundaries."

"I got that, too. And I'm grateful." Amarok wasn't sure how much interaction he'd have with his mother in the future, but he supposed it was a step in the right direction.

He scratched off the label of his beer, lost in thought for a bit. Their relationship would become more of an issue now that she would have a grandchild through him. Deciding he didn't want to have a relationship with her seemed selfish when it meant his daughter wouldn't have one of her grandmothers.

Evelyn came up and rested her hand on his shoulder as she reached over to grab a handful of nuts. "I'm exhausted," she said. "You about ready to head home?"

He slid his empty bottle toward Shorty. "I've just been waiting for you."

She gave him the smile that never failed to steal his breath. "Then let's go, Husband."

They thanked Shorty and, her hand clasped in his, left the bar — only to find his truck decorated with so much shoe polish, balloons and crepe paper, he didn't think he'd be able to see out of the windshield to drive.

"Good thing we hid my car around back," she said, and they hurried to reach it — only to find that the locals hadn't been fooled.

They'd decorated *both* vehicles.

"There are no secrets in Hilltop," Amarok grumbled.

Those who'd lingered to follow them were joined by others who came out from the trees, where they'd been hiding, to razz them and film their reaction.

It took longer to clean the windshield than it did to drive home. While there were some drawbacks of living in such a small town, there were definite advantages, too.

Amarok helped Evelyn out of the vehicle and then seemed determined to carry her across the threshold.

"What about your shoulder?" she asked when he stopped her from going in on her own power.

"It's fine. Almost healed."

"This could break it open again. Are you sure you really want to do this?"

"Call me traditional," he said, and they both laughed as he swept her into his arms.

ABOUT THE AUTHOR

Brenda Novak and her husband, Ted, live in Sacramento and are the proud parents of five children — three girls and two boys. When she's not spending time with her family or writing, Brenda is usually working on her annual fund-raiser for diabetes research. Brenda's novels have made *The New York Times* and *USA Today* bestseller lists and won many awards, including three Rita nominations, the Book Buyer's Best, the Book Seller's Best and the National Reader's Choice Award.